The Culinary Art of Murder
The Alvarez Family Murder Mysteries
Book Six

Heather Haven

The Wives of Bath Press
www.heatherhavenstories@gmail.com

The Culinary Art of Murder © 2017 by Heather Haven

This book is a work of fiction. Characters, names, places, events, and incidents either are the product of the author's imagination or are used fictitiously, and any resemblance to any actual persons, living or dead, events, or locales is entirely coincidental.

The Wives of Bath Press
5512 Cribari Bend
San Jose, Ca 95135

http:// www.heatherhavenstories.com

Print ISBN- 978-0-9892265-9-2
eBook ISBN-13: 978-0-9892265-8-5

Praise For The Series

♥ "Heather Haven makes a stellar debut in *Murder is a Family Business*. With an engaging protagonist and a colorful cast, Haven provides a fresh voice in a crowded genre. We will be hearing more from this talented newcomer. Highly recommended." **Sheldon Siegel. New York Times Best Selling Author of** *Perfect Alibi.*

♥ *A Wedding to Die For* "Wonderfully fresh and funny!" **- Meg Waite Clayton, Author of** *The Race For Paris*

♥ "Heather Haven has kept me on the edge of my seat with *Death Runs in the Family*. I recommend this to mystery lovers everywhere." **Judy M. Winn, Author of** *The Silver Seahorse*

♥ *DEAD....If Only* "There is so much action packed into this book. The characters are terrific. I loved all of them. I will definitely be going back to start at the beginning!" **Linda Strong, Mystery Readers Book Club**

♥ *The CEO Came DOA* "This is a strong work in the genre of the mystery/thriller!" **San Francisco Book Review**

♥ *The Culinary Art of Murder* "This latest installment of Haven's murder mystery series offers a twisty whodunit laced with a healthy dose of suspense. A solidly entertaining mystery" **Kirkus Reviews**

Acknowledgements

A special thanks to Adam Busby, General Manager of The Culinary Institute of America at Greystone and his assistant, Helen Quiroz. They allowed me to see the inner workings of one of the finest culinary arts schools in the world, located in one of the most beautiful places in the world, St. Helena, California. I deviate tremendously from CIA's stellar methods, but at least I had perfection to start with.

While we're talking about the culinary arts, on this book editor Baird Nuckolls served double duty. Not only did she edit the book and make wonderful suggestions, but as a certified pastry chef, she checked my facts for accuracy and recipes for validness. Another thanks to Line editor/proofreader, Paula Grundy. There is nothing too small for her to catch! However, any imperfections within this book are solely my responsibility.

I would like to thank the following people who helped me title some chapters of this book with food puns based on famous literary works. After struggling for two days with only a few to show for it, I reached out to my Facebook buddies, many of whom came through with great titles. Thank you Eileen Bordy, Margie Bunting, Roseanne Dowell, Barbara Ehrentreu, Ana Manwaring, Javier Ceinos Ros, Terry Shames, Russ Taylor, Sherry Troop, and Nora Wittman. I would like to mention that for several days, this task seemed to be Mike Turner's raison d'être. Mike came up with several of the titles used, and I am grateful.

And lastly, where would a writer be without Beta readers? Nowhere, man! So a rousing cheer for Roseanne Dowell and Penny Ehrenkranz, talented writers and professional editors in their own right, and my wonderful readers, who are listed alphabetically: Grace DeLuca, Anahid Gregg, Sue Hornung, Maria Elena Jaquez (making sure the Spanish was A-OK), Sherry Troop and Mary Wollesen. Thank you all! *Muchas gracias*, as Tío would say!

Listed below and in order of non-appearance are all the fine novels, novellas and short stories I had the effrontery to make puns about with my chapter titles:

And Then They Were None – Agatha Christie
A Hitchhikers Guide to the Galaxy – Douglas Adams
Devil in a Blue Dress – Walter Mosley
A Wrinkle in Time - Madeleine L'Engle
The French Connection – Robin Moore
Great Expectations – Charles Dickens
The Adventures of Huckleberry Finn – Mark Twain
The Sun Also Rises – Ernest Hemingway
Elephants Can Remember – Agatha Christie
Lord of the Rings - J. R. R. Tolkien
A Game of Thrones - George R. R. Martin
Brave New World - Aldous Huxley
The Devil Wears Prada - Lauren Weisberger
"A" is for Alibi – Sue Grafton
Alice's Adventures in Wonderland - Lewis Carroll
War and Peace – Leo Tolstoy
Witness for the Prosecution – Agatha Christie
Tender Is the Night – F. Scott Fitzgerald
Watch on the Rhine – John Ringo
The Girl with the Dragon Tattoo – Stieg Larsson
The Purloined Letter – Edgar Allan Poe
The Laughing Policeman - Maj Sjöwall and Per Wahlöö
Twenty Thousand Leagues Under the Sea – Jules Verne
The Last Temptation of Christ - Nikos Kazantzakis
Return of the Thin Man - Dashiell Hammett
To Kill a Mockingbird – Harper Lee
The Silence of the Lambs Thomas Harris
Shroud For a Nightingale – P. D. James
The Picture of Dorian Gray – Oscar Wilde
The Haunting Of Hill House – Shirley Jackson
To Have and Have Not – Ernest Hemingway
Rosemary's Baby – Ira Levin
For Whom the Bell Tolls – Ernest Hemingway
The Maltese Falcon - Dashiell Hammett
Catcher in the Rye - J. D. Salinger
The Spy Who Came in From the Cold - John le Carré
The Sound and the Fury – William Faulkner

Tinker, Tailor, Soldier, Spy - John le Carré
Look Homeward, Angel – Thomas Wolfe
Something Wicked This Way Comes – Ray Bradbury
The Postman Always Rings Twice – James M. Cain
Of Mice and Men – John Steinbeck
Farewell, My Lovely – Raymond Chandler
Pride and Prejudice – Jane Austin
The Name of the Rose - Umberto Eco
Anatomy of a Murder – Robert Traver
The Ipcress File – Len Deighton
From Russia With Love – Ian Fleming
A Farewell to Arms - Ernest Hemingway

These are all classics and well worth reading again and again.

Dedication

This book is dedicated to my mother, Mary Lee, passed but much alive in my thoughts and prayers and always loved. Also to my wonderful husband, Norman Meister, who gives me endless and boundless love, which is not always as easy as it sounds. I would also like to dedicate this book to families throughout the world, solid, having stayed the course, and to the newly forming. The newly formed would be ones like Brit and Matt Gomez, and their infant daughter, Charlotte. I met this young family on a plane recently and was struck by their welcoming of others to encircle their hearth, and share in the warmth that is theirs.

As for the solid, I think of friend and business partner, Baird Nuckolls, and her husband, Neal, together for thirty-three years; my in-laws, Rosina and Bill Krefft, forty years and counting; my family, Grace and Arnie DeLuca, sixty years and still going strong; Debbie and Dean Tedder, Carol and Steve Miller, Bobby and Didith DeLuca; and my heart-sister, Sandra Savarese, and her husband, Steve Thacker. Then there is my own marriage, thirty-five years.

And this book is not only dedicated to couples of all ages and genders but to parents, grandparents, brothers, sisters, step-parents, step-children, half- brothers, half- sisters, and all the others that often make up the modern-day family. To love, to share, and to build lives together is what it's all about.

Families. Long may they thrive.

Table of Contents

The Culinary Art of Murder

Book Six
The Alvarez Family
Murder Mystery Series

Heather Haven

Chapter One

And Then There Were Nuts

"Well, look who's honored us with her presence. Welcome back, Lee. I almost forgot what you looked like, which is stunning, of course."

"I see you got hauled in at the crack of dawn, too. For eight AM on a Monday morning you don't look so bad, yourself."

I stood in the reception area of Discretionary Inquiries, Inc., the family run detective agency, face to face with Stanley, the man who keeps all things sane in our crazy business.

I took in his dark suit and white shirt, and noted the tie. Stanley's choice in garish neckwear added a touch of light-heartedness to his otherwise somber outfits. This one was hot pink with small yellow polka dots.

He shot me a smile. I grinned back. Stanley has worked for us for the past nine years and we would be lost without our office manager and general factotum. The man is an organizing marvel.

"I didn't mind coming in early," he said. "I have to take time off for a dentist appointment at eleven-thirty, so this works out fine. Coffee and rolls are already in the board room. But poor you, weren't you walking the warm sands of a Bermudian beach, hand- in- hand with your man only yesterday?"

"Yes, and drinking tamarind cosmos. I'm not sure where it all went wrong."

"I read somewhere, Lee, when chaos turns out to be a way of life, it's no longer chaos but your life."

"Oh, really? That's pretty heartless for someone not living my life."

"I hid a cheese Danish behind the coffee urn for you."

"All is forgiven."

My name is Liana Alvarez. Call me Lee, but for heaven's sake, don't do it around my mother. She's a lady who would rather eat broken glass than utter a nickname.

I'm the lead in-house private investigator of Discretionary Inquiries, better known as D. I. That is, to everyone except Mom. She doesn't approve of initials, either.

My trip to Bermuda came about because I'd needed a little R&R after dealing with the skullduggery of a visiting research scientist at Caltech. This rogue made off with a bucketful of genetically engineered tomato seeds belonging to the school. Patent pending, the seeds were worth millions.

D. I. to the rescue. During a rushed meeting, the client revealed certain mandates i.e., no police, no publicity, no how. And they wanted the thief caught *pronto* before he had a chance to sell the seeds off.

Word to the wise: never leave a meeting like that to visit the ladies room. In absentia, it was decided I would handle the case 'personally'.

I hate that.

The case found me running up and down the back hills of California, Oregon, and Washington states. Deeper and deeper into the wilderness, through poison oak and marijuana farms, day after day, wearing the same old sweats and sneakers, and gulping down slop masquerading as coffee from dingy motel rooms.

I caught up with the bucket-snatching thief near the Canadian border in a shabby motel held up mostly by mounted dead animals and cobwebs. He wasn't happy to see me and didn't give up without a fight.

I hate that.

Sure, I got the bucket back, but between logging in eighteen-hour days and scrapes and bruises, I was in need of some serious time off. And a good cup of coffee.

After two weeks in Bermuda with my adoring husband of four months, reality bellowed. I whined, but this Monday morning found me back in D. I.'s south conference room dreading the urgent board meeting called at the last minute by Lila Hamilton Alvarez, CEO, mother mine, and She Who Must Be Obeyed.

I stifled a yawn. Aside from Mom, my fellow hostage was kid brother and CTO, Richard Alvarez. We sat awaiting the arrival of the two remaining board members, Ms. Evangeline Packersmythe and Mr. James Talbot.

These ghastly, first-thing-in-the-morning board meetings require you not only to show up, but dress the part. Being a professional, I'd tried to do just that. Colorful, but I like to think classic. Even my long, dark hair was restrained in a conservative bun.

Mom gave me a look that said no.

She appraised each part of my outfit in turn: turquoise pantsuit, clunky silver and coral earrings, bracelet, and matching pin. I think my orange stilettos 'done' her in.

She looked away and sighed, shimmering at the head of the table. By sharp contrast, my cool, blonde mother was dressed in a haute couture silver-gray ensemble, and wearing her ever-present pearl button earrings. Serene, beautiful, and totally in control, this was the mother fate chose to give me. I loved her anyway.

Brother Richard sat as upright in his chair as his slight frame would allow. That would be a half an inch taller than me. I ring in at five-eight. Unlike me, he takes after our mother in the coloring and features department, fair. Unlike her, he drapes his body in faded t-shirts, worn jeans, and all-out dorkiness. What can I say? He's a techie. Brilliant, but still a techie.

"So where are the other two? I thought we had an eight AM board meeting," I said.

"They are due at eight-thirty, Liana," Mom said. " I wanted you here ahead of time to *apprise* you of the situation concerning Ms. Packersmythe."

"Ms. Packersmythe?" I was shocked. What kind of situation could the most straight-laced person in the world cause?

Out of the blue, my brother made his own surprising announcement. You know how people like to grab the attention.

"I can't wait to tell you what's been going on while you were gone. Tío has a lady friend. She's a southern chef."

"What?"

I looked at Mom. If she was as shocked as I was by Richard's words, she didn't show it. But ice princesses tend not to show their emotions, other than pleasure at a subject's bowing and scraping. Or displeasure at them not doing so.

Maybe I hadn't heard Richard right. Maybe my ears were still clogged from the thirty-five thousand feet descent into the San Francisco Airport the night before. I waved a dismissive hand.

"Don't be an idiot, Richard."

"Tío has a girlfriend," Richard insisted. "And you are such a doofus."

"You're the doofus, Richard."

"*Children!*" Mom looked from Richard to me, her voice lowering the temperature of the room several degrees. "This is *not* the conversation we should be having now. The others will be joining us at any *moment.*"

"Sorry," I said.

"Yeah, me, too," Richard chimed in.

"*However,*" said Mom, having the conversation she said we should not be having, "it is true. Let me simply state that Mateo and this woman *appear* to have culinary interests in common."

"But who is she?" I was stuttering.

"Her name is Patricia Durand. Although, I understand she *prefers* to be called...." And here Mom sniffed as if a rotten egg had rolled in under the door. "...*Patsy.*"

Mom rallied. "But that is neither here nor there. The *reason* for this impromptu meeting is Francis called last night to *warn* me that Ms. Packersmythe was *detained* yesterday afternoon at the police station for inciting a *riot* at a car dealership."

Mom sniffed again. It was becoming a habit. She also has a habit of beating you over the head with verbally underlined words just in case you – a moron – can't get her meaning otherwise.

I asked a moronic question. Actually, three of them. "Our Evangeline Packersmythe? Inciting a riot? Old Ramrod Packersmythe? I don't believe it."

"As of late," Mom said, "Ms. Packersmythe has been behaving in a most *uncharacteristic* manner. Her affiliation with this rabble crowd is an example. It is only a matter of *time* before the media links her to the agency. This is *not* the image Discretionary Inquiries should *have* with the public. We have a *reputation* to maintain."

"Discreet and all that," I said.

"Yes," Mom said. "Francis was *most* alarmed, as am I."

To back up, Francis is Frank Thompson, Palo Alto's chief of police, longtime family friend, and Richard's and my godfather. A good guy.

Ms. Evangeline Packersmythe is another story. She is our in-residence accountant and board member. A highly opinionated Vassar graduate about six feet tall, she's probably the most intimidating person I've met in my life. I do not say this lightly. Her size coupled with her demeanor reminds me of a Clydesdale horse wearing pantyhose. I have often envisioned her with the red, white, and gold Budweiser wagon in tow.

"What was the riot about?"

"*Solar* cars." Mom's tone of voice was akin to saying grave robbing. "She *appears* to be anti."

Satisfied on the Evangeline Packersmythe front, I munched on my cheese Danish. "Patsy Durand, Patsy Durand. Why does that name sound familiar to me?"

"I am *told*," Mom said, shifting gears, as well, "Chef Durand is well-known in Arkansas and throughout the eastern seaboard. She is here for the summer at the Palo Alto Culinary Arts Institute."

"That's why you know her name, Lee," added Richard.

"Yes," said Mom. "As a chef, she has attained a *certain* amount of fame. But please *remember* it is Mateo's business whom he sees or does *not* see. Once again, *we* are not here to discuss that. We are here to meet with Ms. Packersmythe to establish the *depth* of her involvement with this anti-solar organization and how it *impacts* the agency. Let us keep our *priorities* straight, children."

Content to have put us in our place, Mom cleared her throat in her lady like manner and relaxed. Silence ensued. Several seconds ticked by as we waited for the others to arrive.

The door sprung open and in galloped Ms. Packersmythe, her nylon encased legs whooshing loudly as they brushed against one another. She stood before us breathing deep, steady, and loud.

"Good morning," she thundered.

"Morning."

"Morning."

"Morning."

The door opened again. In strode the last member of the board, one elderly but debonair, James Talbot. Dressed in one of his ubiquitous three-piece suits and dapperness itself, he gave us a friendly but reserved smile.

Mr. Talbot has taken care of legal matters for the family – personal and business – for as long as I can remember. I'm thinking that when Mom's ancestors came over on the Mayflower, he and a few Native Americans were waving from the shore.

That stated, Mr. Talbot is an expert in the finer points of corporate or anybody else's law. And he is as sharp as the day he received his degree from Harvard. He's also deaf as a doorknob.

"Good morning, one and all," he crooned, twirling his silver cane in a roguish way.

"Morning."

"Morning."

"Morning."

"About time you got here," roared Ms. Packersmythe. Though her voice has been known to chip plaster from walls, Mr. Talbot gestured he still hadn't quite heard her.

"Ladies and gentlemen," Mom shouted. "If *everyone* would please be seated; I will call this meeting to *order*."

Packersmythe and Talbot sat. Mom picked up the gavel to give it a good bang, which would officially bring the meeting to order.

"Madame Chair," Ms. Packersmythe said, before my mother could bang her little gavel. "I believe I know the reason for this meeting. My affiliation with the movement against the Syntar Solar Car Company."

Mom paused mid-bang, but said nothing. She gave a single, strong nod and set the gavel down. Ms. Packersmythe went on.

"I have discussed the matter with – ah – a friend, and we both agree it would be better for all if I no longer participated in any formal public protests against the company. And I would also like to go on record as saying –"

"This is an *off* the record meeting, Ms. Packersmythe," Mom interjected.

"Thank you, Mrs. Alvarez. I had hoped such was the case," Ms. Packersmythe said. "I would like to bring to your attention that yesterday's participation was on Sunday, my day off. However, I now realize my involvement could compromise the agency's position in the community. I will drop off a letter of clarification and apology to Chief Thompson during my lunch hour today. You have my word on it. Will that satisfy the board?"

She gave each of us a 'so-there' look. Mom turned to Talbot, eyebrows raised in question. Talbot turned to Mom and nodded. Richard looked at his laptop. I looked at my watch. Five minutes. Situation remedied. Not a bad board meeting.

The two non-family board members left, just as my phone rang. When I saw it was my beloved uncle, I hopped on it.

"*Hola*, Tío," I smiled into the phone. "You're calling to welcome me back, aren't you? I –"

"*Sobrina, ayúdame*," Tío shouted, more frantic than I'd ever heard him.

Pulling the phone away from my ear, I tried to say something. But after the Spanish words of 'niece, help me,' he cut me off, segueing into broken English, then Spanglish, and then back to rapid-fire Spanish.

The more upset Tío is, the more he does that. Sometimes he rattles off words so fast and furious, I, who am fluent in all three languages, have a tough time keeping up with him. But I got the gist of it. And he was yelling so loud, Mom and Richard got the gist of it, too, and from across the room.

Short and sweet: The head-teaching chef of the Palo Alto Culinary Arts Institute was found stabbed to death in the kitchen pantry. And with one of his own knives.

There seems to be a downside to running a detective agency in the heart of Silicon Valley. My job description says I ferret out cybercrimes. But when I'm not looking, I tend to fall over dead bodies.

It was a good thing Richard warned me Tío had recently acquired a lady friend. Otherwise, I would have been shocked out of my gourd when Tío informed me that said lady friend, one Patsy Durand, was just arrested for murder.

I hate that.

Chapter Two

The Hitchhiker's Guide To Granola

I pulled out of D. I.'s parking lot in my turquoise 1957 Chevy convertible, which some people say matches my eyes. Not true, my eye color leans to violet.

"Were you able to catch Mr. Talbot, Mom?"

"Yes, he's going to meet us at the police station."

My mother graced the passenger seat and my brother monopolized the back. Richard pounded on the keyboard of his super laptop, tweaked to do everything but pick out his ties. That's only because Richard doesn't wear them. If he did, he could have one knitted on the spot.

In the ten minutes it was going to take to get to the Palo Alto Police Department, I wanted to clear a few things up.

"Okay, so we have one problem solved. But I still don't get this other thing. Tío's seventy, a widower, and the one who gives unconditional love while serving up mouthwatering chimichangas. He devotes his life to *la familia* and cooking," I said. "I mean he wants nothing more, right? So when you say, 'lady friend' you really mean a pal who happens to be female, right?"

"Wrong." Richard took a breath, about to continue when Mom took center stage.

"Liana, *during* the time you were *apprehending* the miscreant in Northern California, followed by a *two*-week visit to your in-laws in North Carolina –"

"We weren't with them the whole time," I interrupted. "After a couple of days Gurn and I flew to Bermuda."

"*Regardless* of where you were, dear, or *why*," Mom said, interrupting my interruption, "your uncle has become *romantically involved*."

"So you're saying our Tío is actually dating this woman?" I found myself stuttering.

"You know, Lila," Richard said, addressing our mother by her work name and as if I wasn't in the car. "If Lee is the best investigator Discretionary Inquiries has going for it, we're in a lot of trouble."

"Oh, shut up, you overstuffed techie," I said.

"Children, that is *enough*." Mom took over again. "I haven't met her in person; *none* of us have, but I'm sure we will in *time*. Meanwhile, Richard, please *continue* your background check on Chef Patricia Durand."

I was surprised he or Mom hadn't done something like that beforehand, but that's my family for you, respecters of privacy. Even though we run a snooping kind of business.

With the top down, I yanked my hair out of its bun, and let it catch the breeze. That's the best part about owning a convertible, the wind in your hair. Sure, it takes a quart of crème rinse to get the knots out later, but that's the price of freedom.

"Let me read you what Wikipedia says." Richard put in, unaware of my mental wanderings. "Patsy Durand was born Patsy Ann Turnbull in Farmington, Arkansas, August seventh, 1956, the ninth of ten children. She was named after the singer Patsy Cline."

"Her name really is Patsy and not Patricia?" I turned and gave my mother a sympathetic look. "Wow, that's too bad, Mom. Now you've got to call her Patsy."

"Never *mind*, Liana," Mom said. "Go on, Richard."

"In 1972 she left high school before graduating and married Ernest 'Bubba' Wilkins, fifteen years her senior. She worked as a cook in his roadside diner and was considered a phenomenon by the locals. People flocked to eat her cooking. Bubba Wilkins died in a car accident three years later and left the diner to her. In 1982 she sold it and went to Paris to study at Le Cordon Bleu."

"It's pretty hard to get into the Cordon Bleu," I remarked. "So she must have been a pretty good cook."

"There she met," said Richard, riding over my comment, "another American student, Hayes Durand. They were married in 1983. Upon graduation from the Cordon Bleu, they went to Little Rock, Arkansas, and opened the Golden Cygnet, a restaurant awarded a Michelin star five times."

"Due to Patsy's culinary talents?" I said over my shoulder.

"That's what it says. During that time they had two sons, Wallace and Peter. Patsy filed for a divorce in 1989. They sold the restaurant for an undisclosed amount of money. Then she opened a chain of successful restaurants back east called *Sooie Cochon*."

"Excuse me?" Mom sounded appalled.

Richard went on to explain. "*Sooie* is a call farmers give to their the hogs to bring them in and, as you know, *cochon* mean hog in French. Pretty clever, huh?"

"Clever is not *quite* the word I would use." Mom's voice was testy.

"So the *Sooie Cochon* chain is hers," I said. I looked in my rearview mirror at Richard. "I've never been to one, but I've heard of them. How many are there?"

"Fifteen and counting. It says here she oversees each one."

"That could be another way of saying she's into micromanaging," I said.

"It often is," Richard said. "She's scheduled to open another one in St. Louis next year. According to this, she came up with the idea of combining classic French recipes with traditional Arkansas dishes. It caught the eye of the public. She's written two cookbooks on the subject, both best sellers. Meanwhile, her sons manage the business end, which gives her more time to visit her restaurants, travel, do talk shows, and develop new recipes. She has plans on coming west to Los Angeles and San Francisco. Right here she's quoted as saying, 'westward-ho'.

"*Another* clever aphorism," Mom said.

I stifled a laugh. So did Richard.

"Let me check her finances to see if she's as rich as I think she is."

Richard proceeded to bang on the keyboard again in a manner that made me flinch. He goes through computers like I go through jars of peanut butter. This is after having tweaked them until they are nothing like the machine he initially purchased. He let out a few 'hmmm's and one or two 'aha's' while looking at his screen.

We arrived at our destination and I parked the car. The burning question was did we stay in the car and listen to the rest of what Richard had found? Or did we race inside the station to get the skinny from Chief Frank Thompson? Skinny won.

The Palo Alto Police Station is near and dear to me. Long before I visited in an adult capacity to make out the occasional deposition or do other company business, I was brought here as a child by my father, God rest his soul. For me PAPD stokes up memories of donuts, candy bars, and smiling folks in blue.

Our father, Roberto 'Bobby' Alvarez, started his career as a cop. He pounded the streets of Palo Alto, along with his best friend, Richard's and my godfather, Frank Thompson.

Nearly two decades ago Dad left public law enforcement to start his own private investigative service, Discretionary Inquiries, with the foresight of how the technological industry would need its particular services in the future. Meanwhile, Frank climbed the ladder to become Palo Alto's chief of police. Both couldn't have been prouder of the other.

Dad has been gone three years now, lost to us by an unexpected brain aneurism. Grief still lives close to the surface but you learn to deal. Sometimes I drop by to visit Frank. We talk about Dad, both of us feeling the better for it.

True, Frank gives me lip from time to time about being a PI, but I adore the sometimes-crotchety man. He looks on me like his second daughter, the one he has to keep an eye on.

I knocked and pushed open Frank's office door. He looked up from his neat but crowded desk, his handsome, Denzel Washington face showing signs of strain. Standing, he brushed at his already crisp uniform, not quite in a nervous gesture but one of unresolved energy.

"Lila, Richard, Lee, I've been expecting you."

"Where's Tío?" I looked around.

"He's with Ms. Durand in one of the interrogation rooms. I believe she's contacting an attorney."

"Mr. Talbot has been retained as her lawyer," Mom said, with an air of finality. "He's outside doing the necessary paperwork."

"Good," said Frank. "I was hoping he would be called. I'll have the guard bring him to her when he gets finished. Mateo will probably have to vacate, but I'll keep tabs on where he goes." He picked up the phone, pushed a button, and mumbled a few instructions.

When he hung up, Frank glanced at Lila, giving her a small smile. Mom returned it. This was novel. While not exactly sworn enemies, they had absolutely no idea what made the other tick. And they also rubbed each other the wrong way. You say toe-may-toe, I say toe-mah-toe, that sort of thing.

"So what's going on, Frank?" I looked at him, but he gave me an unreadable stare.

"Why don't we all take a seat?" Frank went to a corner of the room and dragged over a third chair. He put it beside two others then went back behind his desk.

"If Tío is allowed to be with her," asked Richard, sitting down, "does that mean no charges have been brought against Ms. Durand?"

"That's not what we were told." I piped up, still standing. "Tío said she'd been arrested."

"Not exactly," said Frank. "At the moment, she is a person of interest, brought in for questioning. An arrest may be imminent. We're not sure yet."

"What the hell does that mean?" It wasn't like Frank to do a tap dance around the facts.

"Liana," my mother said, taking a seat. "Language, *please.*"

"Sorry, Mom," I rolled my eyes.

Hands outstretched toward me, Frank made a 'sit down' gesture. I sat. There was a moment's silence. Frank's voice was quiet.

"I'm going to outline the facts before you ask any questions." He looked directly at me. "Agreed?"

"Agreed," I muttered.

"Thank you. At six-thirty this morning, Manuel Sanchez, dishwasher, found Chef Jacque Chalifour, head-teaching chef, in one of the pantries of the Palo Alto Culinary Arts Institute, dead from multiple stab wounds. The murder weapon, a butcher knife and the chef's own, was lying beside him."

Frank pronounced the dishwasher's Spanish name with the perfect Spanish accent. Always one with an ear for languages, he moved on to the perfect French pronunciation of the chef's name.

"Why Sanchez would be there so early when his shift doesn't start until nine AM, we have yet to discover. In any event, Sanchez called the police, but before we arrived he split, possibly because he's an illegal. We're checking on that. But it's also possible that Sanchez killed Chef Jacques, then in a fit of remorse returned to the scene of the crime this morning, called us, panicked, and ran. We have an APB out on him."

Frank cleared his throat.

"However, he is not the strongest candidate. Patsy Durand, guest chef at the Institute, had a fight with Chef Jacques in front of students and staff Saturday afternoon. Something about adding fried squirrel to the menu. The discussion became heated. Accusations were flung, such as him being a 'thieving hack' and her being 'nothing more than a cook'. From there it escalated."

Richard looked aghast. "You mean it became physical?"

"Oh, dear," murmured Mom, shaking her head.

Frank nodded. "According to witnesses, he snatched the toque blanche hat from her head, threw it to the floor, and ground his feet into it. She, in turn, ripped the pockets off his white jacket. Then he pushed her. She kicked him in his checkered black and white pants; I will refrain from saying where. Meanwhile, he was screaming he would destroy her while she was screaming she'd kill him."

"This is soooo not good," I commented.

"The upshot is he fired her and ordered her out of the building. She told him he couldn't fire her and he should do something to himself that is physically impossible. That's when she picked up the murder weapon. Witnesses state she threatened to cut off his nose with it. It took several students to pull them apart."

"Uh-oh," I said.

"While Patsy Durand denies killing him, she doesn't have an alibi for the time of the murder, claiming she was home alone and in bed. The coroner says the time of death is roughly between eight and eleven PM Sunday night. And her fingerprints are all over the knife. Motive, means, opportunity." Frank paused then turned to me. "You do the math."

"What do security tapes show?"

"The Institute doesn't have them."

"What?" I was shocked. "I thought every business had security cameras these days."

"Not every. It often depends on the type of business. Banks, liquor stores, and jewelry stores tend to. Apparently, Chef Hayes Durand, owner of the Palo Alto Institute of Culinary Arts, does not believe in them."

"I'll bet he's changing his tune now," I interjected.

"Maybe, maybe not," said Frank. "He feels they are an intrusion of privacy. And they are not required by law. Unfortunately," he added. "Our job would be a lot easier if they were."

"Where does all of this leave Patsy Durand?" Mom's voice was sharper than usual.

"For the moment, we are detaining Ms. Durand for further questioning. Hayes Durand vouches for her and swears she'd never do such a thing. In fact, he wants her released so she can return to his kitchens and take over her classes. Then there's your uncle. He's applying all the pressure he possibly can, very unlike him."

"I've never known you to bow to *any* type of pressure, Francis," Mom said.

"And I haven't," Frank said. His chin raised a notch in a slightly belligerent manner. "However, until we find Manuel Sanchez, arresting her wouldn't be prudent."

I thought for a moment. "Today's clime? Bad press? Possible charges of false arrest? None of the above; all of the above?"

Frank shrugged, but didn't answer.

"So what now?" Richard reentered the conversation again.

"We see what Talbot arranges," Frank said. "Now that her lawyer's here, she'll be taken to another room to confer with him privately. Being Ms. Durand hasn't been charged with anything yet, possible release into her own recognizance or into some upstanding citizen's care, like Mateo or Hayes Durand. Durand is also her former husband and the father of her two sons. They seem to have a cordial relationship; close friends, even."

"That's refreshing," I said.

"He can't say enough positive things about her. Says he's been trying to get her to Palo Alto to teach at his school for years. She only came now because his guest chef had to drop out at the last minute and he was in a bind. Something like that. I don't know much about the world of gourmet cooking. But I suspect I'm about to find out."

The intercom sounded. Frank picked up the phone, pressed a button, and listened for a moment. He replaced the receiver with a deep sigh and looked at me. "Mateo has asked to know when you arrive. Have you arrived?"

"Yeah, sure. But why all the formality?"

Instead of answering, Frank stood and walked to the door.

"Lee, let's go find Mateo, now that he's alone," he said to me. He turned to Mom and Richard, still seated. "You two; okay with staying here?"

They both nodded, but I could tell by the expression on their faces, neither of them knew what was going on. Me, either.

Frank shut the door behind us and we started down the long hallway toward the holding cells. We walked in silence.

"I see they've painted the walls a new color," I said. "Lovely shade of beige."

Frank looked at me with a smile. "You hate beige."

"I know, but this is by way of making conversation." I didn't look at him but kept walking side- by- side, keeping up with his long strides. "When are you going to tell me what's really going on, Frank?"

He stopped abruptly and turned to me. I also stopped, wheeled around, and stared him straight in the face. His eyes flitted about to make sure we couldn't be overheard before he spoke.

"Lee, he said he wouldn't leave the station until he spoke with you."

"Tío wouldn't leave? Why?"

"I think he wanted her to have as much protection as possible."

"Protection? Protection from what? Who?"

Frank didn't answer my question. "Lee, honey, I've known Mateo a long time."

"That's right."

"Same as you kids. Extended family."

"Out with it, Frank. You're starting to scare me."

"He may be professing her innocence, but he's in a panic. He thinks she killed the man."

"Wow. You're sure?"

"Not only does he think she's guilty, so do I. At the very least, she's keeping something back and it's big."

"Like what?"

His face looked pained. "No idea."

"Do you think Tío knows what it is?"

Frank thought for a moment. "No, I don't think so. He seems almost as thrown by all of this as I am."

I started to speak, but Frank rushed over my words.

"Once we find Sanchez – and we will – if he doesn't pan out as the killer – and odds are he won't – I'm going to have to arrest Patsy Durand for murder. It doesn't matter if Mateo is in love with the lady chef or not."

Chapter Three

Devil In A Blue Cheese Dressing

"Liana!" Tío sprang to his feet and ran to me. Swallowing me up in bear hug, he apologized again and again in Spanish.

"Forgive me, *Sobrina*. You come back from vacation and I bother you right away. *Lo siento.*"

"Don't be sorry, Tío. This is important."

"*Si, si.*"

He nodded earnestly, then reached out and held onto both my shoulders with his hands. Looking me directly in the eye, he said,

"My friend, Patsy, you do not meet her yet. But she is a good woman. She do not do this stabbing of the man. She do not. But I fear for her. This is bad."

He looked at Frank, who stood near the door, and forced a wan smile.

"I worry our good friend here. He thinks she is guilty." He turned back to me. "You must prove Patsy is innocent. I know you will do this."

Tío gave me the same look Tugger, My Son The Cat, gives me when he knows it's time for a treat, he can't open the cabinet door, and he's counting on me to do it. Half hopeful, half expectant, fully trusting.

When the cupboard is bare, I've gone out many a stormy night with a raincoat thrown over my pajamas to buy his stupid dried salmon slivers. All it takes is that look. You betcha I would do as much, and more, for Tío.

At twenty and with both parents dead, Tío took responsibility for his younger brother, my father, only five years old. Together, they made the incredible journey on foot from Vera Cruz, Mexico, to Salinas, California, looking for a better life.

Tío's rise from strawberry picker in the fields of Salinas to executive chef at San Jose's famed Las Mañanitas Restaurant is the stuff of which legends are made. While his way around a kitchen is mostly self-taught, he did receive a degree by taking night classes at the San Francisco Culinary Arts School. Tío never for a moment believed he couldn't do it.

Retired now, he cooks six days a week for the two-footed at the San Jose Homeless Services and the four-footed at the animal shelter. My uncle is the busiest retired person I've ever met.

My eyes met his in silence. We gave each other a tenuous smile.

"I'll leave you two to discuss this," Frank said, exiting. He leaned in for a moment before pulling the door closed. "Come back to my office when you're done here, Lee."

I nodded and studied my normally fastidious uncle as he sat back down. His elegant demeanor seemed shaken to the core. Dark, under eye circles and an ashen hue dominated his usually healthy, tanned face. Tío's shirt was not just wrinkled, but looked like it had been taken from the bottom of the clothes hamper.

"Tío, you look exhausted. Have you been up all night? Did you get any sleep?"

He brushed me off. "Do not worry for me, *Sobrina*. I was – " Breaking off here, he reached out for my hand, and pulled me to him. "Do they put the bug in this room?"

I looked around. "You mean, hidden microphones?" I shook my head. "No, Tío, it's against the law. They have to tell you when they're recording what you say."

"*Bueno*." He moved around in the hard wood chair, maybe trying to get more comfortable, maybe antsy. He looked up.

"Liana, *estoy preoccupado*."

"I can see you're worried. Tell me what's going on." I sat in another chair across from him.

"Last night, early, Patsy says she will meet me at our house. I cook for her *Chile relleno en nogada*; it was the plan. She likes poblano peppers and I make this dish the best. Your mother, she is gone for the evening and Patsy and I will be alone. Then she calls."

"What time was that?"

"Six-thirty, I think. She says for me to start eating without her. I say 'no, I cook for you; I wait for you'."

He ran a trembling hand through his thick salt and pepper hair.

"She says she will come soon. But she does not come. By eight I worry. I phone her. No answer. I drive to her apartment – it is close by – and bang on the door. No answer, but I have a key."

"You have a key?" I was shocked but tried not to show it.

"*Si*. I let myself in. Things are thrown around, messy, not like usual."

"You mean, like someone had searched the place?"

"*Si, si*. This is when I feel to call the *policía*. But then, just then, she phones me. She tells me not to worry; she is all right, but I know she is not. I say to her, where are you? She will not say but tells me again she is all right. Her voice is different." He paused before saying in Spanish, "*Estaba asustada*."

"She was scared," I repeated in English, thinking about the ramifications of his words.

"*Si*."

I could see Tío was working himself up. I stood, went behind his chair, and massaged his tension-filled shoulders, trying to relax him a little.

"Okay, Tío, okay. Let's stay calm and try to sort this out. When did she show up at her apartment last night?"

He shook his head. "*Nunca*. Never. She call again to tell me she would not come; I should go home. I say yes, but still, I wait for her. I fall asleep on her couch. In the morning I hear from Patsy. She is at the police station. I come here and see her right before I call you this morning."

"Does Mom know you didn't come home last night? She never mentioned it."

Tío shook his head. "I do not think so. The house is big and your mama and I do not check in with one another. Not always."

I chewed this over.

"So Patsy never showed up. And according to Frank, the chef was killed between eight and eleven PM last night."

"I know this."

"I'm not going to pull any punches with you, Tío. This is bad. She lied to the police. She said she was home when the man was murdered."

He nodded then looked down. "I know this, too."

"Have you told the police you were in her apartment alone at the time she says she was there?"

Head bowed low, he shook it. "They have not yet asked me," he mumbled.

"But it's bound to come up," I stressed.

Tío looked up at me, eyes glistening with tears. "I know this, also."

"Poor Tío. You're in a spot. You could wind up being a witness for the prosecution."

He said nothing.

"But more to the point, you think she killed the man. Obviously, you do."

Before answering, Tío rubbed at the stubble of a beard on his face. It was the only time I've known him to have a five-o'clock shadow, except for the time he had a bad case of flu. Now he had a bad case of love.

"I do not know what to think, but I know how the police work; how they think. Your father was a policeman. They think she is the one. They will not look further."

"You could be right. Their job is to follow the clues and find the most logical suspect. And then they stop looking. That suspect seems to be Chef Patsy Durand."

"*Si,* but she is a good woman, Liana. I swear to you. She would not –"

His words were cut off by the door flinging open, so forcefully, it hit the back wall.

"Matt! Matt, are you in here? They told me you were."

A petite, curvy woman strode in, mature but still very attractive. Straight silver hair cut in a Vidal Sassoon style framed a face devoid of wrinkles. It was also well made-up. Her eyes, blue and vivid, caught sight of my Tío. Although I'd never seen a picture of the woman, I knew straight away this was Patsy Durand. We PI's can put things together like that.

A smile lit up her features. "There you are! Matt, you poor thing. You look like you been rode hard and put up wet."

The way my orange stilettos had done Mom in, Patsy Durand calling Tío 'Matt' did me in. I have to admit, I wasn't so thrilled with her. I mulled this over and stepped aside. My uncle stood with outstretched arms and she rushed into them.

"I'm so sorry. I'm so sorry, lambie-pie," Patsy murmured, reaching up and whispering in his ear. "This is such a mess."

"It's all right," he said in a soothing tone. "We will face this together."

I watched this tender scene with a jaundiced eye. Tío's wife, Richard's and my *Tía* Maria, had been dead six years. They'd had a long and happy marriage lasting more than four decades. I never thought he would care for another woman. But in the autumn of his life had my uncle, lonely and vulnerable, become ensnared by a murderess?

Chapter Four

A Wrinkle In Thyme

They broke free and turned to me. Wherever she'd been, Patsy Durand fared the night's ordeal far better than Tío. If I calculated right, she was around sixty or sixty-one, at least a good nine years younger than my uncle. But still. She looked like she was ready to walk onto a set of a television studio.

She wore black stretch jeans and a fitted, black long-sleeved blouse. Her touch of color was a scarf tied jauntily to one side around her neck, the same shade of red as her lipstick. Every hair was in place, her makeup just so. Considering Tío's condition, it made me furious.

With a smile, she reached out, took my hand, and pumped it up and down. "You must be Matt's niece, Liana. I have been so looking forward to meeting you, sugar."

Patsy spoke with the most southern of drawls. Aside from dropping the 'g' from words normally ending with one, each vowel had three or four syllables bouncing around within it like a rubber ball. She bounced on.

"But I hear you don't hang with formality; everybody calls you Lee. Excepting your mama and this big oaf right here." She smacked Tío on the arm with a laugh. "So I'm going to call you Lee, myself."

"All rightie," I muttered. And coldly, I might add.

She turned to my uncle. "Matt, you didn't tell me what a beauty your niece is!"

She looked back at me and seemed to rev herself up.

"Why, you're as pretty as a peach. Have you ever heard of Elizabeth Taylor? I know you're too young, but you might have seen her on TCM in the movie *Cleopatra*. Or *Suddenly Last Summer*. Anyway, you are the spitting image of her. Those gorgeous violet eyes and that dark hair! Of course, hers wasn't as thick or as curly as yours, but honey, you must stop them in the street with your looks."

Okay, I was mellowing. Maybe her accent wasn't so bad.

"Yes, I've heard of her," I said. "Thank you."

"And Matt tells me you recently got married. I can't wait to meet the lucky man. What's his name? Garth?"

"Gurn." No one ever gets his name right.

"Well, Garth, Gurn, he must be prouder of you than a blue-ribbon calf at a state fair. You tell him I said so."

She threw her arms around me and continued talking in a down-home, intimate, and friendly manner. Mom was soooo going to hate her.

"Anyway, sugar, I don't want you to worry about your uncle and me. All this malarkey about me having murdered that second-rate, short order cook pretending to be a chef. He should live so long. Well, he didn't. But he thought a Turducken was the height of *haute cuisine*. Don't that beat all? But he didn't deserve to die like a slaughtered pig at a barbeque. So, I'll say it again; don't you worry, honey. This will all get cleared up."

Having taken my breath away sufficiently, she turned to face Mr. Talbot standing in the doorway. I hadn't seen him until that moment, so under the spell of her personality. I looked at him now. He, too, seemed caught up in the magic that was Patsy Durand.

"Now that we're all here, let's get this party started," said Patsy. She turned to Mr. Talbot, with a beckoning gesture of a red-lacquered fingernail. "Come on in, Jimmy boy."

Shocked, I sucked in a quick breath. Mr. Talbot, 'Jimmy Boy'? I don't think even his wife would have dared.

Mr. Talbot gave her an indulgent smile, while crossing the room. "I wouldn't call it a party, but as soon as the judge signs off on your ROR, you can leave."

"How about an update," I said. "What's going on?"

I looked from Patsy to Mr. Talbot. He answered, but with a worried look on his face.

"Ms. Durand is not under arrest at the moment. However, it is possible that when Manuel Sanchez is located, the court may reverse its decision. But until such time, she must remain in the Bay Area and in constant telephone contact, or she will be arrested automatically." He turned to Patsy. "You do understand that, don't you, Ms. Durand?"

"First of all, Jimmy," she answered in a voice loud enough to be heard in Los Angeles, "Call me Patsy. And I got it all memorized."

She cleared her throat, closed her eyes, and began to recite.

"A Release on your Own Recognizance or an ROR is a written promise signed by the defendant – me – promising that I will show up for future court appearances and not engage in illegal activity while out on the ROR. And I will answer my phone right away, should they call me. I understand and I'll be a good girl, hon. I won't leave you in a lurch."

He looked at her in a way that showed he hadn't heard the last part.

"I said I won't leave you in a lurch," she shouted. "And thank you, kind sir, for all your help. You really know your way around a clink."

Mr. Talbot relaxed and smiled at her. "Be in my office at four this afternoon so we can go over everything. In cases like these, it's best to be prepared. I'll go see what's holding up those papers."

He looked at Tío and then me. "Until we meet again, I shall bid you adieu."

He turned to leave but paused at the door. "Remember, Patsy, four o'clock. I shall be expecting you."

"And I'm expecting you to get a hearing aid, Jimmy boy," Patsy retorted with a big smile. "I'm getting hoarse trying to talk to you, hear me?"

"I shall think it over, dear lady." Mr. Talbot gave off with a light laugh as he left the room.

Speaking of hearing, I couldn't believe my ears. This stranger made a demand of Mr. Talbot I never thought anyone would or could. Following my mother's lead, I assumed saying such a thing to him was verboten.

Historically, Mr. Talbot has been around since Mom was in rompers, as he is wont to say. But more to the point, I think she's scared of him and I'd like to know how he does it.

I came back from my mental meanderings when Patsy turned to me. "That old coot's a real sweetie, Lee. I can't thank y'all enough for hitching us up. We got ourselves a company lawyer, but he's in New York, and I don't want to bother him with this trifling thing."

"I don't know how trifling murder is—" I started, but she interrupted me.

"Besides, you think Jimmy Boy's a stuffed shirt?"

"Well, no. I don't –"

"You should see Hallsworth Rehnquist," she said right over my words. "Double starched and a stare mean enough to clean out an outhouse. No fun at all." She smacked me good-naturedly on the arm the same way she had done to Tío. "You be sure to thank your mama for me, too. Matt can't say enough nice things about her."

She walked over and put her arms around Tío, smiling up into his face. He looked down at her adoringly. Yikes.

"Of course," she said, "I know you did it because of this *hombre* here, but I appreciate it. Don't think I don't."

"In that case, Patsy," I said, overlooking the fact she'd pronounced the 'h' in *hombre* and the last syllable like the bray of a donkey, "I hope you don't mind answering a few questions?"

She dropped her arms from Tío's waist and turned to me. I gave her a big smile, but wasn't smiling inside. She hesitated then gave me a phony, fifty-kilowatt smile. The only honest thing between us were my orange stilettos.

"Whatever you say, sugar," Patsy finally said.

"While we're waiting for Mr. Talbot to return, why don't we sit down and clear up some things?" I gestured to the hardback chairs.

"Sure, sugar." She sat and turned to Tío. "Matt, I am simply parched. Do you think you could find me a thimbleful of water from somewhere?"

Confused, Tío looked at her then shrugged. "*Como no*, of course." He glanced my way, with a sheepish grin. "She wants me from the room for a while. So, *si*, I will go get the water."

We watched him leave then looked at one another. The smile left Patsy's face to be replaced by sober deference.

"Sugar, I know what you want to talk about."

"Good." I sat across from her. "Where were you last night?"

She leaned in toward me, placing her elbows on the tops of her thighs. "I did not kill that sorry excuse for a man."

"You told the police you were home last night but you weren't. Tío was at your apartment and not only weren't you there at the time, you never returned. It's one thing to have an alibi that can't be proven. It's quite another to lie about one. Now Tío hasn't told the police yet, but it's just a matter of time before it has to come out. He's not going to lie to the police to protect you."

"No, of course not," she said. "I wouldn't expect or ask him to." She pursed her lips together. "I never thought of that."

"Then tell me where you were."

She shook her head. "I can't."

When she saw I was about to protest, her words overrode mine. Again. "Sugar, God as my witness, I can't. At least, not right now. I need to talk to somebody, get his permission."

"This is murder, Patsy. It trumps everything else, any promises you've made, anyone you're trying to protect. If you don't start cooperating, you could be arrested and charged with the crime. And if things continue as they are, it's possible Tío could be charged with impeding an investigation. There's no way I'm going to let that happen to him."

This was the first time I saw her rattled. "Good Lord almighty! I don't want to involve Matt in this. Is there –?"

"He's already involved. He was at your apartment. He knows you weren't there at the time of the murder. And, if called upon, he would have to testify to that."

My voice was sharp and angry and I didn't care. But I did care a second later when Patsy Durand burst into tears just as Tío walked into the room with a small paper cup of water. A look of surprise turning to anger crossed his face.

"What is it you do? What is it you say to upset her like this, Liana? Shame on you, *Sobrina*. For shame."

Chapter Five

The French Concoction

I sputtered, Patsy drew a small hanky out from the wristband of her blouse – Mom would have been impressed – while Tío charged in like a bull. Before anyone could say more, Patsy blew her nose, and waved her free hand dismissively at Tío.

"Matt, don't be silly. This sweet little thing? She hasn't been anything but kindness itself. It's just me, lambie-pie. I think this whole awful mess has just caught up with me."

I can't remember ever being called a sweet little thing, but more importantly, I'd never been charged at by my uncle, as if I were a villain. My feelings were so hurt I sat there like a statue.

Patsy, unaware of our family dynamics, went on with hers.

"And I was hoping the boys wouldn't learn of this until it was over, but it was on the news. They're on their way here, Wally from Little Rock and Pete, Portland. They should be here any minute."

She let out a deep sigh and tucked her hanky neatly back in her wristband. Turning to Tío, she asked, "Did you see Jimmy out there? I need to get out of here." She gave me a meaningful glance. "I have to see somebody about something."

I could feel Tío's eyes never leaving me as he answered her.

"*Si*, he waits for you outside. Everything is done, he says. You join him and I will be there in a minute." He reached out. "Here is your water."

"Thanks, hun," she said, and drank it in a preoccupied manner. She turned to me. "If I don't see you outside, sweetie, I'll call you when I know more. Just give me a couple of hours."

I nodded and looked down. I felt rather than saw her leave the room. Tío came and stood before me for a moment.

"Liana," he said sitting in the chair she vacated, his voice soft and tender. "I owe you the apology. I should not have raised my voice like that. I am tired and more upset than usual, but…that is no excuse."

He reached over and took one of my limp hands resting in my lap. He held it in his with tenderness.

"*Perdóname*. Say you forgive me."

It took a moment, but I squeezed his hand and finally could look at him. "Of course, I forgive you, Tío. I'm sorry if you think I was being hard on her. It's just that –"

"No, no, do not say more," he interrupted. "This is not anything for you. This is for me. I should explain." He took in a ragged breath and cleared his throat.

"Patsy, she is different than any woman I know before. Some might call her tough on the edge –"

"Rough around the edges," I interjected, with a small smile.

Tío smiled, too, then repeated the words carefully.

"*Si*, rough around the edges." He glanced away before going on.

"I know she is not the same as you or Lila or…my beautiful Maria. There will never be another Maria, I know this." His voice broke and he cleared his throat again. "No one will ever take her place with me."

I saw the light. "But you were afraid that once the family met her, we'd compare her to *Tía*, right? And she would show up lacking, right? At least, to us?"

He hesitated. "In part, *sí*. But there is more."

"More?"

"*Sobrina*, you, Ricardo, and your mama, the ones I love with all the heart, have lived a more…what is the word…" He broke off and shook his head.

"I cannot remember. But I have seen more of the world than you. Here in beautiful California, you have the good life. But there are other good lives out there –"

"Tío," I interrupted, horrified. "You think we're snobs."

"No, no."

"Yeah, you do. May I remind you of what I do for a living? Find the bad guys. That's what Discretionary Inquiries is all about; for Richard, Mom, and me."

"Sheltered."

He found the word he'd wanted and said it, as if I hadn't spoken. He even raised his forefinger for emphasis.

"You have been sheltered. And it is one thing to find 'the bad guys' for a living and another to think of having someone like that in *la familia*."

"Tío! Are you thinking of marrying this woman? You've only known her –"

Tío's sound laughter stopped me midsentence.

"No, no." He shook his head. "But we are friends. Good friends. She makes me alive again. And it is good."

I studied his face for a moment. "It is good. I'll give you that. But I think you're selling us short, Tío."

It was his turn to study my face.

"*Quizás*…" He paused, thinking.

"Perhaps? Perhaps what?"

"It is *la culpa*; my guilt. Many days I feel I betray your *Tía*."

"My aunt would want you to be happy, Tío. We all do."

I took in a breath, long and deep then stood.

"But you know what, uncle mine? Stow your *culpa* away for the moment. We have to find out exactly what Patsy's involvement is in all of this. You can't keep this information to yourself much longer, Tío. As it is, Frank is going to wonder why you didn't come forward sooner."

"I did not think it would come to this."

His voice was sad. I ignored it.

"Who else besides me knows you spent the night alone at Patsy's apartment?"

He shook his head. "No one. I tell no one."

"Then don't. Not even Richard or Mom. We don't want to put them in the position of being a party to withholding evidence. Patsy said she'd call in a couple of hours and tell me where she was. It can wait until then. She says she has to talk to someone."

"Who?"

"I don't know. But I want your promise, Tío, if she doesn't call, you will tell Frank what you know. And today."

My mind raced on with possible excuses, which came tumbling out of my mouth as I thought of them.

"You can say you didn't think it was important; you hadn't realized the man was killed during the time you were alone at her apartment waiting for her; something like that. We'll work it out, make it plausible. He'll think you're a knucklehead, but maybe it will be all right." I turned and looked at him. "Promise me."

Tío hesitated then nodded. When he answered, his voice was strong.

"I give you my word. I will do what is right. The Alvarez, we do no less."

"Glad to hear it, Tío. You had me scared for a minute."

Chapter Six

Grape Expectations

I was sitting in my car outside the family home, alone. Tío, Mom, and Richard had gone inside a few minutes before. No one said a word on the short ride home. I knew Tío was emotionally spent, as were my mother and brother. But for the first time in a long time I feared what happened after my father's death was happening again; a deep, damaging rift.

The earth's crust with its fissures, cracks, and earthquakes can take a backseat to human relationships. When Dad died – the patriarch of the family – Mom, Richard, me, and even Tío became lost in our own grief. Not one of us reached out to the other.

An unexpected murder case I stumbled into reunited us, but it was a long, painful, and lonely two years later. I didn't want to go down that road again.

My phone rang and I saw the picture of my husband come up on the screen. All the control and barriers I'd put up came crashing down. I answered, barely controlling a sob.

"Gurn."

"What's wrong?" He knew something was up just by my one word.

I explained as briefly as I could, not just Patsy's involvement in a murder, but Tío's dilemma and what might be happening to the family. Again.

"I'll be right there," he said, and hung up.

I got out of the car feeling like heavy chains were wrapped around my legs. I staggered around the back and toward our 1930s kitchen, the heart of the house. Pushing slightly at the kitchen door, I heard unexpected lighthearted chatter, the fragrance of freshly brewed coffee, and the aroma of hot food wafting toward me.

Mom must have seen the slight movement of the door. She called out.

"Liana, is that you? I was *wondering* how long you would stay in the car. I saw you from the window just a moment ago."

"I...I was talking to Gurn."

"Well, I can't imagine *what* you two had to talk about that *took* so long," she said. "Come *inside*, dear."

I opened the door fully. My mother sat at a table that was set, even a green salad held center court in the middle of the table.

Standing next to my seated brother was Tío, who looked at me with a smile. In his hand, he held a spatula heavy with a steaming, batter-fried chili poblano stuffed with finely chopped meat, fruits, and nuts. I knew what was inside the poblano, because in his other hand was a silver tray laden with three small bowls. Each bowl contained one of three toppings, golden walnut sauce, red pomegranate seeds or chopped green parsley.

He set the tray down on the table and waved a greeting. Then he slid the poblano onto a plate in front of Richard and began the process of dressing the poblano with toppings from the bowls.

Picking up a large spoon, Tío covered the poblano with his sauce or *nogada*. A sprinkling of red pomegranate seeds came next then chopped green parsley. The final result is colorful and delicious. The dish has been presented this way since I can remember.

Paying no attention to the family ritual, Richard gazed at his laptop, grinning from ear to ear. He laughed at something on the screen.

"And here she is, rolling over! Just four- months old. Look at our girl!"

Mom walked toward me and wrapped an arm around my shoulder. She coaxed me inside.

"Hurry *up*, Liana. You're *missing* the videos Richard took last night of my *granddaughter*." She lowered her voice. "This is the second time he's showing them. Proud papa." She continued at a more normal volume, "Stephanie Roberta is *such* a beautiful baby. And so intelligent!"

"*Si*," agreed Tío. "*Bebé preciosa*."

Turning away from the screen, Richard glanced up. "You know it, Mom." He noticed our uncle and flashed him a brief smile.

"*Gracias*, Tío. Hi, Lee. What are you standing in the doorway for? Come on in."

"Liana," said Tío. "I reheat the *nogada* and fry the fresh poblanos. Have some before Ricardo eats them all."

My uncle gave Richard a pretend frown, winked at him, and turned back to the stove. Richard laughed.

"This is my second helping. Lee, you'd better get some before I eat it all."

Mom guided me to an empty chair and I fell into it. She sat across from me, clasped her hands together, and gave me a smile filled with warmth. I looked back at Tío, my eyes following his every move.

He came to the table and set a steaming plate of *Chile relleno en nogada* in front of me. He leaned down and kissed the top of my head before he began the ritual of putting together the dish once more.

"*Gracias*, Tío."

"*De nada, Sobrina*," said Tío. "You are welcome," he repeated in English.

I sniffed the dish, grabbed my fork, and took a bite. Until then I had no idea how hungry I was. Tío watched carefully for my reaction. As I chewed, I groaned out loud.

"Liana," Mom said. "*Manners.*"

"*Bueno,*" Tío said to me with relief, both of us ignoring Mom's edict. "I fear it was not good from being in the fridge all night."

"Well, fear not." I looked at him with a grin. "It's the usual fantabulous."

"Liana," said Mom, "while you've been out in the car and before we began watching videos of Stephanie Roberta, Mateo explained *everything* about last night."

"He did?" I stopped eating then glanced in my uncle's direction, his back to us as he busied himself at the stove. "That's great," I stuttered. "I'm glad it's out in the open."

Actually, I was. I reached out and helped myself to some salad loaded with avocado and drizzled with Tío's seasoned lime and olive oil dressing. Yummy.

Tío turned around and faced me. "I know you say not to tell about last night, but I think it is best."

My mouth was crammed with avocado, so I merely nodded.

"Yes, it was," said Mom, "and I'm *surprised* at you, Liana. Family *doesn't* keep secrets from one another."

"I understand what Tío was going through," said Richard, smiling at me. "I'd lie like a rug to protect Vicki."

"That is different, Ricardo," said Tío, a slight rebuke in his voice. He turned back to the hefty cast-iron skillet on the stove. It was his favorite cooking pan and older than the hills. Picking up a plate from the side of the stove, Tío went on, filling the dish with food as he spoke.

"Victoria, she is your wife, the mother of your child. She is *familia*. While I am fond of Patsy, I was carried away with what you call the knighthood."

"You mean, acting like Sir Galahad?" I swallowed and looked at Tío. "Rescuing fair damsel in distress?"

He shrugged in answer. "Last night I think she may do this terrible deed. But now, in my kitchen, in the day, with *la familia,* I know she do not. It would be out of – how you say – character."

He returned to the table with a plate of hot food and sat down next to me before continuing.

"That is why I will wait until she calls you with the truth of where she was. And then I will go to Frank with everything." And with that proclamation, Tío picked up a fork and took a big bite.

I turned to Richard. "I should like to clarify for you, brother mine, that as Vicki's husband, legally you cannot be forced to give damning information about your spouse. And you can't be charged with obstructing justice if you withheld such information. That's because under California Evidence Code, a spouse has the privilege not to be called as a witness by any party adverse to the interests of the other spouse in the trial and said spouse cannot be penalized. Tío, on the other hand, has no such immunity."

"Wow," Richard said with a laugh. He leaned in and whispered. "I love it when you go all legalese, Sis."

"Never mind," I said. "*¿Entiendas o no?*"

He let out a sigh. "Yeah, I understand. Tío needs to come clean."

Tío laid down his fork and looked at both of us. "And I will do so. But first, I will eat my lunch and shave to be presentable."

"Liana," said Mom, "I think you're *overreacting*. Mateo is merely *delaying* giving information. He's not permanently withholding it."

"Tell that to a judge," I said.

The kitchen door burst open and all heads turned in that direction. Gurn stood in the doorway taking in the scene at the table, a surprised look on his face. After talking to me, it wasn't at all what he'd expected.

I smiled brightly. "Hi, darling! Fancy meeting you here." I got up and practically flew across the room, throwing myself in his arms.

"Dear *boy*," said Mom, rising. "How *delightful* to see you. What brings you home from work in the middle of the day?"

"Hey, Hutchers," called out Richard, with Gurn's nickname from their NROTC days. "Come on in and look at the latest video of your niece, Steffi. She's already rolling over, like the brilliant little girl she is."

Tío had an indulgent smile on his face at Richard's bragging. Then he spoke, rolling the 'r' in Gurn's name and sounding slightly Scottish.

"Gurn, you are in time for my *Chiles en nogada*. I will get you a plate."

My husband looked at them then at me. Green-grey eyes expressing puzzlement and his lop-side smile in place, he leaned against me. In a barely audible tone he said,

"So...exactly what's wrong here? Am I missing something?"

I held him in an embrace and whispered back. "Jumped the gun. Got carried away. Apologies. But you won't be sorry you came once you taste Tío's dish."

I pulled him over the table. Mom cleared a space and Tío picked up another plate.

"Here you are," said Tío beginning the ritualistic sprinkling of toppings once more. "And you have the last poblano, the best."

"The last one?" Richard's face showed disappointment. "Aw, jeesh, Tío. I feel bad. I wanted Vicki to have some. Why don't I save what I haven't eaten for her –"

"*No es necessario*," said Tío, with a dismissive wave of his hand. "I put aside for her already two poblanos, in case you eat one on the way home." Tío winked at Richard.

On the sly, Gurn turned to me again. "I feel like I'm in a Norman Rockwell painting."

"But with a Spanish accent," I whispered.

"I will make more often," Tío said. "Before I can only get the pomegranate seeds late summer and fall, but now a friend has a tree in his hothouse. But eat, eat," he ordered, "before it gets cold."

We all took a forkful of food almost in unison, chewed and choruses of ooohs and aaahs filled the air. We burst out laughing then continued eating in relative silence.

My phone rang. I thought of not answering it, but as I was expecting Patsy to call me, answer it I did. It wasn't Patsy, but Frank.

"Hi, Frank," I said, swallowing before I turned my back on the table. "What's up?"

"Nothing good, Lee," he said.

His voice was sober. We both knew I wasn't going to like what he had to say, but he said it, anyway.

"We have a warrant out for Patsy Durand's arrest."

Chapter Seven

The Adventures Of Huckleberry Flan

"A warrant for her arrest? What happened, Frank?"

Everyone at the table froze at hearing my end of the conversation, the *nogadas* forgotten. I put the phone on speaker and set it in the middle of the table. Frank continued.

"Forensics found several of Ms. Durand's hairs on the chef's jacket and remember, her fingerprints were already on the murder weapon."

"The fingerprints happened when Patsy and Jacques had their argument, and she picked up the knife. The hairs could have gotten there the same way," I said. "It got pretty physical. You said so yourself."

"I agree, but this isn't up to me. She hasn't answered her phone, a direct violation of her ROR. She swore an oath she would be at the other end of her phone 24/7. And she knew she would be arrested if she violated that oath."

I said nothing, but looked up at Tío. Frank's voice rang out in the room.

"Tell Mateo we've been trying to reach her to come in voluntarily, but there's been no response. I don't care to send a car out for her, sirens blaring, but it appears I have to." He paused. "Wait a minute. There may be an update."

We heard muffled voices, as if he put his hand over the mouthpiece. Collectively, we sat mute at the table, the atmosphere snapping with tension. A short conversation took place between Frank and someone else. He came back on the line.

"Never mind. I'm told Ms. Durand has arrived at the stationhouse as instructed. Claims she'd accidentally turned off the ringer on her phone and just now heard the messages. Not that it makes any difference. We have no choice but to arrest her. Hold on."

Again we heard muffled voices, and still couldn't make out the words. Frank returned.

"She's asking to talk to you, Lee. She'll have to be sent to County for the arraignment, but I can give you fifteen minutes in the holding cell if you come over right away. I shouldn't, but I will."

"I'll be right there, Frank. And thank you," I said, disconnecting. I stood, pushing my chair away from the table. A high-pitched grating sound rang out as the legs scraped against the floor. It seemed to echo my nerves.

"I go with you," Tío said, throwing his napkin on the table and rising.

"Me, too," said Gurn, following suit.

"I'll get my bag," Mom said, also standing.

"Wait a minute," I said, waving my arms around in protest. "We can't all go."

"We're not all going." Richard closed the lid on his laptop. "I have to get back to D. I. Someone's got to run the place. But before that, I want to drop by the shop and see Vicki and the baby for a few minutes. I'll bring her the *nogadas* for lunch."

Vicki owns an exclusive hat shop called "The Obsessive Chapeau," selling headwear to the discerning and the loaded.

I looked at the faces of my mother, Tío, and the man I loved. There was no way I was going to get out of letting them tag along without a fight, and I didn't have time for that. I grabbed the keys to my car.

"Okay, let's go." Everyone trooped behind me as I crossed through the family and living rooms, and out the front door. We piled into my car and we were at PAPD in less than ten minutes. I got out and slammed the car door, turning to the tagalong party.

"Frank's not going to let anyone else in her cell but me, folks."

Worried about having Tío by my side and possibly gumming up the works, I took a deep breath to state my case further. Gurn, bless him, took over.

Wrapping an arm around Tío's shoulder, He said, "Tío, why don't you and I take a walk? Then we'll wait out here for Lee to return."

Tío hesitated then nodded. "*Si, si.* We walk; we talk."

With Gurn's arm still around Tío's shoulder, the two men turned away and headed toward downtown Palo Alto. I looked at Mom, who reached out a well-manicured hand.

"Give me the keys to your car, Liana. I'll either wait for you in it, go shopping, or be in Frank's office."

I handed the keys to my mother, who took them, but suddenly became lost in thought.

"Perhaps at some point, I will at least *meet* the woman who seems to be monopolizing our lives."

"I hope it won't be at her trial, Mom."

"As do I." Mom paused and looked into my eyes, a sure sign she wanted the truth and nothing but. "You've met her, Liana. What is your *impression* of the woman?"

"Flamboyant, strong-willed, intelligent." I answered without hesitation. Then I remembered how she'd leapt to my defense during the short time Tío thought I was abusing her.

"And there's something about her that seems like she might be a fair-minded person." I shook my head. "But it's too soon to tell."

"Do you think Mateo's right and she *didn't* kill that man?"

"It's too soon to tell that, either."

Chapter Eight

The Bun Also Rises

I sat in a holding tank, decorated in a shade of pink I wouldn't be caught dead in a ditch wearing. It was more or less like any other police station's holding cell, a secure area designated for short-term use. The fourteen by fourteen space was painted Drunk Tank Pink, a shade claiming to reduce hostile, violent, or aggressive behavior. I would have said Pepto-Bismol, but what do I know. Whatever you call it, the color didn't make me feel any calmer.

My companion gave me a look that said she had no idea how we got to where we were. I could have told her. Murder most foul.

"I think they're madder that I didn't answer the phone than if'n I killed the man." Patsy shook her head.

"They haven't proven yet you committed the crime, but you were free on your word of honor to be on call at all times. You broke your word."

"When you say it like that, I don't sound like such a good person." She shifted around, uncomfortable on the holding cell's hard bench.

Patsy wore another matching jean and fitted blouse combo, this time in royal blue. Finished off by a white neckerchief, once again tied jauntily to one side, I sensed a design theme.

"That danged phone," Patsy said. "I get into more trouble with it than a long-tailed cat in a roomful of rockers. I'd accidentally pushed the mute button. I gotta get rid of that phone."

She looked at me again. Contrition written all over her face, she tried a smile. I didn't return it.

"A man is dead, Patsy. Let's skip the colorful chitchat and get to where you were last night. I'm assuming that's why you want to talk to me."

She nodded and swallowed hard. "Okay, sugar. Let's talk." Her voice lost some of its theatrical drawl and became softer.

"I cleared it with Hayes. He said I could tell you. I was at his place most of last night."

"Your ex-husband, the one who owns the Palo Alto Culinary Arts Institute, right?"

"That's right. His wife Connie tried to commit suicide. He called me around six to tell me she'd just taken a shitload of sleeping pills, pretty much the entire bottle. He was in a panic."

"Why didn't he call the paramedics?"

"She's an assistant professor at Stanford in the Research Science Department. She's on sabbatical leave; supposed to be researching a paper. She hasn't published in a long time. Hayes says that isn't good. He says she has one shot at tenure and it's been a long time coming. If she gets tenure, there'd be a chair that goes with it worth millions in grants. You know about this chair thing?"

"Yes, it's a faculty member who serves as the academic leader and administrative head of a department. It's pretty prestigious."

"Hayes gave me double talk like that, too. It's all a lot of hoo-ha to me, but he says there's a lot of competition in her field."

"And?"

"And if news of her trying to kill herself got out, she not only might lose tenure track, she might even lose her job. Hayes knows how much getting tenure means to Connie. If he could get out of calling in the paramedics, maybe no one would have to know, what with one thing and another."

"What's one thing and another?"

My voice sounded impatient, the way I was feeling. Patsy looked around then leaned closer to me before going on.

"Sugar, I'm getting to it. Keep your shirt on. Connie's clinically depressed. She tries to keep it hidden, under control, but it pops up every now and then."

Patsy sat back, reflective.

"Maybe it's having me around. You see, she has a thing about me. My being here has made her feel more insecure. I wouldn't have come, but..." And here her voice tapered off.

"But what?"

She leaned in again and whispered.

"Hayes asked me. He asks me all the time, but this time it worked out, you know? And he really needed me. So what with one thing and another, I came."

"We're back to 'one thing and another'?"

Patsy glossed over my question. "I owe him that much. The boys, too. And then..."

Her voice petered out again. She paused and blinked. I prodded.

"Patsy, you've got something on your mind. What is it?"

"Nothing, nothing. I swear, sugar. It's just Connie. Hayes didn't know it until last night, but she'd stopped taking her meds. She does that sometimes when she hits a low point. Anyway, when he saw she took the sleeping pills, he wanted something to induce vomiting, so he called me. I dropped everything and went running over. I tore my place apart looking for the Syrup of Ipecac. I always have some with me, left over from having small kids. Hayes knew that."

"So you're the one that trashed your apartment?"

She nodded. "I knew every minute counted. When I got there I made her drink it."

"Got where?"

"Hayes and Connie Durand live in an apartment on the third floor of the Institute."

"I see. Go on."

"It worked right away. The pills were barely dissolved, so we knew she'd be okay."

"Then what?"

"Then I remembered my date with Matt. I called him thinking I would only be late, but right after, Connie became hysterical. She started screaming and crying, throwing a fit, saying she wanted to die. Hayes called her doctor, who said she needed to get back on her meds as quick as possible. Come to find out she'd thrown them away, so the doc had to put in for a whole new parcel."

"Hayes didn't tell the doctor about her suicide attempt?"

"It seemed passed, honey, and Hayes was afraid the doc would want to take her to a hospital for observation or something. There'd be a record. Bless her heart, Connie begged Hayes not to say anything, so he didn't. I told Hayes I'd stay with her until he came back from the pharmacy with the pills."

"That's a lot to do for an ex-."

She studied me for a moment. "Not only is he the father of my two boys, he's had a lot to deal with lately. And we're friends. Sure, he's gone on with his life – haven't we all – but there's nothing I wouldn't do for him. Hayes and I go way back. And I owe him."

"You've said that before. Why? Because you became a culinary star and he didn't?"

She pulled at a strand of hair and tucked it behind an ear before she answered. "Something like that. But our past doesn't have anything to do with this, sugar. I swear."

I merely nodded before going on. "What time did he go to the pharmacy?"

"Let's see." She mulled this over. "Probably by then it was getting on eight."

"When did he get back?"

"Close on midnight."

"That's a long time."

"He had to wait for the doc to call the meds in. Then there was something about special pills not being on hand; had to be hauled in from another pharmacy. Hayes had to drive across town, too, it being Sunday."

I mused for a moment. "So the three of you were in the apartment above at the time of the murder. And you didn't hear anything?"

"It's all been soundproofed. Hayes did that when he moved in. He bought the three-story building about fifteen years ago, when his tour of duty was over."

"He was in the armed forces?"

"Right after we divorced he took a job with the army supervising the kitchens in their overseas commissaries, first in Germany and then France. It was an opportunity he just couldn't pass up. He was even given a commission. But it was hard on him. He couldn't see the boys every weekend like most divorced dads, but there wasn't a birthday or holiday he didn't send a present.

"And he'd call them as often as he could – his fire-cracker boys – sometimes twice a week. That was his pet name for them, 'cause they had his same red hair. They loved it, going all over Europe during vacations with their dad, but they didn't know him as well as they should have. As I say, it was hard, but he wanted something of his own, the Institute."

She paused for a moment, seeming to look inward.

"I think the family drifted apart more than we thought during that time. And it was my fault."

"Hayes started the Palo Alto Culinary Arts Institute fifteen years ago?"

Her face became more animated.

"Yes-sir-ee Bob. He's made a go of it, too. Lives right there on top of it all. One of them newfangled apartments with everything you can imagine, even a workout room. When he married Connie eight years ago, she moved in with him."

"Okay, back to last night, because we're running out of time. During the time he was gone, where was his wife, Connie?"

"She was asleep in their bedroom. I peeked in on her once to see she was all right. I guess a little of the pills got into her system or she wore herself out. She was dead to the world."

"So she was asleep the entire time he was gone?"

"She was."

"Did she ever wake up?"

Patsy shook her head before replying. "Nope. Not once that I could tell."

"That means you don't have an alibi for the time Chef Jacques was murdered."

She said nothing. I went on.

"Where were you between six and seven this morning?"

"I...I left Hayes' place around four. I drove home but didn't go in, just sat in my car chewing things over. How much he and I had changed over the years. How it was my fault Connie went off the deep end. I feel bad about that." She paused. "I must have drifted off around five, still sitting in my car. I didn't know Matt was inside waiting for me. Anyway, I didn't wake up until the police were tapping on my car window. Scared the living daylights out of me. They had me follow them to the station."

"So you don't have an alibi for the time of Manuel Sanchez's disappearance, either. This doesn't look good."

A look of fear pathed itself across her face.

"What am I going to do? I'm in trouble; Lord knows I am." She snatched at my hand. "Find out who did this, Lee. Please help me."

Something in me didn't want to get involved in this. Maybe the fact she wasn't telling me everything or the nagging feeling she could be guilty. Or both. My laugh was light but forced.

"Honestly, I don't know that you wouldn't be better off hiring the type of PI who concentrates on investigating this type of thing. My specialty is non-violent, white-collar crimes. You know, Silicon Valley stuff."

"I've read a few newspaper pieces about things you've done. And Matt says you're the best ferret in the business. It's so cute how he rolls his 'r's on that word and everything."

She chuckled for a moment then stared at me with the scared look again. I steeled myself and became firm.

"You know uncles; they tend to be prejudiced. Besides, you've got a good lawyer. Mr. Talbot may be old, but he's one of the best. And maybe the police will find out who really did it, if it wasn't you." I gave her what I hoped was a non-accusatory look. "But if it was, this is the time to say."

I stared at her. She stared back.

"Lee, I swear on the lives of my two boys, who I love more than God's little green earth, I didn't kill that monkey butt."

"Word to the wise, Patsy. Don't call the deceased names. It doesn't make you look a very sympathetic character."

"I was being kind. He was a lot more than that, honey." Some of the old Patsy spirit resurfaced. "Did you know he deliberately hired illegal immigrants then made them give him part of their salary in exchange for silence? What kind of lowlife does something like that?"

"Hmmm. What you're saying is, there might be several people who'd want to see Chef Jacques dead?"

"Honey, you could line up folks that wanted him dead from here to the barnyard – and in double rows – starting with the mother of his children. I hear tell she can't get child support unless she threatens to take him to court. Then there's any of the ladies at the school. If you were under forty and female, and didn't sleep with him, he'd flunk you out. And none of the real chefs at the Institute could stand that fraud, especially Dexter. He was up for the same job but lost out to him. By the way, Jack Chalifour was about as French as my big toe, even though he let off he was."

She'd pronounced his last name cauliflower, but I didn't feel the urge to correct her. "If he was so awful, why did your ex- keep him around?"

"You'll have to ask Hayes that. All I know is, that skunk fought me at every turn on everything. He even wrote a nasty letter, filled with nothing but lies, to *Chefs Talk Out Magazine* hoping they'd print it. They didn't, but if ever there was a piece of vermin who didn't deserve to breathe the same air as the rest of us, this was the one, sugar." She paused. "Not to speak ill of the lard-ass dead."

"Of course not." But that was one lard-ass motive if ever I heard it.

Patsy twisted her fingers together before she spoke. "Do they have the death penalty here in California?"

I nodded my head. "Yes, but it's rarely used. If convicted, you'd more than likely spend the rest of your life in prison, but I think you're getting ahead of yourself."

"Oh lawdy, lawdy, lawdy." Her voice was small, almost childlike. "I'll pay you whatever it takes, whatever you want. Just help me. I'm begging you."

"It's not a question of money, Patsy." I paused. "And this word 'lawdy', it's southern for Lord, right?" She nodded. "I just want to be clear about things."

"Lee, sugar, help me," she repeated then added, "Please."

"Patsy, I can't be in direct competition with the police. They know what they're doing. Let them do it."

"Then do what they don't do. Matt says you're the whistle-stomping best at finding out the truth, no matter when it happened. Find out the truth. That's all I ask. If not, they're going to railroad me into this, I know it."

Maybe it was because she looked so small and helpless, a direct turnabout from the larger than life Shakespearean-like character I'd witnessed earlier. Or maybe I'm just self-destructive. I'm going with the latter.

"Let me think about it," I heard myself saying. "But if I do," I added, "it's more for Tío than you."

She reached out and crushed me to her in a hug. "Honey lamb, when you get to be my age, you learn to take what you can get."

I looked at my watch. "My time is up. Mr. Talbot wants to see you. Meanwhile, more advice. Don't answer any questions without your lawyer present and don't give the police the password for your phone, either. They have your phone, right?"

She nodded then shook her head. I was confused.

"Do they have it or not?"

"They have my phone," she said, "but I don't have a password on it."

"Oh, lawdy."

"I can't remember passwords. I'm cyber stupid. And they've had my phone since I came in."

"Double lawdy. Well, tell Mr. Talbot. He'll need the heads-up."

"I will. Thank you, Lee."

I stood to leave, took a few steps, but turned back to Patsy.

"Don't thank me yet. Because if you're guilty, you're going down. And you'll be glad if it's life without parole, so I can't get my hands on you."

She studied me for a moment. "You love your uncle very much, don't you?"

"You bet I do."

"Then I'm glad I'm not guilty."

I glared at her long and hard. Her steady gaze met my glare. I was the first to break.

"I'll get back to you later today on whether or not I'll take your case."

Chapter Nine

Eggplants Can Remember

I knocked on Frank's office door, pushed it open, and was surprised by what I saw inside. I'm not sure how many men it takes to make a gaggle, but I would say a gaggle of men were sitting in Frank's office, seven in all.

Reading from left to right the first four were Frank, Gurn, Tío, and Mr. Talbot. The other three were unknown to me, but given what was going on, it had to be Hayes Durand, plus the Durand boys. I use the word 'boys' loosely – as they looked to be in their early to mid-thirties.

The older of the two leaned against the free space of a wall checking his smartphone. Wearing a crisp blue dress shirt, red tie, and navy slacks, he looked like a New York buttoned-down executive. The other, a year or two younger, sat on the floor, back against the wall, like he should be playing drums for a rock band. Shaved head, tattoos, body piercings, and shredded jeans. The whole nine yards.

My eyes lit on Gurn. Dressed in California casual, pink shirt, tan slacks, and looking like an ad for GQ, he was perched on a corner of Frank's desk reading his mini-iPad.

Tío, Hayes Durand, and Mr. Talbot sat in the hardback chairs previously occupied by the others of the Alvarez Clan a short time before. The seated men were silent, lost in their own thoughts. Frank was behind his desk doing paperwork, pointedly ignoring the featherless gaggle.

Mom was suspiciously absent. Probably too much testosterone crammed into one space. Or maybe she was window-shopping the stores on Palo Alto's main drag, something she'd alluded to. We Alvarez women never miss an opportunity.

I cleared my throat and all seven men snapped to attention, looked at me, and began talking at once. I held up my hands and gestured for silence.

"Hold it. Hold it, gentlemen, please. One at a time."

For a split second silence descended. Then Mr. Talbot was the first to go solo.

"There you are, dear girl." He nimbly got to his feet and crossed to me, silver cane in hand. "I take it I'm now free to see my client." He turned to give a generic wave to the room at large. "Ta ta for now, gentlemen."

As he passed by on his way out the door, he paused and said in hardly more than a whisper, "Lee, you and I should reconnoiter later today. Shall we say at my office? Six o'clock?"

"I haven't decided yet if I'm taking the case," I whispered back.

"Of course you will, dear girl. Of course, you will." Tapping the side of his nose several times with his forefinger, he exited.

I'm going to be honest. I have no idea what it means when a person taps the side of their nose, especially in a 'conspiratorial' way. But I was not going to be coerced into taking on an investigation on behalf of Patsy Durand, no matter how voting members of the gaggle cast their ballots.

I crossed the room to my uncle and leaned down. "Tío, how are you doing?" He smiled and nodded.

I glanced at Gurn with one raised, questioning eyebrow. My husband gave a low-keyed thumbs-up gesture and went back to his iPad.

Satisfied the two men I loved most were okay, I focused on the man sitting next to Tío. He wore khaki pants and a white shirt covered by a dorky red vest, a tad too small for him.

"You must be Hayes Durand. We haven't officially met."

I extended my hand then withdrew it. I noticed both his hands were unnaturally red, ending in swollen, stiff fingers. Nonetheless, he leapt up and grasped my hand with these seemingly, useless digits as if it was a lifeline.

"I am. And you are Lee Alvarez. Sorry about this," he said, gesturing to his hands. "They were burned a few months back in a fire, but I'm told I will make a full recovery, eventually." He spoke with a cultured southern accent, quite pleasant to the ear, and went on. "How's Patsy doing?"

The two boys rushed forward, not waiting for an answer. The taller, older one's voice nearly covered his father's final words.

"Yes, how is Mama? Is she okay?"

"You must be Wally." I extended my hand again.

"Yes, ma'am. Wally, ma'am." Wally 'ma'amed' me even though he was around my age. He took my hand in a very polite way, and squeezed it gently. I love southern manners. That's one of the reasons I fell in love with Gurn. He hails from North Carolina.

I pointed to the other son, coming to his brother's side. "That makes you Pete."

"Yes, ma'am, I'm Pete." He reached out and the same southern manners applied. Civilities done, however, Pete jumped at me. "How's Mama doing? Really?"

"She's holding up." I smiled at Pete. "Really."

"She's tough, boys." Hayes' voice was gruff, almost like he was trying to convince himself more than them.

I turned to Frank, who didn't say a word but stared at me with a scowl on his face. He probably didn't like the idea I might interfere in a police matter anymore than he liked his office being turned into a waiting room. I wondered why the men were there in the first place. I decided to do my godfather a favor. All things considered, he can be a good guy.

"Gentlemen, I have an idea. Why don't we take a walk to Discretionary Inquiries and give Chief Thompson back his office? D. I.'s offices are about two blocks away. What say, gentlemen?"

Mumbling assent, everyone except Frank followed my lead as I marched to the door. I opened it, stood aside, and the men trooped out.

I exited, too, but turned and leaned into the office. "See you later, Frank."

He waved me away without looking up. Gurn came to my side and grasped my hand, as if to assure me he was there in support. Marriage can be wonderful.

We passed through the corridor and came out to the larger, main room of the station. Officers in blue were busy at their desks. Several dozen men and women, all shapes and sizes, were sitting across from the officers, waiting on plastic chairs against a far wall, or pacing the room.

On this side of a glass partition, a desk sergeant was filling out a form, while listening to the voice of a woman on the other side. It sounded like there was a line of chattering, annoyed people directly on the other side. I thought I recognized the voice blasting above everyone else's.

Nah, I thought. Couldn't be.

I turned to Gurn. "What did I miss while I was talking to Patsy?"

"A peaceful demonstration at a car dealership gone amuck."

"I've heard about this."

"Solar power at its not so finest. But you don't bust up cars because it isn't as advertised," he said. "A few were arrested, some were detained for questioning, most are only giving their names and addresses and then are free to go."

No wonder Frank looked so harried. And why the Patsy Durand Gaggle was confined to his office. A frazzled, young officer I knew only as Mike opened the door for us to pass through.

The woman giving the desk sergeant what for turned to me as I stepped through the doorway. Ms. Packersmythe. That's right. She was dropping off a letter of apology on her lunch hour.

"Good afternoon, Ms. Alvarez. I am delighted to see you." She had a legal sized envelope in her hand, but what drew my attention was the tall, thin man at her side. Resting an arm around one of her massive shoulders, he didn't look like he was chained in position. In fact, he looked downright happy.

"I want you to meet someone, Henry," she said to the thin man, satisfaction oozing from every pore. She turned to the desk sergeant. "You. This is our place in line. And kindly alert Chief Thompson I wish to see him. I have a letter for his perusal."

After her declaration, she reached out and grabbed the man she called Henry by the wrist, and dragged him in my direction. He came fairly willingly. For the first time I paid attention to the fact her medium brown hair, usually worn in a tight bun at the back of her neck, had been cut shorter. Wonder of wonders, Ms. Packersmythe was sporting an almost stylish bob.

"Ms. Alvarez," she said. "May I present Henry Encino? Henry, this is Liana Alvarez. She works with me at Discretionary Inquiries. Henry is a concert pianist with the San Mateo Symphony Orchestra," she added with pride.

"In the junior seat, a fairly new position," he clarified, reaching out a long-fingered, elegant hand to shake mine.

I gave him my paw while observing he was about ten or fifteen years younger than Ms. Packersmythe, and definitely more easy going. That's often a musician for you, even of the classical variety.

"Evie's told me so much about you," he said.

Evie? Well, I never. First Jimmy Boy and now Evie. Next you know, people will start calling Lila Hamilton Alvarez, Lulu. While I mused on this, he went on.

"And she's told me so much about your family's business, Ms. Alvarez. It's a pleasure to meet you. And call me Hank, if you like. A lot of people do except Evie, of course. She can be very prim and proper."

He looked at her with a slight chuckle. She blushed and looked away, a small, feminine titter rising up from her throat.

Okay, so I was in an alternate universe. I should have known it when I saw the gaggle of men in Frank's office. Speaking of gaggles, I remembered the troop waiting behind me.

"It's a real pleasure to meet you, Hank. I'd love to stay and chat, but I'm afraid I have to get back to the office."

"I'm on my lunch hour, Ms. Alvarez," said Ms. Packersmythe. "In case you were wondering."

"Oh-ah. No, I wasn't." I turned back to Henry Encino. "I hope we can become more acquainted one of these days."

"Delighted," he said with a warm smile. "Another time." He turned to Ms. Packersmythe. "Back into the breech, Evie."

They both turned at the same time and rejoined the front of the line at the window, him slipping an arm around her waist. Or trying to.

I exited the building and glanced behind me. The Gaggle Parade was in place. Tío and Gurn were on either side of me. Three steps behind, father and sons chatted quietly, the older man showing each son warmth and compassion.

Tío saw me glance their way. "He does his best to be a good father, even from a long distance away."

In that one statement I understood that my uncle not only knew Hayes Durand, but liked him. Tío went on.

"Their mother, she is a good person, too. I know you will help her, *Sobrina*."

"Of course, I will."

Whoops.

"Now I have the easier breath," he said, and smiled at me.

I tried to smile back. But I'd done it. I was committed. Or maybe I should be committed.

We passed my car and Mom sat in the passenger's side reading her Kindle. As it was a gorgeous April day, the car windows were down. I reached in and touched her on the shoulder. She looked at me, I gestured that the group and I were hoofing it, and mouthed the word 'office'.

My pantomime skills must be improving, because Mom nodded, slid over to the driver's seat, and started the car. Before she could drive off, however, Gurn went around me and opened the passenger door.

"Change of plans, sweetheart," he said to me. "You seem to have everything under control and I need to get back to work."

This was the middle of April and the height of the tax season. Gurn being a CPA – actually, owner of Hanson Accounting Firm – this was his busiest time of year and he'd just returned from a two-week vacation. Yet he still dropped everything and came running.

Before I could say anything, Gurn leaned down and spoke to Mom. "Lila, can you drive Tío and me home before you go to the office? My car's there."

"My pleasure," she said.

"*Si*," said Tío. "It is time for me to prepare meals for the shelter, now that I know all will be well."

Then my uncle turned to the Durand family waiting on the curb. Tío stood tall and said with no small amount of pride, while looking directly at me, "I leave you *caballeros* in the very best of hands."

I was so dead.

Chapter Ten

Lord of the Onion Rings

Gurn opened the passenger car door and gestured for Tío to get in. Then he winked at me. "You take care of what you need. I'll see you later."

I leaned in. "I can't wait to find out what you and Tío talked about. But whatever it was, darling, thank you." I kissed him lightly on the lips.

"A worried man in love is something I know very well. And you can thank me later tonight," he whispered, opening the back door and jumping in.

During the short walk to the office Hayes Durand came to my side. The boys dropped behind, matching our gait but giving us distance and privacy. Whether or not their father had requested it, I didn't know. But he used the walking time to approach the subject I'd been planning to address later on in my office. Without looking at me, he said,

"How much do you know about Patsy and me?"

"Not much."

"We met at Le Cordon Bleu Paris. I was twenty-one, Patsy twenty-five. Being the only Americans enrolled, and both from the south, we became friends right away."

"I noticed the accent," I said with a smile. "Where are you from?"

"Vienna, Georgia. My parents have a pecan farm there or I should say, had. It sold a short time ago. My parents are elderly and my brother, Quinn, was running it until his death. I was injured in the same fire."

While his words came easily enough, I could feel deep emotion behind them. He took a cleansing breath.

"Now my parents are in assisted living."

"I'm so sorry. May I ask what happened?"

"One of the hazards of having a barn filled with hay is they are combustible." He shot me a wry smile. "The doctors say I'll get back pretty much all of my mobility one of these days. And I can finally drive a car. What's hard is not being able to write. I'm a big letter writer. I even keep a journal. Although, right now it's painful to sign my own name."

His words were followed by a remorseful laugh, which tapered off into a soft smile. I returned it.

"Were you and your brother close?"

"In some ways. I used to write long, long letters to Quinn. In fact, he knew everything about Patsy and me. How I was a rich boy and she a poor girl. Just like in the movies."

He stopped speaking again. We may have been walking down University Avenue, but he seemed to be strolling down memory lane.

"I loved her from the start. Patsy didn't feel the same way; she only wanted to be friends. But I couldn't help myself. She was the prettiest, most dynamic, and talented girl I'd ever met. And her artistry in the kitchen was second to none. I could tell right away she had the gift."

"What gift is that, Mr. Durand or should I say Chef Durand?"

"It would be Chef Hayes, but call me Hayes. We're not at the Institute now."

"Call me Lee all the time. So what's this gift, Hayes?"

"Why, the gift of culinary genius. Didn't you know she had it?"

A startled look came to his face. Recovering, he flashed me a smile tinged with humility and warmth. I found I'd taken to the guy, tacky red vest and all. I returned his smile.

"Sorry, no."

"With your uncle in the field, I thought you'd know Patsy's reputation, Lee."

"Don't assume I know anything. Better to assume I know nothing."

He laughed before going on.

"Then let me explain. A lot of people can cook and do it very well. Some, like me, teach. And I do it very well. But now and then you meet a person who elevates the craft to darn near magic. Mateo has that skill for the most part. Look at what he did with Las Mañanitas. Took a so-so Mexican restaurant and won the James Beard Award for Outstanding Chef twice. Although now he's retired, they're struggling to keep the reputation going."

"It seems to me those of you in the white-hat-food-game keep track of what others in the field are doing. True or not true?"

"True. It's a small world, epicurean-wise."

I mulled this over. If Patsy was to be believed, the question then was how Hayes Durand got snookered into hiring a womanizing, blackmailing, deadbeat dad for his head–teaching chef? Why hadn't Chef Jacques' reputation preceded him?

I'd have to find out later. The streets of Palo Alto weren't the place for a potentially explosive confrontation. Not with the butcher, the baker, the candlestick maker looking on.

"So Patsy has the gift, you were saying."

"Yes, indeed; from the beginning. You should have seen her then! Even the snooty teachers were impressed. So young, but so talented. The little girl from Arkansas was the talk of Paris during the three years we were there. They even loved the way her southern accent butchered their French."

He laughed again, but sobered.

"Seriously, though, Patsy could master the most difficult tasks in one or two tries while the rest of us were floundering. Slam, bam, thank you ma'am. She'd make it her own, adapt it, take it to a whole other level. Then she'd use that knowledge and blend traditional dishes together; create a whole new masterpiece. She loved to try French country combined with downhome southern, even then."

"I'd say her marriage of French and southern cooking has served her well."

"Much better than ours."

Those words were spoken in a softer tone, so much so, I almost didn't catch them. He looked behind him as his two sons walked about fifteen feet away, chatting together, oblivious to us.

"But more on that later." He cleared his throat and went back to his ex-wife's brilliance with a spatula.

"Patsy could go by the book, too, when she had to. Heck, it was like she wrote *Mastering the Art of French Cooking*. Julia Child had nothing on her. You know, when we graduated she was offered a position at Epicure Restaurant in Le Bristol Hotel, Paris. Three Michelin stars."

"I'm impressed."

"You should be. Chefs can wait all their lives for an invite to a place half that good and it won't happen. For a beginner; unheard of. But what did she want to do? Continue with her fusion ideas. Go her way."

Just then we turned the corner and faced the three-story edifice built of gold-beige sandstone standing on an angle at the two corners of Forrest and Gilman.

The Honor Blythe Building, named for a turn-of-the-century society matron, is one of the few non-campus buildings constructed of sandstone from the Stanford University campus. The quarry is spent, but some of these noble buildings live on.

D. I. doesn't own this historic building, more's the pity. The Republic Savings of Palo Alto, located on the ground floor does. However, because Mom was largely responsible for it being listed as a historic monument, the bank gave D. I. a ninety-nine year lease.

"Saints alive," exclaimed Wally when he caught up with us. "Where did this come from?"

"Man, oh, man," said Pete. "Ain't this something?"

Hayes' sons seemed taken with this peaceful and serene oasis in the midst of a busy small town, with its nod to bygone days. Of course, Hayes knew of the cobblestone courtyard complete with a three-tiered stone fountain decorated in vivid blue and green colored mosaic tiles.

"Sometimes when it all gets too much for me," Hayes said, pointing to an Oak tree, "I come here and sit under the shade of that tree, boys. It's over two hundred years old."

He added the last bit with a certain amount of pride, as did nearly everyone who lived and worked in Palo Alto. As a taxpayer, this was his courtyard as much as anyone else's.

I took over the tour. "The windows in the building are the original hand-blown, beveled glass from the eighteen hundreds. You can see how the irregularity of the panes catches the sun's light. Let's go inside the lobby. All the glass fixtures were designed and executed by Tiffany and Company."

"Well, I swan," murmured Pete, as we walked inside.

"I've got an idea." I pushed the elevator button to call down one of the crankiest elevators I'd ever met. It began its slow, clattering descent from the third floor.

"You three ride up in one of the most ancient public elevators still in operation. It only holds three passengers, and I like to use the stairs, anyway."

Before anyone could reply, I dashed to the stairs and took them two at a time, no mean feat in four—inch stilettos. I knew I could beat the stupid thing to the third floor – it's so old and slow – and I wanted a moment for a one-on-one with Richard.

Out of breath, I hurried across the burgundy-colored, plush carpet toward the end of the hall. I barely glanced at the gold leafing on the double, black ebony doors that read:

Discretionary Inquiries, Inc.
Data, Information and Intelligence
Room 300

I pulled at the ornate brass handle, and the door opened on silent hinges. Stanley looked up. I leaned over his desk until we were eye to eye.

"Now listen, Stanley, I have to make this fast."

He sat up straighter and came to attention. "All ears, Lee. Missed having you around for the past two weeks saying cloak and dagger things like that."

I lowered my voice, despite the fact no one else was in the waiting room.

"There are three southern gentlemen on their way up. Send them back to my office."

"Shall I order hot biscuits and gravy?"

"Only if you're hungry. They're the Durands, father and sons. Tell them I'll be with them in a minute. Is Richard in his lair?"

"Came in about twenty minutes ago."

"Great. Thanks, Stanley."

I waved a goodbye and headed toward the back, forbidden section of our offices. That would be D. I.'s heartbeat and also Richard's domain, Information Technology.

Andy, Richard's second-in-command, was guarding the gate, so to speak. He knows me and passed me through without the standard interrogation. With so many secrets contained within, very few non-IT people are allowed back here, even employees. I burst open Richard's office door and caught him tinkering with a bunch of wires and a small box.

"Richard, stop whatever you're doing. I haven't got a lot of time. I'm meeting with Durand and sons in my office, but meanwhile, I need you to do some fast research."

He dropped his screwdriver, swiveled his chair to his desk, and opened his laptop.

"Shoot."

"First, find out everything you can on Chef Jacques Chalifour."

His fingers rested over the keyboard. "Already did that. With a name as unusual as that, he wasn't too hard to find."

"Then Hayes Durand, owner of the Palo Alto Culinary Arts School."

"Him, too. Just let me know when you're ready to hear it all."

"Not now, later. He's got a wife, Connie something; don't know what her maiden name was."

"Doesn't matter. I'll find her." He finally began to type.

"She's supposed to be clinically depressed. See if it's true and what you can dig up."

"I won't be able to get medical records so fast, but I'll see if I can find someone who can verify what you've learned."

"The two sons, Wallace and Peter Durand. Mid-thirties. They manage Patsy's restaurants. Get me whatever you can on them."

"Yes, milady."

"I guess we're going to have to do a cursory background check on all of the students enrolled at the Institute or at least the fourteen living on premises."

"You mean I'll have to do a cursory background check on them. Already on it. Supposedly, none of them have access to the Institute when it's closed, even the ones living in the dorms. The assigned keys are numbered and can't be copied."

"I'll need a list of who has those keys."

"Of course, your majesty. Is that all?"

I ignored him. "No. Lastly, let's see what we can find out about the missing dishwasher, Manuel Sanchez. Let's make him number one."

"Already did that. Something about his name triggered a red flag for me. You've got a few surprises in store. I'll leave you in suspense, but text you what I found."

"Thanks."

"By the way, Chef Patsy Durand is worth over a hundred mil, in case you're interested."

I let out a soft whistle. "It pays to cook. The Durands should be in my office by now. How about filling me in on the rest later?"

Richard gave me a quick salute. I crossed to the door then turned back.

"You saw Vicki and the baby. How are they?"

"The absolute best. Vicki sends her love," he said, suddenly grinning. "I'll text the video I took of Steffi last night. Her favorite aunt should be up-to-date on her achievements."

"I'm her only aunt, but I want them, anyway," I said opening his office door. I paused for a moment. "Sorry I was a little testy earlier, brother mine."

"When was that?"

"Conference room, D. I., earlier."

"Oh, that. Forget it. So was I. That's board meetings for you."

We both grinned at one another. I looked at my watch.

"Gotta go. See you."

"Not if I see you first."

I groaned. Sometimes the nerd in Richard just has to come out.

Chapter Eleven

A Game Of Scones

"Sorry to keep you waiting," I said, opening the door and rushing inside. I spoke before I saw who was or wasn't in my office. I stopped short when I found only Hayes Durand in the room standing before my latest acquisition, a Sergio Bustamante bronze and resin piece. Part cat, part bird, part human and all fantastical, the colorful piece sat atop a black pedestal, begging to be admired.

"Where are your sons?" I looked around as if they might be hiding behind a piece of furniture.

"I asked them to stay in the waiting area so you and I could finish our conversation in private. There are some things I want to say without the boys around. The chairs out there look comfortable and the coffee is excellent, I must say."

He held up a mug wearing the Discretionary Inquiry's logo in maroon and grey. Or as Mom would say, claret and slate. However, 'a rose by any other name' still hangs true. Call them what you want, D. I.'s color scheme is drab and ugly. There. I've said it. I've said it and I'm glad.

"Good, I can talk to your sons later." I moved behind the desk and sat down. Hayes turned away from the large statue. He took a seat in one of the two hand-painted chairs in front of my desk.

"You have a very colorful and whimsical office. Actually, it's more like a small museum."

"Thank you. I like to keep myself amused and entertained when I'm in here pretending to work."

He laughed dutifully, and there was a moment of silence. I got right to it.

"So you said earlier your marriage was not so good. Exactly why did you two divorce twenty or so years ago?"

Hayes took a long sip of coffee, probably to give himself a chance to think. He let out a deep sigh and leaned forward.

"Look, I wasn't even twenty-two when she got pregnant with Wally. Then Pete showed up thirteen months later. Patsy and I, we really tried to make a go of our marriage. I knew she was just letting me ride her coattails; she was so brilliant and such a go-getter. One day I came home from taking the boys to the park -- we were in Arkansas by then -- and she sat me down and told me it was over. She couldn't do it anymore."

"How did you feel about that?"

"Frankly? A part of me was relieved. I didn't want to run a restaurant. It can be a twenty-four hour a day job. I wanted to teach. Help other talents. Teach them all I know then turn them loose. Maybe one might turn into another Patsy."

He paused.

"Besides," he said looking down, "it's hard to be that close to the sun. You get your wings singed." His reference to Greek mythology's Icarus wasn't lost on me.

"So the divorce was a mutual thing?"

"Yes, in many ways. She is, and always will be, my best friend. Even if I haven't seen her for years." He laughed then shook his head. "But I can't live with her any more than she can live with me."

"Does your wife know this?"

"Connie does when she's on her meds and is all right. But some days she just…gets lost."

"Tell me about your murdered chef."

"He'd been with me for about six months."

"What exactly was he in charge of?"

"He coordinated the classes and scheduled the students. Chef Jacques monitors – or monitored – the classes. The school runs on two shifts. There are two morning classes, which go from seven AM to one PM. The afternoon classes go from two to nine."

He took a deep breath.

"Thirty students in the morning, in rotation between two teaching chefs. Thirty students in the afternoon, two other chefs. We keep it fifteen students per teacher. Otherwise, they don't have the 'hands-on' time necessary for mastering the craft. Sixty students in all. We're small but mighty."

It sounded a little like a speech given to perspective students or written in a brochure. I'd check it out. Or ask Richard to do it. Ha ha.

"What was Chef Jacques' typical day?"

Hayes thought for a moment. "A lot of his job was to follow through with keeping the chefs and the students on track, but he would step in and teach, if necessary."

"On track?"

"Certain things have to be taught in order for students to get their degree and for us to keep our accreditation as a professional school."

"Do you set those standards?"

He shook his head. "Uh-uh. The state does. It has protocols in place for becoming an accredited school and staying accredited. Every year we have to send in documentation proving to the state we are complying with their rules. Every other year we have an onsite visit. I'm responsible for those."

"Was there anything else the dead man did?"

"His was a hard job. As head-teaching chef, he helped grade students' work, and stayed on top of their learning. But the biggest part of his job was keeping some pretty high-powered personalities, teachers and students alike, in line. That didn't seem to be a problem. He could be intimidating."

"A person like that often makes enemies."

Hayes shrugged, seemingly reluctant to reply. When he did, it was on the vague side.

"As I said, it's not an easy job."

"Tell me about the other four chefs. What are their names?"

"Chefs Dexter and Oliver teach the morning classes. Chefs Barbara and Aurélien teach the afternoons."

"How long have they been with you?"

"Let's see." He thought a moment. "Dexter's been with me since he graduated from here. That would be ten years. Barbara five, Oliver and Aurélien, two; they came within weeks of each other."

For the second time he pronounced Aurélien's name as if it was a combination of two English words. Airy – a breezy room – and the second, the word lean. I sat on the urge to say the Frenchman's name correctly. Been hanging around my mother too long.

"What do they teach?"

"What every chef needs to know. Food safety, storage, and the different methods of preparation in poultry, fish, meats, vegetables, sauces, fruits, and desserts, whether they are cooked, baked, fried, grilled, broiled, raw and so forth. And, of course, butchering a slaughtered animal."

"Butchering?"

"Each student has to be able to butcher a side of beef, which is roughly three- hundred pounds, in under thirty-minutes."

I blinked. He explained further.

"For steaks, chops, filets, the different cuts of meat. Then there's game animals, too. I thought you knew that, being the niece of a well-known chef."

"You'd think, wouldn't you?"

"It doesn't mean all chefs do that on a daily basis," he clarified. "There are many chefs who specialize. But each chef needs to know the basics of butchering."

I thought about what I knew of my uncle's traits. "And they use their own knives for that. No one else's will do."

"Of course not. Each chef invests in his or her own set of knives. It is a must. But to continue, we have one guest chef each spring who demonstrates their own particular skills in the lab. The lab seats sixty. Six chefs in all, not counting me. Two years ago the guest chef was your Uncle Mateo. Farm to Table, Mexican Style."

"I remember that."

"This year it's Patsy. We were lucky to get her, even though she is my ex-. She's filling in for the guest chef who got ill at the last minute, Chef Bob. He's had a hernia operation. Insisted on subbing, once she knew of my dilemma."

"The way I heard it, you asked for her help."

"Maybe I did." He gave me a weak smile. "I can't remember which one of us brought it up first."

"And what is it exactly you do?"

"I manage the administrative part of the program and oversee the day-to-day running of the kitchens, ordering food, tools, and supplies, things like that, along with my assistant, Nancy Littlejohn. And I usually try to keep my hand in with a class or two. But now I can't do much."

"Sounds like the chef business is a lot of work."

It seemed like an effort for him to come back to the present. He feigned a smile before speaking.

"It is. For all concerned. We usually put in twelve, thirteen-hour days, six days a week. It's not for the faint of heart, as my momma used to say."

"How long is this program?"

"Twenty-four months long."

"What's the cost?"

"Seventy-five thousand dollars, but ninety-five percent of our graduates find jobs right away."

"Quite a career investment, seventy-five grand."

Hayes got a tad prickly. "We have student loans, scholarships, and grants, just like other schools. If they have the talent and drive, we help them out in any way we can."

"Tell me about Patsy's role in all of this."

"Patsy didn't kill anybody," he shouted. "She had nothing to do with it."

Chapter Twelve

Braised New World

His reply was so vehement, his voice so loud, I was taken aback.

"Whoa. I meant as a teacher, how does she contribute to the program?"

He rubbed his forehead with delicate fingers. "I'm sorry. I'm just overwrought. I've lost a chef, my pearl diver is missing –"

"Your what?"

"Pearl diver. It's slang for a dishwasher. Not that it's all Manuel did. He did all sorts of things for Chef Jacques. He functioned more or less as his assistant. People like that aren't as easy to replace as you might think."

He pulled himself together and tried to give me a smile long on southern charm. It failed. Even he knew.

"But you asked me what Patsy contributes. As this year's guest chef, she demonstrates the French country approach to southern stewed meats. There are dozens of stews using alligator to squirrel, as well as the standard pork, bird, and beef. Seasonings and sauces make all the difference."

"I had alligator once. It tastes like chicken."

He fought back a smile. "Not if you have chicken alongside it. Then it tastes like alligator."

I nodded, deciding to leave the squirrel out of this conversation. We have one living in our backyard and he's just the cutest thing. Or she is. It's hard to tell the gender of a squirrel at a glance.

"How did you feel about Chef Jacques?"

"To be honest, he wasn't a good fit. And I'd had others, including Chef Dexter from the Institute, vying for the job. Naturally, I'm sorry he's dead, but I...ah...it was a mistake to hire him."

"So why did you keep him on?"

He threw his head back while exhaling air with a hissing sound. He shook his head still looking at the ceiling.

"The truth? He talked me into a contract I should have never signed."

"What kind of contract?"

"It was a five-year ironclad contract with a penalty clause. If he was let go for pretty much any reason outside of strangling a student, I had to pay him twice his monthly salary for the run of his contract in one fell swoop."

"That's a helluva contract."

"I know. Chef Jacques had four and a half years to go. If I fired him, it would have made a serious dent in my profits. But we were trying to work things out."

"Were you?"

I didn't say more, but here was a crackerjack candidate as a killer. According to Patsy, he'd spent hours getting meds for his wife, had access to the crime scene, and motive up the wazoo.

Hayes looked away. His jaw clenched and on one side a cheek twitched, probably from tension in the muscles. I ignored it and pushed on.

"So with that in mind, do you know anybody besides you he might have been blackmailing? I mean he did blackmail you into giving him the job, didn't he? Maybe he did that sort of thing with somebody else."

Hayes jerked in the chair as if an electric shock went through him. "What makes you say that? Did someone tell you that? Not Patsy. She never –"

"Easy," I said, with a smile. "Nobody had to tell me; it makes sense. What was it he had over you?"

Hayes sat for a moment glaring at me then hung his head.

"Oh, God, this is like a nightmare. I did want him to go away, but I didn't want him dead. I didn't kill him. I swear."

"What did he have over you?" I repeated the question and stared at him. He hesitated to speak. I decided to reassure him.

"Don't worry, I'm not the blackmailing kind; too much conscience. But I have to know these things if I'm going to help Patsy."

Hayes nodded then swallowed hard. He brushed a hand over his mouth, as if it were dry.

"Need some water?" I swiveled in my chair, reached inside the small fridge at my feet, and pulled out an individual bottle of Perrier.

He nodded his thanks, unscrewed the lid, and drank nearly half of it down. I wasn't sure when he would start talking again, but I let him take his time.

"There was no contract. I made that up, hoping I wouldn't have to tell the truth."

"Now that it's out, let's hear it."

"When he came to interview for the job, he acted like he knew something I wouldn't want other people to know. At first, I thought he was crazy or I was reading something into his words that wasn't there. I ignored it and asked him to tell me about himself. He said everything I wanted to know was right there on his CV."

He paused. I could see he was revisiting the incident in his mind.

"He sat across the desk from me, smug and condescending, just looking at me. He finally said how sad it would be if anyone found out about Connie's background. I said what has my wife got to do with this? We're talking about your qualifications for the position of head-teaching chef."

Hayes squirmed around in the chair and brought the bottle of water to his lips. He drained it dry and set it on my desk with a clunk.

"He made it very clear. I remember his exact words. He said, 'It's about her being up for tenure at that classy college of hers. How would they feel if they knew she was caught stealing expensive jewelry in Baton Rouge?'"

He looked at me from across the desk.

"It all happened before I met her, when she was seventeen. She told me about it after we were married. She was too young to have an arrest record, but she did spend some time in Juvenile Hall. That was how they found out she was clinically depressed. Sometimes the illness manifests itself in peculiar behavior."

"So he threatened to expose your wife to the university if you didn't give him the job?"

At first, Hayes didn't say anything, but nodded his head, a look of shame clouding his face.

"This has to remain a secret," he suddenly blurted out. "Connie has already threatened suicide. If it came out about her thefts in Louisiana, coupled with her condition, she could lose her position at Stanford. Then there's no telling what she might do. Promise me you won't tell anyone."

"Unless it's pertinent to the case, I see no reason why it should come out."

He let out an audible sigh of relief. "Thank you."

"If you had to say who you think might have done it, who would you name?"

"I couldn't even hazard a guess. Everyone is above suspicion." He paused. "Except, of course, Chef Dexter. He did not take losing the job to Jacques as one would expect a gentleman to do. But I'm sure he wouldn't –"

He was about to say more, but his phone rang with one of those chimes that suggests a tune but never really gets around to delivering one.

He pulled the phone out of his vest pocket and scanned the digital name. He looked at me.

"Sorry, it's my assistant. I've got to take this." He opened the phone. "Nancy, why are you calling? Is something wrong?"

He listened briefly, his face blanching white. When he hung up, he stood and turned to me.

"I have to leave immediately. Nancy just discovered we had a break-in. One of the storage freezers has been emptied of all its contents, including about ten thousand dollars' worth of crab and lobster."

Chapter Thirteen

The Deviled Food Cake Wears Prada

"I'll drive you," I said, rising.

"That's all right, I'll call Uber," he said. "I'd walk back to the police station to get my car, but I'm in a hurry."

"Don't be silly. I'm right here." Before he could agree or protest, I was at the door, purse in hand.

"I can't believe this." He became preoccupied with his troubles, repeated this phrase again and again, while walking down the hallway. Then he turned to me. "What is going on? It's like someone is trying to destroy the Institute."

We hurried into the waiting room, Hayes' face troubled and glum. His two sons stopped reading magazines, rose, and stared at us in silent alarm. Hayes rushed to them and spoke softly.

Stanley stopped what he was doing and looked at me, expectantly. "The game's afoot, right?"

"A-car, actually. That's if Lila has returned with mine yet. Has she?"

"She has."

He snatched up a set of keys at a corner of his desk, and thrust them toward me. I grabbed the jangling keys out of his hand and turned to Wally and Pete.

"Okay, boys, I still need to interview you. Do you want to wait for me here or do it later? I should be back in twenty minutes. Either way, I'd like to do it sometime today."

"For heaven's sake, why must you talk to them?" Hayes jumped into the conversation, his temper flaring white-hot again. "Aren't they going through enough now? Their mother's in jail on a murder charge!"

This unexpected roar of anger caused Stanley and the Durand sons to freeze in place, eyes darting first to him and then to me for my reaction. I faced a man I was finding on the volatile side, either by nature or driven there by the situation.

"I'm afraid I must insist." My tone was calm and quiet.

"Daddy, that's all right with me," said Pete, reaching out a hand and touching his father on the arm. "Do you need us with you? If not, I'd just as soon wait here and get this over with. Maybe I can help."

"Me, too," said Wally, stepping forward. Both sons seemed to be aiming for peace. "But it's up to you, Daddy."

Hayes fought for control and forced a smile. "No, no, of course not. You would just be in the way, boys, if you went with me. I don't know what got into me." He turned to his sons. "You two stay here and wait for Lee to get back."

"In that case, let's go." I turned back to Stanley. "If anyone asks, I'm driving Mr. Durand to the Palo Alto Culinary Arts Institute, but I should be back in twenty minutes at the latest."

My phone gave the cluck-cluck it does when I have a text message coming through. Then it rang.

"I have so missed your high drama," Stanley said in a small aside, as I paused at his desk to look at the name of the incoming call.

"And I've missed your lies." I looked at the number of the incoming call and answered. "Gurn, is this urgent? If not, can it wait about twenty minutes?"

"I'll leave you a voicemail," he said.

"Thanks, darling," I said and disconnected.

On the short ride toward El Camino Real, I was formulating a plan. I glanced at Hayes, looking worried and chewing on his thumbnail.

"Your missing dishwasher, Manuel Sanchez. How long has he been with you?"

"He was hired by Chef Jacques. The last one had been with us for over two years, but up and quit, leaving us in the proverbial pickle. Manuel was somebody Chef Jacques knew, but not your average dishwasher. Nosy and a belligerent sort. But I guess he does his job. I have little interaction with him."

"Does he have a habit of just not showing up for work?"

Hayes shook his head. "No, he's been pretty reliable."

"So this is unusual."

"Yes."

"What's his schedule like?"

"We try to keep overhead down, so he works a split shift. We have him wait until there are dirty dishes from the morning classes. He comes in around nine, works for four hours then goes on a four-hour break. He returns at five and stays until nine, doing the same thing for the afternoon classes. He gets lunch and dinner. One of the perks."

Five minutes later we arrived at the square, three-story building on the corner of El Camino Real and University. A large, royal-blue and white sign on the side of the building, three-stories high, announced the Palo Alto Culinary Arts Institute.

Hayes opened the car door, but turned back to me. "Thank you. I'm sorry about earlier."

"Forget it. Hayes, it would be better if you don't mention to anyone where you've been or who I am. And that includes your assistant. Have you got that?"

He shook his head. "I tell Nancy everything. She's my right hand."

"Please don't. It's crucial that you don't mention any of this to anyone right now. Later on, when we have more of a handle on what's going on, we'll see who we can let know what."

He stared out into space for a moment then turned to me. "Ordinarily, I wouldn't agree to this, but anything for Patsy."

"And while you're at it, don't hire a replacement for Manuel yet. And if he returns, call me immediately."

Hayes let out a short laugh, more like a bark.

"Replacing him is the least of my problems, Lee. The staff is spooked. Several students have talked about leaving. Parents are threatening to remove their children from the Junior Chef Program. If I can calm everybody down and resume classes, then I'll need to replace all the food that was stolen from the freezer. Nancy's coming up with a list now. If I have to wash the dishes myself, that's what I'll do."

"I think I have a solution for that, but we'll talk later. I'll be in touch."

He hesitated, as if he was going to say more. Then Hayes shook his head imperceptibly, grabbed the door handle, and got out. With a brief wave in my direction, he hurried into the building.

Taking out my phone, I read the text that cluck-clucked at the office right before the call came in from Gurn. The noises a phone can make. The long text from Richard meant the missive had been dictated to Siri, his personal cyber slave.

Lee, let's talk later about the others. Here's what I have on Manuel Sanchez. Fifty-three years old, served fifteen years in San Quentin for armed robbery. Paroled June of last year. Arrested for petty theft six months ago and should have served three more years, but was released under the supervision of Jacques Chalifour, who gave him a job.

Side note, Lee: This is why Sanchez's name rang a bell with me. I remembered reading about him in the papers. Sanchez robbed the shoe repair store right down the street from D. I. He was charged with reaching inside an open window and taking a black pair of men's shoes. Said they were his, which they turned out to be, but didn't have the money to pay for the repairs. The bill was eighteen dollars and thirty-one cents. The parole officer said he would have gone back to jail if he hadn't been hired by Chef Jacques.

Well, shut my mouth, as Patsy would say. So Manuel Sanchez owed Chef Jacques big time. In turn, it wasn't much of a leap to say Chef Jacques probably felt he owned Manuel Sanchez body and soul. From what little I was learning about the chef, I'm sure he used that hold for all sorts of nasty little jobs.

I couldn't wait for the official lowdown on Chef Jacques Chalifour and texted Richard as much. So far, the dead chef sounded like a cad and a villain. I felt a surge of sympathy for Manuel Sanchez. Imagine, facing an additional three-year jail sentence for an eighteen dollar tab. Shades of *Le Miz*.

I sighed, hit my voice mail button, and listened to my man's voice. After four months of marriage the sound of it still made my heart flutter. He'd be home at seven, packing turkey and cheese sandwiches for dinner, with french fries. And P.S. he added, he loved me to pieces. Now there's a man who was a keeper.

I turned the car around and headed back to the office. I was looking forward to interviewing the Durand boys. Were they as charming, laidback, and innocent as they appeared to be? I couldn't wait to find out.

Chapter Fourteen

"A" Is For Abalone

The door opened. Wally Durand sauntered in with a far different demeanor than he showed earlier. Just under six feet, he had twinkling blue eyes and straight, red hair same as his father's, but styled in an early 60s mode. That and the buttoned-down clothes made him look like a clean cut, preppy throw back to a simpler era. It was a time when folk songs and banjos were all the rage, and the Kingston Trio hung down their heads with Tom Dooley.

I wasn't even born yet, but my dad had every song Joan Baez put out, so I knew the period well. Plus her father was a Stanford professor, so around Palo Alto she's a queen.

Where was I? Oh, yes. The door opened. Wally Durand sauntered in and blah blah.

"Hello, lovely lady," he drawled in a charming, flirty sort of way. He gave me a smile that said he was interested in sharing more than information with me.

"Thank you for waiting for me, Wally." My tone was slightly formal, just in case it was necessary to ward off a side order of unwanted romance. Even if I wasn't a fairly new bride, I don't mix business with pleasure. Way too complicated.

Wally came to my side of the desk, giving me a slight yearning expression, while leaning in on me.

"A privilege and a pleasure," he said.

His voice was soft and suggestive. I glanced up and saw he'd missed shaving a spot directly under his chin. Plus his aftershave, a lemon-lime mixture, made my nose itch. So much for sex appeal.

"Please have a seat," I said, gesturing to the other side of the desk with my left hand and flashing my ring finger adorned in glittering, marital symbols.

The sapphire wedding band was new, designed to go with Gurn's great-great-grandmother's engagement ring. A one-an-a-half carat blue-white solitaire surrounded by sapphires, it was given to her by a besotted Union officer to seal the deal and soften the blow of the south losing the war. They were married for fifty-six years. Let's hear it for Great, Great Granny Charlotte Louise Parkington.

"I see you're married," he said, sitting down.

"Yes." My answer was firm and non-negotiable. "I understand you arrived in the Bay Area sometime today?"

"Yes." He managed to imitate my tone of voice on the same word. I tried not to show my irritation. He seemed to find that amusing.

"I flew from Little Rock nonstop. As soon as I saw CNN, I hopped on the first plane. I drove the rental straight to the police station."

"What time was that?"

"I got here…" he paused to look at his watch, "…about two hours ago. It was a five-hour flight, and with the time change, we landed around twelve-thirty, your time. Want to know the flight number?" He looked at me with an impish grin.

"That would be helpful."

"American Airlines, flight 3254. I'm good at remembering numbers."

"Do you happen to have your boarding pass?"

He reached in both pockets, dug around, but came up empty. "Sorry, sugar, I must have thrown it away."

Wally was lying. I decided not to call him on it. My look was, I hoped, noncommittal.

"Thank you, anyway," I said, smiling. "Where are you staying? In case I need to reach you?"

"The Park Stanford. But don't call me there, sugar. Jolene might answer the phone." He blew me a lascivious kiss then winked.

I'd had it. "Wally, we're on a tight time frame and need to keep this strictly professional. I'm trying to help clear your mother of murder charges."

He drew back, a sullen look crossing his face. From somewhere inside he found a smile.

"Sure, sugar. Just showing you some friendly, southern charm."

"Right now I could use some California cool."

"Don't you want to know who I think did it?"

"Okay, who do you think killed Chef Jacques Chalifour?"

"That Nancy Little...something or other. Daddy's assistant."

"And why would that be? Did you see them argue? Notice any altercation between the two?"

"Well, look at her. She dyes her hair red, yellow, and purple, dresses in black, and has a bunch of chains wrapped around her. No telling what somebody like that will do."

"But you never actually saw her and Chef Jacques together?"

"Sugar, I never even met the man and I only saw her a couple of times. Truth be told, I haven't seen my daddy since Uncle Quinn's funeral. I don't know what's going on at the Institute."

"Really? Your father's business and you know nothing about it? And you a businessman, as well?"

I stared at him. He stared back. Then Wally turned his head to the side, but glanced back at me and chuckled.

"Why, Miss Lee, I do declare. I believe you're trying to lay something at my feet."

"Certainly not." I placed a smile on my face. "It's just that, if nothing else, your father might have made a comment or other over the phone to you in one of your conversations. Something that might have helped you form an opinion."

"Frankly, I heard precious little about Chef Jacques from Daddy. He and me, we don't talk shop. When I'm in town, I usually stay at a hotel and I don't even go to the Institute. And when I'm home in Little Rock, I'm busy with my own life. I got married last month. Jolene. A blond bombshell."

"Congratulations."

He leaned forward and whispered. "She's not half as pretty as you, but her father owns a chain of liquor stores that do well. Tell me, sugar, does your detective agency do well?"

"Didn't we just visit this? Down, boy."

He let out a light laugh. I tried not to barf.

"Has your mother or father ever mentioned anyone who had a grudge against the chef? Someone who might want to do him harm?"

Wally shook his head. "Honest, sugar, I don't know a thing other than what I told you. I wish I did, so you and I could spend more time together." He winked at me.

I stood. "In that case, thank you very much for your time. I think we're done for now."

His flirty look changed to one of concern. He rose, saying, "But you're still going to help my mother? I know she's a character and all, but she'd never do anyone in, for all her big talk. Doesn't have it in her."

I stood up straighter. "Rest assured, Discretionary Inquiries will do its best to help clear your mother's name. Would you mind asking your brother to come in? And again, thank you."

I made the mistake of extending my hand in that farewell-fellow-well-met gesture to indicate the meeting was over. He took my hand in both of his and yanked me over the desk toward him. He went into his sultry routine again.

"I was thinking you and I could meet later for a drink or something. It's awful lonely in a town where you don't know anyone, sugar."

I leaned in close enough to count his nose hairs. "Let go of my hand, sugar, or you will regret it as surely as the Robert E. Lee steamed down the mighty Missisip."

He hesitated for a moment, released me from his grip, staring into my face. "Well, you're a spirited little heifer, aren't you?"

I stood on my side of the desk, feeling like I needed a shower. "Please ask your brother to come in."

Wordless, he pivoted, walked out, and slammed the door.

"Wait a minute," I said to the closed door. "Did he just call me a cow?"

Chapter Fifteen

Alice's Adventures in Wonder Bread

Pete Durand strolled in presenting the exact opposite image than that of his older brother. It wasn't just his tattoos, shaved head, ripped clothing, and pierced body parts, he didn't have one sexual overtone in his demeanor. Actually, he looked scared.

Before I could say a word, he launched into his protest, speaking faster than I thought any southerner could do.

"Listen here, Lee, my mama could no more kill someone than I can fly to the moon. I'm serious now, dead serious. I met that lowlife charlatan, who called himself Jah-quees. He's no more French than my billy goat back home. I'll bet his real name was Bubba or something."

"No, it was Jacques. He was French Canadian. Quebec."

"That don't make him French. And he always had it out for Mama, too. He didn't like her because she was smart, smarter than him."

He took a quick breath and launched into phase two.

"She would tell me how he was always yelling at the men and pinching the women. She thought he was skimming money off the top. Ordering stuff, writing a check from the Institute, but getting a kickback from the vendors. And that's not all he did. A real lowlife, like I say. It's no wonder somebody topped him. But it wasn't my mama."

He paused here, glared at me, and took another breath. I took the opportunity to jump in.

"You have a billy goat?" I gave him what I hoped was a disarming smile.

It must have worked, because he let go of some of his prickliness and smiled back.

"I do. I call him Homer, because the first book he ever ate was The Iliad. I was finished reading it, anyway."

"I never finished my copy. Maybe I should."

"Maybe you should, yes, ma'am. It's a bit long in the tooth, but worth it."

He took another moment to relax and flashed a larger smile at me. First impressions don't always count, I decided then and there. I found on closer inspection, he was probably an intelligent, likable guy.

"Sit down, won't you, Pete? I just have a few questions."

He took one of the chairs across from me and glanced around at the surroundings.

"This all South American?"

"Mostly Mexican, but a little of everything."

"My favorite is the Mesopotamian period. They rival anything from Egypt. Although some of the artifacts from the Aztecs are impressive. They had a big collection of weapons, but then their main goal was to kill everybody in sight; offer them up to the sun god. A little barbaric for my tastes."

He grinned at me. I found myself grinning back.

"You sound like a pretty learned guy."

He looked down at his attire.

"Don't let my clothes fool you. They're just part of my protest. Way back when, after I graduated from college, I wanted to teach art literature. That doesn't fly in my family. If it isn't food related, you can't do it. But I have a dual degree, Art History and Business Administration, so now I manage the image of the restaurants."

He raised his hands as if he were holding a marquee.

"'Downhome Arkansas Cooking with a Touch of France'. That slogan was mine. Marketing, PR, that kind of thing; that's what I do."

I had never heard the slogan before and wasn't particularly awestruck. He must have read my mind, because he leaned in.

"Actually, the slogan stinks, but Mama liked it and apparently, so do the customers. Sometimes the simplest rather than the cleverest wins the day."

"I see you've lost a bit of your southern drawl."

"It comes, it goes, depending on the weather."

"On the weather?"

"Yes, ma'am. On whether or not it's called for." He winked at me, not in the lascivious way his older brother had, but in a charming 'aren't we all too clever by half' way. I laughed then forced myself back on track.

"Pete, I'd like your opinion. You've met Chef Jacques."

"Not more than a couple of times, but I had him figured out, all right. He wasn't a person to hide who he was."

"Tell me about him."

"Always looking for a free ride. Or to steal from somebody. I don't know why Daddy kept him around. Oh, he did his job all right, I expect, but it wasn't enough to justify the way he treated people."

"Like how?"

"The way he leered at the ladies made me want to throw a bucket of cold water on him. But he was ill-mannered and rude to everybody, man, woman, and child. Always looking to put somebody down. If there wasn't a real reason, he'd invent one. And the way he talked to the hired help was pitiful. If anybody spoke to our employees like that, they'd be fired on the spot."

He thought for a moment. It seemed something new crossed his mind.

"Except for his errand boy, Manuel Sanchez. He was real careful about how he talked to him, but then any sensible person would be. That one looked like he'd kill you as soon as talk to you. That's why I'm sure he's the one who carved up Jah-quees. Find him, you'll find your killer."

"Let's get back to the chef. When did you first meet him?"

"Let me see." He thought a moment. "Maybe six months ago. I had a week with nothing to do and thought I'd visit. He was different then."

"Chef Jacques?"

"No, Daddy. Bless his heart, he's under a lot of strain. Like that hissy fit he threw in the waiting room earlier. He was always the calm one. But that's what happens when you have lowlife like that Jah-quees hanging around, sucking the lifeblood out of you."

He sat for a moment, thinking. Then he leaned back, letting go of anger and resentment.

"But it wasn't just that. I don't think Daddy ever got over the way Uncle Quinn died."

"Your father mentioned something about losing your uncle in a fire."

"Daddy was visiting the farm at the time. He and his brother got caught inside the barn when it caught fire. Only Daddy got out, but his hands got burned bad. We had to have a closed casket at the funeral; nothing much to put in it. Daddy took it real hard."

"Condolences on the loss of your uncle."

Pete gave a curt nod but said nothing. I went on.

"Why don't you tell me about your father's second wife?"

"Connie was always sweet to me. Had a big brain back in the day, lecturing everywhere on world hunger and seaweed. But all that's stopped now. She's got some real problems. Daddy says she's a handful, but that don't stop him. That's Daddy. He tries to handle everything."

He added the last bit with a certain amount of tentative pride. It was like he didn't agree with his father's choices, but because he couldn't do anything about it, he may as well be proud.

I went back to the subject of the dead chef. "Can you tell me anything about Chef Jacques? Friends, enemies, things like that?"

He shook his head. "To be honest, I steered clear of him. But when Mama showed up at the Institute four weeks ago, they locked horns and never let go. I heard an earful about his shenanigans every time I called her. So I've been driving down now and then to make sure she's all right. You know, Portland isn't all that far by car. Maybe eight hours if you put the pedal to the metal."

"Do you mind me asking what sent you to Portland? I thought you lived in Little Rock, like the rest of your family."

"That's where my wife's folks are. I took some time off. We've been visiting them for nearly a month now. Set to go back home next week."

"Did you drive from Portland last night?"

"Ah...yeah...I left late, drove straight through and showed up early this morning." His eyes blinked and flitted around the room, only to come back and rest on me.

And I had another liar on my hands.

I didn't say so aloud but he still clamped his mouth shut. I could sense him pull back, watching what he said, not being as forthcoming. I tried to egg him on.

"So you left Portland before you knew your mother was being questioned for murder? Merely a coincidence?"

"Yes, ma'am." He cleared his throat. "I didn't know anything about it until I heard a news bulletin on NPR this morning somewhere near Sacramento. Nearly drove off the road."

"Anything in particular bring you here?"

"No, just wanted to see Mama. See how she was doing."

Again he was lying. I decided to change the subject, see if I could get him to open up if we talked about something else.

"Your brother says he hasn't visited your father in a year. Does that sound about right to you?"

"I'm surprised he showed up even now," Pete said with a small laugh.

"Why is that?"

"Wally takes care of Wally. And he gets what he can from people. He has four assistants who do all the work, making sure the restaurants run like they should. One of them, Ruthie, she does everything he's supposed to be doing. Molly's another one. But then, they're in love with him. In fact, I wouldn't be surprised if he didn't let each one think he'd marry them one of these days. That was until Jolene got the dubious honor. My brother's a real ladies man. Did he hit on you when he was in here?"

"Ahhhhh...."

"I thought so. In some ways, that Jah-quees fellow reminded me of my brother. I think that's another reason I detested him."

"The chef or your brother?"

"Take your pick." He gave off a laugh. "I'm just kidding, Lee. Wally and I get along like two hogs in a slop pen."

I had no idea how hogs in a slop pen got along, but I wasn't sure Porky Pig would have approved of the comparison.

"What does your mother think of Wally's questionable ways?"

"She doesn't see them or anything else bad about him. Blinders, just like any proud mama. Oh, she sees what I'm up to, all right, but then I don't have Wally's winning ways. He's the favored son." He shrugged, as if making sure I understood he wasn't looking for sympathy. "I'm used to it."

I was silent. He went on, more to himself than to me.

"Or as used to it as I'm ever going to be."

Chapter Sixteen

War and Pizza

When Pete left I picked up the phone, hoping my brother was still around. It was after five and I'd have to hurry if I wanted to get to Mr. Talbot's office by six. It was across town and the Bay Area rush hour traffic was going to be its standard madness. Richard answered on the fifth ring.

"Glad you're still there, brother mine."

"Was about to call you. Wanted to give you the info on the dead chef. Not a very nice man."

"Do tell."

"Jacques Chalifour. No middle name. Fifty-six years old. Went to a now-defunct culinary school in Chicago back in the early eighties, so it was a bear getting his records. But when I did, I came across a comment made by one of the instructors. I'll read it." Richard cleared his throat. "Jacques Chalifour shows promise, but is lazy and likes to cut corners. Also he is often distracted by the ladies."

"I didn't know they put information like that down in a cooking school, Richard."

"Neither did I, but I guess a school is a school. After he graduated, he had several small jobs in restaurants and hotels – cleaning, cutting vegetables, and making soups – then whammo, got a job at the restaurant in the Hotel Marmaduke as executive chef in the early nineties. It looks like he married his way into the job."

"Do tell."

"His father-in-law was the hotel manager. Anyway, he gambled all his earnings away and his wife divorced him after six years. He lost his job shortly after and made his way to Las Vegas where he was involved in a hit and run. But get this, the charges were dropped when he started dating the woman whose leg he broke when he struck her in the crosswalk."

"I don't believe it. What?"

"True, I swear. He married the woman, who was seven years his senior, and they have three children, a son and two daughters. After he mortgaged her house to the hilt, and emptied her bank account, he deserted her and the kids, and went underground. He surfaced in San Francisco a short time ago. His wife only found him after he got this job. He owed five years of back child support."

"He sounds like the kind of man who gives the male sex a bad name."

"Not any guy I'd want to hang out with, Lee. I've got some pictures of him, if you want to see what he looked like. Not a bad-looking dude before he ran to fat."

"Yeah, send them on. By the way, did you find out if he was skimming profits off the top?"

"That's a toughie. I'm still looking into it. But if he was, he probably had help from someone inside. Or at least, someone who looked the other way."

"Manuel Sanchez? Nancy Littlejohn? Hayes Durand?"

"Or anyone of the chefs or students. Nothing stands out."

"Oh, lawdy."

"Sorry about that. I'm just a fact checker, not a miracle worker."

"I know. Good job, Richard."

"Thanks, Sis. Okay, gotta go. I have a lot of other –"

"Wait a minute," I interrupted. "While I've got you on the line, do me a favor. Find out if Wally Durand was on American flight 3254 this morning from Little Rock; I don't think he was. And then I need the last twenty — four hours' worth of calls made by all four of the Durands."

"Why don't you try asking them to give you access to their phones?"

His voice held the edge of exasperation I find so endearing. I tried to be reasonable.

"Something tells me this family has a few things to hide. I'd rather get a call list from you."

"Excuse me, sister mine, but it's Houdini's day off."

"Ha ha," I said.

"No, seriously. I don't know what you think our department does," he said. And hotly, I might add. "But getting a list of phone calls made on private lines in this day and age is not easy."

"If it were easy, I wouldn't be asking you. You are, after all, the master of the difficult and the conqueror of the impossible."

I added the last part to smooth any ruffled feathers. He still squawked.

"And if the phones are encrypted," he went on, as if I hadn't spoken, "it's not going to happen. Steel yourself for that. What's up, anyway?"

I could tell his curiosity was peaked.

"Are you going to do it or not? Come on. Your department can get through practically any firewall."

"I'm not sure I can pull Andy off the board game problem–" He interrupted himself. "You've heard about that?"

"No. Should I have?"

"Sometimes, Lee, I like to remind you of other things we do in IT besides serve your latest whim."

He went on without waiting for me to reply.

"We've been working on Bucko Rancho Games, catering to eight year-olds and younger. It's looking like the game writer introduces hidden codes that corrupt competitor games on the user's computer, forcing the kid to play only their game without any problems. Sabotage, pure and simple."

"You're going to put that on hold, though, aren't you? After all, this is for Tío."

"I don't know that I can."

"Sure you can."

He hesitated. I waited him out. Curiosity won the day.

"All right. But tell me, what's up?"

"I need to find out just how many secrets a slop pen can hold."

Another pause. Then he exhaled sharply.

"I don't know why I bother to ask. When do you need all this, your majesty?"

"A.S.A.P."

"Naturally. So what's a slop pen?"

"I have no idea. But we're about to get into one."

"Maybe *you* are. Sounds messy to me."

Chapter Seventeen

Witness For The Praline

I raced into the waiting room, having given myself only twenty-minutes to get to Talbot's office. Stanley, who was bending over doing some sort of filing, stood up and dramatically threw himself against the wall as if I might run him down, otherwise. Sometimes he can be such a smartass.

Pretending he wasn't there, I passed him, and headed for the door. I was stopped by the un-dulcet-like tones of Ms. Packersmythe.

"Ms. Alvarez," she boomed. "A moment of your time."

"Oh, ah," I replied. "I really can't. I must be go –"

As if I hadn't spoken, she descended upon me. Grasping me by the arm, she pulled me in the direction of her office.

I've only been in her office once before in the ten years she's worked at D. I. It's a colorless, sterile place. Being neat as a pin only added to its austere look. A desk, rows of tall file cabinets, and one rinky-dink chair for a visitor, filled the space.

While her office was not particularly small, her weighty, carved wood desk took up about ninety percent of the space. Reminiscent of the imposing monument of power used by a seated judge in courtrooms, I waited for a bailiff to command 'all rise'.

"Ms. Alvarez," she rushed on once she closed the door. "As we are both women of the world –"

"Are we?"

This was news to me. I would have thought we were two women short. Oblivious to my words, she began to pace the free area of the room, forcing me to step aside each time she came my way.

"Today you met my betrothed. I do not as a rule bring my personal life into the work place, but I thought as you had met Henry and formed a distinct bond –"

"Did we?"

Ms. Packersmythe continued to ignore me or wasn't listening; I'm never sure which. She went on pacing, maybe using all of her mental powers to marshal her thoughts.

"And as you are newly married –"

"Oh, ah."

Yes! There I was on firmer ground. I am married, I remember the ceremony clearly.

"You, too, married late –"

"Did I?"

Okay, I was thirty-four, so I guess we can say that. For the first time since we came into the room, she turned and looked at me.

"I realize, I am a few years older than you –"

Eleven to be exact, but who's counting.

"But here is the truth of it," she said.

She came closer, hands on hips. All six feet of her stared down at me.

"I am with child."

Being a well-brought up little girl, I've read a lot of the Bible, compulsory reading in most Sunday schools. The words 'with child' and 'begot' were everywhere. Long and short of it, Ms. Packersmythe had been begetting, and was pregnant.

I resorted to murmuring 'oh ah' again, rather than 'good gawd, woman, why are you telling me this?'

She went on.

"I don't have a lot of friends, Ms. Alvarez, as difficult as that is to imagine."

'Oh, ah' time, for sure. I gave it everything.

"No, no, I speak the truth." Her protestation was loud and firm. If there was a mirror somewhere in the room, I'm sure it cracked. "I know only too well the jealousy and envy of those less secure in who they are. You needn't try to sugarcoat it for me."

"Oh, ah."

"I am a loner, a woman who prefers the company of ledgers and numbers to people. That is, until I met Henry. He has won my heart."

Feeling more and more like I was in the middle of a Shakespearean soliloquy, I saved my 'oh, ah' for a later time. She wasn't listening to my part of the conversation, anyway.

"That said, I am a few years older than he. He's thirty-two; I'll be forty-six next month."

Ms. Packersmythe came closer, dark eyes piercing mine. As I was still looking up at her, I nearly fell over backward. Steely-faced, she grabbed me by the shoulders, steered me to the rinky-dink chair, pushed me into it, and cantered behind her desk. Court was in session.

"Now, as to the reason I have asked you here. Henry has asked me to marry him several times, even before the unexpected news of the child's arrival. I have not yet given him my answer. The truth is –" And here she resumed her thinking.

I glanced at my watch. Time was a-wasting. At this rate I'd never make it across town by six. Oh, what the hell. I decided to sit back, focus in on Ms. Packersmythe, and see what she wanted. Finally, words poured forth.

"Henry has a secret. I'm not sure what it is, but I know I cannot marry him until I find out. I've asked him repeatedly to tell me about his past, but he refuses. I know nothing of his family or former life. All I know is he's from Rochester, New York."

She stopped and looked at me. I tried to enter the conversation.

"Did you want me to –"

Silly me. She went on right on talking.

"You see, Ms. Alvarez, I am a woman of substance."

Literally? Figuratively? Financially? Help me out here, I thought. But as 'oh, ah' had filled many a gap in this conversation, I muttered it. Or maybe I just thought it. She kept on talking.

"Yes, I am woman of importance. I am looked up to in the Palo Alto community. Not only is it the vital work I do here at Discretionary Inquiries, but I am a founding member of the Peninsula Accounting Club, serving as vice president the last four terms. I have a small house in the heart of downtown Palo Alto, completely paid for. My home is worth a great deal of money in today's market. There is my savings account of no less than one hundred thousand dollars. I realize that to someone like you that doesn't sound like much –"

"No, no, it all sounds good to me," I interjected lest she, too, thought I was a snob or something. I'd had enough of that for one day. Now that we were actually conversing, I ventured on.

"Ms. Packersmythe, what is it you want from me? A little sleuthing into his past? As a valued member of the agency, I'm willing to do whatever you need. Within reason," I added.

She beamed at me. "How very astute you are. No wonder you are the most sought after investigator we have."

"Well, I don't think I'm the most sought af–"

"Before I agree to become his bride," she interrupted. "I need to know if he is merely dallying..." And here she hesitated in putting her thoughts into words. "...with my affections."

I jumped in. After all, I'd like to get to Talbot's office and then home sometime before the new millennium.

"Okay, 'nuff said. I'll find out the skinny. So what we know is, his name is Henry Encino, thirty-two years old, hails from Rochester, New York, and is a pianist with the San Mateo Orchestra." I stood. "That's more than enough to start with." I got up and headed for the door.

"Ms. Alvarez."

I stopped and turned back at the sound of her voice, now not so brusque, not so loud. She gave me a soft smile.

"I should mention that I care deeply for him. If you find his character to be exemplary..." She paused and took a deep breath. "I would be very pleased."

My heart went out to her. Maybe she was more of a woman of the world than I thought. Maybe I was, too.

"I'll get back to you as soon as I can. Try not to worry too much."

"Thank you. And I am entrusting you to keep this conversation between the two of us."

"Of course."

I left her office, wondering when I would find time to sneak this little tidbit of sleuthing into my agenda. I didn't need to bother Richard or the IT Department with this. One of the many handy-dandy tools PIs have access to finds all sorts of information on the populace at large. Knowing this, I have been hiding my weight for years.

Chapter Eighteen

Tenderloin Is the Night

I climbed the stairs to our garage apartment around eight-thirty that night. I was tired, but the smell of french fries moved my legs up and onward.

Opening the front door, I helloed man and cats, and the queen couldn't have had a better reception. Maybe no twenty-one gun salute, but two cats came running like I was covered in catnip. Better yet, my man came running as if he hadn't seen me in days.

Run Tum Tugger, also known as My Son the Cat, was the first to arrive. The white and orange guy leapt into my arms, meowing the story of his day. Gurn's sweet little Baba Ganush (I Bite your Tush), a long-haired, grey and white fur ball, stopped at my feet. She rose on hind legs and pawed the air, silently begging me to pick her up. I reached down with my free arm and grabbed onto her.

There is a Chinese proverb that goes, "The gods created the cat so that man may stroke the lion." Hear, hear.

Gurn arrived and the four of us hugged – cats, man and woman – until Tugger figuring enough was enough, strove to break free. Ever the copycat, Baba struggled to be let down, too.

Once liberated of feline entanglements, Gurn and I embraced, sharing an intense and lingering kiss. I am one lucky lady.

He pulled back and smiled at me. "I've been waiting all day to do that." I saw a look of concern come to his face. "You look tired, sweetheart. How was the rest of your day?"

"Long. Glad to be home."

I kissed him lightly on the lips, threw myself on the couch, took off my shoes, and crossed my legs at the ankles atop the ottoman. I wiggled my toes and looked at the man I adored.

"Thanks for dropping everything and coming to my aid today, darling."

"Always, sweetheart. You'd do the same for me."

"You betcha." I grinned at him. "How was the rest of your day?"

He returned my grin then threw himself on the couch beside me. We both reached out and clasped hands. Gurn let out a deep sigh.

"Same as yours. Long. Glad to be home. Lots of tax returns and extensions needing to be filed. It'll all get done. I've got a good crew. How'd your meeting go with Talbot?"

"Oh, well enough. We've hatched a plan. I called Hayes. He was reluctant at first, but came around. Did you know Frank's men found traces of human blood inside the Institute's freezer, the one that was robbed? Did I tell you about that? Or did I find out after you left? Today has just been one thing after the other."

"No, but Rich mentioned it a little while ago."

"My brother's in the know."

"But he didn't know whose blood it is."

"Nobody does. They have to run tests on the blood type and results should be back tomorrow. Chef Jacques was Type O. If it's O, it could be his."

"Or not," Gurn reminded me. "That's the most common type by far. I'm Type O."

"Me, too. And to further complicate matters, there's total access to that particular freezer. Even though there'd been expensive meats, seafood, truffles, rare herbs, anyone could have gotten in there. The ME has determined it's unlikely Chef Jacques was killed then moved to where he was discovered. She's thinking he died on the spot. Still, it begs the question, what was human blood doing in the back of the freezer? And whose is it?"

"If it's only a trace, it's possible the chef was first attacked in the freezer but then ran to the spot where he ultimately died."

"Oh, great. I hadn't thought of that. Or maybe it's our missing dishwasher's blood. Anything is possible at this stage."

I grabbed my forehead with my hand and groaned. Sarah Bernhardt couldn't have done it better.

"It's such a mess. I don't know whether I'm coming or going."

Gurn stood up, took one of my hands, and pulled me into his arms. Brushing his lips on my forehead, he said,

"You're tired and you're hungry. Let's leave it for now. Time for dinner. French fries are warming in the oven."

"Smells wonderful."

"And ham and cheese sandwiches are in the fridge."

"I thought you told me turkey and cheese earlier."

"Cook's discretion." He gave me a big smile. "Either way, it's sandwiches. Nothing gourmet. I thought we'd have something different tonight."

"Works for me."

Arm in arm, we strolled into the kitchen. I leaned my head on his shoulder and relaxed for the first time that day.

"Did you feed the cats?"

"I did. Fresh water, too. You can give them some treats later, after you clean out the litter pans. I left that for you."

"You're too good to me."

We both laughed. I looked up at him, sudden tension filling my body again.

"I just remembered. What did you talk to Tío about on your walk this afternoon?"

"Oh, yes. That." He put on his oven mitts and opened the oven door. "Get the sandwiches from the fridge, would you, sweetheart?"

I pulled open both doors of our refrigerator, looking for the food, while he kept talking.

"It seems Patsy is writing a new cookbook on southern and Mexican fusion, focusing on Arkansas."

"Isn't that Tex-Mex?"

"Don't let any southerner hear you say that. The Tex is short for Texas, which is the Wild West, and pretty much what we eat here in great abundance."

"What's the difference? A tortilla with grits and ham hocks?"

"Actually, grits topped by chorizo is fantastic."

"You know, you're right. I've had that combo. And shrimp and cheesy grits are just the best."

I found the sandwiches, and brought them, plus extra mustard, to the table. Gurn met me there with the pan of hot, crispy fries, which he placed on a trivet. The table was already set with paper plates, paper napkins, and plastic utensils. We live such a grand life.

Gurn sat down then looked at me. After a beat of silence he said, "Lee, sweetheart, promise me you'll stay calm."

"Uh-oh."

"Patsy wants to do the new cookbook in collaboration with your uncle. Seems his knowledge and reputation would give the book a lot of credence."

"What?"

I stared at Gurn with an opened mouth. He said nothing but returned my stunned look with a steady gaze. I went back to the fridge.

"I need some wine." I reached inside one of the doors for an already opened bottle of wine.

"Bring two glasses," Gurn said. "And if there's some tequila, we might want to start with that. There's more to tell."

I froze with the bottle of chardonnay and glasses in my hands. Gurn gestured for me to return to the kitchen table and sit. I did and waited, not even breathing. Gurn looked at me with sympathy written all over his face.

"Lee, sweetheart, this is his life."

"*Dios mio,* you've called me sweetheart twice in less than a minute. You're going to tell me something really, really, really horrible, aren't you?"

"After the book is finished, Patsy has asked Tío to do a twelve-month book tour with her across the United States, demonstrating the glories of combining Mexican and southern cooking. She calls it *South of the Border, Arkansan Style.*"

While talking, he pulled the cork from the half-full bottle and emptied equal amounts into both glasses. I snatched my glass, and swallowed half the liquid without even tasting it.

"This can't be happening."

I threw back more wine, wishing it *was* tequila, or a martini, or something more potent and numbing. Despite everything, I felt a burst of pride over Tío's accomplishments.

"Of course, she asked him to do this with her. He's a well-known chef who specializes in Mexican cuisine, two-time winner of a James Beard Award, and handsome as all get-out."

I sat for a moment. Gurn was silent but watching me for any signs of a breakdown. He hadn't touched his wine yet and I'd nearly finished mine. That's what this kind of news can do to a person. My voice sounded sad yet resigned, even to me.

"He's going to do it, isn't he?"

"He hasn't decided yet."

"What if I let her rot in jail? That's the ticket. Then he can't go anywhere with her. What if I don't get involved in this? Let nature take its course. After all, it's to my benefit she stay in jail."

"Do you think she did it?"

I didn't respond. Instead, I reached across the table for his glass of wine, having finished mine. I glugged it down noisily, thinking all the while.

Gurn stood, went to the fridge, and took out a fresh bottle of chardonnay. He grabbed the corkscrew from the drawer next to the refrigerator, and extracted the cork from the elixir of life in about two seconds flat. He poured wine into my former, empty glass and slid it to his side of the table.

"Well, do you?" He sat back down.

I finally answered. "I just don't know."

Gurn's eyebrows shot up. He gave me a smile.

"Which means despite everything you've just said, you're going to find out."

"Yup."

"And because it's Tío, you're going to work your tail off to prove her innocence unless or until you find out otherwise."

"Yup."

"And there we are." He picked up his wine, lifted the glass in a toast, and took a sip.

"Gurn, darling," I said, reaching for a sandwich. "You know how much I hate it when you're right."

"Yup."

Chapter Nineteen

Watch on the Rind

Six AM the next morning found me knocking loudly at the side entrance of the Palo Alto Culinary Arts Institute. At seven the teaching chefs, students, and administrative staff would start trooping in. It had been previously arranged with Hayes Durand I'd arrive earlier than the scheduled nine o'clock this one time so I could look around before anyone else showed up.

I'd rung the service bell minutes before, but since no one answered, I thought banging on the door was in order. I was about to take out my phone to call Hayes, when the door creaked open so slowly, I almost thought it was doing so by itself.

A woman, quivering in a washed-out blue chenille bathrobe, peeked around the door. She was a small, bird-like creature, with dark hair, pale skin and high cheekbones.

"Yes? What is it?" Her voice matched her looks, vulnerably delicate. That was it, of course. The woman seemed too fragile to be standing on her own two feet. I recognized her even though her online photo had been grainy and blurred.

"Mrs. Durand?"

Instead of replying, her large brown eyes darted from left to right. Then she looked back inside the building, as if the question was too difficult to answer on her own and she needed help with it. Under normal circumstances, I would have said that it was possible I came across as intimidating to such a slight, thin woman, but that couldn't have been the case now.

Not enough sleep, a headache from too much wine, combined with one of my uglier getups, a disguise I save for when I want to remain in the background. Should anyone glance my way, they're more than happy to leave me there.

Gone was the Sanguine Orange polish from nails cut to the quick. Farewell new Hermes Shantung silk twill dress and knee-high calf-skin boots. Bye-bye designer jewelry, including my wedding rings.

Standing in my knockoff black Crocs, I wore a clean but shapeless white shirt, and baggy black pants. My facial features were distorted by wire-rimmed glasses and fake buckteeth any beaver would be proud to chomp down a tree with. Guaranteed to add fifteen years, my crowning glory was a wig of uncontrollably thick, wiry hair, salt and pepper in color. Bushy eyebrows pasted over my own matched the wig. I was a real bow-wow.

This getup inspired Richard to make out my work papers in the name of Arbela Einstein. Apparently, I bore a striking resemblance to the discoverer of $E = mc^2$.

Ghastly, yes. But intimidating? No way.

"My name is Arbela," I said keeping my voice as nasal but as flat as possible. "I'm the new hiree. I've been sent by the employment agency."

She stared at me, lower lip trembling. I smiled, which was not easy with my new buckteeth.

"Oh, and here's your newspaper."

I offered the paper to her and she backed up as if it were a snake. We both stood staring at one another. After what seemed like an internal deliberation, the current Mrs. Durand shuddered, drew herself up, and took the paper.

I felt that somehow this was a huge step for her. Then she spoke, hesitating over every other word. Chances are she'd never be on a debate team, but I tried to pay attention to what she said, anyway.

"Yes, thank you. That's what I came downstairs for. My husband isn't up yet. He had a late night and wanted to sleep in. And Nancy isn't here yet." She faltered. "Are you the new assistant cleaning specialist?"

Excuse me. We're calling a dishwasher a cleaning specialist now?

"Yes, madam." I was polite without being southern. It can be done.

"There's no one here, I'm afraid. Nancy won't arrive for another hour. I don't know…"

She broke off, eyes blinking rapidly. The queen of hesitation stared at me. Harkening Albert Einstein's theory of relativity, I decided to get my mass moving in any direction.

"Would you like me to wait outside?"

I made the suggestion but hoped the answer was no. My sole purpose in arriving hours ahead of time was to do a little snooping. Mrs. Durand made another mammoth decision.

"No, I suppose not," she bleated. Hesitating yet again, she turned leaving the door open, and walked inside.

I stepped over the threshold, shut the door, and followed her. We passed through the cream-colored waiting room with comfy looking, oxblood red leather chairs. Brushed white oak tables were splattered with brochures and photos. Beyond a large archway was a huge, high-ceilinged room containing the bulk of a culinary school's necessities.

On one wall, professional ovens, refrigerators and a freezer sat side by side under a line of high windows. Through the paned glass, the morning showed grey and overcast, throwing a gloomy pallor over everything.

Connie Durand flipped on the overhead lights and we trotted on. We came first to several long eating tables surrounded by enough chairs to hold dozens of diners, again in white brushed oak. Butcher-block counters separated this area from the teaching kitchens, four in all.

As we passed through each kitchen, I noted six-burner stoves, dual sinks, and more counters holding blenders, food processers, and mixers. Labeled bins and stools were beneath the counters. Copper and stainless steel utensils, pots, and pans, sat on shelving above, ready for the upcoming day.

To express this in southern terms, I didn't care diddly-squat about what most of this stuff did. But a few passes through Sur La Table© has shown me these were gadgets serious cooks took seriously. Tío's kitchen has many of these toys, but not all. He gets the job done but is big into double duty.

Our travels stopped on the far side of the room. Black two-tier steel carts, four of them, loitering just outside a doorway. Stacked with dirty glasses, dishes, utensils, pots, and pans; they looked like they were waiting for me. Oh, goody.

We stepped over a threshold into a narrow, windowless space. Against the wall, a metal counter ran on either side of an enormous, silver machine. This machine looked suspiciously like a carwash, and probably could hold a European pocket car in a pinch. It was filled with clean tableware and utensils of every size and description. On the right of the machine were two enormous, stainless steel sinks flanked by scrubbing paraphernalia and rubber gloves.

The whole room was about fifteen feet long, eight to ten feet deep, with a walkway of about four feet wide or just enough to maneuver around in. At either end, more shelving held thick, white commercial dinnerware, neatly stacked by type. Mounds of flatware sat in shallow, plastic bins.

"I'm sure you know how to use this."

She pointed to the silver machine's dials, switches and gewgaws. Having not a clue, I nonetheless nodded sagely, noting that one of the fake eyebrows was sticking to my upper eyelid. I glanced away, reached up, and patted it back in place.

"I don't know what you should be doing," said Mrs. Durand, in a voice that sounded lost, confused, and dare I say again, hesitant? She stepped back into the main room, warbling on.

"I'm afraid I don't know much of what goes on in here. I was just coming down for the morning paper. Perhaps you'd like to look around?"

"Yes, madam," I said, close on her heels and trying to understand her flaccid mutterings.

"I'm afraid Nancy isn't here yet." She'd said that before, but repeated it again. "Nancy's the one who handles employee forms and such. Maybe you would like to look..." And here her voice dribbled off. "Oh, dear. I already asked you if you'd like to look around, didn't I? I just don't know..."

I saw where this was going or rather wasn't. We could be talking round-robin for another forty-minutes. I decided to take the situation in hand again.

"Yes, madam, you did. Please don't worry; I'll be fine. Thank you. Please don't let me keep you from what you were doing upstairs. I'll be fine."

"Oh, yes." She looked around her. "What did I come down here for?"

"Newspaper?" I gesture to the *Chronicle* in her hand.

"Yes, yes. The paper," she trilled. "I'll leave you then, shall I?"

"Yes, madam. I'll wait down here until Nancy arrives. Thank you."

I watched her cross back over black and white tiles to a plain but serviceable staircase. The staircase hugged one corner of the wall and went up to the second floor, the Durand apartment.

With great care, Mrs. Durand put the hand with the folded newspaper on the banister. Gathering up the bottom of the bathrobe in her free hand, she revealed small feet enveloped in fuzzy, brown slippers. As I watched her plod up the stairs, I had an instant rush of foreboding, coupled with pity.

She finally disappeared at the top of the landing. I tore across the large room toward the bottom of the staircase and stood for a moment. I strained my ears for any sound. A slight creak of hinges then a click told me a door had closed behind her. I looked around me.

Tomb silent. Just the way I like it.

Chapter Twenty

The Girl With The Dragon Fondue

I pulled my phone out of my pocket and checked the time. Forty-two minutes until people supposedly arrived. It could be sooner, it could be later, but at least there was enough time for a cursory look at the first floor.

Richard kindly sent the city's blueprints of the building to my phone. I perused them again. Three stories and a basement. Four in all. The ground floor where I stood held the classrooms, kitchens, large-scale appliances, and loading dock. In the basement below, the event room, lab, offices, supplies, and dead storage. The Durand's apartment, second floor. Fourteen dormitory style bedrooms for select live-in students were on the third or top floor.

Interestingly enough, you couldn't access the student dormitory from inside the building. You had to use the outside stairs or elevator. Students were not allowed on the lower floors from nine-thirty PM to six-thirty in the morning. And Hayes was adamant I couldn't go into any student room unless I asked the student's permission.

Hoping it wouldn't come to that, I concentrated on the lower three floors. A tall order combined with a full-time pearl-diving job, but it all started with the first step.

A hallway off the large room had two doors. They wound up being a broom closet and stairs leading down to the basement. Next to them, two elevators running between the basement and the first floor sat side by side, the larger one marked service.

Racing back into the large room, I stood in the center and pivoted, eyeballing everything. I decided to start with the walk-in refrigerator next to a walk-in freezer.

Being paranoid, I checked the doors of both the fridge and freezer for access out before I went inside. Both had inside handles, and no way of being locked without a key. They also had alarms with a two-way speaker system. No chance of someone getting locked inside accidentally and not being able to alert the world. Hopefully.

The fridge was stocked with every perishable and edible item known to man and then some. Nothing jumped out at me, except six-pounds of Beluga Caviar, worth almost as much as a bucketful of genetically engineered tomato seeds. Okay, maybe not that much, but I'd never seen so many expensive fish eggs in one place in my life.

A glance inside the looted freezer showed it to be empty, with no signs of blood anywhere. But then its Clorox-y smell meant it had been cleaned within an inch of its life, slated for restocking in the early afternoon.

Finally, I came to what had to be the pantry. This is the room I really wanted to take time checking out, as that's where the murder occurred.

Sometimes a pantry is called the dry store, according to Google. Whatever, the room was about thirty-by-thirty, with floor-to-ceiling evenly spaced open racks holding non-perishable foods, spices, cooking oils, flour, and so forth.

The metal racks were in rows on either side of a center aisle. Each rack held a variety of monstrous containers, like the stuff at Costco, where you, too, can buy sixty-gallons of extra virgin olive oil.

A small, folding stepladder leaned against one wall. Nearby, an empty, heavy-duty platform truck with large wheels sat ready to be loaded.

Sadly, the yellow crime scene markers were missing from anywhere in the room. That meant the police were satisfied they'd found any evidence there was to find and had removed the crime scene tape.

The idea the police are idiots, is probably left over from black and white movies of the forties – which I love nonetheless – where actors like Humphrey Bogart or Tom Conway showed cops to be utter fools on celluloid. In real life they aren't.

I pushed the door completely open, and the pungent odor of bleach was almost overpowering. That was my second heartbreak. This meant that after the police finished with the crime scene, the room had been released to either professional cleaners or somebody's aunt who believed that cleanliness was next to Godliness.

The sum total of these two parts meant the chances of me finding anything helpful was zilch. But I stepped inside, closed the door, and put on my rubber gloves, anyway. If Margaret hadn't been my middle name, it probably would have been Hope.

Not to brag, but what I often have over the police is a bull-headed resolve. It's helped me crack a case or two. I also have the luxury of working on only one crime at a time, coupled with a strong hunch-ometer. My hunch-ometer right then was telling me to hurry up. I only had fifteen minutes left until the inmates started arriving.

I shook off the eeriness, total quiet, and claustrophobic feeling that a multitude of stuff being crammed into a small space can often give you. Especially when that space is filled floor to ceiling with row after row of the imposing multitude. Instead, I concentrated on the paper version of Frank's crime scene report, first shared with Patsy's attorney, Mr. Talbot, and then with me. It was about as detailed as you can get.

What caught my eye was the bit about splashes of blood called blood patterns, which led from one of the racks in the front of the room to the right back corner. The patterns suggested the killer chased the chef, trapping him at the rear. There the man had been stabbed six more times, twelve in all, with two fatal thrusts to the heart. It had a frenzy to it that even startled my godfather's experienced firsthand knowledge of crimes.

The report became my map, now that the blood had been eradicated for good and the room was up to health code standards. Guided by the words, I went from the front to the back, scrutinizing each shelf, aided in my search by a small, but high-powered flashlight. The stench of bleach became stronger the closer I got to the back. My eyes began to water.

Several rows down and on the other side, I did find one of those yellow, half pencils. Often used to fill out forms at the DMV or to count your strokes at miniature golf, it lay on top of a fifteen-pound can of black olives. Half hidden by the metal rim of the can, it could have been left by anyone and at any time, before or after the crime. It wasn't exactly a 'eureka' time, but I picked it up and tucked it in my pocket.

Squeaking hinges at the front of the pantry alerted me the door was being opened. Not wanting to be seen, I hunkered down in the back, far corner of the room, more out of instinct than thinking it through. I waited.

There was a moment of silence and then from the front of the room, came a cacophony of sounds. Clanging and ripping metal, falling and splintering glass. Everything crashed down, breaking against one another. What the hey?

Came the dawn. The first metal rack in the front of the room had fallen over, pushing on the next and the next. Heavy racks falling one on top of the other. Like dominos. Front to back. Coming at me.

I looked up to see several large cans of Crisco quivering on a top shelf. Then the entire rack filled with hundreds of pounds of deadly projectiles rained down on me.

Chapter Twenty-one

The Purloined Lettuce

Just before the contents from the shelves made contact, I did a swan dive to the center aisle and rolled into a ball. I covered my head, hoping I wouldn't get hit by too much flying debris.

A mammoth jar of peach preserves landed on the tip end of my big toe – ouch – and shattered into a million, shard-laden pieces covered in sugary goo. A can of peas struck me on one elbow's funny bone then clunked to the floor, only to spin away like a top. A cloud of white dust rose from a broken fifty-pound bag of flour.

Once I knew the avalanche was over, I sat up, covered from head to foot in flour. In particular, an inordinate amount of flour attached itself to the foot slathered with peach preserves.

Coughing, I tried to stand on wobbly feet, if for no other reason than to get above the dense cloud of floating flour particles. Thus begun a round of coughing, hacking, and sneezing. So charming.

"Who's in here?" It was a woman's voice, harsh and confident, coming from what sounded like the front. Because racks on the other side of the aisle nearest the door were still standing, I couldn't see the person. The voice went on before I could answer.

"What have you done? Show yourself, immediately. I'm calling the police. There's an intruder in here."

I heard the voice of a man, not as strident, saying something I couldn't understand, what with me coughing my head off.

"Wait, wait," I finally got out when I could talk. I tried to go on. "It's me, the new dishwa... ah...assistant cleaning specialist." The last few words were garbled, as I started coughing again.

"What?" Man's voice.

"What's that you say?" Woman's voice.

More garbled male and female conversation from them. More coughing from me.

"Come out from there," demanded the woman. "Who did you say you were? Come out, I say."

I looked at the mess before me, like the aftermath of a nine point oh on the Richter scale. At my feet lay the police report, covered with something suspiciously gummy, like honey or the wretched peach preserves.

"Not sure I can!" I managed to say before more coughing ensued followed by a bout of sneezes. I bent over, half driven by my ailments, but mostly to snatch up the report. I crammed the icky paper into my pants pocket trying not to think about how gross laundry day was going to be.

"I might not be able get through the mess. I'll try, but maybe not."

Tears came to my eyes from the coughing and I swiped at them with flour and preserved covered fingers. A dough-like mixture formed on my fingertips. This was just getting better and better.

Finally, the two people made an appearance at the front and stared down the aisle at me. The man was dressed in whites. He looked stunned for a moment then chortled.

"Can't you see, Nancy," said the voice of reason attached to the chortler. "She can't get through until the aisle gets cleared."

"Call the police, Dexter," was the woman's reply. She pushed at spiked, short dark hair tinged with royal purple dye.

Okay, got the lineup. Nancy Littlejohn, administrative assistant. Dexter Fuller, teaching chef. Frosty the Snowman, me.

"No, no," I managed to croak. I moved toward them, trying to pick my way through broken bottles, gunk, olive oil, and smashed pickles. And let's not forget about being covered with flour.

"My name is Arbela Einstein and I've been hired as your new assistant cleaning specialist."

I took a cautious leap over several jars of ginger that hadn't broken, crunched on some errant coffee beans then dodged a small crate of dried apples. The couple watched me, she with suspicion, he with glee.

"Don't tell me that's the new pearl diver, Nancy." He studied me, giggles turning into full-blown laughter. "This is just too rich."

"Stop laughing, Dexter," said Nancy. "This is vandalism. I'll have her arrested."

"Now wait a minute," I said, in between hacking and dodging. "Nobody needs to be arrested. I can explain all this."

About half way down the aisle, I took a skid on a slick patch of EVOO. I grabbed onto the nearest rack still standing on the other side of the aisle. A puff of flour billowed from me. Dexter found this hilarious.

"Nancy, she works here," said Dexter. His slender body shook with mirth.

Nancy wasn't having any of it. "That well may be, but she isn't supposed to be here until nine. And what is she doing destroying everything in the pantry?" She gave him a hard glare, which had no effect on him whatsoever.

"When she makes her way up here, we'll have to ask her," he guffawed.

I found it annoying at how they talked about me like I wasn't in the room. Along those lines, Dexter suddenly pulled himself up to his full five-ten or so, glared at her, and became quite serious.

"Besides, I've been telling you for years to stop putting the heavy cans on the top shelves. Put them at the bottom. I've told you, Nancy – I don't know how many times – one of these days those shelves are going over." He pointed an accusing finger at the miscreant fallen shelves, dead soldiers all. "Just an accident waiting to happen. I'm writing this down."

The chef removed a smallish blue book from his apron pocket and produced a yellow, half-pencil. He made quick notes while Nancy rolled her eyes.

I finally arrived at the front of the room. I gave a quick glance to the left. A small, opened stepladder that hadn't been there before caught my eye. It stood right in the middle of where the first shelf had been when it was upright.

"Are you all right?" Dexter looked up at me with a titter. "Underneath all that flour?"

I opened my mouth to answer, but gathering more momentum, Dexter overrode anything I might have had to say. He turned back in Nancy's direction.

"It was just an accident waiting to happen," he repeated, obviously still in his I-told-you-so mood. "You're lucky she doesn't sue."

"Sue?" Dressed in a fashionable black Goth ensemble, Nancy's already pale face lost even more color, vaguely resembling my flour-covered mug. "Sue? Sue?"

She turned on me with the biggest fake smile I've seen in a long time. Even though she was no longer in her first youth, the metal of her braces glinted in the overhead lighting.

"You're not going to sue your new employer, are you?"

"No, madam," I said, finding the nasal twang for my voice again. "But I would like to go home and change."

"What happened?" Nancy ignored my request. "How did the shelves go over...what was your name? Einstein?"

"Yes, madam. Arbela Einstein."

"What's going on here?"

Hayes' voice, authoritative and curt, rang out from the doorway. We all froze in place; on his home turf, he had that kind of command. He stared at each of us like royalty about to call for one or two beheadings. When recognition finally came to him about me, his eyes grew wide and his jaw went slack.

"Le...." Catching himself before completely saying my name, he made a quick recovery. "Land sakes alive, what happened here?"

Nancy ran to his side like a first-grader about to tattle on one of the other youngsters in the schoolyard. "This is the new dishwasher, Chef, and look what's she's done."

"I didn't do this," I retorted. "I was at the back of the room when it all came down. I was trying not to get creamed."

"Are you all right?" Hayes looked at me with concern.

I nodded, felt an itch, reached up and scratched my wig with one hand. Flour poofed around my head. Hayes fought back a smile then returned to his lord of the manner routine.

"Never mind all that. We have no time for accusations. Classes start in a half an hour." Hayes was positively regal in his fiefdom. "Nancy, call the cleaning service from yesterday, and tell them to come back here immediately."

"Yes, Chef," said Nancy, scooting around him and heading for her office.

"Chef Dexter, don't you have something you need to prepare for this morning's baking classes? I believe you are making chocolate éclairs today."

"Yes, Chef," said Dexter with a slight bow, a quick turn, then vanishing in the direction of one of the kitchens.

"You," Hayes pointed a finger in my direction. "Go to the ladies room and clean up. There's a shower, towels, and clean uniforms. Then come see me in my office. In the basement. Twenty minutes."

"Yes, Chef," I parroted.

He turned on his heels and without a backward glance, left the room.

"It's good to be king," I muttered, shaking myself like a dog. Loose flour floated down around me like soft snowflakes.

Jeesh, what I do for a living.

Chapter Twenty-two

The Laughing Pomegranate

The idea of getting out of the flour-encrusted, goopy and disgusting clothes, showering, cleaning my wig, glasses, buck teeth, plastic shoes, and finding a uniform that remotely fit within twenty minutes would have made me laugh under ordinary circumstances. But these were no ordinary circumstances.

The shoes cleaned up in a jiffy, but the wig took a full ten minutes. To remove what I could of the flour, I beat it against the sink until my arms ached. The wig needed to be washed, but that wasn't going to happen. The fake eyebrows were a total loss and besides, I had neglected to bring more glue with me. Lesson for the fatheaded: Murphy's Law. If it can go wrong it will. Be prepared.

The flour residue in the wig made it even stiffer. I pulled a chunk down over my forehead and eyebrows then glanced in a mirror. Staring back at me was an Old English sheepdog that looked like it had done battle with a windmill and lost. I gave a short bark, climbed into some whites, shoved in the false teeth, and threw on my reading glasses.

I knocked on Hayes' door twenty-two minutes later. If he called me on being two minutes late, my plan was to slap him upside the head, southern style. One can only take so much.

"Come in." Hayes' voice still held the king of the realm quality.

I opened the door, slipped in, and closed it behind me. His demeanor changed instantly from King Lear to Huck Finn.

"Lee! What happened in there? When did you get here? I didn't even know you'd arrived."

He leapt up and came over to my side of the room. Grasping my arm, he guided me to the chair in front of his desk. Being treated like a fragile doll has its moments but this wasn't one of them.

"I'm all right, thank you," I said, shaking free of him.

"I couldn't believe my eyes when I saw you and that catastrophe in the pantry. Here, sit down. Are you really all right?"

"Other than a few scrapes, bruises, and the black and blue toenail, I'm fine, Hayes," I said, with a tone of finality in my voice.

"I'm so relieved. I wasn't even told you were here. Why wasn't I told you were here?"

I took a breath to answer then thought better about it. His wife, Connie, had known I was here. After all, she let me in. But I decided not to throw her under the bus.

Hayes didn't press me for an answer, thank gawd. "What happened in there?" He asked the question again.

I hesitated. "Not sure."

"Chef Dexter said something about the racks being top heavy. Is that why they came down?"

"It could have been. Although, an opened step-ladder that hadn't been there before seemed to show up." I studied his reaction.

"Red metal?"

I nodded.

"That's one of the two we keep at either side of the center aisle for our higher items."

He thought for a moment then a look of fear came to his face.

"Wait a minute, Lee. You don't think somebody stood on top of the ladder and pushed those racks over on purpose? Good Lord almighty, you could have been killed!"

Hayes began to tremble in his chair, lost in the reality of what happened. Seeing his quivering hand resting on his desktop calendar, I reached a soothing one of my own across his desk. I did some back-peddling. Nothing would be accomplished by terrorizing the staff, especially their leader, at this point.

"I'm sure the ladder was already there. I just didn't see it."

Bald-faced lie. It hadn't been there. When it comes to sleuthing I'm not the knucklehead I often pretend to be, a sometimes useful and deflective image to present in my line of work. But my lie served no purpose. Hayes wouldn't be soothed.

Jerking his hand from beneath mine, he shot to a standing position. He crossed the room and stood with his back toward me, facing a series of photographs hanging on a wall. I came to his side. After a brief moment, he turned to me, tears brimming over in his eyes.

"Lee, if someone deliberately pushed the racks over, that means that whoever killed Jacques is still here." His voice took on an exasperated and desperate air. "What do they want? What's going on?"

"Give me some time to find out."

My voice was quiet but firm. He shook his head.

"I should close the Institute. My life savings is invested in it, but I don't want to be responsible for anyone else's death." And here he broke down, shoulders shaking with each sob.

I knew better than to reach out again. Nonetheless, I persisted.

"Forty-eight hours, Hayes. Otherwise, we may never know who really committed the crime."

"Well, it isn't Patsy!' He hurled the words at me.

"What makes you so sure?"

"I know her. Like nobody else. She doesn't kill people in the real sense of the word. Yes, she smothers them to death with her talent and ambition. But actual murder? No."

"Under the right circumstances anyone could become a murderer."

"I'm not saying she wouldn't defend herself or her sons if they were physically threatened. But all she wants in her life is to create recipes and cook. She has a fire in the belly. She'd never jeopardize that."

"What if someone stood in her way?"

He shook his head firmly. "Never. Besides, if she was driven to something like that, she'd shout it to the world. She has never been one to hide from the consequences of her actions."

"Okay then. We need to prove it. Forty-eight hours?"

He didn't say anything, but stared off into space. Just when I thought he wasn't going to answer, he looked at me.

"You'd better get to Personnel and fill out your W-2 form, Ms. Einstein. Did you bring your social security card with you?"

"Yes, sir," I said with a smile.

Chapter Twenty-three

Twenty Thousand Leagues Under the Seafood Salad

""Oh, m'gawd," said a female voice, the words drawn out in surprise. "It's like a steam room in here. Isn't the fan working?"

I turned to face a smiling young woman, probably around twenty-five. Long, honey-colored hair was pulled up and deftly styled at either side of her 'beanie' toque. That's sort of a weird-looking, flared white hat, shorter than most other chef headgear. She gave it a lot of pizzazz. The rest of the uniform consisted of black and white checked pants and a white jacket.

Devoid of makeup, her face glowed not only with youth, but natural beauty. She may have been a chef-in-the-works, but she was a gorgeous one. I, on the other hand, was none of the above.

She stepped into the room. "You're new, aren't you?"

"Yes, I am."

"Hot enough in here for you?" She laughed. I didn't "How about this?"

She hit a switch on the wall. A steady drone sounded. I looked up at a huge fan in the ceiling, previously unnoticed by me, blades turning faster and faster until they became indefinable. She stuck out a hand.

"I'm Brit Poynter." She gave me a radiant smile. "My first name is really Britomart. My mother was a Lit major and named me after the lady knight in *The Faerie Queene* by Edmund Spenser."

She threw back her head and laughed showing even, white teeth without a hint of a filling in any of them. I could have hated her if I wasn't so tired. Brit looked at me.

"You've never heard of the poem, have you?"

Actually, I had. It's one of the mind-numbing literary works you have to read your freshman year in college, so your parents feel you're being punished sufficiently for spending their money on a higher education. But, as I was playing a part, I shook my head.

"No, nobody has," she said. "That's why everybody calls me Brit."

Yanking off the rubber gloves I'd been wearing for the past three to four hours, I pushed a wrinkled, prune-like paw toward her. We shook hands.

"Hi, Brit. I'm Arbela. And thank you for that," I gestured to the fan, blinking back the sweat pouring down my face. I brushed at the hair in my eyes, then raked at fake bangs that felt more like a Brillo pad than not. "I didn't even know the fan was there." I had developed a lisp. I think my buckteeth shifted.

"You're job's tough enough without all the heat and steam." She stared up at the ceiling fan. Then she turned to me. "I'm surprised Nancy didn't show you how to use the fan."

I wasn't surprised in the least. Nancy Littlejohn turned out to be a bitch of the first order. Brit continued her light chatter.

"It looks like you're almost done. You're a lot faster than Manuel. I can't believe he didn't show up yesterday or today. Though, maybe after what happened, he had to take a couple of days off. I guess he and Chef Jacques were closer than I thought."

But her voice sounded doubtful. Given what I'd heard of the man, I was doubtful, too. I went into my act.

"That must have been such a shock," I said. "Finding the chef dead like that. Stabbed!" I clucked a little and shook my head in sympathy.

"It was like oh m'gawd. I mean, really. I mean, like, really?"

I tried to find the subject of her words, but unable to, decided to move on.

"How long have you been studying at the Institute, Brit?"

"This is my second year. I graduate in June. Then I hope to work as a chef at somewhere like the White House. I love the White House, you know?"

"Well, for one thing, it's so white."

She looked at me for a moment, then burst out laughing. "Hey! I see you have a sense of humor, Arbela."

"It pops up every now and then."

"Did you get a chance to look around? I was told you got here early this morning."

She gave me a smile that didn't look like she was on a fishing expedition. But as I returned it, I wondered how she knew when I'd arrived. We both stood smiling for a moment before I continued.

"A little bit. Mrs. Durand opened the door for me."

"Oh, yes, Connie. She's on sabbatical. Stanford, you know."

"So I understand," I said, remembering both Patsy and Hayes had told me the same thing. Being on sabbatical from a prestigious school such as Stanford usually meant a person had all their wits about them, to say the least.

As if reading my mind, Brit looked around her then leaned in.

"You'd never know it from the way Connie's been behaving lately, but she suffers from periodic bouts of depression. I think she's in one now. When she's all right, she's one of the country's leading authorities on the oceans' seaweed and it's processes. Says farming it could end world hunger. I thought I might specialize in cooking with seaweed and went to one of her open-forum lectures. She was amazing. But I don't think so. It's too restrictive."

"When was that? The lecture?"

"Oh, the beginning of the term. Sometime in September."

"Brit, you seem to be a fount of knowledge, so let me ask you. How well did you know Chef Jacques?"

Her smile was replaced by a grimace and a frown. She didn't answer, but looked away.

"I hear he had a thing for the ladies," I persisted, watching her.

She shot me a look of suspicion.

"What makes you ask that? Did anyone say something?"

I turned back to the dishwasher, my new nemesis. Removing trays of clean glasses, I stacked them on a white two-tier steel cart. Black for dirty, white for clean. Simple and orderly. I replied without looking at the younger woman.

"No, no, Brit. I just wondered that's all. If he was a man with wandering hands, I'm sure glad I wasn't here when he was. I wouldn't like him groping me."

"And he would have, too," she said with gusto. "But don't worry. The other chefs are great."

"That's a relief. I've met Chef Dexter, briefly. He works the mornings, right?"

"Yes, he's awesome. And Chef Oliver's good, too."

"What are the others like? Chef Barbara and Chef Aurélien, right?"

Without thinking, I'd given the French pronunciation to the name Aurélien, which meant when the word is said, it should be half swallowed and very nasal. She stared at me. I did some fast talking.

"I…ah….understand Chef Aurélien is French."

"Yes, he is. But those two teach the afternoon classes, so I don't know much about them. But I see them around from time to time, at parties and banquets, those sorts of things. Chef Airy's accent is so thick sometimes I can't understand what he's saying. Everyone calls him Chef Airy. Not whatever you said. Your French is pretty good."

She, paused, studying me. I swear, French gets me in trouble every time. Giving her a bucktoothed smile, I vowed then and there to cut back on any and all accents.

"I'm originally from New Orleans," I said, making it up on the spot. "My grandmother was French."

"That's nice." She thought a moment, seemingly distracted then went on. "You'll probably never connect with any of the chefs; they're pretty busy. But if you ever meet Chef Oliver, stand back. The worst halitosis I've ever experienced. But his Salmon Wellington is to die for. And he knows everything about fruits and vegetables. He even makes brussels sprouts taste good. And he can carve up the side of a steer in, like, thirty minutes, but they all can."

"So I've heard."

Her face took on a dreamy look. "Chef Dexter is the best, of course. I hope to be that good someday. No one can touch his *millefeuille*."

She actually said it correctly, 'meel-foy'. I was impressed, but had no intention of saying so. Brit went on.

"It's a thin, buttery, and flaky pastry. Used in Napoleons," she explained.

Tío makes this pastry all the time, only he calls it *milhojas*, which is the Spanish version. Whatever you call it, it's fattening as hell. I went back to the slaughtered chef.

"So except for Chef Jacques, it sounds like a good group." I cooled my jets with the pronunciation of his name with a French accent.

"Yeah, well, him." Her upper lip curling in disgust, Brit's voice became a whisper. "He wasn't really French, you know. He just pretended to be. Anytime Chef Airy was in the same room with him and he'd put on airs, Airy'd start to growl."

"So Chef Airy didn't like him?"

"He hated him. He called him an imposter. It was so cute the way he said it, too, with his heavy French accent. He was always coming on to all of us females, although he left Chef Barbara alone. She's married to a bodyguard."

"That would be Chef Jacques, not Chef Airy," I clarified.

"Yes, of course. He didn't care what you looked like. Even you wouldn't have been safe...I mean..."

She gulped and stuttered. "I mean, he hit on all the girls, not matter what they....I...ah..." Her voice came to a full stop and she blinked at me. She was a nice kid, so I decided to help her out a little.

"I know what you mean, Brit. With some men as long as she's female he's going to want to jump her bones."

Gratitude at me bailing her out of the faux pas helped her relax. She stepped closer, preparing to unload more.

"Actually, he did more than that. He was like a sicko! He'd bring a few of us girls into his office and if we didn't let him feel us up or sometimes do more, he'd threaten to give us a bad grade."

"Did that happen to you?"

She nodded but didn't say anything.

"Did you take it to Chef Hayes? Surely, he wouldn't allow any of his staff to behave like that."

Given what I'd learned from Hayes during my interview with him, however, it was entirely possible he felt helpless at stopping anything Jacques did. Blackmail can have long-reaching arms.

Brit stood still for a moment, thinking something over in her mind. "It stopped for a while when Rhonda was here. Right after her first visit with Chef Jacques, she came in wearing new outfits and expensive jewelry. Then she graduated early and applied for all the plum jobs. Recently, she got an assistant chef job on a cruise line. I forget which one. While she was here, Chef Jacques left us alone, but he started in again a few weeks ago."

"Why didn't anyone go to the Powers That Be to complain?"

"My friend, Sandy, went to Chef Dexter and told him." Brit looked around and lowered her voice. "She knew Dex was keeping a log on Chef Jacques."

"Was he?" I considered the smallish blue book I'd seen him writing in earlier. "What does this log look like? Is it blue?"

Her face took on the look that happens when you know you've let the proverbial cat out of the bag. Sorry Tugger.

Brit physically backed up, but her words rushed on. "Yes, but you won't tell anyone I told you, will you? Sandy's on scholarship, like me, and neither of us want to be involved in any trouble."

"Pinky swear. But nobody actually did anything about Chef Jacques's behavior?"

She shook her head. "I think a lot of us were scared; we just avoided him. Things went missing around here and a couple of the girls got blamed for them, especially the ones who threatened to complain or went to Dex, like Sandy." She rushed on. "Even though I don't think she had anything to do with the rest."

"What rest?"

She took a deep breath and ran a straightening hand over her pristine whites. "When you get a little more experienced, one of your jobs is ordering food, like you'd do for a restaurant. So you can get the hang of ordering in bulk."

Brit gulped and paused, as if gathering up courage. She looked around her before going on.

"Three cases of Alaskan strawberries disappeared. Then a week later a double order of white truffles never showed up, but was paid for. Really expensive. Sandy's name was on both orders. She swore she didn't have anything to do with it, but it didn't look good. Anyway, they were black marks on her record and when some new copper pots disappeared a few weeks later, everyone looked to her. It was awful. She cried for days." Brit lowered her voice. "We can't afford to make any waves or get in bad with the school."

I was incensed over this attitude, but tried not to show it. I smiled.

"Regardless, there are laws against this type of harassment in the workplace, and certainly in a place of learning, Brit. You could file a formal complaint."

I barely got the words out when Nancy came barreling into the room.

"What's going on in here?" She turned to me. "Don't you have pots to scrub, Einstein? You don't get paid to gossip with the students." She turned to Brit with a slightly softer, but firm tone. "You'd better get back to class. Chef Oliver is demonstrating how to carve a crane out of Japanese radishes. You won't want to miss this."

She gave the girl a frozen smile, but stepped forward and into her personal space. Brit backed up and, skirting around the two of us, fled the room. Nancy turned to me.

"And you need to remember your place, Einstein. You are not here to fraternize with the students."

She stepped into my personal space, as well, probably wanting me to think she could squash me like a bug if she chose.

Putting aside my black belt in karate, I had a good four inches in height on her. My initial reaction to any enforced intimidation is to stand my ground and look the bully in the eye. In this case, the thought of picking her up and throwing her in the dishwasher for a thorough cleansing came to mind.

However, subservience was the role I was playing that day. I gritted my teeth, stepped back, and nodded.

"Yes madam," I whispered.

"That's better." She preened before adding, "Now get back to work." She pivoted and stomped out of the room. It was all I could do not to throw a clean plate at her purple hair.

Chapter Twenty-four

The Last Temptation Of Crust

Let's face it, I'm a little softer than I like to think. Washing an endless supply of dirty utensils and hauling heavy trays back and forth from the dishwasher to the carts in a windowless room at over ninety degrees heat took their toll on me.

Not to mention – but I will – I was also responsible for cleaning out the johns, and 'maintaining' the garbage and trash containers. On the hour, every hour, my job was to check on the heavy-duty trashcans holding thirty-five gallon black garbage bags scattered around in specific spots. When these devils on wheels were full, I'd roll them to the outside loading ramp, down the incline, and to one of three side-by-side large dumpsters set against the wall of the building.

I'd tie the heavy, messy, and smelly bag closed, lift it out of the container, and throw it inside a dumpster. My first time out at ten AM, I saw the nearest dumpster was already loaded with full black bags, what I took to be the previous day's garbage. Not to complain, but that meant I had to roll the containers to the second dumpster. Every footstep counted when you're as tired as I was.

Once the containers were emptied, I rinsed them out, dried them, lined them with a fresh garbage bag, and rolled them back to one of the kitchens for further use.

The only time scurrying students or teachers looked at me was if I accidentally got in their way or they stepped on me. Otherwise I was invisible. Good for my line of work. Bad for my toes.

The morning found me loitering when and where I could, studying potential suspects. There was an air of edginess about everyone, nervous laughter and anxious looks. I chalked this up to the violent death of a colleague, even a disliked one.

The students were a concert in whites. Thirty in all watched, cooked, and learned from their betters, easily identifiable by stove-pipe style white toques.

The toque originated in Greek orthodox monasteries during the Middle Ages, when dissident chefs often took refuge with other educated members of society. They distinguished themselves from the monks by wearing a white hat, instead of the black worn by monks. The hats got taller as time went by. The Big Mac isn't the only thing that became supersized.

Chef Oliver's white toque leaned to the left, sort of like he did. He was a small man with a concave chest and lousy posture. I never got close enough to smell his breath.

On the other side of the room in the baking area, Chef Dexter was teaching his class the art of creating an éclair, start to finish. After baking, he filled the insides with a creamy mixture then slathered the top of the pastries with melted chocolate. The whole process made my mouth water. I'm a girl who likes her éclairs.

I noticed each chef carried with him his basic knives of the trade in a soft-side nylon case. Each case contained interior knife slots and sturdy handles ensuring safe cutlery transport. The canvas could roll and unroll at will. And they willed the unrolling a lot.

Chef Oliver was small, but he could wield a knife with the best of them. Meats, fruits, and veggies never stood a chance. Several large radishes met their demise disguised as a white bird.

Chef Dexter did a neat trick using the flat side of one of his larger blades. He crushed mounds of dark chocolate into dust before putting the chocolate into a double boiler to melt. I was glad I wasn't a Hershey bar.

But on the upside, both men were easily understood and called out the names of their students repeatedly. I saw quickly who was who.

The only student I wanted to know more about was Brit's friend, Sandy. A pretty, brown-haired girl, along the cheerleader type, she didn't look a day older than nineteen. I suspected she was, though, and had one of those faces that looked perennially young.

Sandy had an easy, but shy laugh. When she glanced my way, her smile was genuine and warm. Instinct told me she wasn't a person of interest, even though she'd had a history with the dead man. To me she seemed more a victim than a predator.

But her last name was Macintosh, and hoot man, I'd run a check on her to be sure she was as sweet and as innocent as I perceived her to be. Or have Richard do it. I was busy taking out the garbage.

While observing the group, I leaned my aching body against the doorframe to my room of horrors. Just then Nancy Littlejohn marched by like a master drill sergeant ready to send the troops out on a thirty-mile hike. Now here was a person of interest.

Body language in the kitchens changed instantly. Everyone stood more at attention, even the chefs, and stopped any little chatter going on between them. It became 'serious business' when she was around.

Nancy had a similar effect on me. I did an about face and went back to work, hoping I would last until the end of my first shift.

Morning classes ended at one PM, when everyone would eat what had been prepared by the students. According to the schedule, the afternoon classes trooped in at two. I would return by five and start washing dishes dirtied by the second round's gang. My last cleanup was supposed to have me finished and out by nine PM. Dishes used after I left were to be rinsed and set aside by students after they cleaned the kitchen areas. Very regimented.

I left at the end of my first shift, went home for a quick nap and showed up again at five for the second half of my job. I was looking forward to meeting Chefs Aurélien and Barbara.

I could see why the deceased chef left Chef Barbara alone. The lady was into bodybuilding. Maybe even weight lifting. Her muscles rippled with every move. Sort of Arnold Schwarzenegger with a bra. And she seemed to have a particular enthusiasm for whacking large chunks of meat with a butcher knife that bore a remarkable resemblance to a hatchet. Even the students observed her from a respectful distance.

To be fair, Chef Airy also wielded an impressive blade, a shiny, stainless steel ten-inch boning knife, all the while screeching in French. *Oo la la,* he could slice up a side of cow for a *boeuf bourguignon* or French beef stew, even faster than I've seen Tío do it. But then, Tío wasn't trying to impress a group of students.

All in all, there didn't seem to be one of these culinary artisans who wasn't used to hacking, slashing, or spearing just about anything with their kitchen weaponry. I was surprised they didn't yell *en garde* before they struck.

The second set of white-clothed students were pretty much like the first, but tended to be more under Nancy's thumb than the morning crew. Like me, Nancy worked a split shift, but came and left at will. You never knew when or where she was going to put in an appearance or whom she would corner about something. What was interesting was she seemed to have no life outside the Institute.

That night, while loading up the last of the dirty dishes, I did a recap. My split-shift job consisted of three major tasks. The first being cleaning dishes, either by dishwasher or by hand, which included far too many pots and pans. Thank gawd for rubber gloves. At seeing my nails, my manicurist was going to sob bitter tears.

The second task was periodically cleaning the bathrooms. And the less said about that the better.

The third and most harrowing task was garbage maintenance. The day had seen me hauling containers of garbage, morning and afternoon, in several scheduled excursions to the dumpster.

Five minutes to nine, I rolled the last of the garbage outside to the well-lit dumpster area. Filling up the second dumpster, I threw the last several bags into the third, wondering, once again, if it was too late to become a nurse.

Right then the privately owned garbage truck arrived. I stood to one side and watched. Two men in bright-blue coveralls sat in the truck. One leapt out, opened the first of the three dumpsters, and began pulling out the large black plastic bags. The driver stayed in place, but seemed to be in charge of raising and lowering the forklift at the back of the truck.

With speed and know-how, bag after bag from the dumpsters was loaded onto a forklift, electronically raised up, and then thrown into its open top. I watched this job with new appreciation.

Whoa, Nellie. While I was pondering on how I could get a little miniature forklift to follow me around, something struck me.

According to the Institute's schedule, the garbage was picked up six days a week, the last pick-up being Saturday night. Sunday the Institute was closed. Finding the slain body of the head-teaching chef early the next morning had closed the Institute before classes began again on Monday. If the dumpsters were emptied Saturday night and with the two-day closure, there shouldn't have been any garbage when I went out Tuesday morning with my first load.

Yet there was. The first dumpster had been full. My mind raced.

Meanwhile, a garbage man – or should I call him a refuse collector, if I'm an assistant cleaning specialist – jumped on the running-board of the truck, and grabbed hold of a sturdy looking handle bar. He waved to me in a friendly manner as the truck started slowly out of the driveway.

I chased after them.

"Wait, wait," I yelled over the din of the truck's motor.

The driver jerked to a stop, leaned his head out, and stared at me, waiting. He was young, and had a friendly smile. I jumped onto the running-board, alongside the second man.

"Listen," I said. "Did you come here yesterday?"

The man next to me on the running-board spoke first. "Yes, ma'am. We come every day except Sunday, unless they have a party or something."

"About four times a year they have a party on a Sunday," said the driver, chiming in. "When they do, we show up special, on a Sunday night. Those three dumpsters are loaded after one of their parties."

Both men laughed.

"But you were here yesterday, Monday, around this time?" I was persistent.

The driver, still smiling, picked up a clipboard with several sheets of paper on it. He perused it for a second.

"Yes, ma'am, we showed up yesterday at nine-oh-six PM. See?" He turned the clipboard in my direction. "Although it wasn't worth it."

"Why wasn't it worth it?" I looked from one man to the other.

"Nothing there. Right, Dan?" The driver turned to the running-board man.

Dan picked up the conversation. "That's right. Not a thing."

"Not like today," I said, "where you had fifty or sixty bags?"

"Sixty-three, ma'am. Full load," said the driver. "See? Wrote it down." He turned his clipboard in my direction again.

"You keep meticulous notes," I said.

"Yes, ma'am," they said in unison again.

"Customers like that," the driver added.

"Saw on TV you had some trouble in there yesterday," Dan said.

"Yeah, a murder," added the driver.

"Really? I hadn't heard," I plastered a big smile on my face. "I don't supposed you'd let me open up one of those bags to see what's in them?"

The driver plastered an even bigger smile on his face before he said, "No, ma'am. Once they're inside the truck you'd need a court order. People's privacy and all that. Company rules."

"Thank you, gentlemen." I hopped down with a sigh.

They gave one another a quick glance before the driver shrugged and said, "Sure thing, ma'am. You have a nice day now." With a smile, he put the truck in gear, and pulled away, the running-board man waving goodbye again.

It didn't take a rocket scientist to figure out the likely scenario. Someone stole the food from the freezer, put the contents into black bags, and threw the lot into the dumpsters, probably late Monday night. In any event, it was after the garbage truck showed up for collection and left empty-handed. Did I suspect this to be true? Yes. Did I have proof?

No. And proof I needed. I returned to the dumpsters, opened the lid of the first, held my breath, and hopped inside.

For a garbage container it was surprisingly clean. I then remembered Nancy telling me that part of my job was to wash them out twice a week, Tuesdays and Fridays, with a Lysol/water spray. Today was Tuesday. Lawdy, lawdy, lawdy, could this job get any worse?

I bent down. Several smaller scraps of paper, a larger, balled up one, another paper clinging to a piece of wood, and a wilted broccoli floret caught my eye, all obviously escapees from a black bag or two. I scooped them up.

"Einstein!" The sharp and dreaded voice of the drill sergeant reverberated inside the empty, metal dumpster. Startled, I jerked upward and bumped my head on the metal lip.

"Ow." I rubbed the sore spot, as Nancy leaned over the railing of the loading dock. She looked down into the container.

"Einstein, are you paying attention to me?"

"*Jawol, mein Kapitän,*" I muttered under my breath, remembering my ninth-grade German. I crammed what I'd found into my pants pocket.

"Yes, madam?" I said louder. "Can I help you?"

"Ah, good," Nancy said. "I see you're getting a jump on the job. Very good."

"Ah...yeah....right. Tell me, Nancy, did the Institute have a party last night or some kind of get together?"

"Certainly not! Our head-teaching chef was murdered Sunday night. And the Institute was closed yesterday."

"Can you think of any reason why there would have been garbage put into the dumpster after the daily pickup last night? Could one of the neighbors have used it?"

"Of course not. There are no businesses open late at night and no residential homes. In all the time I've been here, we've never had anyone add to or take out any of our garbage." Her tone was haughty and dismissive. "The idea is absurd. And as it's not important, I suggest you get back to your job."

Her orders went on without allowing a response from me.

"The Lysol spray is in the utility cabinet. There should be a container sitting beside it that screws onto the hose. Fill it half way with Lysol, put it on the hose, and wash out each dumpster. After that, you're free to go home."

You never saw a PI work as fast as I did. I was out of there within fifteen minutes and on my way to a hot shower and vats of Bengay.

Chapter Twenty-five

Return Of The Thin Mint

Usually, California is into water conservation, so Gurn has shown me how to take a shower, military style. Turn on shower. Get wet. Turn off shower. Soap up. Turn on shower. Rinse off. Turn off shower. Stand down. Not spa luxurious but does the job.

Not this time. I took a shower that only ended when the supply of hot water ran out. I'd leaned against the tiles letting the hot water run over my aching muscles. That was after I came inside the apartment, gave a brief hello to awaiting cats, ran to the shower, stripped off, and left my clothes on the floor.

Tugger and Baba were aghast. The standard greeting they expect is a lot more along the lines of hugs and kisses, finished off by a round of treats. Following me into the bathroom, each sat outside the shower, staring at me through the glass door, hoping I would mend the error of my ways. About fifteen minutes into my shower, they gave up and wandered off.

Finished and wrapping my terrycloth robe around me, I saw both cats playing with things they pulled out of the pockets of my discarded clothes. No doubt the delectable aroma of garbage attracted them. In particular, Tugger was battling with the scrap of paper attached to a piece of wood.

As I hadn't had a chance to examine what I'd looted from the garbage bin, I sat down on the floor cross-legged next to the four-footed kidlets. Much to their displeasure, I snatched the booty from them, being sure to get everything they had.

I tried to throw the broccoli in the trashcan, but Tugger would have none of it. A clever paw made a grab. He chomped down on this disgusting lifeless veggie like it was manna from heaven. Baba went to him and sniffed his mouth, as if he was eating something so tantalizing, she wanted half. He didn't share.

I reminded myself to give them their expected treats as soon as possible. Do not deny your cat treats. You will only suffer for it.

But before I did so, back to work. I inspected each item I'd taken from the bin, no matter how seemingly insignificant. Still sitting on the floor, I held up one tiny scrap no bigger than my thumbnail. Torn at one side, it had a neat, triangular end on the other. I just made out the numbers 5473 before Baba made a lunge for it. She swallowed it before I could get it away from her.

Such is the life of a PI living with cats. Especially, if you're sitting on the floor with them. Playtime. I should have locked myself in a room before I started my investigations.

But I was sure the scrap came from an invoice. I'd seen several like invoices pinned to the bulletin board for incoming deliveries. All with numbers in the upper right hand corner.

Next was Tugger's second favorite after the broccoli, a scrap of paper with a partial image of a lobster tail. It was attached to a sliver of wood, probably broken off from one of the crates. The wood looked new and clean.

Part of the stolen items were crates of lobster tails. Here was the proof I needed. Maybe not admissible evidence in court, but good enough for me.

Hayes told the police he thought someone was trying to discredit the school, i.e. stealing expensive items not to resell, but to destroy. Food left to rot, causing at the very least waste, disruption, and angst.

But if Hayes was right, did that discrediting go as far as murder? Or was the murder a separate issue? My gut told me the two were linked.

I remembered the balled up paper and looked around. Not seeing it, I reached inside a pocket of my pants. There it was, caught in a fold. No wonder the cats couldn't pull it free.

After a brief struggle, I extricated it. Taking the time to smooth it out on the floor, despite interference from my feline kids, I saw most of the top was missing. The partial words 'of Na' written in green told me which end was which.

When I'd filled out the work papers for the job, I sat across from Nancy Littlejohn at her desk. She had several writing pads prominently displayed. The words 'From the Desk of Nancy Littlejohn' was emblazoned across the top of each pad. In green. Interesting.

But what was more interesting was the remainder of the sheet was covered with Hayes Durand's name written in cursive. Neat little rows. Neat little writing. Someone was practicing Hayes' signature. Was that someone Nancy Littlejohn?

Office assistants have all kind of duties and rights. Some even sign checks for their employees, duplicating their signatures. Maybe Nancy was one of those assistants.

And yet another thing to find out.

Meanwhile, I stored my booty in a plastic bag out of the cats' reach, and went to give them their treats.

Chapter Twenty-six

To Grill A Mockingbird

"So how was your day, Vicki?"

I stood at the kitchen counter, a chilled martini in one hand, the other spooning cheerios into my mouth. I remembered to put the phone speaker on just as I heard her answer my question.

"From the sound of your voice," she said, with a laugh, "better than yours. You sound tired. Tell me about your day."

I picked up my cereal and phone, crossed to the kitchen table, and sat down. I settled in for a chat with my sister-in-law. No matter how brief, it was always welcomed.

Vicki is a wonderful addition to our family. Each Alvarez member contributes his or her own uniqueness to the family, but Vicki gives us a large dose of sweetness. And heart.

"My day, by Lee Alvarez." I cleared my throat. "Exhausting. And far too boring to go into. How's my niece?"

"Well, at the moment, I am stroking her head. She's asleep and I plan to follow her lead in about fifteen minutes. But I love ending the day with a call from you."

"You are such a sweetie to say that, but don't let me keep you. What's that hound of a brother of mine doing?"

"He's cleaning up the kitchen, but he's nearly done."

"No kidding? How did you manage that?"

"He had a choice between changing the baby's diaper or cleaning the kitchen."

"Gotcha."

"Richard's becoming very domesticated. He even grilled rib eye steaks tonight."

"Do tell. No, don't," I said. "The steaks were seasoned with kosher salt and fresh ground pepper then grilled until medium rare. There is no such thing as a well-done steak in our family."

"As Tío says, 'The animal is already dead. There is no need to kill it twice'."

"Only he says it in Spanish."

Vicki and I shared a long moment of laughter at the family's idiosyncrasies. Then she asked, "Where's Gurn?"

"I'm on my own until around midnight. He's getting last minute tax returns ready for the April fifteenth deadline. Did Richard fill you in on what's going on?"

"Yes. If you hadn't worked so late, I would have had you come over for dinner. I don't like you not having a proper meal."

"Don't be silly, Vicki. I just love stale cheerios, overripe bananas, and milk long past its expiration date. Good for the constitution. How's your shop doing?"

"Made a sample hat for the holidays."

"Getting a jump on the season?"

"Have to. It's a cloche with multi-colored beading that looks and moves like tinsel. Not sure if it's going to work. Right now it looks like I'm a flapper."

"How about adding flashing bulbs, like they do on Christmas trees?"

"Then I'd be a flapper with bad taste."

We laughed again. Laughter. The instant vacation.

"And I've been tweaking another hat for the Sweet Pea line," she said.

Vicki designs all the lids sold at the Obsessive Chapeau herself, and has a fairly new line for tykes. Her latest is a pink, blue, yellow, or green bouclé newsboy cap with the kid's name hand sewn on the crown in beads.

I understand it's a hot seller, even though Steffi wore the prototype for fifteen seconds, and screamed like a banshee until it was removed. The cap has been living in the back of their closet ever since.

"But never mind my store." Vicki went on with a critical edge to her voice. She can be such a mommy. "Richard says you're working too hard."

"You're not kidding. My respect for people who work the BOH of restaurants has gone through the ceiling."

"What's BOH?"

"Back of house. In particular, pearl divers are now my most heroic characters," I followed with a hasty explanation. "That's a dishwasher. But everybody works their tails off. I've had a firsthand taste of how hard Tío worked to get where he was…and is." I let out a big sigh. "Every bone in my body aches. I'm just a wimp."

"No, you're not." Vicki as usual, defended me, even to me. "You're a thinking, of-the-mind detective, who is trying to do hard, manual labor. Even though you keep up your ballet and do karate, that doesn't mean you can haul trays of heavy dishes and silverware all day long without getting a few aches and pains." She inhaled deeply after that long, run-on sentence. "If nothing else, it requires a whole other set of muscles. But you're in good shape. In three days' time, you'll have this down."

"Oh, gawd," I groaned. "You mean I have to go back for another two days?"

We both burst out laughing.

"Tell you what," she said. "Let me go relieve Richard of kitchen duty, so you two can talk. I'm sure he's almost done, anyway."

While waiting for Richard to come to the phone, I stood and stretched. Ballet is my passion and Vicki's comment reminded me I needed to do a barre. I hadn't done one in a day or two and felt the tightness throughout my body. I vowed to do so the next morning, no matter how much earlier I had to get up.

"*Hola*, sister mine," said Richard, coming on the line. "Glad we could take a meeting. I've got a few things to tell you."

"Same here," I said.

"Me first, Sis. Finally got something back on the Durand boys. Wallace Quinn Durand, age thirty-five, was a problem child, even from the beginning."

"Middle name given for the brother, Quinn? Or is it a family name?"

"Seems to be a family name. Great grandfather, grandfather, and recently deceased uncle. To continue, Wally was caught stealing money from the Cub Scouts cookie fund in the third grade and he got a girl pregnant in the tenth. Those are just the highlights. He'd get in trouble and his mother bought him out consistently."

"Wow. No wonder Pete is full of resentment about him. How did you find out about this?"

"Door-to-door visitations. It pays to talk to the neighbors, especially ones who think the Durands are 'too big for their britches'."

"You flew someone to Little Rock to talk to the neighbors?"

"I did. Nothing like the personal touch and this is for Tío. Back to where I was going with this, being Conrad's from the south –"

"Conrad? From your department? The one with the ascots and pullover sweaters?"

"The same. He dresses funny, but –"

"I don't think he dresses funny."

"Well, you wouldn't. I think he dresses like an eighteenth century fop," said Richard. "And he spouts English sayings like 'pip, pip and cheerio', but all with a southern accent. Completely weird for a computer analyst. But he's good at codes. Where was I? Stop getting me off my train of thought."

"Choo-choo!"

Silence.

"Sorry. Go on, Richard."

"Thank you. Conrad is from Macon, Georgia, so he fits right into the culture. And he didn't say so, but this assignment suits him. He might make a good investigator one of these days."

"And he certainly dresses to Mom's liking. It's no secret that Lila Hamilton Alvarez likes her agents to dress like their posing for either *Gentleman's Quarterly* or *Vogue*, depending on the gender. I've gotten strangely used to it."

"You just can't say on track, can you? And don't say choo-choo again."

"Richard, I thought we were having what is called a con-ver-sa-tion," I said, enunciating each syllable. "I didn't know you were giving a lecture."

"Well, I am. Or trying to. It's late and we all need to get to bed. So hush." He cleared his throat before going on. "Tomorrow morning Conrad heads to the courthouse to see if he can dig up anything else on Wally. Possible pending charges, outstanding warrants, things like that. You know, he recently got married. Jolene. His third."

"So he collects wives like some men collect ascots?"

"Only Conrad collects ascots that I know of," Richard said, pointedly. "But I think collecting three wives by the time you reach your mid-thirties is on the excessive side."

"Vicki will be glad to hear it."

"And the women have to sign a pre-nup or no deal. Mama Patsy's edict. By-the-by, wife number two was the daughter of the neighbor, Conrad tells me. She lasted four months, so he's one bitter dude."

"Who's bitter? The neighbor or Wally?"

"I was referring to the neighbor, but maybe both. She left him. Seems he was 'catting around'. That's the neighbor's words, by the way. Conrad will fly back tomorrow night with any updates. And by the way, Wally was on an AA flight, but the day before."

"That's why he didn't show me his boarding pass. Tell me about Pete."

Richard paused, probably looked at the screen of his laptop.

"Thirty-four years old. Honor student all the way. As the neighbor said, 'not a lick of trouble from that one'. Has a teaching credential, not that he uses it. Married his childhood sweetheart, Allison, thirteen years ago. No children, but from all reports they're still trying. Little league coach. Even plays the guitar, like I do."

"But I'll bet not as well," I said, with a loyal edge to my voice.

My brother laughed. "You're prejudiced. But Pete Durand comes across as an all-around good guy."

"On paper."

"On paper," Richard agreed. "But he did have a gas charge on his credit card in Sacramento last Saturday."

"So he also arrived a day earlier in the Bay Area than he said. You've got nothing else on him?"

"All I've found out is he's been staying at the Park Stanford Hotel. Alone. No wife. She's still in Portland."

"Isn't that the hotel where Wally and his wife, whatshername, Jolene are? Did you do any looking into her background?"

"A little. Other than her being a cheerleader, Junior Miss, and winning Miss Arkansas Moonshine Honey, there isn't much else. Had a couple of DUIs last year. License suspended."

"You got a picture of her? What does she look like?"

"Looks a little like a tall, blonde Barbie doll, but maybe I'm being sexist."

"It wouldn't be a first. But for you to admit it, speaks well of Vicki's influence on you."

Richard harrumphed and went on, changing the subject. "What I do know is a woman matching Patsy's description asked for both Wally and Pete at the front desk of the Park Stanford last Saturday."

"The day before the stabbing?"

"Right. The clerk remembers her because she had a heavy southern accent." Richard paused again before saying, "Here's a novel idea. Why don't you just ask them why they were all here a day early?"

"Richard, brother mine," I said as condescendingly as I could. "It's not a good idea to tip someone off you're checking out their movements." I dropped the act. "Although, sometimes the element of surprise can make people reveal things they wouldn't ordinarily reveal. Maybe I should do just that."

"Told you," he smirked. "But not tonight. It's close to ten. Besides, the boys went to visit their mother and didn't leave the jail until it closed up for the night. They stopped off at a diner right after. They're still there."

"How do you know that?"

Richard stuttered. I let out a hoot of laughter.

"Why, you bad boy. Did you put a tracer on their cars?"

"Yes, I did and you may as well know I've got someone keeping tabs on the hotel, too. Wally's wife is there. You're not the only one who's going the extra mile for Tío."

I stopped laughing and became silent.

"Lee? You still there?"

"I am."

"I can feel you thinking. What's going on in that mind I have come to fear?"

"I'm thinking this might be a good time to visit Wally's wife at the hotel. I have a hunch she figures more into this case than anyone suspects."

"Miss Arkansas Moonshine Honey? You've got to be kidding. What could she possibly have to do with any of this?"

"Ah! There's my prejudiced, un-politically correct brother. Glad to know you haven't changed too much."

"Never mind that. Just stay out of trouble."

"Now, how can I do my job and stay out of trouble?"

Chapter Twenty-seven

The Silence Of The Lambchops

Within twenty minutes I was dressed and at the Park Stanford. It's a lovely hotel right on the El Camino Real, part of the historic mission trail. Also known as Route 82, it passes through or near the historic downtowns of many other Peninsula cities, including Burlingame, San Mateo, Redwood City, Menlo Park, Palo Alto, Mountain View, and Sunnyvale.

From the hotel you can walk to the Stanford Shopping Center and a few nearby restaurants. This can be a nice stroll, if you don't mind having a bajillion cars whizzing by at sixty-miles an hour.

I pulled into the parking lot, handed my car over to a valet service – love those – and went inside the hotel. I stopped at the front desk and was surprised to see Mr. Anderson behind the counter. He usually only works days, and I understand he has done so for decades. I've visited many relatives and friends at the hotel throughout the years, usually here for a Stanford event, and Mr. Anderson is a mainstay. He's friendly, professional, and always remembers your name.

"Hello, Mr. Anderson. What are you doing here tonight?"

"Why, Miss Alvarez, how nice to see you," he said, giving me a wide grin. "We're all taking turns on the evening shift for the next few weeks. Mrs. Lombardi had hip replacement surgery. But how remiss of me. I should be addressing you as Mrs. Hanson now, shouldn't I? I understand you're married. Best wishes to you and the Lt. Commander." Mr. Anderson grinned again, displaying even, but yellowing teeth.

"Thank you. Actually, I kept my maiden name."

"Ah! A modern woman. We get many of those around here, some on their honeymoons," he said. He leaned over the counter toward me. "It's never made any couple less in love, from what I can see."

We both chuckled. I was not quite certain why Mr. Anderson kept up on who was who in Palo Alto, but he did. And as an investigator, it was sometimes useful to me.

He straightened his back, adjusted his tie, and became more formal. "So now, Miss Alvarez, what can I do for you?"

"You have a Mr. and Mrs. Wallace Durand staying here. I wondered if you could give me their room number?"

Mr. Anderson looked scandalized. "I can't do that, Miss. You know we're not supposed to give out the room numbers of our guests, even to someone as distinguished as you."

I didn't know how distinguished I was, but I tried for a distinguished smile.

"Fair enough. How about ringing the room? Seeing if anyone is there? Like Mrs. Durand?

"If you're looking for the lady, I can tell you I saw her go into the Menlo Grill about a half an hour ago. She hasn't come out yet, so I'm sure you'll find her there."

He nodded in the direction of the bar, a very fine watering hole. I've had many a cocktail there, my second favorite being their Fire and Ice. My first, a martini. They make a smooth-as-silk one.

I thanked him and entered the bar. The main feature of the room is, of course, the booze. Bottles of every concoction with an alcohol content stand side by side on shelves backlit by attention-grabbing colors. Even the bar, itself, is a tempered glass lit from within, glowing in shades of green and yellow.

The room was nearly empty, which I found surprising but helpful. For sitting at the bar, dressed in all white, was a young woman strongly resembling a live Barbie doll. I stealthed to the opposite end, watching her down the last of her drink.

The bartender, a young, costumed lad wearing a black bowler hat and red and black striped vest, hurried over.

"Good evening, miss," he said, wiping down the bar in front of me with a damp cloth. "And what can I get for you?"

Remembering the martini I'd had only a short time before, I withdrew a twenty from my purse. I waved it in front of him.

"I want water, shaken but not stirred, and poured into a martini glass. Don't spare the olives. And this is for you." I slid the twenty across the bar toward him.

Not even a little surprised, he took the bill, and shoved it into the breast pocket of his vest. He proceeded to make me the most watered down martini I'd ever had, solid H_2O. Meanwhile, I kept an eye on Jolene Durand. After a minute or two, she looked in my direction, but it was really the barkeep she was seeking. When she caught his eye, she called out.

"Hey, sugar, can I have another margarita down here?"

Apparently 'sugar' is a southern form of address akin to 'hey you' for the rest of the world. When I thought about it, I found it preferable.

"Be right there," he called out with a smile. He turned back to me. "Here you go, miss." He set a sparkling martini glass in front of me and shot me a brief smile.

"Thank you," I said.

He then crossed to the other end of the bar and picked up the empty glass in front of Jolene.

I studied my surroundings. A foursome sat at a back table in front of a crackling fire, long on atmosphere and short on heat. Other than that, there was no one else in the bar except for Jolene and me. And of course, the bowlered barkeep.

While Jolene waited for her new drink, she looked sad, beaten down. Her head hung low the same way Baba's does when Tugger, the alpha cat, steals one of her toys. I'd call it hangdog, but Baba's a cat.

The barkeep set the margarita in front of Jolene and she took a long drink. I made a note to keep the door to the liquor cabinet locked on the off-chance Baba might head for it when Tugger steals her toys once too often. Maybe I should buy two of every toy. Give Baba more of a chance.

Whoa. I mentally slapped myself across the face, came back to the here and now, and strolled in Jolene's direction.

The phone rang behind the bar. The barkeep answered the phone and became engrossed in a conversation with his back to the customers. Perfect timing.

I caught Jolene's eye and raised my glass in a form of a greeting. It was a good way to see if she was receptive to having some company.

She gave me a fleeting smile, raised her glass in answer to my salute, brought it to her lips, and drained it dry. I walked over and sat on the stool next to her.

"Hi," I said. "I see it's just you and me in here tonight. My name's Lee."

"Well, hi there, yourself, Lee."

She reached out and grazed my shoulder with her free hand in a greeting. Super friendly, super drunk.

"My name is Jolene." She looked at her glass. "Empty. As soon as he gets off that phone, I'm getting another one of these. They taste like limeade only they pack a real wallop, you know?"

"I had four of those once and the next morning woke up under my friend's coffee table. Her mother was pissed."

I looked at Jolene's face, young, vulnerable, and very, very sad. Against my best interests, I said,

"You should go easy on those, Jolene. Maybe have some pretzels." I pointed to the small crystal bowl.

"Sure," she said agreeably, reaching out and taking a handful of the snack. She nibbled on one. "Although, it doesn't make any difference. Here I am, stuck in this place. No husband, no car, nothing to do."

"Really," I said, thankful she'd brought up the subject I was dying to bring up, myself. "Where's your husband?"

"Oh, he's off with the car visiting his mother. She's in jail. She killed somebody."

I nearly choked on my water. "Did she?"

"Hell, I don't know. I hope she did. Get her out of my hair." A look of regret passed over her face. "I shouldn't say that. Wally loves his mother. The witch," she added. "I shouldn't say that, either." She gave me a smile showing charm and innocence rolled into one.

"Don't pay any attention to me, Lee. I'm just bored. And drunk. Even if I had a car, I'm not supposed drive. Too many of these."

Jolene's phone rang. She reached out and picked up her cell sitting on the counter near her small purse. She looked at the number.

"Oh, Lord," she said, a worried frown coming to her face. "It's my sister." She pushed a button. "What's wrong, Rhonda? Why are you calling me so late? It must be past midnight at home."

Rhonda, Rhonda, where had I heard that name recently? It came to me. From Brit at the Institute. Rhonda's an unusual name, but someone else in the world had it, I was sure. Coincidence? Or was this the same Rhonda purported to be an assistant chef on the high seas?

I strained to hear Jolene's conversation with her Rhonda. The barkeep strode over, with a big, 'what's your next drink going to be?' smile on his face.

"Go away, go away," I said in barely more than a whisper. Startled, he backed off and began to clean glasses. Jolene saw nothing of this interaction. She was bending over the phone cuddled in her hands, her voice barely audible.

"Oh, Rhonda, honey. The doctor says sometimes you get morning sickness at all hours. You know that. Don't cry. It's all going to be all right."

Despite her words, tears came to Jolene's eyes.

"Now, you go back to bed, sister girl, and get some rest. I'm going to see you soon." She paused, listening. "We can't leave yet, but day after tomorrow. I promise."

Jolene disconnected. She wiped tears from her eyes.

"I just lied to my baby sister, but she's got a lot on her mind, you know? She doesn't know the real reason we're here. Well, at least why we *were* here, before that rapist got murdered."

Chapter Twenty-eight

Shroud For A Salad

Jolene made a wild gesture of anger and nearly fell off the stool. I reached out to steady her. Her hands flew to her head, grabbing at it, like it might fall off.

"I'm so dizzy. I wonder why?"

"How many of those did you have, Jolene?"

"I don't know. Five maybe." She looked at me. "I think I'm going to throw up."

I stood and wrapped my arm around her waist, just as she slid off the barstool. She was surprisingly light, but she grabbed onto my shoulders, anyway. The barkeep came over, concerned.

"I tried to cut her off, but Mrs. Durand doesn't take that well. Is she going to be all right?"

"I think so," I said. "Do I need to settle anything with you?"

"Nah," he said. "I'll just put it on the Durand tab like I always do. She's in room 1543. The keycard should be in her purse. Last night her husband wasn't around, so I helped her to their room. She's a sweet lady, but she can –"

He broke off speaking and brought his fisted hand to his mouth, thumb pointing to his lips, and tipped his head back. The universal sign for a drinker. He shook his head with sadness.

"But we try to look out for her," he continued. For one so young, he had a surprisingly paternal bend to his tone. "Like I say, Mrs. Durand's a sweet lady."

"What's your name?"

"Everett, miss," he said with a smile.

"Everett, when I get back, I'm going to give you a nice tip," I said over my shoulder, half carrying Jolene to the door.

"You already did. No worries."

He smiled. I smiled back.

"You're a good kid, Everett."

"Thank you, miss," he said.

After a brief elevator ride, I managed to get Jolene past the living room and bedroom of their suite and into the bathroom before she threw up in the john. Better out than in.

I was struggling to walk her towards the bed, when I heard the door to the suite burst open.

"Jolene? You in here? You all right, honey?" Wally came running through the suite into the bedroom, just as I sat Jolene on the side of the bed.

He didn't seem surprised to see me. In fact, he gave me a nod, before he sat next to his wife on the bed. I backed away and he put his arm around her. She leaned into him and began to sob.

"I'm sorry, I'm sorry, Wally. I don't know what gets into me." Her sobs became full-blown crying. Wally wrapped both arms around her.

"Hush now, honey. Don't you worry about it, Jolene. Tomorrow we'll find ourselves an AA meeting. We'll both go. I've been knocking back a few too many, myself. We'll get right as rain soon enough. I love you, Jolene, I surely do."

He kissed her tenderly on the forehead. She looked up into his face.

"We got to do something about Rhonda, Wally. We got to go home."

"I know, I know. We will. But the police won't let us leave right now. You know that."

She didn't say anything, but nodded and hugged him. Holding on to her, Wally rocked her back and forth like a small child. He looked up at me and gave me a sad smile.

Up until that point, both acted as if I wasn't in the room. And under ordinary circumstances, I would have been long gone. But I stayed in the doorway of the bedroom. I needed a few answers, and I wasn't going anywhere until I got them.

"You lay down now, honey. Get some sleep," Wally said, standing up.

He bent down, removed her shoes, and lifted her legs onto the bed. After covering her with a throw, he came to my side. We both stepped into the living room of the suite, Wally closing the bedroom door behind us.

"I ran into Everett."

"The bartender?"

"Yes, ma'am. He described you to me, told me how you was taking care of Jolene. I'm sorry about this, truly. Jolene's a good woman, a fine woman, but we got to get this drinking under control. It don't help her daddy owns a chain of liquor stores. And other things that cropped up aren't helping, either. It isn't her fault. Not all of it, leastways."

Everything about Wally was different. Gone was the cocky womanizer, the shallow, in-for-himself man. He sounded like he cared about his wife.

"When you say 'other things', Wally, are you talking about Rhonda?"

A shocked look crossed his face. He stared at me for a split second.

"You know about Rhonda?"

"Yes, but you need to tell me more."

He hesitated. I glared at him.

"And I'm not leaving until you do."

"Then we'd better sit down. It's a long story."

He crossed to a silvery, grey leather sofa. I sat across from him in the matching chair. Wally looked down, obviously thinking about what words to choose.

"Look, Jolene and Rhonda, they didn't have the best start to their lives. Oh, their daddy does all right in his business, but their mama ran off when Jolene was six and Rhonda was one. They were more or less on their own, except for a nanny when they was still young. They were both pretty girls and made bad choices in men. You might even say I was one of them."

He gave a self-deprecating chortle then cleared his throat.

"Anyways, when Jolene and I started seeing each other, Rhonda took it into her head she wanted to be a chef. Try to be another Patsy. It was the first time she ever wanted to do something other than run around wild. So I called my daddy, enrolled her in his school. I was only trying to help."

He looked up at me with a pained expression, shook his head, and looked down again. I picked up the conversation.

"So you arranged for Rhonda to come to the Institute, where she met Chef Jacques."

Wally jumped in, his voice filled with contempt.

"He seduced her. And he scared her. Here was her one chance to make something of her life and he said if she didn't sleep with him, he'd flunk her out. That dirty old man was old enough to be her father. Hell, her grandfather." He paused. "Anyways, she got pregnant. We haven't told Rhonda yet that vermin is dead. We thought we'd wait 'til we got home."

"So the story about her getting a job as an assistant chef on a cruise ship was just that, a story."

He nodded. "She didn't want the other students to know. She has some pride. She came home. But Jolene and me couldn't let this go. He destroyed her life."

"Did your father know any of this?"

"No. Rhonda didn't want anyone to know. But we decided to come here and tell him, anyways. Face-to-face. Daddy needed to know. I mean, what was a man like Jacques Chalifour doing working there? Pete felt the same way."

"How did your mother feel about all of this?"

"Well, she always thought both girls were too wild for their own good. She never liked me marrying into that family. But she still was shocked at how Daddy could hire a man like that. That's one of the reasons she agreed to teach at the Institute. She wanted to be here seeing for herself what was going on."

"Where were you Saturday night when the chef was killed?"

"Right here at the hotel. Jolene and me were together in the bar most of the night. Then we came upstairs and went to bed. I swear."

"What time did you leave the bar?"

"I don't know. Ten-ish, I think."

"Was that the reason for the Big Lie?"

His eyebrows rose. "Ma'am?"

"Come on, Wally. You were in the Bay Area before Chef Jacques was killed. Not after. It was a foolish lie, easily checked out. Were you, Pete, and your mother going to have a showdown with the man who made your wife's sister pregnant?"

He hesitated then leaned back against the cushions in almost a relaxed surrender. "Yes. But we never got to do it. I swear. "

"You never got a chance to tell him?"

He shook his head slowly. "No. Next thing we knew the blaggard was dead. Just like that," Wally snapped his fingers, "He's dead."

"And problem solved."

"Yes ma'am."

"You realize you are all probably suspects in the chef's murder?"

He looked to the bedroom door. "That's why Chief Thompson said we all had to stay put. Even though Mama's locked up, once the chief found out Jolene, me, and Pete lied about being here, he said we had to stay until it all got ironed out. But I have to get my wife home. She's all Rhonda's got. And it's making Jolene nuts not be able to be with her."

"You sound like you love your wife."

He gave me a shy smile. "Yes, ma'am. Three times the charm. As long as Jolene will have me, I'm hers."

"So why the bad-boy act in my office the other day?"

"Look, I have a reputation with the ladies or had one. I thought if I acted randy enough, you'd tell me to go away. Maybe I could take Jolene home, away from all this. He was dead. Like you said, our problem was solved."

"Wally, your problems might just be beginning."

Chapter Twenty-nine

The Picture Of Dorian Gravy

The next morning came early to this twenty-first century scullery maid. I worked my duff off for the first half of my split shift. Close to one I staggered past the loading dock and into the backyard. Armed with a bottle of cold water, and a soggy, leftover ham and cheese sandwich from dinner two nights before, I collapsed under a tree.

According to Hayes, it was mandatory that teachers and students share the meals prepared in the classes, not just for the taste, but for the camaraderie. All the afternoon teaching chefs had arrived and both they and the morning chefs were enjoying the fruits of their students' labors for one hour before the second lot trooped in. That's what crepes stuffed with sweetened ricotta cheese and covered with a cherry sauce will get you. Full attendance.

Ordinarily, I would be the first in line. But it was a good time to explore the rest of the building during the one-hour everyone was sharing lunch.

While munching on my sandwich, my eye caught a half window at the base of the building, usually the type found in basements. I checked my watch. Time to get moving. But before I got the energy to stand, I studied the second story, Hayes and Connie's apartment.

As well as the inside staircase I'd watched Connie Durand climb the other day, the apartment also had a back, outside concrete stairway. It ended at a small landing and a sturdy looking door. To the side of the landing, a large, six-paned window, framed by tieback white sheers looked down on me. Probably the apartment's kitchen, I thought.

At that moment, Connie Durand, dressed again in her blue chenille robe, stepped into the sightline. She seemed to be talking to someone I couldn't see. I got to my feet, and backed up near the trunk of the tree. I was shielded in the shadows of limbs and leaves, in case she glanced down.

But she didn't. She was in what appeared to be a heart-rending conversation with someone out of my line of vision. Just as I pondered if it was Hayes, a tall, lanky man came within view, closing in on her. Both profiled in the window, he proceeded to talk to Hayes' wife in an animated but angry way.

What the...? Henry Encino! What was Ms. Packersmythe's true love, the father of her unborn child, someone I was planning on investigating when I came up for air, doing here?

I strained my ears, but couldn't hear their conversation. No doubt, double-paned windows. I hate double-paned windows. A working sleuth's enemy. Only the loudest of sounds can be heard through them.

Fortunately, the windows had been recently cleaned. Even though I couldn't hear the words, I could see the two players as clearly as if they were on television.

By the looks on their faces, whatever they were discussing was serious, very serious. In fact, at one juncture Henry Encino took Connie by the shoulders and shook her. Then he embraced her hard. She hugged him back for all she was worth and began to cry into his chest. It was like watching a soap opera with the sound turned down.

Just then the back door of the Institute flew open. Nancy stepped out and slammed the door closed as hard as she could. Not only could I hear it, I could feel the vibrations from where I stood.

She took a stance on the small landing. Legs spread apart, hands on hips, glaring at me, she looked ready for a shootout. Gunfight at the OK Corral.

"Einstein, what are you doing out here? It's not time for your lunch hour, and when it is, you should have lunch with the others."

I was ready for her. "I have an appointment at the DMV in half an hour. Chef Hayes said it was all right."

"Oh, he did, did he? Well, I'll talk to him about that. The morning classes are done and they'll need clean utensils for the afternoon sessions, which start at two."

I capped my bottle of water, put the remnants of the sandwich back in the bag, and glanced up at the window on the second floor. Connie and Henry disappeared, probably at the sound of the slamming door. They could've heard it in China, double-panes notwithstanding. I turned back to Nancy.

"They're done. The clean dishes are on the white carts ready for the afternoon classes, madam," I said, crossing the narrow lawn toward the building. "I finished them earlier. I didn't want to roll them out during the morning classes, so I left them covered and in the hallway. With a large sign that said 'clean tableware'. I left a note on your desk to that effect." I paused. "Madam."

I hadn't actually talked to Hayes about anything. And I certainly hadn't left a note on Nancy's desk. But I can lie with the best of them. My purpose was accomplished. Nancy was thrown.

"I haven't been in my office. You know we're all expected to stay upstairs with the students for lunch. Chef Hayes is adamant about that. As for me, I never miss the opportunity to break bread with the students."

And that's enough to put you off your feed, I thought.

She went on. "Well....so...well...you've done them."

"Yes, madam."

"That's good." She stuttered. "But in the future should you decide to deviate from the normal schedule, you need to run it by me first. Not just a note downstairs. Is that clear?"

"Yes, madam."

We glared at one another, me thinking she had a mad on and I having no idea why. Thoughts whirled through my brain.

If Chef Jacques had been skimming profits off the Institute, was Nancy Littlejohn in on it? Had she been romantically involved with the man? She was in her early forties and beneath that bitchy exterior – which some men might call feisty – she was an attractive woman. Besides, like I told Brit, with some men as long as she's female he's going to want to jump her bones.

But another theory was she'd been pilfering money on her own, if Hayes' signatures on that scrap of paper meant anything. Maybe Chef Jacques caught her at it, wanted in, and she killed him. I liked that one. I gave her a bucktooth smile.

I couldn't tell what she was thinking about me, but I'm sure it was something involving extra work under near inhumane conditions. I was already getting a crackerjack experience at being Cinderella before she went to the ball.

"Very well," said the wicked stepmother. "I'll check what you've done. If it's acceptable, we'll see you at five."

She turned to leave, then spun back on me. "And if they're not satisfactory, I will be back for you."

Without waiting for a response, she marched inside, slamming the door again behind her. After only a split second, I chucked my lunch in a nearby trashcan, and looked around to see if anyone else was in the vicinity including the soap opera couple from above. Had they returned into view? *Nada.*

Hotfooting it to the half window I'd spied minutes before, I bent down. Sure enough, it was the basement, a window near the ceiling of a long hallway. After another look around, I gave the window a yank upwards. Unlocked. Just how I like them.

Chapter Thirty

The Haunting Of Porterhouse

I held my breath, slid inside the window, and dropped to the floor. I had an hour, and hopefully, I wouldn't get caught, at least if everyone stayed upstairs at lunch. Let the sleuthing begin.

Even though the only light in the hallway was from the half window, it was sufficient. The day was bright and sunny and the basement had been painted off-white. The floor was also white, done in large, blocky ceramic tiles. Boring, but it was, after all, the basement of a cooking school.

Off the hallway were six rooms, five unmarked, and one labeled Personnel, Nancy Littlefield's office. I gave the knob a quick turn. Locked. Using my picklock tools, I was in her office faster than you can say Jack Robinson, although why you would want to say that eludes me. I dashed off a quick note with what I'd told her outside, left it on her desk, and looked around. Other than the filing cabinets, which I might have to peruse at a later date, it held little interest for me.

I closed and relocked her door and looked down the hall. Without a lot of time to think about where to begin, a larger, arched door looking important and regal beckoned to me. It had one of those silly locks set in the doorknob, which can be opened more or less with a nail file in not more than ten seconds. I opened it in less than five.

Similar to a ballroom, it was decorated in oak paneling. Large oak wine barrels, and a swath of enlarged photos of past students and teachers dressed in whites and smiling happily completed the decor. This had to be the Events Room. Orientation, graduation, and parties were held here, but it was now empty and unused. No doors leading to closets or storage room. I closed and relocked the door.

The lab held nothing other than a modern kitchen workspace, with three monitors facing semicircular, tiered desks and chairs, sixty in all. Even with its overhead camera, it had a Romanesque feel to it, like a small amphitheater. What cabinets there were, were empty. Lone salt and pepper shakers decorated a butcher block counter.

I made quick work of a shared office by the five in-residence chefs. Name plaques identified each desk. There was no sign of a Chef Bob, the desk now being used by Patsy. I chose to search that desk first, her being my client.

If you can tell anything about a person by the contents of their desk drawers, a plethora of info was being given out on Patsy Durand. The top drawer held dozens of newspaper clippings on the stats of *Sooie Cuchon's* competitors. They were stapled together by restaurant, some info highlighted. One drawer was filled completely with pricy make-up, a few as yet unused. A bottom drawer contained books on how to manipulate the stock market – as if – and a Danielle Steel novel, obviously read many times. The last drawer contained handwritten recipes with one, thick notepad completely filled with wild squirrel recipes. Apparently, the right amount of vinegar used at the beginning of cooking makes all the difference.

I checked out the other chefs, choosing the afternoon's first. No reason; desks closer to the door. Strongwoman Chef Barbara liked to knit. Skeins of yarn in soft colors filled drawers along with snapshots of her half-grown children and husband. I didn't know his name, but judging by the looks of him, Bruiser would have fit.

Chef Aurélien was neat, neat, neat, with copious notes in French on each of his students' strengths and weaknesses. One drawer contained a stash of high-quality chocolate candy. I snatched a couple of pieces, not having finished my sandwich. When needs must.

Moving on to the morning's culinary experts, Chef Oliver was a slob, but I made quick work of going through his stuff. The only thing of interest was a receipt for a new butcher knife to the tune of six hundred dollars. I took a picture of the receipt with my camera and went to the fifth and last desk.

I took more time with Chef Dexter's desk. He was a serious fellow jotting down notes on his finances. He recently put in a bid on a two-bedroom, one-bath bungalow in a nearby neighborhood. A scandalous amount of money, but that's the Bay Area for you.

The blue book seen by me and mentioned by Brit was nowhere to be found. Maybe Chef Dexter had a hiding place for it or kept it on him at all times. It wasn't that large. But I did unearth another half-pencil, like the one I'd found in the pantry and saw the chef use the previous day.

The smaller office next door was Hayes'. The owner of the Institute collected droopy plants. About six fought for space on his one and only high, narrow windowsill. The walls were covered with framed pictures of him posing with the famous and not so famous of the culinary world. On the desk were more personal-type photos, him with his boys, Connie or Patsy, with Patsy winning the women-folk subject three to one.

I reflected for a moment. It must be hard for a second wife to live in the shadow of the glorious and famous first wife, divorce notwithstanding. I wouldn't be happy if Gurn kept photos of ex-girlfriends on his desk, let alone had there been a former wife. But Gurn is a smart man, who doesn't live in his past. Not sure I could say the same for Chef Hayes Durand.

A small glass cabinet contained three shelves of identical, thick black journals. Nine by twelve inches, sixty were stacked within, side-by-side. I remember Hayes mentioning he kept a journal, but I hadn't realized it was his *raison d'être*.

I crossed the small room and pulled on the flimsy door of the cabinet. Locked. A good yank would have opened it, but I used my pick and was in in less time than it takes to mention.

Each journal had a handprinted white label on it, with the date and year. Running January to December of each year, they stood side by side in their binders. However, the current year and the year before were missing. I mused on this. His hands were burned the past November, stopping the journal in its tracks. And this year there probably wasn't one, as he couldn't write. I felt sorry for the guy. To some people writing down their thoughts and feelings is a critical part of life.

One of my pals at college kept a journal. Only being female, she called it a diary. She wrote in her diary religiously, carried it everywhere with her, jotting things down as the urge overtook her. I never had that urge. I'm from the school of thought that doesn't believe in putting anything down in writing that can't be read aloud to the Supreme Court.

Hayes' journals started in chronological order, covering forty-five years, long before he knew Patsy. I pulled one out at random, labeled 1988, and flipped to a page.

Fluid, legible writing revealed the author's innermost feelings, fears and hopes. That year his marriage to Patsy was thriving, as was their new restaurant in Arkansas. He worshipped the ground she cooked on. But he was a man filled with angst on nearly every page, almost like he knew it wouldn't last.

I'm going to say it's unusual for men to keep a diary, but not unheard of. However, I was surprised Hayes stored them in his office. One possibility was he didn't want his second wife to get hold of them, given what I'd just read of his goddess-like adoration of Patsy.

I replaced the 1988 journal and relocked the cabinet, checking my watch. Ten minutes left until lunch was over and people came trickling down. I wiped the sweat from my brow and sniffed my underarms to make sure my Degree antiperspirant was still working. This rushing through people's lives had a franticness about it that was challenging, especially when wearing a hot wig.

The remaining locked office was Chef Jacques'. In I went. The room hadn't been cleaned yet, but was scheduled for the following day. The desk and shelves were covered with dirty black smudges from our boys in blue checking for fingerprints. Even the desk drawers were left open, which made my job a little easier.

I pushed items around with the half-pencil, but didn't find much. Other than a bottle of vodka, half full, and two girly magazines, both in a lower drawer, there wasn't much to tell of the man's life. Probably anything really telltale about him had been taken by the police. I'd have to grill Frank about it later.

Ever listening for any sounds of someone descending the stairs from above, I stuck my head inside another room and switched on the overhead light. The room held masses of dishware, flatware, and pots and pans stacked in neat rows on steel mesh shelving. I hurried along the makeshift aisles, giving everything a cursory look.

Time was running out. I zipped to the next room. It held furniture and linen, probably brought into the Events Room as needed. Round and square tables, counters, and dozens of stacked chairs stood at the ready. Three huge laundry hampers on wheels held folded tablecloths and napkins, all of a high quality, and sorted by their colors of white, blue and green. I crossed to the hampers and rooted through; just to make sure they held linens from bottom to top. They did.

What struck me first was the overall cleanliness of the rooms. No dust, no cobwebs, nothing. A cleaning service was used frequently, and so far, every corner of the Institute looked like you could eat off the floor. I prefer a table, but it's nice to have the option.

The other thing was the initial outlay of money to run such an enterprise. There had to be tens of thousands of dollars' worth of stuff needed to maintain a cooking school. I had no idea.

My watch told me I had two or three more minutes before the lunch ritual was over. Even at my breakneck speed, there was still one more room, the equipment storage room, to go through. It would have to wait. I exited, relocked the room, and went up the inside stairs that led to the ground floor hallway.

I slowly opened the door and peeked out. Nobody. Luck was with me, so I stepped out and closed the door. I hadn't taken two steps when Nancy rounded the corner, saw me, and stopped short.

"There you are. I've been hoping to find you, Einstein. Did you finish early at the DMV?" I opened my mouth to answer. "Never mind, come with me."

And danged if she didn't open the door to the basement and descend the stairs. I was hot on her trail.

Nancy pulled out a set of keys, went to the one room I hadn't gotten to yet, and inserted a key in the door. For whatever reason, the lock wouldn't turn. She shook the doorknob several times in frustration.

I fought the urge to take over and get the job done with one of my picks in my normal five-second interval. Instead, I placed my subservient self behind her.

"What the…" she muttered. "I've never had problems with this door before." She jiggled the knob a few more times and banged at the door. It finally gave. "There!"

Pushing the door open, Nancy hit the wall switch, and the room was flooded with light. She stepped inside. I followed.

This room was the biggest, save the Events Room. Used to store stacks of trays, multi-tiered baking racks, portable ovens, refrigerators, and freezers, it was filled to capacity.

Even two six-burner stoves with two ovens apiece, one below and one above, dawdled here.

Each appliance was accessible but clearly unused, either shrink-wrapped or with their heavy-duty electrical cords bound up and taped to their sides.

Nancy was nattering on about something, but I wasn't paying any attention. Something caught my eye, a large freezer chest in a corner, its cord plugged into a wall outlet.

"Nancy, do you store any food down here?"

"What do you mean? Of course, not. We have two walk-ins on the main floor, one's a refrigerator and the other's the freezer."

Her eyes followed my gaze.

"Who plugged that thing in? I'll have to speak to Chef Hayes about this. Do you know what it costs to run these appliances?"

I ignored her and made my way to the back of the room and toward the freezer. Nancy followed me, talking all the while.

"Where are you going? Come back here. I want you to help me carry up these trays. We'll have to use the service elevator, and I need your help. Einstein, pay attention to me."

"Oh, shut up."

I pulled the freezer lid up. Nancy, shocked by my reply, stared at me.

"What? What did you say?"

I turned to her, put my forefinger in her face while making a shushing command, pulled out my phone, and hit my speed dial.

"Frank, it's me. I've found your missing dishwasher, Manuel Sanchez. You'd better get back to the Institute. The freezer chest is in the first storage room on the left side, down in the basement. I'll be waiting for you."

Nancy Littlejohn turned away from me. She looked inside the freezer, screamed, and fainted dead away. I caught her before she hit the floor. I knew underneath that tyrannical exterior was a total wuss.

Chapter Thirty-one

To Have And To Haddock

"Manuel Sanchez is dead?" Mom looked at me.

"Frozen like a popsicle. Well, not completely," I amended. "It takes more than forty-eight hours to freeze a human body, especially if the freezer hasn't been on beforehand."

I blurted this out, turned, and looked at my family sitting around the dinner table, which included Vicki, Richard, little Steffi, Tío, Mom, Gurn, and me. The Institute was closed for the remainder of the day. I had no idea what the next day would bring. But I hoped not another dead body.

Tío had taken pity on this poor working girl and her husband with plans of a take-out pepperoni pizza for dinner. Inviting us to a feast, we were devouring crown roast of pork with apple and sausage stuffing.

Yum yum yummy, but not really the time nor place to go into details about a dead body. Consequently, the family sat staring at me, forks in hand. All except Steffi, who slept in her carrier on a chair beside her mother.

The popsicle line had overstepped the boundaries of the family's dining etiquette. I know my face showed my chagrin. My eyes brushed over each member of my family.

"Sorry."

"It's my fault, Liana," Mom said, taking the blame. "We know the rules. I shouldn't have asked the question. No discussion of the agency or other inclusive business at the dinner table. It doesn't do Mateo's food justice."

Indeed, it didn't. The first course had been crab cakes, followed by a knife-and-fork grilled Caesar salad, served with glasses of sparkling *Cavas Freixenet de México*. I got Vicki's share of the sparkling wine. Nursing mom and all that.

The entrée was roast pork and stuffing, served with baby carrots with a touch of cinnamon and brown sugar. A gorgeous Pinot Noir from the Northern Baja region of Mexico accompanied the meal.

While we drink wines from other parts of the world, only Mexican wine is served at the table on special occasions, a tradition started by my father.

What was the occasion? None. Other than Tío trying to stay occupied while the love of his life languished in jail on a murder charge. Maybe multiple charges. So breakfast, lunch, and dinner at the Big House was a gourmet extravaganza, for sure.

I shoveled another helping in my mouth. The real killer of the two men was going to have to be found before I could no longer fit into my clothes. I took another piece of Tío's homemade rosemary and olive bread and slathered it with sweet butter.

My reasoning for that particular evening's indulgence was because I'd been sweating all morning confined to that horrible pearl diver room. Naturally, when I mentioned that to Mom, she replied, 'Liana, horses sweat, men perspire, and women glow'. Well, if that's the case, you could have seen me glowing from outer space.

But I was looking forward to Tío's *Flan de Naranja y Leche Condensada*, a new take on his traditional *Flan de Naranja*. Both desserts used candied orange peel made from fruit picked from our own tree mid-January.

After dinner, we made our way to the family room. Bellies full, there was just enough room to slurp down decaf coffee and Tío's homemade *bizcocho*. And we could now deal with business matters.

Once seated, Richard said, "That was good work, finding out about Jolene's sister, Rhonda. That's why the boys arrived a day earlier than they said they did?"

"That's their story," I said. "Consequently, not one of them has a decent alibi for the time of the chef's death. And they all had reason to off him."

"Liana." Mom's voice rang out in chastisement. "That's crudely phrased, I must say." She took a sip of her coffee.

"Crude but true," I retorted, shoving a *bizcocho* in my mouth.

The Mexican *bizcocho* is a cookie very similar to the Italian biscotti, but lighter in texture. They're made with lard, and there is no substitute for the lard, according to Tío. He uses a sweet Madeira wine in the mix, and often serves the cookies after dinner with coffee.

Richard shook his head in disgust. "The more I look into Chef Jacques' background, the more of a lowlife he seemed to be."

"But that doesn't excuse what happened to him," said Mom, still in her chastising mode. "He was a living, breathing human being."

"Same with Manuel Sanchez when it comes to it," Gurn said.

"Of course. That goes without saying," I declared. "But we can say it, if it makes everyone feel better."

Gurn threw back his head with laughter. He really does get me.

"Without going into any of the gory details," said Vicki, sitting in a corner of the room and discreetly nursing Stephanie under a baby blanket, "How did Sanchez meet his end? I sure hope he wasn't trying to get out of that freezer while he froze to death." She shivered at the thought.

"I saw the prelim medical report," said Richard. "He was already dead when he went into the freezer."

I picked it up. "He had his head bashed in and there were cuts and bruises on his wrists and hands, as if he'd tried to defend himself. His blood type matches the traces they found in the freezer from where the lobster tails were stolen."

"Maybe he was trying to get away from his assailant," said Vicki. "This is all so sad."

"According to the ME," I said, "he was killed with a mallet around six-thirty Monday morning soon after he'd made the phone call to the police. They found the mallet a block away in some brush. Fingerprints wiped clean."

"Does this not clear Patsy?" Tío entered the conversation and turned to me, with hope ringing in his voice. "She was at the police department in the morning."

I could tell what was going through his mind. For as awful as it was to have another person murdered, if it tagged someone else for the crimes and freed Patsy, it was all to the good.

"Probably not, Tío," said Richard, reaching for another bizcocho. "The crime could have been done within the time frame she claims to have been sleeping in her car."

"No, no, no," Tío protested. "You grasp at the straw."

"I'm with Tío. That doesn't make sense," said Vicki. "I've never met Patsy," Vicki went on, "but I understand she's barely five feet tall. How could she swing a mallet that hard then lift a man by herself and put him in a freezer?"

"That's exactly the argument Mr. Talbot is going to the judge with," I said.

"Playing devil's advocate," said Richard. "She could have had an accomplice."

"An accomplice?" Tío scoffed. "Do not make the absurd statement, Ricardo. Who would help her do such a thing?"

"Somebody who loved her?" Richard kept going, formulating the idea as he went along. "Someone like maybe one or both of her sons or her ex-husband or –" He gulped and stopped talking, staring at our uncle.

We all turned and looked at Richard then Tío, not saying a word. But I knew what my brother was thinking. Someone like Tío.

Chapter Thirty-two

Rosemary's Bagel

"Lee, be reasonable." Gurn punched his pillow in frustration and settled down in bed.

"I won't be reasonable. The idea that Tío could hurt anyone is ridiculous. I'm surprised you and my brother even went there."

This was the first major fight of our marriage. I was so angry I was sputtering.

"To accuse the sweetest, most gentle man on the face of the earth –"

"Nobody's accusing Tío. I only agree with Rich's premise. The way Patsy doesn't have an alibi for where she was Tío doesn't have one, either. There's only his word he spent the night at her apartment alone. He could have been with her at the Institute."

I turned on Gurn. "Helping her kill two men? I mean, really?"

"Sweetheart, darling mine, I don't think that." Gurn looked at me with simple sincerity. "I'm only telling you what others who don't know the man might think. What the law might be pressured into thinking. He has no one to corroborate where he was, if it comes to it."

"He shouldn't need to, Gurn."

"No, he shouldn't," Gurn agreed then added again, "But if it comes to it, he doesn't."

There is a problem in being married to a rational man and leaning that way yourself, upon occasion. When the truth hits you in the face like a wet mackerel, you tend to know it, even if you can't smell it. I threw myself down on the bed.

"You're right. Patsy Durand is heading into the home stretch as the number one suspect and Tío is pulling up the rear. A trifecta."

"A trifecta is three horses, not two. It's a pari-mutuel bet in which the bettor must predict which horses will finish first, second, and third in exact order."

"What are two horses winning? A twofecta?"

"A perfecta. Both horses finishing in the exact order. It's also called an exacta. Then, there's win, place and show."

"How come you know this? Were you a jockey at some point?"

"No, they have to be a bit smaller than me. Usually around one hundred and fifteen pounds."

"That's a lot smaller."

"They're small but mighty."

"What makes you say that?"

"I once had a friend who was a jockey. Rode the Kentucky Derby a few years back and won. And for the record, I'd hate to have taken him on in a dark alley."

I settled under the bed covers. "There's so much about you I still don't know."

"You'll have a lifetime to learn," he said, leaning over and giving me a kiss on the nose. Then he pulled back and looked at me, puzzled. "How did we get to talking about horse racing?"

"I'm not sure. Oh, yes. Our geriatric Romeo and Juliet potentially sharing a cell together. I have to make sure that doesn't happen."

"And I'm sure you will." He chuckled and shook his head. "Life with you is never dull."

"Keep thinking that, darling. When are you heading back to D. C.?"

"Next week, but I'm only gone for one day. I have to show up at the Pentagon when they say." He shrugged. "It could be worse."

"It has been worse, at least from my point of view. Knowing you were off in Afghanistan or Syria, gone for days or weeks. It sure works for me, just having you sit at a round table with a bunch of generals in Washington. I'm sure the Pentagon knows they benefit from you having been on the ground risking life and limb. You're in the know. I am consumed with pride."

"Thank you, sweetheart. I guess you could say I've had hands-on experience."

"Do you miss it? The excitement? The danger?"

"Not really. Besides, now I have you for excitement and danger."

"Keep thinking that, darling. But if you can help keep the men in uniform safer, we both want you to do that."

"You bet. That's my job. Help find ways to keep the casualties to a minimum. But enough of that." He sat up and studied me. "What's that silky thing you're wearing? A peignoir?"

"No, it's just a nightgown. A peignoir is a set. It means both a nightgown and a matching robe." I leaned into him and looked up at his handsome face, now sporting a bit of a blondish stubble. "You might say a peignoir is a perfecta, but the right lacy, silk nightgown can be a winner."

We both laughed. I love a man who appreciates my sense of humor. Smiling at one another, Gurn reached out and ran a hand through my hair, brushing it away from my face. Then he stroked the fabric covering my shoulder.

"Well, I love it. Beautiful. Just like you."

"Did I tell you Patsy said I reminded her of Elizabeth Taylor?"

"Several times. I think you look like you. Beautiful you."

He leaned in and kissed me then pulled away.

"Hey, you have to get up by five-thirty. Maybe we should just go to sleep."

I leaned in. "With you going away on a mission?"

He laughed. "That's not until next week."

"I still want to do my patriotic duty."

"In that case, the United States of America salutes you."

Chapter Thirty-three

For Whom The Bell Pepper Tolls

I hadn't heard from Hayes about the Institute being open and when I called, no one answered. Curiosity getting the better of me, I decided to go whether I heard from anyone or not.

Not sure if I'd been outed, I put on my disguise and arrived at the Institute shortly after eight. The door was unlocked and the lights were on. I stepped into the foyer and crossed into the main room of the Institute. Standing near a workstation, Hayes Durand and Nancy Littlejohn were deep in conversation. Both stopped talking and looked my way.

I thought I looked bad but Hayes looked like he'd been embalmed by a fly-by-night funeral service. Pale, waxen skin drained of color made his reddish hair and eyebrows stand out like a neon sign.

Nancy Littlejohn, however, positively glowed in her Gothiness. It's always surprising to me how some people thrive on turmoil, tragedy, and chaos. Sauntering in my direction, she folded her arms across her chest. She raised one eyebrow and stopped in front of me.

"Well, good morning, Lee Alvarez, private investigator," she said pointedly. She turned and looked at Hayes, who wore a sheepish grin on his face.

"Sorry, Lee," he said. "She suspected you weren't who you claimed to be when you found Manuel's body in the freezer. I had to tell her."

I glared at her then shrugged. "Okay, so you know." I looked across the room to Hayes. "Does anyone else know?"

"No, not yet. Only Nancy," said Hayes.

I turned back to his assistant whose dark hair was now edged with hot pink.

"Can you keep your mouth shut about it? Or what?"

She lost some of her bravado. "Of course, I can keep my mouth shut. You don't even have to ask such a thing. After all –"

"Greatly appreciated." I brushed past her and went to Hayes. "How did the rest of your staff and your students take yet another death within these walls?"

He sagged into a nearby chair at one of the eating tables.

"I should have called you, Lee. I'm sorry. We're closed for the foreseeable future. I've stopped answering the phones. They're ringing off the hook with parents saying they're pulling their kids out of school. Five students have already quit, demanding their money back. Thank God I have insurance for this type of thing."

"I told you paying premiums for catastrophic insurance was a good thing," said Nancy.

She went around me and stood near Hayes. He glanced up at her then turned away before he spoke.

"I thought it meant earthquakes, not...not murder."

A low volume wail escaped his lips before he burst into sobs. Hayes reached for his face with trembling hands and continued to wail.

Nancy knelt down beside him. Reaching up, she stroked his hair in a loving, familiar way. He reached out and took her free hand with one of his wounded ones, coaxing it onto his lap. Also, in a loving, familiar way. All-rightie. Love in bloom.

I heard a noise and turned toward the sound. Connie Durand stood in the doorway, staring at the scene. She wore the same blue chenille bathrobe, the front now stained with what looked like mustard or egg yolks. Wordless, Hayes' wife pivoted and walked away. I followed.

"Mrs. Durand." My voice echoed in the empty foyer.

She paused at the bottom of the stairway, with one hand on the bannister and the other holding up her long robe. I noticed she wore a different pair of slippers, bright green.

"You should leave," she said. Her voice had none of the quaver it held before. "Nothing can be done here."

I didn't like the sound of that. The finality of her tone took my speech away, not an occurrence that happens often. I watched her climb the stairs wondering if she thought she was talking to the pearl diver or knew she was talking to me.

"She's right. You should leave. Nothing can be done here."

I turned around at the sound of Nancy's voice, snarky and contemptuous.

"Is that your opinion or a directive from your boss?"

She hesitated, her face softening a bit. "The Institute is closed, Ms. Alvarez. Classes may resume tomorrow. That is, if every student doesn't quit and we have any students left to teach." Nancy's lower lip quivered, but she forced a smile.

"I'm sorry. I know you're only trying to help. But we may be beyond helping." And with those words, she spun around. She headed to the kitchen area and probably back to Hayes, who sat staring into space.

I didn't stick around to find out. I crossed the room to the door of the basement, flung it open, and took the stairs down two at a time.

The equipment storage room was unlocked and much of it looked the same, save for the empty space where the freezer had been. This time the police scene tapes dominated the corner, ordering people not to step into the scene of the crime. So I didn't.

But I sat on the tile floor just outside the cordoned-off area and studied it. Sometimes being on the scene triggers thoughts of a new scenario. This time it didn't.

Frustrated, I tried to distract myself, and took out my phone to do research on a new subject. Why had Henry Encino been here the day before and what connection did he have to Connie Durand?

I plugged his name and age into D. I.'s search engine, but nothing came up on him in the Rochester, New York area. Then I tried New York State. Nothing. I spelled Encino with an 's' instead of a 'c'. I tried Harry instead of Henry. Then I tried just the last name of Encino. Twenty-two people registered, but not one was a man in his thirties.

Okay, time to call Richard. He answered his phone on the first ring.

"What's up, Lee?" He sounded hurried and impatient.

"Where are you?"

"I'm at the office. Been here since four. I've been piecing together information the team collected. All the keys to the building have been accounted for and the fourteen students who live onsite are in the clear. Where are you?"

"I'm at the Institute, still wearing my disguise. But I don't need it anymore. The Institute is closed until further notice."

"I thought that might happen. Fallout from discovering the body of Manuel Sanchez. You have to find out who did it, Lee."

"Thanks. No pressure there."

"Sorry. Do you want to know what else I've got?"

"Yes, but first, I have one more thing for you to do."

"Of course you do."

I gave him the highlights of Ms. Packersmythe and her intended, Henry Encino. I left out the part about her being pregnant. Whoa! It just struck me. Two women pregnant, Rhonda and Ms. Packersmythe. One young and fragile, one not so young but in her own way, maybe just as fragile. With this kind of stuff, you have to tread lightly.

In any event, Packersmythe's condition wasn't relevant at this point and might lead to unnecessary conversation. We had a lot of ground to cover. Richard, too, seemed to want to stay on the salient points.

"You've used the D. I. search engine for Henry Encino in Rochester, New York, and got nothing?"

"Right."

"So he's not who he says he is?"

"Right."

"Yesterday you saw this man in a heated and seemingly intimate discussion with Connie Durand in the Durand apartment?"

"Right."

"And he is also involved with Evangeline Packersmythe?"

"Right."

He let out a sigh. "Okay, I'll put someone on it."

"Thank you, Richard. Keep me posted. If you can't find him in the New York area, let me know. I've got a few other ideas, but I don't want to sway your thinking. What do you have on Connie Durand, by the way?"

"Let's see." There was a pause, his breath becoming rapid. He was probably searching for files on his computer.

"Ah, here we are. Constance 'Connie' Durand, age forty-five. Born in Baton Rouge, Louisiana. Maiden name Enright. Both parents are dead, and left a considerable fortune. Three brothers and two sisters inherited. Mrs. Durand is not only rich, but smart. She went to Princeton, and then MIT for her doctorate in microbiology. Her research into algae as a food source for third world countries led Stanford University to offer her an assistant professorship. For the past few years her career has stalled out, due mainly to her being in and out of hospitals for treatment for depression. I haven't been able to get all the medical records so it's not crosschecked yet. She married Hayes Durand eight years ago. No children, but I'm still checking."

"Richard, did you verify the boys were where they said they were the night of the murder?"

"We're still on it."

"Is Frank forthcoming on anything the police found out about their alibis?"

"He can't be, Lee. He's already closer to the situation than his superiors are comfortable with. He's told me that much."

"I was afraid of that. Send someone to talk to the staff at the Park Stanford. Is Conrad back?"

"Yes, he is but, boy, did Mom hit the roof with what this is costing us. I know, I know," he jumped in, "It's for Tío." He paused. "I'll send Conrad to the hotel this afternoon, ascot and all."

"Have him get some sort of statement from Everett, the barkeep. What did you find out about Hayes Durand?"

"Hayes and Quinn Durand born in Vienna, Georgia, September eighteenth, 1958. Their parents owned a –"

I interrupted Richard's narrative. "Wait a minute. Are you saying his brother was his twin?"

"Yes, they were identical twins. I thought you knew that."

"No, I didn't. All I heard was Quinn died a little over six months ago in a barn fire."

"I was about to get to that. The police suspected arson. The blaze was so intense nothing was left but charred bones, so forensics thinks an incendiary material was used. If their parents hadn't seen both sons go into the barn to get the horses out, and only one come out, no one could have known who it was. And before you ask, the horses got out fine, but the barn collapsed on Quinn before he could escape. Hayes tried to get him out, but the flames were too intense."

"He mentioned that's how his hands got burned. So Quinn died a hero of sorts, rescuing the horses."

"Yes, he did, not that he was one beforehand."

"Tell me."

"It seems Quinn made some bad investments, some of them at poker tables in Vegas. He nearly drained the family business dry."

"Which was growing pecans," I said.

"Right. The parents came out from the sale of the property with just enough money to live in a retirement home, as long as Hayes helps them out from time to time. Anyway, the Collingsham Retirement Center speaks highly of Hayes' contribution to their support."

"Another hero."

I was silent. Once again, always one to fill in a void, Richard spoke.

"I've got a couple of publicity shots of Hayes and Quinn picking pecans off the trees when they were teenagers. One shows both together. Want me to send it to you?"

"I wouldn't say no."

I heard him bang on his computer and a second later, my phone gave off a 'ping' alerting me I had a message. I opened it and saw a picture on my screen, small but clear.

"Got it."

"One's on a ladder reaching to the top of a pecan tree. The other stands with a hand on the ladder looking up at his brother."

"With a huge smile on his face," I added. "Which one is which? I mean, who's Quinn and who's Hayes? It's hard to tell with twins."

"Look closely. It's easy in this case. See? Quinn was the one with the darker hair, standing on the ladder. It's not a shadow. Hayes, as you know, is a redhead."

"I thought they were identical twins."

"They are...or were," said Richard. "But sometimes you can have small differences even if the DNA is identical. Something about anomalies in the womb. Look it up. Anyway, in the case of Hayes and Quinn, that's how people told them apart. Hair color."

"Well, I s'wanee."

"Is that one of those down-home, southern sayings?"

"It is. I find I love them. So expressive."

"That's all we need. You. More expressive."

"Changing the subject," I said, pointedly. "What have you got on Nancy Littlejohn?"

"Wait a sec." The sounds of more banging on his computer. "Nancy Claire Littlejohn. Except for one incident, a boring existence from what I can tell, other than being related to George Littlejohn who settled in New Hampshire in 1630. Forty-one years old. Went to Gunn High then Santa Clara University. A 'C' student but managed to get a BA in business administration. Parents currently live in Alviso, but she's estranged from them."

"What's the one incident?"

"Elder abuse."

"Not so boring."

"No, but the charges were withdrawn by her parents. So true or not true? Since then she's devoted herself to the culinary institute almost 24/7 for the past three years. Seems to have no other life." He paused. "Ah…Lee…"

"Yes, Richard?"

"About last night. Before we go on, I never meant to suggest that Tío had anything to do with these murders. I'm sorry if I gave you that impression. I could tell how upset you were."

"I'm glad you don't think he could have done something like that."

"I just wish he wasn't so damned devoted to Patsy Durand."

"I know, Richard. Tío does come across as if he'd do anything for her."

"But not something like that." Richard's voice was firm.

"Of course not."

"But he has no problem putting you in the line of fire, Lee. I don't like that."

"What do you mean?"

"Two men have been killed. I'm sorry if Patsy Durand has been arrested for the crimes, but I don't like it that you're nosing around where they were murdered. You might get hurt."

Nothing gets my back up more than someone, especially my kid brother, thinking I can't take care of myself. I had been toying with bailing on this, but now I was going to stick it out.

"Don't be silly. I won't get hurt, Richard, but I promise to be careful."

Something in my peripheral vision caught my eye. Another yellow, half-pencil sat on the second shelf of a steel rack, beside a microwave. Because of sitting on the floor, it was almost eye level with me.

"Richard, gotta go. Thanks for your help. Keep me posted."

Hanging up without waiting for a reply, I put on a rubber glove, reached for the half-pencil and bagged it. This one I would turn over to Frank for possible fingerprints.

Then I returned to the teaching chefs' office in the basement. I was determined to find out just how many of these yellow half-pencils were strewn about the place.

Did all the chefs use them? Or were they a particular favorite of Chef Dexter's? And were they a clue or were they red herring? For the record, I hate red herring, pickled or penciled.

Chapter Thirty-four

The Malted Falcon

Not only did I find three more half pencils in Chef Dexter's desk, but the logbook containing detailed grievances against Chef Jacques made a miraculous appearance. I picked it up and leafed through the small, blue book.

Detailed logs can go a long way in helping to fire an employee after a certain time period. The California Labor Code for termination is tough. It's necessary for the employer to collect hard evidence proving the employee is not sufficiently doing the job. Otherwise, a business can be sued up the ying-yang for firing someone.

I remembered Hayes telling me Chef Dexter had applied for the head-teaching chef position. Had Dexter known about Chef Jacques blackmailing Hayes to get the job? Or had Hayes asked Dexter to keep a log, as the two chefs worked closely together? Or was it Dexter's own idea? The most frightening 'or' came last. Or had Chef Dexter, tired of waiting for a job he thought should be his, slashed his way to success?

Whichever way it was, I was holding onto the logbook. I reached behind me and slid it halfway down the waist of my pants then tightened my belt to keep it in place. Uncomfortable, but secure.

I had a feeling I should probably turn it over to Frank, but took a couple of deep breaths and chanted loudly until the feeling passed. After all, Frank couldn't tell me anything he discovered regarding the murders; he was restricted. I had to find stuff out on my own. So the logbook would be my late night reading until further notice. Restriction worked both ways.

Back to Chef Dexter. I hadn't seen him since he taught his class on the ins and outs of éclairs. I was going to have to track the man down and get some answers. Answers, answers, answers. Everybody had to give me some answers.

Maybe I could prevail upon Frank to spill a little. Whoops. I was becoming unrestricted.

My phone rang while I was making my way to Hayes' office. I looked at the time. Eight-thirty AM. Then I looked at the caller I.D. Speak of the devil.

"Just thinking about you, Frank."

"Lee, we did a rush job on the other fingerprints besides yours that came up on the freezer. They found Patsy's."

"Oh, brother."

"There's more and it's bad. Really bad. They found DNA on the freezer, too. It turns out to be Mateo's."

"What? How the –?"

"I know, I know," Frank interrupted. "Patsy's fingerprints and your uncle's DNA on the freezer holding Sanchez's body. Sweet Jesus," he added in a softer voice.

"No." I balked. "This can't be right."

"I'm sorry, hon. Evidence is evidence. And there's nothing I can do about it. It's out of my hands. We're bringing Mateo in for questioning, as a possible accomplice in Manuel Sanchez's murder. We don't know if we can tie him into Chef Jacques Chalifour's murder, as well, but the prosecutor is sure going to try. The squad car should be arriving any minute to pick him up at the house."

I said nothing, disconnected, and ran out of the building to my car. By the time I got to the Big House, the police were driving away. I saw the back of Tío's head in the rear window.

Chapter Thirty-five

Catcher in the Rye Bread

It was still early enough in the morning for the day to have a soft glow about it, but every room in the Big House was flooded with sharp light. I raced inside and saw my mother and Gurn sitting in the living room, tense to say the least.

Gurn had his phone in his hand. Surprise covered his face when he saw me. "I was just calling you, sweetheart. I'm glad I hadn't left for work yet."

"I can't believe this," I said, my voice breaking. "Tío brought in for questioning on a murder."

Gurn rose and pulled me into an embrace. He broke free just as fast and looked into my face.

"Don't you worry. We'll fix this."

I'll love this man for the rest of my life, if for no other reason than saying those words. I looked up at him with gratitude.

"Yes, we will," said Mom. I turned in her direction. She went on. "I got off the phone moments ago with James Talbot. He's on his way to the police station. There's nothing to do now but wait."

"I hate waiting," I mumbled. "It's the hardest part of the job."

Mom wore a grey and yellow, light, wool robe buttoned up to her neck. Rule of thumb: the more upset she is, the higher the robe is buttoned. It had a stranglehold on her now. I went and knelt by her side just as Vicki entered from the kitchen wearing a front carrier holding a sleeping Steffi.

I stood, happy to see Vicki. Her presence has the most calming effect on me. I think she wears O de Valium or something.

"Vicki! When did you get here? Who's minding the store?"

"Just now," she said, embracing me, Steffi caught in the middle. "When Lila called Richard at work, he called me. He's on his way. He should be here any minute. My new assistant will open for me. Trial by fire. Did the police take Tío away?"

"Yes, they did. This is ludicrous, *ludicrous.*" Mom sat still in the chair, legs crossed primly at the ankles, her voice shaking with emotion.

"Here, Mother Lila," Vicki said, crossing to her mother-in-law, as she unsnapped the baby carrier. She lifted out Steffi. "There's nothing more soothing than a sleeping baby." She handed off Steffi, who cuddled in Lila's arms.

"Thank, you, Victoria." Lila stroked the top of the baby's head then gave Steffi a soft kiss, but looked unconvinced. "I guess things will be all right."

"We'll make this all right, Lila," said Gurn. "The thing to do is not to panic. Tío is innocent, and we'll clear him."

Just then Richard burst through the front door, noisy and fast. "I came as fast as I could!"

"Shhh," said Mom.

"The baby's sleeping," Vicki added.

He looked around at all of us then focused on little Steffi. "Oh, sorry." He lowered his voice. "Tío's been arrested for murder? How did this even happen?"

"He hasn't been arrested," Gurn said. "He's been brought in for questioning as a person of interest."

I took over. "Frank says it's about finding Tío's DNA on the freezer where I discovered Manuel Sanchez's body."

Mom scoffed. "This is absurd. *Absurd.*"

"I agree," I said.

Vicki weighed in. "There has to be a reasonable explanation for why it's there. I remember Tío teaching a couple of classes at the Institute in the past."

"That was two years ago, Victoria. But why should he go down now to the basement?" Mom looked at me. "Isn't that where the freezer was located?"

"That's one of the first things we need to find out," I said. "Has the freezer always been in that location, a locked room in the basement? Maybe it was brought upstairs at some time when Tío was teaching there."

"I wonder if Tío's been there recently, especially during Patsy's tenure," Richard said. "If not, two years is a long time for DNA not to be compromised."

"I was about to say that," Gurn said. "Other people had to have touched the freezer during that time. How did his DNA get there and stay there? Realistically, it has to be more recent."

"We need to talk to Tío," I said. "Find out exactly when he was last at the Institute and where he went." I turned to Mom. "Did you say Mr. Talbot was heading for the police station?"

She nodded. I could see her attention was on Steffi, who was beginning to fuss. Gurn reached down and took Steffi from Mom, who handed her over, gladly.

Steffi settled down in the crook of Gurn's arm. He looked down at her lovingly. I pushed on with Tío's problem, filing Gurn's Love Of Baby for another, less hectic time.

"Maybe if I can't talk to him," I said. "Mr. Talbot can give me some answers."

"Somebody put it there," Mom said. Her voice was hard and angry. "*Deliberately.* Tertiary DNA transfer."

"That sounds like the number one explanation," said Gurn. "Any bodily fluid, such as sweat or saliva, can be transferred easily enough."

"And if left undisturbed," Richard added, "it can stay there for an undetermined length of time, but I don't think as long as two years."

I thought this through. "Someone went to a lot of trouble to set Tío up."

"And maybe Patsy, as well," Vicki said, reaching out and taking the baby from Gurn. "I don't know Patsy, but from what I heard, it doesn't sound like something she'd do. I think she's the type of person who'd be more direct about killing someone."

"I agree," I said. "I'm beginning to think someone is trying to randomly incriminate anyone and everyone. Like throwing spaghetti on the wall, hoping some of it will stick."

"I have never thrown spaghetti on a wall," said Lila. "It sounds *most* unsanitary."

"My vote is it's someone inside the Institute," Gurn said.

"I don't know," said Richard. "Jolene, Wally, and Pete have motives. Maybe one of them did it and Patsy deliberately got herself arrested to protect them."

I was dubious. "Doesn't sound like Patsy to me."

"Mother love, Liana, can be very strong," said Mom, pulling herself out of the chair. "Very well. We need to resolve this. I will go change. Maybe it's time we *aggressively* searched the Institute."

"Hold on, Mom," I said. "First off, I've been doing just that. Right before I got the phone call from Frank, I found this." I pulled the blue logbook from its resting spot on my backside.

"I see you've been sitting on evidence," quipped Gurn. "But what is it?"

"A log kept for the past six-months by Chef Dexter on Chef Jacques's offences at the Institute. There might be valuable information inside. Someone has to read it."

"Give it to me." Gurn reached out a hand. "I'm good with logbooks."

"I thought it was more columns of numbers you excelled at," I said, with a fleeting smile.

"I like to feel I'm versatile." He returned my smile.

"What about your April fifteenth tax deadlines?"

"This is more important," said Gurn. "I'm not the only qualified accountant at the firm. I'll tell them to divide up the work. My group will get it done. I'll stay here today and read this book cover to cover. Why don't you take off your wig, sweetheart? I don't think you need it, anymore, and it looks hot."

"You're right." Snatching at the wig, I yanked it off, crossed the room, and threw it in the designer trashcan in the corner.

"We've gone past the point where a disguise is necessary. I think it's time everybody knew who I was. More leverage."

"So what you're saying is, Liana, there is nothing to be accomplished by going back to the Institute? Are you sure?"

"Yes Lila, I am," I said, thinking of her more as CEO than a mother. "D. I. needs to launch a full frontal attack. We have to pull everyone off anything else they're doing and concentrate on finding this murderer."

"I agree with her, Lila," said Richard.

He stared at her, not as her son, but work partner, the same as me.

"For all we know," said Vicki, joining ranks, "Tío may have been charged with something by now."

"I don't know if we can go as far as pulling staff off everything else." Lila faltered. "The agency has ongoing projects with important clients. You are asking us to virtually close down business. Our reputation could suffer irrevocably."

"We have to," I said. "Tío being hauled in as a possible accomplice puts more urgency to the matter than before. And it will only be for a day or two. But if it's more, so be it."

"Once again, I agree with Lee," said Richard.

"So do I," said Gurn. "Using the agency's total resources may be the only way to save the man."

A somber heaviness overtook all of us. Even Steffi was quiet. Okay, she was sleeping, but she was quiet.

"Very well. I bow to the majority." Lila's words hung in the air, quiet, but firm. "I'll call personnel and have them assign every agent we have to this. Then I will make calls personally to the clients most affected."

"Okay, we need to get to work," I said. "Richard, alert all of IT."

"On it," said Richard, picking up his phone. "What are you going to do, Lee?"

"Think. I've got to come up with a more likely candidate than Tío for these murders."

Chapter Thirty-six

The Smelt Who Came In From The Cold

I looked across the coffee table in the family room at the five of us gathered there: Lila, Richard, Vicki, Steffi and me. Maybe Steffi didn't count at this point; she wasn't doing any research.

We each had spent an hour or so on our assigned tasks, searching the Internet, gathering data, making phone calls, and compiling information via D. I.'s resources.

Gurn was absent, choosing to go over the logbook in his office in the garage. Fewer distractions. In the interim and being the sweetheart she is, Vicki ran out and brought us back lox, bagels, and cream cheese. I munched on the last of mine now.

"First of all, do we have any new developments?"

Lila jumped in, reading from her notes. "On a professional note, our clients have *graciously* agreed to a forty-eight hour extension period. After that, they *may* consider taking their business elsewhere."

"Them's the breaks," I said.

"Indubitably," Lila said.

"We'll deal, Lila," said Richard.

"We will, indeed," she agreed. "Meanwhile, Patsy's arraignment was set for today, but has been *postponed* due to additional pending charges of Manuel Sanchez's murder. Mr. Talbot says *if* she can get bail, it will probably be *upwards* of twelve million dollars."

"Can she get her hands on that kind of money?" I turned to Richard.

"Most definitely," he replied. "She is the queen of an empire. I'm not saying twelve million dollars' bail is chump change for her, but almost. Every year her empire grows. She is one driven and smart business woman."

"Hmmm," I said. "With her stuck in Santa Clara jail, her empire is probably suffering."

"Her stocks are down significantly," said Richard. "And I've got some bad news about this Henry Encino. Just saw it in my message folder."

"Who's Henry Encino again?" Mom looked at me with a raised eyebrow.

"The man Evangeline Packersmythe is involved with," I said.

"That should be, 'the man with whom Evangeline Packersmythe is involved', dear." Lila became Mom momentarily and gave me a you-should-know-better look.

"I'll put that in my message folder, Mom. Thanks. Go on, Richard."

Lila and I turned our attention toward him. He cleared his throat, a smile playing on his lips.

"He's got a wife and kid back in Lafayette, Louisiana; has for five years." Richard looked at me.

"That's too bad," I said. "Anything else?"

"They're still digging."

"The more we look into him, the worse it gets," I said. "Starting off with his involvement with another women in the Bay Area, Connie Durand, as well as our own Ms. Packersmythe."

"Excuse me?" Lila turned a questioning eye at me. "Have I missed something?"

"This is why we all need to be here and come up to speed." I proceeded to tell them about the scene I'd witnessed the day before between Connie Durand and Henry Encino.

Lila was stunned. "He has a tie-in with Connie Durand? Possibly romantic?"

"If Henry Encino is involved romantically with Connie Durand," asked Vicki, "Did Chef Jacques know he was married to someone in Louisiana? Was the chef blackmailing either one or both of them, like the others?"

"Crap," I said. "I hadn't thought of that."

"Language, Liana." Lila looked around at all of us. "That means Henry Encino should go on the list, along with Connie Durand."

"Oh, lawdy, lawdy, lawdy," I wailed. The thought of telling Ms. Packersmythe the father of her unborn child might be a killer as well as a womanizer, caused me to shiver. "This is all too much." I turned to Richard. "See what else you can dig up on him, and thanks for the update."

"Now that we've got everyone on this, I've got stuff coming in all the time," he said. "But I'll keep you up to the minute."

I turned to Lila. "Speaking of updates, Is there anything on Tío? Any info from Talbot?"

"No charges yet. After being interviewed," Lila said, "Mateo will *probably* be released under his own recognizance. Mr. Talbot has been keeping in touch with the prosecuting attorney's office. He's well respected there."

"Man, between Patsy and Tío this family is keeping the Talbot Law Offices busy," remarked Richard.

"Mateo should be home soon. Francis just texted me and said he will drive him home when he's done." Lila gave each of us a worried smile.

"But it's not over yet," I said.

"No," she replied. "Mateo could be arrested at *any* time. It's more or less up to the prosecuting attorney, if he feels there's enough to make a case. Sometimes not preferring charges *initially* gives them more leeway for a tighter case later on."

We turned to the sound of the swinging door opening between the kitchen to the dining room. Gurn came in carrying the logbook. He had a slight grin on his face.

I waited for him to pass from the dining room into the family room before I asked, "You look like you've got something. What?"

"I found use for the speed-reading course I took last summer. According to this," Gurn said, gesturing to the small, blue book, "One evening about a week ago, Chef Dexter overheard part of a heated discussion between Chef Jacques and somebody out on the loading dock. Chef Dexter saw Jacques Chalifour clearly. But the person he was talking to stood in the shadows and spoke softly. Dexter couldn't get close enough to hear or see who the other person was."

"Man or woman?"

"He couldn't tell, Lee."

Gurn paused, turned to a page in the logbook, and read. "He heard Jacques Chalifour say, 'You'd better watch your step. I could blow the lid wide open'."

"What the hell does that mean?" My voice held an exasperated challenge.

"No idea," said Gurn, easily. "I'm just reporting in."

"Sorry, darling," I said. "Of course, you are. I'm just so sick of not knowing what's going on. And the names of the villains keeps changing, too."

"I know. You hate that."

He gave me a full-blown smile. I returned it, temper slightly diffused.

"Back to the logbook," I said. "What else does it say?"

"Right then is when Chef Jacques saw him –"

"Chef Jacques saw Chef Dexter," I said.

"Yes. Jacques moved forward in a 'very threatening manner'. Direct quote from the log. Chef Dexter knew he was outweighed by about sixty pounds. Being a sensible man, he got out of there and fast. End of story. There are a few comments about the difficulties in getting rosemary/kosher salt from Israel, but mostly the entries are about Chef Jacques' bad behavior."

"So who did Chef Dexter see in the shadows?" I mused out loud.

"At this point," said Lila, "It could have been anyone."

"It's time to compile all our information, brainstorm, and make a list of suspects." I picked up the legal-size yellow pad.

"Richard, you're the fastest typist in the room. How about you listen to what we throw out, and make a readable list for all of us? We'll need to refer to it from time to time."

"Good idea, Liana," said Lila.

"I was doing that, anyway," he said.

"The two deceased men are Chef Jacques Chalifour and the dishwasher Manuel Sanchez," I said. "I think we're all in agreement that whoever killed Chef Jacques more than likely killed Sanchez."

Richard and Gurn nodded.

Lila said, "Agreed."

"Sounds reasonable," Vicki murmured.

"Good," I said. "Let's start with the people who have motive, means, and opportunity."

"I think it's going to be a long list," said Richard.

"Unfortunately," Lila said.

I read from my scribbled notes. "Chalifour's long-suffering wife, Edna. Before he came to California, he set up a two hundred and fifty thousand dollars insurance policy payable to her upon his death. A strong motive."

"Yes, she really needs the money," said Richard. "However," he went on, "she lives in New Jersey and we just found out she attended her son's band practice Sunday afternoon, three thousand miles away. So unless she hired an assassin --"

"Which is unlikely," Gurn interjected.

I nodded in agreement. "So she's out."

"Mrs. Edna Chalifour, out," repeated Richard, typing.

"Now let's deal with the people who were on scene," I said, going back to my notes. "According to witnesses, Patsy Durand and Jacques Chalifour had a long standing feud, with a verbal and physical fight the day before he was stabbed. And she admitted her prime motive in being at the Institute was to try to save it from going under, due to the deceased blackmailing her ex-husband, a man with whom she's on good terms."

"And the father of her two children," Lila added.

"Definitely deep roots there," I said. "Patsy lied about where she was at the time of the chef's murder and has no alibi. She had means, opportunity, and motive, big time."

"And what would be her reasoning for killing Manuel Sanchez?" Richard stopped typing and looked at me.

"Maybe he knew or saw something," offered Vicki.

"True," I said. "Maybe he tried to take over where Chef Jacques left off in the blackmailing department. Remember, from all accounts, Sanchez was as unsavory a character as our dead chef. And Patsy has no alibi for his time of death, either."

Richard resumed banging on the keyboard. "Topping the list of suspects – still – is Patsy Durand," he muttered.

"Jolene and Wally Durand, even Pete Durand, have strong motives," said Gurn, "given what we've learned about Jolene's sister, Rhonda. And none of them has a reliable alibi for that night, do they?"

"No," I said. "It was Everett's night off, the usual barkeep, and the woman replacing him was busy and had a bad cold. Conrad says she can't say for certain whether Jolene and Wally were in there or not. In any event, she didn't recognize them from the photos."

"Conrad spoke to Pete, too," said Richard. "Pete claims to have spent the night alone in his room reading."

"I can't keep up with the players," said Vicki. "Who's Conrad again?"

"Our newest operative," I said. "Kid with the ascot."

"Oh, yeah," she muttered.

"Let's look at the boys with a critical eye," I said. "Not only was there the thing about Rhonda and the baby, but their father's business was being destroyed by Jacques Chalifour. Double motive. They know the layout of the Institute very well. Any one of them could have snuck in that night and killed him. The boys have keys to the Institute. Hayes told me."

I took a breath and went on.

"For the record, I'm ruling out Jolene. She tends to turn her anger inward. I don't think she'd strike out at someone, even a guilty party. I think she'd drink herself into oblivion."

"Psychology 101?" asked Richard, with a wink.

"Internet," I replied, winking back.

"Here's a possible scenario for Jolene," said Vicki.

"Oh, no! Not another one," I said.

"Maybe Chef Jacques attacked her, and she defended herself," she said.

"He was a sexual predator," agreed Gurn.

"I'm still saying no on Jolene. From what I've seen of the lady, it's not her style, even if she was about to be raped. And I don't think she could keep such an act to herself."

"Maybe that's why she's drinking so much," said Vicki.

"And here's another thought," Gurn said.

"Oh, my gawd!" I wailed. "We're supposed to be clearing this up, not adding to the mix."

"If we're brainstorming, we're brainstorming," Gurn said firmly.

"True enough," I conceded. "Go for it."

"The boys could have gotten together, committed both crimes, and framed their mother. They are the heirs to her empire. If she were out of the way, they'd have tens of millions of dollars to their names."

"Collusion?" I thought it over. "Maybe."

"And, as you say, there is something more those two aren't telling," Richard said.

"There is, for sure," I said.

"And murder could be it," said Lila.

"I've left phone messages for them," I said. "So far, neither one has returned my calls for a further interview."

Richard bent over his laptop. "Wally and Pete Durand. Motives, strong. Means, strong. Opportunity strong. Following Lee's wishes, Jolene, temporarily out."

"Thank you. Let's move on to the father, Hayes Durand," I said. "Strong motive. He's the one being blackmailed. Opportunity, of course. It's his business."

"But those burns on his hands," said Vicki. "Can he even grip a knife, much less stab somebody with it?"

"Not according to his physical therapist," Richard said. "I talked to him myself. He says Hayes appears to have extensive nerve damage in his fingers. He may never regain full use of his hands."

"That's a pity," remarked Lila. "And how strong is his alibi?"

"Granger's Twenty-four Hour Pharmacy, with a pharmacist onsite all the time," said Richard. "He swears Hayes came in at eight, ordered the prescriptions, and hung around waiting for them to be done, which was after eleven."

"Three hours is a long time to wait for a prescription to be filled," I said.

"It was seven of them," Richard said. "And there was a delay with the doc phoning the scripts in. Plus one had to be brought in from another pharmacy. It was a long time, but there's a waiting area off to the side. The pharmacist saw Hayes out of the corner of his eye. He didn't pay attention to him every minute, but Hayes was definitely there. Another patron saw him, too. "

"Do we know that patron's name?"

"Cynthia Robbins. In her interview, she said she remembered seeing him half asleep in a corner, wearing white pants and shirt. She thought he was an ice cream vendor."

"Okay, on to Nancy Littlejohn," I said. "Did she, too, feel the pressure of Jacques Chalifour's blackmailing schemes? Did she silence him in fear it would come out about her having an affair with her boss?"

"You mean Hayes Durand is having an affair with Nancy Littlejohn?" Lila looked shocked.

"Yes, ma'am," Richard said.

"*Fifty Shades of Grey*, right?" I grinned at Lila then sobered.

Richard went on. "Neighbors stated that for several months, Hayes has been spending one or two nights a week at Nancy Littlejohn's apartment. He wasn't there that night, of course."

"Maybe Nancy was being blackmailed and didn't want knowledge of the affair to come out," offered Gurn.

"Or maybe she flipped out at having Jacques ruin her lover's business," I said.

"Either way," said Richard, "she has no alibi. Claims she was home alone watching television."

Vicki looked at all of us. "What about Connie Durand? Is she a possible suspect?"

Lila shook her head. "Not in *my* opinion. If Connie was going to do such a thing, wouldn't she kill her husband instead of the chef? Or the other woman? And is she *physically* capable of either? She's such a small thing."

"A weak but troubled woman," I said. "But let's not be fooled by outward appearances."

Lila was insistent. "I thought she was sleeping off the drug overdose the night of the murder. Patsy saw her."

I was just as insistent. "Patsy said she looked in on her only one time. Connie could have been faking. She really doesn't have any more of an alibi than Patsy does."

"Maybe our blackmailing chef knew about Connie's affair with Henry Encino, if that's what it is," said Lila.

"Connie Durand certainly has a hidden agenda," I said. "Like the rest of them. But does that make her a killer?"

"Just got a text," said Richard, looking at his phone. "Henry Encino was playing the piano in front of twelve hundred people Sunday night from eight to ten-thirty. Then he went out for drinks with other members of the orchestra. He's in the clear for the chef's murder, and thus, Sanchez's murder."

"He may still be a scoundrel and contemptible person, but there's a relief." I looked down at the yellow paper.

"Moving on to Chef Dexter. He lost a job to Chef Jacques unfairly. There's his motive. He has keys to the Institute, so could enter and leave at any time. Opportunity. And the chefs often leave their knives in assigned but unlocked drawers in the kitchens. They all know that. There's the means."

"And he has no alibi," said Richard. "Says he was home alone, sleeping."

"I suspect he, too, is hiding something," I said.

"Another secret?" Gurn grinned at me.

"We are awash in them," I said.

Richard said as he typed, "Chef Dexter, means, motive and opportunity. Strong. Alibi, weak."

"What about the other chefs at the Institute?" Lila looked at me.

"Praise the Lord, Chefs Oliver, Aurélien, and Barbara have unshakable alibis," I said. "Chef Oliver was at the opera with his wife and children and didn't get home until after midnight. *Aida*; long-winded. And Chef Aurélien spent the evening at his men's club performing in *The H.M.S. Pinafore* in French. He played Buttercup. I understand he was a sensation. Friends took him out for drinks afterward. And Chef Barbara spent Sunday night with her husband and mother-in-law playing cards."

"Do any of the students at the Institute seem likely?" Lila looked at me.

"Only one that we can find," said Richard, jumping in. "The rest have been cleared."

"Sad to say, Brit Poynter is the candidate," I said. "Which is too bad, because I like her. She told me she's had run-ins with Chef Jacques from the first. She's too gorgeous for him not to have been drawn to her like a fly to honey."

Gurn looked doubtful. "That's a fairly weak motive."

"Yes," I said. "But if he threatened to destroy Brit's blooming career, it becomes a stronger one. You saw how it affected Jolene's sister, Rhonda. Chef Jacques was known to abuse his power. And she, too, I suspect, is keeping a secret."

"Good God, another one," said Gurn.

"If that's the case," Lila said, "Chef Jacques might have known what that secret was."

"Brit Poynter says she was home alone," said Richard. "She has an apartment in Menlo Park, but there are no corroborating witnesses."

"And like everyone else at the Institute," I added, "she knew where the knives were kept. She could have grabbed his at any time. Maybe she arranged to meet him there, he let her in, and she killed him."

"And didn't you tell us Chef Jacques was gunning for Brit's friend, Sandy somebody or other?" Vicki looked at me.

"Yes, but Sandy Macintosh is in the clear," I said. "She was in Santa Rosa visiting her mother. She got a traffic ticket on the way back at eleven-thirty PM. Sometimes breaking the law can work for you."

"Wow," Richard stopped pounding on the keys directly after I finished talking. "This is an insidious lot."

"Yes," Lila agreed. "But we have too many innuendos and not enough facts."

"I agree," said Vicki.

"True," I said. "So after all this, what do we wind up with?" Guilty of bad grammar, I looked at Mom. "Or with what do we wind up...with...oh, rats. Never mind." I turned back to my brother.

"Richard, can you print out that list for us? Let's see who we can eliminate."

"A paltry few," observed Gurn.

"Sure thing." Richard banged a little on his computer, and I heard the printer in the small office set up in the corner of the family room light up and churn out paper.

I picked up the five copies and handed them out. We read in silence.

Suspect	Motive	Means	Opportunity	Alibi
Patsy Durand	Strong	Yes	Yes	No
Tío Alvarez	Strong	Yes	Yes	No
Wally Durand	Strong	Yes	Yes	Weak
Jolene Durand	Strong	Yes	Maybe	Weak
Pete Durand	Strong	Yes	Yes	Weak
Hayes Durand	Strong	Yes	Yes	Yes
Connie Durand	Weak	Weak	Yes	No
Henry Encino	Weak	Weak	No	Yes
Chef Dexter	Strong	Yes	Yes	No
Brit Poynter	Medium	Yes	Yes	No
Nancy Littlefield	Strong	Yes	Yes	No
Edna Chalifour	Strong	No	No	Yes
Chef Barbara	Weak	Yes	No	Yes
Chef Oliver	Weak	Yes	No	Yes
Chef Aurélien	Weak	Yes	No	Yes
Sandy Macintosh	Medium	Yes	No	Yes

Looking at the list, I nearly passed out. I rallied long enough to say, "*Dios mio*, three days as a scullery maid and nothing to show for it but dishpan hands and a page full of suspects."

"Six are eliminated," said Lila, "If we trust the alibis."

"True," I said. "But Patsy and Tío are still in the lead."

"Sweetheart," said Gurn. "You're selling yourself short. You're good at what you do. Never mind the list, which I'm finding more confusing than not. After talking to these people and observing them, what does your gut tell you is going on?"

"Okay," I took a deep breath and tried to calm down. "Almost everyone is hiding something. And it's getting in the way. Whether it's something big, little, benign, dangerous, I don't know. But I do know until I get to the bottom of the secrets, I can't get much further. And something's been nagging at me almost from the beginning. Give me a minute."

I closed my eyes and took another breath. My eyes shot open. I got up and walked around in a circle.

"Is this what they call, 'genius at work'?" Richard turned to Vicki.

"Shush, Richard," Vicki and Lila said, almost in unison.

Gurn choked down a laugh.

Ignoring everyone, I began to pace.

"*Dios mio*, wait a minute. Wait a minute. Could it be? Or not be? Do I have this right? Or do I have this wrong?"

I stood thinking again. Everyone looked at me. Actually, gawked.

"Richard, I want you to get your gang to check on a few more things for me. I've got an idea."

"Is it good or are you desperate?" asked Richard.

"Good and desperate." I looked around at my family. "If I can work this out, what do you think the chances are we can get everybody together 'to take a meeting' at the Institute? Otherwise, we may be eliminating this group's secrets until I file for social security."

"That's a clever idea." Gurn looked up at me. "Haul in the suspects and let them duke it out. I like it."

I sat down on the couch next to him and slid closer. Just feeling the warmth of his body made me feel saner. I went on.

"I'd like to have all the people with or without solid alibis in the same room and find out who's the biggest liar. Maybe one will trip up the other. Refute any untruths being made."

"With Patsy in jail, her being there might *not* be possible." Lila studied me with an expression of puzzlement peppered with dismay. Sometimes she acts like I'm one pencil short of a full box.

"I think Frank, he could arrange it." Tío said from the doorway of the dining and family rooms. Next to him stood Frank.

Chapter Thirty-seven

The Sound and the Curry

"Tío!"

"Frank!"

"Mateo!"

After our exclamations of surprise, I leapt up and ran to their sides, wedging myself in between them.

"We didn't hear you," said Mom from the other side of the room.

"Either of you," said Richard.

"Pretty stealthy stuff, gentlemen," Gurn said, with a smile. "We could have used you in Special Ops."

Tío returned his smile and walked in the room. "I know how to push at the swinging door silent, like a cat."

"And you four were so busy concentrating," said Frank, following him. "I don't think you would have heard a bomb go off,"

Frank paused and gave me a quick hug before saying. "Why do you want to have everybody gathered at the Institute, Lee? Who do you think you are, Hercule Poirot?"

His eyes sparkled with his true feelings, so I ignored the jaundiced tone of his voice. It was all for show, anyway.

"Because to catch this murderer we need to expose all these secrets. And a way to do that is to have everybody together in one room."

"Mateo and I were talking about something like that on the way over," Frank said.

"This all is, how you say, 'too glib' I think," said, Tío.

"Too pat," I said. "If you mean the case only has superficial plausibility, then it's too pat."

"Thank you, Madame Dictionary," said Richard. "Go on, Tío."

I stuck my tongue out at my brother. Nobody saw me, including him.

Tío went on. "I know I have never been in the storage room."

"Aha!" Vicki stood and pointed a finger at Tío. "That's what we thought."

"That means your DNA on the freezer was a tertiary transfer," said Gurn."

Tío looked a little puzzled.

"A third person," Frank said, jumping in to explain. "Someone who deliberately put it there to frame you, Mateo."

"Exactly," said Mom.

She and Frank exchanged glances of a united front. The second in less than a week. Well, I never.

Aloud, I asked, "Tío, when was the last time you were at the Institute? Can you remember?"

"*Como no*," he said. "Of course. Friday last I went to join Patsy. Just she and I. The day's classes were over, but she arrange to have the kitchen open for another hour. She wanted to make tortillas with pulled squirrel, guacamole, and barbeque sauce as an experiment before she show it to the class. We do together."

"So you touched just about everything in the kitchen, right?" Gurn looked at Tío. Tío nodded.

"*Si*. It was late when we finish, so after, she wash the dishes, I dry. Together we put everything away. We do not want to cause extra work for the staff."

"On behalf of someone who was staff," I said. "I thank you."

Gurn probed more. "What happened to the towels you used to dry the dishes and your hands?"

Tío shrugged. "I put it in the laundry hamper outside the door for used linens. Like always."

Gurn looked at me. I looked at him and nodded.

"That's when it probably happened. Someone was watching. Then that someone took those towels with your DNA on them and rubbed down the freezer."

"But what about Patsy's fingerprints?" Richard looked from one to the other. "How did they get on the freezer?"

Frank jumped in. "Apparently, she'd sent for several crates of frozen catfish to show the classes how to make a particular dish and needed to store them. It wound up she used Styrofoam containers, but she was down there looking beforehand. Or so she said."

"But is it true or is she just saying that?" My frustration rang out. "Oh, how I wish I could get them all in one room and force them to talk."

"I think I can make that happen," Frank said, clearing his throat. "It might cost me a dressing down by my superiors, but I think I can pull in a few favors and have Patsy at the Institute for a couple of hours, probably tomorrow morning." He looked around at all of us, his gaze resting on Tío. "If you believe in her innocence, Mateo, I'm willing to give her the benefit of the doubt."

"I do," Tío said.

My voice wavered. "I'm not so sure, Tío. She's holding something back, just like the rest of them. And it could be murder. If you can do what you say, Frank, let's just see what happens when we put everyone together tomorrow and stir up this culinary pot."

Chapter Thirty-eight

Tinker, Tailor, Soldier, Pie

Before we'd decided to 'line up the usual suspects', I'd made a mid-afternoon appointment for a jail-time visit with Patsy. I didn't cancel. One last–ditch attempt to get her to tell-all.

However, with the Institute closed, I had a few free hours before I met with her. Never one to let slave labor go untapped, Mom commandeered my services meanwhile.

A short time later found the two of us heading to Palo Alto's Rinconada Library, formerly called the Main Library. Life goes on as they say, and even with all the chaos happening with the Alvarez Clan, the yearly month-long fund drive for the library was in full swing.

Discretionary Inquiries is a long-standing contributor to the library; books are our friends and all that. I was to help Mom drop off two hundred assorted cupcakes donated by the agency for an afternoon party promoting children and reading.

Both the "Butter and Nothing But the Butter," a local bakery, and the library are about five minutes away by car and in a direct line. You gotta pass one to get to the other. *Mucho* convenient. Get a good book, and snarf down a pastry either coming or going. If you play it right, both ways.

We picked up the ready-to-go boxes of cupcakes. Actually, I did the picking up. Lila Hamilton Alvarez doesn't lift boxes if she can instruct others in the finer points of doing so. As instructed, I piled them into the trunk of her Jag, and won the battle of not stealing a cupcake for myself. Feeling virtuous, we delivered all two hundred to the library intact.

I had the foresight to combine the delivery of the cupcakes with the return of three books due back the next day. Once I helped arrange the goodies on trays, I left the kitchen area and toddled to the returns desk, still not having snitched one single cupcake. Sometimes my self-control astonishes me.

On my way to the returns desk, I passed dozens of children and one or two teenagers. A few whispered quietly together, others engaged in reading, but all were doing their best to respect the silence required within.

I'm sure Ben Franklin was smiling down from somewhere at seeing yet another generation of youth using a public library. I know it brought a smile to my lips.

I stood with the three books in my hands at the return desk. About to say something to the assistant librarian, I noticed a tall, lanky man lurking around the reference section, some ten feet away. Within a flash, I realized it was Henry Encino.

He hadn't seen me yet. Just as I was wondering if he, too, was involved with the library's fund drive, Connie Durand came around a corner. Gone was the faded chenille robe, replaced by a blue and green plaid dress, nipped in at the waist. Her hair was combed, and held back with a headband. She even wore a little makeup. Connie was searching for someone, a look of desperation dripping from her face.

Deborah Kerr had the same look when she took a long walk in the rain while sick with pneumonia in Graham Greene's movie, *The End of the Affair*. Only in Deborah Kerr's case, rain dripped from her face, as well as desperation. Connie's face may have been bone dry, but it still had the same expression of hopelessness, the abandonment of anything good coming into her life.

Once past Graham Greene and his literature, I took stock of the situation. Connie wouldn't recognize me, me not wearing my Arbela Einstein getup. However, having met Henry Encino as myself – and recently – this presented a problem.

Thus, I dropped down to a squat behind the returns desk, capturing the stares of a few nearby kids. Putting my forefinger to my lips, I gave a small shushing sound to the gawking children and stayed out of sight.

Kids being kids and used to the silly ways of adults, they merely shrugged and went about their business. The assistant librarian, used to my silly ways, merely shrugged and went about his business. I was good.

"What on *earth* are you doing, Liana?"

I looked up to see my mother staring down at me. Her expression of surprise turned to one of annoyance. The librarian – one smart cookie – stepped away to the other end of the counter.

"I said --" Mom began.

"Shhhh!" I put my finger to my lips. "Ignore me, Mom. Just ignore me."

She didn't, of course, but leaned down and whispered, "What *are* you doing?"

I gestured in the vague direction of Henry Encino and Connie Durand.

"Here, here," I hissed, thrusting the three return books in her hands. "Return these, please. And ignore me. Please."

Mom finally got the message, took the books and went to the other side of the returns desk.

"Excuse me," she said to the librarian, who was pretending to read a magazine. "I'd like to return these books for my *daughter*." She delivered her next line very pointedly. "Then I will go wait *outside* in the car."

"Smooth, Mom," I muttered then peeked around the corner of the desk.

Henry wasn't paying attention to us, so intent was he in a pantomime with Connie. Using gestures similar to an aircraft ground handler guiding a big plane, he signaled for her to meet him at the back of the stacks. She nodded and turned in the direction of his gestures. They both scuttled away.

I stood, intending to shadow the scuttling couple. I said nothing of my behavior to bystanders or my mother. I've found it's best not to offer any explanations in circumstances like these. Nobody cares or believes you. Besides, I was one of the cupcake fairies. Don't mess with me.

Speaking of cupcakes, a small bell rang several times. Apparently, that was the signal the party was about to begin. Youth from everywhere closed books or stopped whispering, and rushed in the general direction of prearranged tables and chairs on the other side of the large room. Attending adults followed.

All except Mom. Head held high, she walked in the opposite direction, toward the exit nearest the parking lot.

That left the three of us, Henry Encino, Connie Durand, and me heading toward the mystery section. They walked down one aisle, I the next. Darting my head into spaces between shelved books, I kept a constant eye on them. The couple stopped in a corner in front of Carolyn Hart's books. I love her Death on Demand series. I'd try to snag one later.

But back to the job. Once I knew they were staying put, I removed several books from the shelving. I was in the perfect location, but the two subjects were speaking so softly I couldn't hear everything they were saying. But I could see perfectly.

Looking around her, Connie withdrew a small item from the pocket of her skirt. She opened her hand and showed it to Henry. His face went white. I couldn't make out exactly what it was, but it looked like a small piece of gold jewelry. He snatched it from her with a loud exclamation, more primal in sound than an actual word. Connie shushed him. The way her face wore a look of desperation, his took on one of grim determination.

Connie studied him for a moment, her look of despair replaced with one of fear. She glanced around her again. I pulled away from my vista spot, lest she catch me spying on them.

"Excuse me," said a youthful voice. "Are you going to be checking out that Stephen King novel?"

Startled, I turned to see a teenage boy peering at me from behind thick glasses, one hand carrying a half-eaten chocolate cupcake, the other a skateboard.

I looked at the two heavy books I'd removed from the shelf in my hand.

"No, no," I whispered, shoving both books at him. "Here, take whichever one you like."

The skateboard clattered to the tile floor, as he grabbed for the books. The sound echoed throughout the stillness, ostensibly attracting *mucho* attention. I scooted around him and walked away, hoping to keep from being noticed.

Just as I arrived at the end of the aisle, a tearful Connie came whizzing by me. She was too upset to see much of anything or anyone, but I turned around, just in case. I also took a step back into the aisle, thereby avoiding a collision with Henry, who flew by a second later.

"Wait," he called out, his voice husky and filled with great emotion. "Wait for me, Connie."

"I only wanted *The Shining*," said the teenage boy, coming up behind me and shoving the other book in my hand. The skateboard was now tucked under his arm, but he still carried the cupcake. His face broke into a smile.

"You like Stephen King? I think he's cool."

"Yes, he is." I watched as Connie exited the building, Henry close on her heels.

"I just finished *Misery*," the boy continued. "You read *Misery*?"

"No, I haven't."

"It's good. You should check it out."

"I will definitely do that, but at another time. Gotta go," I said re-shoving the book into his hand. I turned to leave, hoping to catch the couple outside, so I could tail them.

"Wait," the boy said, using the same word as Henry, but without any of the emotion. I stopped to look at him. He went on.

"They're giving out cupcakes in the kids' section. Don't you want one? They're good." He shoved the last of his in his mouth.

I couldn't help but smile.

"Thanks, but I don't do cupcakes." Liar, liar, pants on fire.

I made a quick exit to find both subjects getting into their cars, and pulling out of the parking lot in separate directions.

With a toss of a mental coin, I opted to follow Henry. I ran to Mom's Jag, leapt into the passenger seat, and got the chance to finally yell the words,

"Follow that car! I've been waiting most of my life to say that," I added.

Mom shook her head in disbelief. "Sometimes I wonder at your sense of humor, Liana. So that's Henry Encino. What were he and Connie Durand doing at the library?"

"I have no idea, but it seemed to involve a piece of jewelry. But they sure didn't want to be seen by anybody."

After a few blocks, Henry parked in the lot of an Italian eatery, specializing in the best pizzas in the world, so said their sign. He got out of the car. After we parked, I turned to Mom.

"Lila," I said, now in total work mode, "Stay here. No need to draw attention to ourselves. Let me see what's going on first."

I was in luck. The restaurant had a large, plate-glass window showing most of the inside area. Sun streamed in, making the patrons very visible. I cautiously peered in, hoping to see Henry without him seeing me.

It was easy. Waiting at a front and center table, was Evangeline Packersmythe looking up at him. All smiles now, he gave her a quick kiss on the cheek and sat down across from her at a cozy table for two. She poured him a glass of wine from a waiting bottle of chianti. In front of her was a glass of water.

Yeah, that's right, I thought. Expectant mothers don't drink alcohol. He may not be a murderer, but that didn't keep him from being a two-timing louse. It was all I could do to keep from marching inside, picking up the glass of wine, and flinging it in his face.

But tomorrow was another day. The Hercule Poirot get-together. When truth will out. I felt a pang of sorrow for the happy mom-to-be.

Chapter Thirty-nine

Look Homeward, Angel Food Cake

Elmwood Jail houses female arrestees who have not yet been arraigned, along with the rest of the county's female prisoners. Patsy Durand fell into the first category.

Quickly looking over the visitation rules, I saw I was good. There wasn't a snowball's chance in hell I'd carry a weapon inside the jail, and even less that I'd wear a slit skirt or shorts, expose major portions of my torso, back, shoulders, chest or midsection, or wear transparent, strapless, halter, spaghetti straps, bare midriff, or tank top clothing. And forget about wearing attire displaying obscene language or drawings. Versace would be scandalized, not to mention my mother.

The day was still gorgeous, so I put the top down on the convertible and aimed the car for Milpitas. It was a quick run south on 101, one of the Bay Area's main arteries. Then I crossed Highway 237, also called the 'forgotten highway'. That bit of cement runs north to south at the bottom of the Bay. I listened to the Everly Brothers the entire way and arrived at 701 South Abel Street in Milpitas in a great mood and with ten minutes to spare.

I'd never been to this facility before and it was impressive. Elmwood is a large, gated community that doesn't keep people out but rather, in. The only notion it was a jail was the obligatory surrounding high fence and cameras. If you looked close enough, the security was A Number One. They were just low-key about it.

I parked in a lot typical to the Bay Area, which meant not enough trees to shade cars left to bake in the sun, and put the top up. Stowing my bag and cellphone in the trunk of the car, I crossed the parking lot, carrying only my ID and car keys.

Waiting for me on the other side of the security checkpoint were two guards, one man and one woman. The man looked like a linebacker. The female guard did, too, only with dangle earrings. Flanked on either side, I was escorted not to one of the visiting rooms but to the kitchen area.

In the midst of a kitchen the size of a kids' playground and filled with oversized mixing pots, stoves, ovens, and refrigerators, stood Patsy. She was dressed in the new and much heralded retro prison garb. That would be black and white striped top and pants with the words 'Santa Clara County Department of Corrections' stenciled in bright green across the chest. Looking very much at home, Patsy moved cooks and volunteer prisoners around like a cop directing traffic at a busy intersection.

"Cecil, sugar," she called out to a large young man standing over a mammoth mixer. Wearing the same type of uniform as Patsy, Cecil looked like a Kodiak bear in zebra stripes. Had he and the mixer been filled with helium, they could have been in the Macy's Thanksgiving Day parade as balloons.

"Just enough to form soft peaks," Patsy went on. "You're whipping the cream, not beating it into submission. Otherwise, you got butter, sugar."

Cecil turned and gave her a little-boy grin. "Yes, Chef. Sorry, Chef."

"You're learning, Cecil. You're learning. My granny would have been proud of your Brunswick stew yesterday."

Everyone there wore similar garb, except the guards and several middle-aged people dressed in whites. One woman wearing a chef's toque hurried over to Patsy. She judiciously carried a large spoon filled with some darkish liquid.

Patsy saw me and gave another one of her dazzling smiles. "Lee! Sugar! Haven't see you in a coon's age. Come on in and meet the gang. Everyone, this is my hound dog of a sleuth, Lee Alvarez."

Friendly greetings sounded throughout the room from guards and prisoners alike. I gave a global wave instead of barking, and hurried to Patsy's side. The lady chef in white stood nearby with a smile.

"How are you?" Only it came out 'hahwahya'. Sammy was obviously from Boston.

"Good, good," I said, somewhat thrown by all of this.

She turned to Patsy. "Chef, what do you think of the roux now?" While Patsy took a taste off the spoon, the woman anxiously awaited the verdict. "Simmered it longer, like you said, Chef. It makes a stronger taste."

"It surely does, Sammy. It'll do fine." Patsy gave her a big smile and the younger chef preened in its brightness.

"The world needs her food, Lee," said Sammy. "She can't stay in jail." A rotund woman, Sammy turned back to Patsy with nothing less than worship in her eyes.

"That's the goal, Chef Sammy," I said.

"Chef Sammy's quite a lady," said Patsy, punching her colleague good-naturedly on the arm. "She's responsible for filling the bellies around here. Her title is Certified Chef de Cuisine."

Sammy looked at me with a laugh. "That means I know string beans are better for you than bacon fat."

There was a round of laughter from those nearby, especially Cecil.

"Once Chef Sammy and the others heard I was here, they were chomping at the bit to get me into the kitchens. Sammy's not half-thrilled, even though she knows what she's doing, all right."

"Thank you, Chef," Sammy giggled. "But we can all learn from someone like you."

"I promised to teach her how to make *poisson chat en croute*. That's catfish wrapped in pastry dough, French style. But with an Arkansas twist; stuffed with green peppers and laid on a bed of spicy black-eyed peas."

Her pronunciation was ghastly but the dish didn't sound half bad.

"Of course, that's not for here," Patsy said. "It's for her own personal consumption; her husband's from Tennessee."

I looked around at the kitchen. "This looks like a pretty big operation."

"Sure is," said Sammy. "We prepare twelve hundred meals a day at Elwood."

Patsy took over. "It's something about the California Code of Regulations. Prisoners are entitled to a hot breakfast, cold lunch and hot dinner, all produced under the guidance of a registered dietitian – that would be Sammy – who ensures the meals meet federal guidelines. All the penal kitchens in this neck of the woods turn out about fifteen thousand meals a day. That's a lot of flapjacks, sugar."

Sammy laughed like Patsy had said the funniest thing she'd ever heard in her life. I worked up a smile.

"While I'm in here," Patsy said, "I'm helping out a little. Giving them a few tips. Training the volunteer inmates. Like Cecil." She pointed to the Kodiak bear kid. "The kid's got talent. Never stepped into a kitchen before he served time, but his instincts are just fine. When he gets out of here, he's going to come and work for me in my St. Louis restaurant. That's where he's from. I hear tell he can steal a car in less than sixty seconds, but now he can make a possum pie almost as good as me. That's what counts."

Cecil stopped what he was doing, stood at attention, and shouted like he was on the drill field. "Yes, Chef. Thank you, Chef."

Patsy turned to me. "You hear the way to a man's heart is through his stomach? It's also a way to his soul. Many a man – and woman – has been saved by doings in the kitchen."

"Before we go any further," I said, "tell me there isn't really a possum in that pie."

Patsy threw back her head and laughed. Sammy did likewise. It was like I was at the Punchline Comedy Club, for all the laughs. Patsy went on.

"Its name comes from the fact the pie is playing possum. You don't know what's in it until you cut it open. Everybody's recipe is a little different. Mine is the best, naturally."

"Naturally," I said.

"We start with a baked pecan and shortbread pie crust. After it cools, we add a cream cheese filling flavored with honeysuckle extract. Then a layer of thickened Crème Anglaise, followed by a layer of chocolate mousse, all topped with whipped cream. Of course, the honeysuckle flavouring is my own little secret. Keep it to yourself, hon."

"Done."

Patsy turned back to the other chef. "Sammy, you'd better get back to your roux."

"Yes, Chef." Chef Sammy hurried away.

"And them biscuits you made were a lot lighter today," Patsy called after her. "It's using forks to mix them that does the trick."

She walked over to Cecil. "You watching the pie shells, Cecil?"

"Yes, Chef. Two more minutes of baking, Chef."

"You use unsalted butter this time? They get too burned otherwise."

"Yes, Chef. Apologies, Chef."

"We all make mistakes, Cecil. And you used bittersweet chocolate to make the pudding?"

"Yes, Chef."

"No more instant pudding crap?"

"No, Chef. Won't happen again."

"Possum pie is a *Sooie Cochon* tradition. If you're going to be working for me, we only use the finest ingredients. And everything, and I mean everything, is made from scratch."

Cecil drew himself up to his full height, which looked to be slightly under seven feet.

"Yes, Chef. Nothing but, Chef."

I envisioned the queen dealing with the improprieties of her royal court going on forever. "I need to talk to you, Patsy, and I've only got thirty minutes. Can we go somewhere private?"

"Sure thing, sugar. I hope you got something good to tell me."

Before I could answer, she walked away. I followed close on her heels. Then she stopped abruptly and I nearly ran her down. Patsy turned and shouted to Chef Sammy, now filling steel trays with cooked greens of some sort.

"Sammy, I'm using your office for a while. Hope that's okay."

"Of course, Chef. At your disposal."

"Thank you, Sammy," Patsy said.

We walked toward a corner office constructed mainly of glass windows, with an inset glass-paned door. Maybe it kept a conversation private, but you certainly wouldn't want to change clothes in it.

Patsy held the door open for me to pass through. She went to the other side of the desk and sat behind it. She looked at home. Me, not so much.

"They got a good budget here," she said, with a smile. "Can order pretty much anything but truffles and caviar."

I studied her face. "So how are you doing, Patsy? Really?"

"Glad I can be in these kitchens. They're not mine, but it's a good distraction from what's going on."

"It looks like you're running the place. With most inmates, it would be the other way around."

She laughed but sobered almost immediately.

"Now what's on your mind, sugar? I know you didn't come here to learn about a kitchen. Matt says your idea of cooking is ordering take-out."

I skipped to the chase. "You know I found the dishwasher's body in one of the Institute's freezers yesterday?"

"Jim Talbot called and told me. That's why I'm still in here, sugar. They were supposed to arraign me this morning, so I could post bail. Now they got another forty-eight hours to make up their minds whether they're going to charge me or not. But I'm hoping this puts me in the clear."

She broke out into a broad smile.

"I'm afraid it doesn't."

Her smile vanished as quickly as it had come.

"That's too bad. I don't mind saying I'm getting a little nervous, Lee. I'm beginning to think I might be stuck here for the rest of my life. What are you doing about it?"

I opened my mouth to tell her I'd see her the following morning at my interrogation soiree, but decided against it. As they say, forewarned is forearmed. I changed the subject. "I know about Rhonda and her pregnancy."

"I know you know. Just because I'm in here doesn't mean I don't know what's going on. Wally told me he spilled the beans to you." She settled back in the chair. "Sad little girl. But both those girls are. Jolene and Rhonda never had any good upbringing, but Rhonda didn't deserve to get knocked up by a man older than her father. But what's that got to do with me being in here?"

I didn't answer that question, either, but prodded.

"Is that the reason the boys showed up in the Bay Area earlier than they said? Is that why you met them at their hotel Saturday? Rhonda's pregnancy?"

A momentary look of relief passed over her face. Then she answered with the fastest patter I've heard yet from a southerner.

"Yes. Petey plans on adopting Rhonda's baby when it's born. They've been trying to start a family since he and his wife got married. Rhonda says she doesn't want to have anything to do with a baby. Wants to give it up, go somewhere, start a new life as a chef. She's giving it to Petey. She's already signed the papers."

"Is that legal?"

"Honey, with enough money you can make practically anything legal, but yes, it is. It just takes a little doing. Petey wanted to be here in person to tell Jacques he'd fathered a child with Rhonda and have him sign over his parental rights. We worked it out where Petey'd offer him a hundred thousand dollars to sign the papers. Go up to half a mil, if'n we had to. I was going along to make sure that lowlife didn't try to hold the baby ransom for any more than that, like the worthless piece of donkey dung he was."

"That explains you and Pete. But why was Wally involved in it?"

She paused for a moment, seemingly searching for the right words.

"After we straightened out the business about the baby, the three of us planned on confronting Hayes, as a family. Tell the boys' father he had to let that man go. It didn't make sense. The business was suffering."

"But you never did?"

"Never had to." She leaned forward, lowering her voice. "The next night Connie tried to commit suicide. Hayes finally admitted to being blackmailed into hiring him, on account of Connie's past. Then someone did the world a favor. The devil was slain."

Patsy sat back, ruminating.

"It's just like Hayes. Taking that man on, trying to save the woman in his life. He wanted to do the same thing with me when we were married. Be the white knight galloping in on a horse. But I never needed any saving. Except now, sugar. I'm hoping you'll save me. I didn't kill either one of those men. I swear."

"You realize when this comes out about Rhonda's pregnancy, it's going to make your family's motives for killing Jacques all the stronger?"

She gave me another one of her dazzling smiles. "But it don't have to come out, does it, sugar? Aren't you under some kind of seal of the confessional?"

"You have me mistaken for Father Brown, Patsy. I'm just a lowly PI, and as an officer of the law, I'm required to give any pertinent information to the police that would help them solve a case."

She leaned forward again, a look of fury crossing her face. "What's going on with my family is personal and private. It has nothing to do with the death of that rattlesnake. Or that dishwasher, neither. You better not drag my boys into it any more than they already are. I'd rather confess to killing those men, myself, than see anything happen to my boys."

Well, well, well. How right Mom was about mother love.

Chapter Forty

Something Pickled This Way Comes

I walked into the parking lot pondering my conversation with Patsy. She was one tough cookie. But was she capable of murder?

Ignoring the sound of a vehicle accelerating its engine nearby, I mused on.

When Patsy got 'riled up', she seemed to be a person who held a grudge. I'd just riled her up and it wasn't a pleasant experience. Had Chef Jacques riled her one too many times and paid the price?

The racing of the nearby motor became louder, but not quite as loud as the pounding of my heart. I had to face it. Patsy could have killed those two men, no matter what Tío said. Or wanted.

I felt a sourness in my stomach and looked up. I'd managed to pass my car by two rows. Turning around, I eyeballed the Chevy's location, called myself a ninny, and went in between parked cars until I came to the first drive lane.

In the midst of crossing it, I heard the gunning of a motor and squeal of tires. I turned. A white van was bearing down on me going faster than I thought possible in a parking lot. And I was right in its path.

Fortunately, I'd done a barre that morning, so I was pretty limber. I twisted my body to the right and went into a quick *plia* followed by a *jeté*. I heard a 'snap'.

The combined execution of these ballet steps not only would have made Madam Pleyeskeiva proud, but served their purpose. They propelled me up into the air and to the side. I landed on the hood of the nearest parked car with a thunk. The van screeched by so closely, I felt the breeze of it.

Splayed out on the hood of a BMW, I looked into the windshield of the driver's side. A man sitting behind the steering wheel stared wide-eyed at me. As he was stunned and I'd had the wind knocked out of me, it was a staring game for about five seconds.

Then he threw his car door open and jumped out. A man in his early fifties and of average height, he had a Good Samaritan look about him. This despite wearing an opened shirt revealing many gold chains on a hairy, barrel chest.

Meanwhile, I slid off the hood of his car, onto the pavement, and sat in a stupor. My body was in shock and couldn't feel anything yet. But I wondered what had made the snapping noise. Was it my ankle or my shoe? As I was wearing new Christian Louboutin Choca Criss Sandals, I could only hope it was my ankle.

"Oh, my God, lady," the man said, squatting down. "Are you all right?"

"Oh, no," I said, spying the dark blue patent leather heel lying in the middle of the lane.

The man misunderstood my cry of dismay. "I'm calling 911," he said, pulling out his phone.

"No, don't do that," I said. "I'm fine. But my new shoes are ruined. And I just bought these!"

"What?" Thrown, he paused in the midst of hitting the emergency number and gave me a puzzled look.

"I'm okay."

"Are you sure, lady?"

I struggled to my feet. He rose with me. Standing wasn't easy with one foot in a five-inch spike and the other in a broken shoe, but I managed.

"Really, truly." I assured him and leaned against his car. "Just give me a minute to catch my breath." I gave out a slight giggle. "I'm glad I didn't dent anything on your car."

"Don't worry about it. You're sure I can't do something for you? Call the police or something?"

"No, no. Besides, there are plenty of police around here if I need one. But you can go get the heel of my shoe out of the road before someone runs over it. Maybe I can have it reattached."

"Sure thing," he said. He gave a nervous glance both ways before he crossed into the lane. "You know," he said in a raised voice, "it looked like he was coming right for you. Never seen anything like it."

He picked up the heel, glanced both ways again, and scampered toward me. "I'm telling you, it was like he was aiming that van for you."

He handed me the heel to my shoe. I took heart. It looked like it could be reattached. Maybe the day wasn't a total loss.

I stretched out my limbs to see any damage done to me or my clothes. Other than the shoe, I seemed pretty much intact.

"You keep saying 'he'," I said, hobbling in the direction of my car. "Did you see the driver?"

He looked startled again, but fell in step with me. "No, I didn't. It all happened so fast. I just assumed it was a man, because the van was so big. It could have been a woman driving, I guess."

"You didn't happen to get the license plate number, did you? Even a partial would help."

"Sorry, I didn't notice. As I say, it came out of nowhere."

"Yeah, I know what you mean. I was too busy getting out of the way, myself."

"Are you sure you're all right? You need some coffee or something? I could go get you some coffee."

"I'm fine." I smiled at this nice man, who was trying so hard to be a good caregiver. "I don't want to keep you from…coming or going. Whichever you're doing."

"Don't worry about it. I'm going. I just saw my business partner. He's awaiting charges."

"Oh, I'm sorry," I said, for want of anything better to say.

"Don't be. He was stealing me blind. I hope he swings."

We arrived at my car and I beeped the door unlocked. I turned back to the man, hoping he would go away so I could absorb what happened. And make a few phone calls. Who on the list owned a white van? I gave him a big go-away smile.

"Thanks again. I'm fine now. Really."

"Nice car," he said, no longer paying attention to me. "'57 Chevy convertible. Looks like the original paint job."

"It is."

He reached inside a pocket and pulled out a business card. "If you ever want to sell it, give me a call. Reinhart Motors. I'll take it off your hands for a good price. That is, if I'm still in business or don't go to jail for shooting my ex-business partner."

"You don't want to do that. You'd wind up in here like him. But I understand the food is pretty good."

He laughed. I did, too. Then he sobered.

"Well, you take care of yourself, young lady. I don't watch many cop shows, but it looked to me like that van tried to run you down. You broke someone's heart lately? Or something worse?"

I slid into the driver's seat before answering.

"I'm thinking something worse," I said more to myself than him.

Chapter Forty-one

The Postman Always Grinds Twice

The Big Reveal Day had come. I was so nervous it was like I forgot to wear underwear.

Basically, if what I suspected was true, lives would change irrevocably. If not, I was about to make a total ass of myself, whether it was covered or not.

I usually never have a problem with making an ass of myself; just goes with the territory. But a lot was at stake this time, several people's happiness and a woman's freedom, possibly even my beloved Tío's freedom.

It had been a sleepless night making sure I had the truth of it all. But with help from Richard's data, snuggled into a sleeping Gurn, and both cats purring by my side, I finally had things in order. I hoped.

"The white van belonged to Manuel Sanchez," said Richard in a soft voice. "Elwood's security tapes from yesterday afternoon confirmed the license plate number. It's still missing."

"Well, that adds insult to injury," I said, "stealing the murdered man's van and trying to run me down with it."

Richard and I hovered in the doorway of the Palo Alto Culinary Arts Institute, about to enter. Close on eight AM, Mom, Gurn, and most of the suspects were already inside. My brother and I were taking a quick meeting for any updates I needed to hear before I joined everyone.

We were spotted, however, by Nancy Littlejohn, who stomped toward us with heavy-duty attitude. She took a possessive stance in the doorway, like she owned the building. "This is ridiculous, summoning us all here like this," she said. "Just who do you think you are?"

Hayes' assistant glared at me. I gave her a bright smile, forced from the core.

Here, once again, was a woman who positively glowed in the midst of chaos. While nearly everyone else was struggling to keep it together, including me, Nancy seemed luminous.

Still wearing chic, black clothing, the ends of her short, ebony hair had been dipped in a rainbow of bright colors. Blue, green, purple, red, orange, and yellow framed her face. Silver chains wrapped around her neck and dripped down her slim body. She almost made this Goth thing work.

She repeated herself. "I said, just who do you think you are?"

I resisted the urge to smack her, just as Hayes came up from behind and placed a tentative hand on her quivering-with-outrage arm.

"Nancy, please," he said. "Come and sit down."

She turned around and went back inside. I stepped over the threshold into the foyer. The room was chillier than usual, and I was glad I'd chosen to wear my red silk gabardine pantsuit. Hayes wore a cotton bomber jacket zipped up to his neck.

By contrast to his assistant, the owner of the Institute looked like death warmed over. Purplish bags under his eyes contrasted his ghostly pallor, making the color of his hair stand out all the redder.

I looked beyond the mismatched couple, at those already assembled around the eating tables of the Institute's kitchens. Wally and Jolene sat side by side, she biting her fingernails, he playing with his smartphone.

Wally wore a yellow shirt with a green tie under a lightweight jacket. Khaki slacks completed his preppy look. If Jolene had spent only one day at an AA meeting, it did wonders for her, although the sad look was still in place.

The puffiness I'd seen at the bar was gone, replaced by soft but well-defined features. Dressed again in stark white, a V-necked, long- sleeved sweater dress emphasized her curves. Platinum hair gleamed under a shaft of light coming in from the morning sun.

Pete sat at a separate table, studiously reading content from his phone. He wore a faded maroon T-shirt and jeans. He, too, covered the shirt with a lightweight jacket. Such are mornings in the Bay Area, even sunny ones. Some say bracing, others say cold.

At the end of the table, Chef Dexter was also dressed in jeans. He wore a long-sleeved T-shirt, black emblazoned with the Sharks logo in teal and white. He sat across from Brit, a vision in a lavender slack suit and matching blouse. She was paging through a magazine, every now and then glancing at the man who sat across from her.

Chef Dexter rarely made eye contact with the woman, but stared down at his clasping and unclasping hands. Elbows rested on the table then not. Resting then not. Trapped, hot energy radiated from him. He was the only one in the room who looked warm.

Connie sat alone in the corner of the room, staring at a small painting on the wall. Enveloped in an oversized, grey sweat suit she wrapped her arms around her in a comforting manner. Her dark hair was back to being drab, uncombed, and in disarray. The brown, fluffy slippers had made a reappearance on her small feet. But there was something else about her. She seemed aware of her surroundings, but not engaged.

Two people had yet to arrive, both unexpected to everyone save the police and the Alvarez clan, including Gurn. Henry Encino had promised to be there any minute. Frank had texted me he and Patsy Durand would be arriving soon from County jail.

My gaze followed Nancy and Hayes as they made their way to the tables. Ignoring his wife, Hayes sat next to his assistant, drew in a deep breath and closed his eyes, as if he wanted to be any place but here. I was with him. Bermuda sounded good to me.

Tío was in one of the kitchens whipping up omelets, so silently you could hardly tell he was there. But there were the sounds and smells of frying butter and eggs.

The hour was early and most people hadn't eaten yet. I would have preferred he wasn't cooking for this motley crew, but that's Tío. He's a big believer that food, like music, has charms to soothe a savage breast or, as some would say, a savage beast. For the record, it's 'breast' but either way, making breakfast kept Tío busy. That was my goal.

Leaning in the arch of the pantry with arms crossed over his chest, Gurn looked relaxed but kept this party under a watchful eye. If ever I wanted to be married to an ex-Navy SEAL who knew how to defend life and limb, this was the time. Just a feeling.

The door to the Institute opened. Almost as one, we turned in the direction to see who was standing in the doorway. A uniformed officer checked his list and allowed Henry Encino to enter.

Surprised, Connie rose and ran to greet him. It was the most animated I'd seen her. They hugged tightly and murmured something to one another, unheard by the rest of us. Eyebrows rose everywhere. Hayes opened his mouth to speak, but decided against it. He lapsed into silence once more.

Another officer came to Connie and Henry, ushering them back to where Connie had been sitting. He drew a chair over for Henry to sit in. Henry glanced in my direction, his gaze settling on me. He gave me a curt but not unfriendly nod. I returned it.

An ominous silence descended. No one spoke, not even Nancy. But her disdain and displeasure at having to be there was apparent. She fiddled with several silver rings on her fingers, giving furtive glances to the Institute's door.

She couldn't know we were waiting for Patsy, but I could tell she sensed something big about to happen. The door sprung open again. In marched Frank with an uncuffed Patsy, dressed again in her royal blue jeans and shirt. Two policemen stood nearby.

Upon seeing Patsy, the two boys leapt up and ran to her. Frank backed up, giving them more space.

"Mama," said Pete, rushing to hug Patsy. "What are you doing here?"

"Are you all right, Mama?" Wally came to the woman's other side.

There was a moment of hubbub, everyone focusing on the formerly incarcerated mother being greeted by her sons. Patsy reached out arms like a mother hen spreading feathered wings over her chicks. She pulled her sons in tight.

"I'm fine, just fine, boys. Let's not make a fuss."

Lila and Richard joined Frank off to the side, standing quiet and in alliance. I wondered if Mom had her gun with her. I'd decided not to bring mine. Hopefully, it wasn't the wrong decision. We'd find out.

Hayes rose, came halfway across the room, and reached out a helpless hand. Dropping it to his side, he asked, "Really, Patsy? Are you all right? I'm so glad to see you. Are you sure you're all right?"

She murmured something indicating yes then looked past him into the kitchen area at Tío. Her eyes glistening, she nodded an acknowledgment to my uncle. He smiled back as he came around the counter carrying two plates of steaming food. He set one in front of Jolene.

"You eat this, Señora *Durand*. It is good for you."

She smiled up at him. "Call me Jolene, please."

"And you will call me Tío. ¿*Si?*

"*Si*," she said laughing. She picked up a knife and fork from the center of the table and began to eat.

He set the other plate in the empty spot next to Jolene.

"Come sit down, Patsy," Tío said, his rich voice filling the room. "I make the omelets for you and everybody else. For you the mushroom, just as you like it. Come eat while it is hot."

Sniffling back raw emotion, Patsy broke free from her sons, wiped her eyes, and gave Tío a trembling smile. "I'll be right there, honey lamb. I've been missing your cooking like crazy the past few days."

Trailed by her sons, she crossed the room to the table and sat down. Tío returned to the kitchen and brought out two more plates for the boys.

"It's freezing in here," said Patsy in a surprised tone, rubbing her arms to warm them. She looked directly at Hayes as she said it.

"I'm sorry," said Hayes. "The room is cold from the furnace accidentally being shut off all night. I put it back on a few minutes ago. The room should warm up soon." He returned to his own chair without saying more, but kept a steady gaze on Patsy.

Both boys sat and drew in their chairs around their mother in a protective manner. Tío set two steaming plates on the table in front of the boys.

"I don't know how much food I can eat, Mr. Tío," Wally said to my uncle.

"It is just Tío," my uncle said with a smile.

"I don't know about me, either," said Pete, agitation ringing in his voice. "I don't think I could eat a thing."

"You will try," said Tío. He turned to the rest of the group. "I make for all of you, as well, in the next few minutes."

He rested a quick hand on Patsy's shoulder. Patsy reached up and gave his fingers a quick stroke with her own. She watched him return to the kitchen to make more omelets.

"Well, I'm so hungry I could eat a horse," Patsy said, picking up her knife and fork. "Boys, eat your breakfast. We're all here for a reason. I'm sure Lee knows what she's doing."

She looked at me and paused. All eyes turned to me, waiting for what was next. Patsy went on.

"So just what *are* we all doing here, hon?"

I blinked.

Just what, indeed? I mean, Hercule Poirot, indeed. But I couldn't think of any other way to flush out a killer. The game was afoot. Wait a minute. That's Sherlock Holmes. Oh, gawd. I am so screwed.

Chapter Forty-two

Of Rice and Men

"Thank you all for coming," I said in my best debate team voice.

"As if we had any choice," Nancy grumbled. She gave a quick glance to Frank Thompson, chief of the Palo Alto police, and moved restlessly in her chair. Hayes shushed her absentmindedly, coming out of some sort of reverie, if only for the split second.

"Yeah, I swan," said Pete to me, now picking up Nancy's attitude. "This sucks." He did a quick turnaround, not just physically but in temperament. "But at least I get to see you, Mama." He leaned toward her and took her hand in his.

Patsy gave her younger son a quick smile and looked away, pulling her hand free in a gentle but firm action. She began to eat again.

"Now that we're all here," I said, "let me start by introducing myself. My name is Lee Alvarez and I am a private investigator."

"Big deal," said Nancy. "I bet you don't even have a license."

"Actually, I do," I replied in an easy tone, squelching the urge to smack her.

"I work for Discretionary Inquiries, Inc., an investigative service that normally deals with cyber and intellectual property thefts. But through a set of circumstances, we have been looking into the murders of Chef Jacques and Manuel Sanchez. We're working in cooperation with the Palo Alto Police Department. I, myself, have been undercover here for the past few days –"

"You're the pearl diver," Chef Dexter interrupted, pointing a finger at me in an aha sort of way. "I recognize your voice. You clean up good."

"No way," exclaimed Brit, staring at me wide-eyed.

"Way," I said. "But back to –"

"Now you know what you're going to look like in twenty years," Brit said, with a laugh.

"Well, let's hope not," I said.

"If there's any justice," Nancy said, her voice covering mine.

"Thank you all for sharing your comments," I said loudly. "But if I may have the floor, please."

I looked around me. All were silent, giving me their full attention.

"We're here this morning because of secrets. It's time to bring them out in the open."

Everyone glanced around, uncomfortable with the idea. I went on.

"Let's begin with the first."

I crossed to a table where my briefcase sat. I pulled out Chef Dexter's logbook. He sat bolt upright in his chair.

"Hey! Where did you get that? I've been looking all over for that. You have no right."

"Chef Dexter, your logbook was an interesting read," I said, going and standing in front of him.

"Give that back to me." Leaning across the table, he made a grab for the book. I backed up. Frank stepped forward. The chef looked his way then after a moment, sat back down. I went on.

"It will be returned to you shortly, but first I want to ask you why you were keeping it."

He looked at me then Chef Hayes. His bland face developed a sneer. "The job of head-teaching chef should have been mine."

"Now, Dexter, I told you –" Hayes said, in a reasonable tone.

"You told me," mocked Chef Dexter. "You told me nothing. Suddenly all the work I'd done around here meant nothing. You hired that charlatan, who wasn't even a good cook. That job should have been mine. And I was going to prove it."

Hayes looked like he'd been physically struck. "I know, I know."

He glanced at me. Then he looked at Connie, shame written all over his face.

"There were extenuating circumstances, Dexter. I had to do it. I'm sorry."

He hung his head and said no more. Nancy reached out and stroked the side of his face with her hand. Hayes didn't seem to notice.

"But you had a double reason, didn't you, Chef Dexter?" I turned back to the slender chef. "Putting the job aside, Chef Jacques was hitting on Brit."

"He hit on every woman in the place," said Chef Dexter. His tone became guarded.

"He never got anywhere with me," said Brit. She threw down her magazine in disgust. "I told you that the other day."

"No, he didn't. But you did fear him. Maybe one of these days you might have given in. Especially, as he had something on you."

I turned at Chef Dexter again. "That must have rankled you, him taking your job and then trying to take the woman you loved."

"What are you talking about?" Nancy's tone was demanding and queen-like. "The staff never has personal relationships with the students. It is forbidden. A chef," she added pointedly, "could be fired for such a thing. And the student dismissed."

"Probably that's why they both kept it secret." I glanced back to Chef Dexter and Brit. "But even if you might be fired or dismissed from a school, you can't always tell the heart what to do. Right, Brit?"

She gave me a fleeting smile. "It's even worse. We've been secretly married since February."

"Brit! Don't say anything more. Please." Chef Dexter's voice had a pleading tone to it.

"Cool it, Dex," Brit said. "It's out. They know. Besides, what's the difference now? The school is probably closing. You'll be out of a job, anyway." She turned back to me. "But how did you find out?"

"You slipped up and called him Dex on the first day we met. And every time you talked about him, your tone sounded more intimate than just teacher and student. That made me delve into your lives a little further. A Reno marriage is a matter of public record. I'm suspecting you were both together the night Chef Jacques was murdered, but couldn't say so."

The couple stole a glance to one another then turned back to me with a nod.

"A belated congratulations to both of you." I came and stood in front of Chef Dexter. "Here's your logbook."

I set it on the table and reached inside my pocket for three half pencils. I set those in front of him, too.

"These are yours, as well. If I were you, I'd keep a closer watch on them. I keep finding them at murder scenes."

He sucked in a quick breath. I winked at him.

"You're next, Nancy Littlejohn," I said, turning abruptly. "Let's get to you."

"You know what, lady? Up yours." Nancy leapt out of her chair. "I don't have to sit here and listen –"

"Yes, you do," said Frank, stepping forward. "Unless you want to be arrested for obstruction of justice." Frank came and stood in front of her, his six-foot frame towering over her shorter one. "So sit down, Ms. Littlejohn. You'll leave when I say you can."

Reluctantly, Nancy sat down, crossing her legs and folding her arms across her chest in a belligerent manner. "Police brutality," she muttered. I looked down at her.

"Along the lines of hidden romances, how long has your affair with your boss been going on, Nancy?"

She uncrossed her legs and sat upright. Hayes appeared not to have heard me. After a fleeting glance in his direction, Nancy turned to me.

"I don't have to tell you anything," she said.

"You started seeing each other about six months ago, right?"

"So what?" She fairly spat her words. "You think a man like Hayes could be satisfied with a mouse like her?"

"Nancy! Stop this." Hayes came to life, resuming some of his lord of the manor attitude. "You have no right to insult my wife that way. Watch your manners and your mouth."

Nancy looked at Hayes in amazement. "Why you pompous ass," she shouted.

"Okay, easy, the both of you," I said. "Let's take it down a notch or two. This is only the beginning."

They stopped glaring at one another and turned hard stares on me. I crossed the room and stood in front of Patsy and her two sons. Pete reached for his mother's hand again. Wally put a protective arm around her shoulder. Their mother shook them both off.

"Boys, I'm fine," Patsy said. "What's on your mind, Lee?"

"First off, how did your fingerprints get on the freezer downstairs?"

"Oh, that. It's like I told Frankie over there." She looked across the room at Frank who gave her a passive, business-like nod.

"I was down there looking to see if it was a good place to keep the catfish I had flown up from Mississippi for one of my classes. None of the other chefs wanted me to keep them in the regular freezer because of the stink, they said. But I didn't like the idea of traipsing up and down from the kitchens to the basement. So I bought a half dozen cheap Styrofoam coolers, used them, and threw them away after. I showed Frankie the receipts, too."

"How did you know about the freezers downstairs?"

"I don't know," Patsy said, her tone becoming vague. "Someone suggested I look downstairs at that freezer as an alternative."

"Who was that?" My question was sharp, followed by another one. "Who suggested it?"

She shook her head. "I don't know, sugar. It could have been anyone. Maybe Nancy Girl?" She turned and looked at Nancy Littlejohn.

"It wasn't me, bitch." Nancy gave a good imitation of a snarling dog.

"Hey, watch your language," said Pete. "That's my mama you're talking to."

"That's all right, Petey," said Patsy. "Consider the source, I always say."

"So Patsy went downstairs shortly after to check the freezer out." I raised my voice so it echoed throughout the room. "But I doubt if it was Nancy who suggested that. When I asked her if they stored anything in the freezers in the basement, she was pretty definitive about the answer being no."

"That's right. It wasn't me." Nancy snarled again. Someone throw her a chew toy.

I turned back to Patsy. "When did all this take place?"

"About two weeks ago. I haven't been in the storage room since."

"And everyone knew you went downstairs to look at that particular freezer?"

"Just about everybody. It wasn't a secret, sugar."

"Good 'nuff. So on to your secrets, Patsy. At first, you told me your sons arrived in the Bay Area the morning you were arrested for murder. And that turned out not true, didn't it?"

Quick, guilty looks transpired between the three. The boys turned away, Patsy faced me squarely.

"I told you all of that yesterday," she said. "Why they were here the day before."

"Not quite all of it. I know the part about Jolene's sister, Rhonda, and the baby. And important though it may be, I'm talking about a bigger subject. The one that had been bothering you and your sons for months."

Patsy stared. "I'd rather not say."

I smiled. "I'm afraid I must insist."

Patsy continued to stare me down, finally saying, "It's a family matter, having nothing to do with this." Her tone was firm and unyielding.

"On the contrary, Patsy. It has everything to do with this," I said.

"Mama, you don't have to say anything more," Wally said, turning on me. "This is really none of your business, Lee."

"Like I said then, Mama," said Pete. "And I'm saying it now. I'm sure it's nothing more than Uncle Quinn's death."

"Hush, Petey." Patsy's voice was firm. She turned back to me again. "You're airing our dirty laundry in public, Lee," said Patsy. She smiled at me, but it looked like it was carved out of stone. "I don't hold with that."

"I'm sorry, Patsy. I genuinely am. But this is a double homicide – actually, triple - so personal feelings don't matter right now. It didn't have anything to do with Chef Jacques Chalifour, did it?"

Patsy hesitated and looked from one son to the other, almost seeking permission. Wally offered a small shrug and looked away. Pete nodded.

"No, it didn't," she said. She paused before plunging in. "It was Hayes, himself. The boys and I wanted to meet face to face to discuss the changes in their father. They had been telling me for months something was wrong. Once I saw for myself, I called them and they flew here in secret. It was a discussion better done between the three of us in person. Not over the phone. We didn't want Hayes to know."

"What changes? Specifically?"

Again Patsy hesitated. Wally picked up the slack.

"Ever since the time he watched his brother die in the fire, Daddy's been different. I can't explain it. Small things."

"Like all of a sudden he eats pastrami," said Pete. "He hated processed meats before."

"You boys have an overactive imagination," shouted Hayes from across the room. "I've got a lot going on. A wife who doesn't take her meds, a failing business, and, yes, my brother died six months ago. I don't know what you all want from me! I can't pretend to be the same person I was back then."

I went and stood in front of Hayes. He gathered himself together, closed his eyes, and leaned back. In a calm and contrite voice he said, "I apologize for the outburst."

"I understand," I said.

Hayes didn't open his eyes, but nodded. I studied him for a moment then turned away.

"There is someone else in the room that most of you do not know. At least, judging by the expressions on your faces when he came in."

I walked to the corner of the room where Connie and Henry, huddled together. "And that would be Henry Encino aka Henry Enright."

"That was Connie's last name before she married Hayes." Patsy's voice rang out in the large room. "Are you her younger brother?" She leaned forward, scrutinizing Connie.

"No," I said, before Henry could answer. "Not her brother. Henry is her son."

After a few exclamations of surprise, Patsy took back the floor, her tone taut and demanding.

"I never knew you had a son, Connie." She turned to Hayes. "Did you that know, Hayes?"

His eyes wide, he shook his head, a shocked look covering his face.

Patsy turned and looked at Connie, indignation spilling over. "Why didn't you tell somebody?"

Connie looked at Henry and he at her. Both seemed reluctant to speak.

I jumped in. "Let me explain. According to hospital records in Baton Rouge, Connie gave birth to a baby when she was barely in her teens."

"Thirteen," said Henry, finally speaking up. "She was thirteen. Hardly more than a baby, herself."

I studied mother and child, who were not looking at one another but clasping each other's hand so tightly their knuckles were white. Connie began to sob quietly. I took over again.

"And as with a lot of families who have an unexpected arrival, the family kept the baby, but the grandmother became the mother and the mother was passed off as the older sister."

"I only found out about it a short time ago," said Henry, brushing at his eyes. "My 'mother' made a deathbed confession. Told me she was actually my grandmother." Henry looked at me. "That's when I knew I had to find Connie again."

"Let me make an educated guess," I said. "You lost touch with one another as brother and sister, probably due to the differences in your ages. That can happen."

I turned to Henry.

"You were at home, still in grade school. Connie was off at MIT getting her degree. She got an offer from Stanford, met Hayes, married him, and began a new life out on the west coast."

"I was trying to put the past behind me." She smiled at Henry. "I didn't deserve to have the love of my son. I was unworthy," she whispered.

"That's ridiculous, Connie," said Henry. "You deserve to be happy."

"Well said, Henry." I stood before him. "Meanwhile, you grew up, went to music school, and joined a symphony orchestra on the east coast. Long and short of it, you'd drifted apart."

He looked up at me with tears in his eyes. Connie began to shiver. My voice became gentle.

"But then you found out she was really your mother. That made everything different. That's why you took the job at the San Mateo Symphony Orchestra. You wanted to get to know Connie, not as your sister, but as your mother. When was that?"

"I arrived in the Bay Area sometime in January. We weren't trying to deceive anyone," said Henry, with a defiant edge to his voice. "We weren't. But after I came I found out things were complicated. Connie and I decided to keep our relationship a secret for a while, until they got sorted out."

"This doesn't make sense," said Nancy. "Why be ashamed of it?"

"We're not ashamed of it." Henry's voice was indignant and angry. "How dare you say that?"

"Henry, please. It doesn't matter." Connie squeezed his hand, but addressed herself to me. "It isn't that we were ashamed. It's just that he came back into my life so suddenly...and...I'd been having some problems..." Her voice, starting out strong, tapered off.

"I was the one who suggested keeping a low profile," Henry said to me. "For various reasons," he added.

"What reasons?" My voice was sharp and echoed in the large room.

He didn't reply, but shook his head.

I persisted. "You were mother and son. I agree with Nancy. Why not let the world know? Who or what were you hiding from, Henry?"

"We weren't hiding," He protested, spirit rising within him.

I pushed. "Then why the phony name? Why did you change your name from Enright to Encino?"

"When Connie told me what was going on, she was really scared. And I didn't want to put anybody on their guard. So I borrowed the name from a friend of mine at school, who was also a Henry. I sat behind him the entire time in school; Henry Encino and Henry Enright, but he goes by Hank. We were the same age and look kind of the same, too. Hank said it was all right if I borrowed his name for a while."

"Hank's the one with a wife of five years," I said. "And a son."

"Good God. I forgot about that. But I didn't think anyone would check up on me."

"You even kept the secret from Evangeline Packersmythe, didn't you?"

"I told Evie yesterday, I swear. At lunch. I knew she'd understand. I was doing this for my mother, for God's sake. It wasn't supposed to be this way, but when I saw what was going on here –"

"You keep saying that, Henry," I said. "What exactly was going on?"

He broke off and took a deep breath. "Like I told Evie, Connie has always had mental and emotional problems, intellectually gifted as she may be. I wanted her to go to the police, but given her background, she felt she couldn't. So I was trying to help her gather evidence." He stared at Hayes then turned away.

"And in order to do that," I continued, "you'd visit her in secret. You'd come in the back entrance and go directly to the apartment during the day while everyone was downstairs working. Sometimes you'd meet at the local library, but always in secret."

Henry nodded, but said no more. I turned to look at Hayes.

"And you never knew. Now, why is it you never saw them together, Hayes? Or even suspected something? I mean, that's pretty oblivious."

"I guess I've been preoccupied with my business, as well as my brother's death. I haven't been paying the attention to my wife as I should have." He looked at her. "I'm sorry, Connie. My apologies for my behavior."

Wordless, Connie turned away and leaned into her son, who wrapped a protective arm around her shoulders.

"Or," I said, "maybe one of the reasons you didn't know is because you've been spending a lot of your spare time elsewhere as of late." I gave a nod in Nancy's direction. "Something new and different for you. Your times with your wife have been geared to what suits your purpose."

"What do you mean by that?" Hayes demanded.

I didn't answer him but turned back to Connie and Henry. "You ever see a movie called *Gaslight*? It's an oldie goldie, with Ingrid Bergman and Charles Boyer."

Confused, Henry shook his head and looked around him. Others shook their heads.

"I saw that on TV," piped up Jolene. "In the middle of the night. It's about a woman being driven crazy by her husband."

"A gold star for Jolene," I said, "It's a wonderful black and white movie from the forties based on a play, *Angel Street*. Made around 1944. It's about a man who is driving his wife crazy for purposes only known to him. Until the end of the movie, that is."

For the first time Connie glanced at me with a sharpness I hadn't seen in her before. Henry looked up at me, too, eyes narrowing with understanding.

"Isn't that what both of you decided Connie's husband was trying to do to her? Trying to drive her crazy? Using her illness against her? After all, you come from a very rich family. There's a lot of money at stake. With her out of the way, Hayes would have millions at his disposal."

I looked across the room to Hayes. Hayes lurched to his feet, knocking his chair over.

"What? I never. I never married Connie for her money. I love her. Nancy means nothing to me. This is crazy, this." He pointed an accusing but shaky finger at Henry from across the room. "If she told him that and he believed her, then they're both insane. The fruit doesn't fall very far from the tree. Mentally ill, the two of them. They both should be committed."

"No, we're not," Connie said, but in barely a whisper.

"That's exactly what she was afraid you'd say," shouted Henry. "You'd try to have her committed if she went to the police. But we found the locket and the truth will come out, Hayes."

Henry rose and stared back at him, both men in battle stance. An officer up righted Hayes' chair. He took Hayes by the shoulder and pressed him back into the seat.

"You sit down, too, Henry," I said, moving in front of him. "It's going to be okay. This will work out, I promise."

Henry searched my face for something and satisfied, sat down.

In silence I strode back to Hayes, who was breathing heavily with his eyes closed. Even though the room had warmed up considerably he still had his bomber jacket zipped up to his neck.

"Your turn, Hayes."

"I have nothing to say to anyone here. This is highly unorthodox, all of this. I have a good mind to call my –"

"Don't get het up, Hayes —" I interrupted him, but turned to Patsy. "It is called 'het up', Patsy, right? Same as riled up. Meaning annoyed or excited?"

She nodded dumbly to me.

"Good," I said. "It's time to get to the biggest secret of all, Hayes. Your brother, Quinn. He was a remarkable man, clever and smart. Some could say he was a Renaissance man, a man with great creative talents going in a lot of different directions. Others might call him a jack of all trades; master of none."

"That would be an unkind and unjust thing to say," Hayes muttered, still not opening his eyes.

"Maybe, maybe not," I said. "According to the information we could find on Quinn, he had a bachelor's degree in fine art. At one time or another he'd been a painter, an actor, singer, racecar driver, even a magician's assistant. He did all those things fairly well, but apparently not quite well enough to make a successful living at any of them."

"He lost interest, that's all."

Hayes' voice took on a protective edge. I went on as if he hadn't spoken.

"Unlike you, who seemed to have the golden touch in the epicurean world from the get-go."

Hayes opened his eyes. "He took care of our parents. I was here living my life and he returned home to take care of our parents."

"Yes, he did. But another take on it would be he returned home because he had nowhere else to go. He'd run up significant gambling debts in Vegas. It was time to lick his wounds, so to speak."

"I think that's an unkind assumption, Lee," Hayes said with some heat. "He was needed there. Our parents were failing. I couldn't be there, myself, so he went."

Shrugging, I crossed to my briefcase. I withdrew a sheet of paper from it and walked back to Hayes. I turned the paper around, a bank statement, and held it in front of him.

"And while there, he ran the pecan farm into seven hundred and fifty thousand dollars' worth of debt. That was after he spent the profits. The farm was about to be foreclosed due to his excessive spending. At least, that's what the bank says."

"I won't speak ill of my brother."

"And when the bank let you know what was going on, you flew to Georgia for a showdown with Quinn, didn't you? Try to sort this all out. I mean, here you were, a successful entrepreneur, running a successful culinary arts school. That and thanks to the proceeds from your first marriage, as well as your current marriage, you actually are quite solvent, despite what you said earlier."

He looked me dead in the eye. "I don't know where you're going with these innuendos but I resent this kangaroo court. I'll be contacting my lawyer to see about filing charges when we are finished here."

"Are these coming across as innuendos, sugar? I meant them as accusations," I said, in a dismissive manner. I leaned in on him, my voice hardening. "What was the real reason you returned home to Georgia?"

Hayes was silent. I regarded him for a moment and walked back to the table again, my devil-red heels making a high-pitched clicking sound on the tiles. I returned the bank statement to my briefcase and pivoted back to Hayes Durand. I could feel everyone in the room holding their breaths.

"I'm waiting for an answer."

"As I said before, I went home to help our parents out," he finally said, through gritted teeth.

"Actually, you went home to help yourself out. You saw your opportunity and you took it. Because when you and your brother were there at the same time, you started a fire in the barn. You deliberately killed your brother, in order to assume his far more successful life. Didn't you, Quinn? Because that's who you are. Not Hayes Durand, but Quinn Durand."

Chapter Forty-three

Farewell, My Lasagna

After a few well-placed gasps, the room sat in stunned silence. They looked from me to Hayes. Frank, a surprised look on his face, nonetheless, moved toward the man in anticipation of him trying to run away.

I, myself, expected Hayes to leap to his feet, do something. He didn't. His was a steady gaze, focused on my face. Then he burst out laughing. The sound echoed in the large room.

"You know, you're probably the biggest crazy in here, Lee." He pivoted, addressing everyone in one fell swoop. "This woman is nuts."

Gurn stepped into the room and came to my side.

"That may be so," I said, "but that doesn't change the fact that you are Quinn Durand, and that you murdered your brother, Hayes Durand, six months ago, and more recently Chef Jacques because he knew who you were. And then Manuel Sanchez, who either saw you kill him or knew more than he should have."

He shrugged and held up his hands. "Prove it. Prove I'm not Hayes Durand. Yes, I was fingerprinted in the army, but the barn fire destroyed my prints. And my brother, Quinn, was never fingerprinted. I know that for a fact. Our DNA was identical. You can't prove a thing." His tone was smug.

"Ah, but I can." I was just as smug. "All we have to do is wait."

"Wait? Wait for what?" He stuttered. I could see his mind trying to work this out.

"All of what you say is true, but there are certain anomalies that can take place within the womb, which can affect the babies. For instance, there is a case study of a twin girl whose umbilical cord was twisted, cutting off a certain amount of nourishment. Consequently, while her twin sister weighed in at seven and a half pounds at birth, she was around five. All her life she was thinner and smaller than her sister. There was no difficulty in telling them apart."

"So what?" He gave me a half smile. "My brother, Quinn, and I looked the same. We were identical."

"Not quite," I said. "Your natural hair color is dark brown. Hayes' was red. That's how everyone told you apart. Right before you killed your brother and started the fire in the barn, you dyed your hair red. You've continued to dye it ever since. All we have to do is wait to see what color it comes in when you don't have access to red hair dye."

Hayes/Quinn stared at me for a full five- seconds. Then in one quick movement, he grabbed Nancy by the arm and sprung from his chair, jerking her into a standing position.

From inside the pocket of his jacket he withdrew a handgun. Before any of us could do anything, Quinn wrapped one arm around Nancy in a stranglehold and drew her in front of him. With the other hand, he pressed the gun to her head.

"Gun," Frank said, in a loud, clipped tone.

At the sound of that one word, those trained in law enforcement, separated and went immediately into defense mode, just short of withdrawing their own guns. Even Lila.

"Nobody move," yelled Quinn. "My hands work a lot better than I pretend they do. Don't make me prove it by pulling the trigger. Stay right where you are or I'll kill her."

I just knew he was going to say that.

"And this is a semi-automatic gun," he said, for those not in the know.

Which wasn't me. I was close enough to see what it was. So were Gurn and Frank. Lethal with a capital "L." Quinn continued with this line of threats.

"I can take down five or six of you before you get me."

"Nobody's taking anybody down. Let's talk this through," said Frank, taking a few steps forward and becoming a negotiator.

"I said nobody move," screamed Quinn. "Or I swear to God I'll kill as many of you as I can."

Frank not only stopped coming forward, but backed up to his original position.

"Easy. Let's take this easy. Whatever you say, Quinn. Whatever you want," Frank said. "There's no reason for anyone to get hurt."

Nancy began to shake all over. Huge tears ran down her cheeks. I found myself feeling sorry for her. I couldn't stand her, but she didn't deserve this.

"Quinn," I said. "Let Nancy go. Take me instead. Nancy's no good to you. Look at her. She'll probably pass out or something. And she has an attitude problem."

Nancy came to life again. "How dare you," she directed at me.

"I'm a better choice," counter-offered Gurn. "I've got a plane. Take me and I'll fly you wherever you want to go. It's gassed up. We can leave right now."

"What? Shut up," said Quinn, confused by all his wannabe dance partners. "Just shut up. Everybody stay right where you are. I don't want to shoot anybody, but I will if you force me."

He took several steps backward pulling Nancy with him. Glancing now and then over his shoulder, he seemed to be backing up toward the loading dock and freedom, only a few yards away. When he neared the first kitchen, his gaze rested on me again. We locked eyes.

"Except for you, Lee Alvarez. You're the cause of all of this. If it hadn't been for you, I would have never been discovered."

The room went deathly quiet. Quinn turned the gun away from Nancy's head and pointed it at me. I heard the click as he released the safety, about to pull the trigger.

Everything happened at once. Gurn pushed me out of the way and threw himself in my place. I staggered sideways, but remained upright.

Simultaneously, a round, heavy black thing came out of the kitchen area. The 'thing' pushed Quinn's hand holding the gun toward the heavens. A terrifying report sounded as the gun went off midway between us and the ceiling.

The black thing came back into view again. It struck Quinn on the side of the head with a loud clunk. Hayes' brother did a small sidestep then crumpled to the floor.

Nancy let out a long, ear-piercing scream. Then she, too, crumpled to the floor. I knew it. The woman's a chronic fainter.

My uncle emerged from the shadows of the kitchen holding his favorite black cast-iron skillet in his right hand. He looked down at the two people lying on the black and white tiles.

"*Basta*," he said. "Enough."

"Wow, Tío," I said. "I sure didn't see that coming."

Chapter Forty-four

Fried and Prejudice

"I didn't think you'd come," Quinn said.

"I didn't think you'd ask me," I said.

It was four days later. I was back in Milpitas at the Santa Clara Correctional Facility, this time the medical facility of the men's division. An armed guard was stationed at the clinic's door.

Five empty beds, the sixth held Quinn Durand. I stood at the bottom of Quinn's and saw his right ankle was cuffed to a metal bedpost. Then I noticed his hands. Not nearly as inflamed looking as before, he held them in a natural position across his chest.

Despite the setting and his head being wrapped in a white bandage, Quinn Durand wore a smug, condescending look on his face. Between the headwrap and two black and blue eyes, he reminded me of a dime-store swami who'd gotten into a fist fight. But this was a remorseless killer of three people. For want of Tío's cast iron skillet, Gurn or I would have been the fourth.

"What do you want, Quinn?"

"You always get right to it, don't you Lee?" He gave me a warm and friendly smile. "Come in. Take a seat. Stay awhile."

"I have things to do. I repeat, what do you want?"

"You see, that's where you and I differ. I have all the time in the world. In here with nothing to do but lie back and think."

"There's only so many minutes visiting time, so if you have something to say, you'd better say it. By the way, where's Nancy? I understand she's here every visiting hour."

"Yes," he said, letting out a martyr's sigh. "What can I say? The woman's in love. And, just between the two of us, she is a lady who likes her drama. I have a way of providing that, I surely do."

He looked at me and laughed. I was silent, so he went on.

"In answer to your question, I'm only allowed one visitor at a time, so I asked Nancy to go away. She left a few moments ago. Now that she knows who I am and have no wife, she wants me to marry her. Can you imagine?"

"Not really."

"But I suppose I could do worse. Should I marry her? Give me your honest opinion. What do you think, Lee?"

"I think you're playing with me and if that's the case, I'm leaving. I have a lunch date."

The lunch date was with Mom and Patsy, their first such meeting alone together. Why they invited me, I don't know. I was either a buffer or a referee. Or maybe a court jester set before the queens. Whatever, I was more nervous about meeting the two of them than being where I was. Quinn's face sobered.

"Don't leave, please. I feel in the mood for a chit-chat." He reached out a beckoning hand. "And as I lie here, Lee, one of the things I want to do is apologize for trying to shoot you. It was very rude of me."

He looked at me and smiled then straightened the covers around him in a fastidious manner before going on.

"Also, I keep wondering how you found me out. I pride myself on being clever and thinking of every detail, large and small. I like a well-planned event. For instance, turning off the heat in the building the morning you called us together for your big denouement."

"So you could wear a jacket and hide a gun in it, in case I had you figured out."

"Small but important details. And larger ones." He displayed his hands, rapidly turning them front to back again and again. "See?"

"Your burns aren't nearly as bad as you pretended."

"No. I am a master of illusion. The magician's assistant wound up knowing more than the magician. Makeup and an artistic way of holding my hands, created the illusion they were much more useless than they actually were. I even fooled the doctors."

"And damaged hands solved a multitude of problems. Fingerprints, handwriting, and teaching the students how to cook."

"Doing this to myself was painful, but worth it. Putting the fingerprints and handwriting aside, I am lacking in some of the accomplishments of most chefs, even though I am, as you say, a renaissance man."

"I never thought that. More like a jack-of-all-trades."

He gave me a callous stare, the smile leaving his lips.

"And I never thought of you as anything more than a bothersome pest. Although I did try to eliminate you several times on general principles."

"The dry storage room and the parking lot."

"Yes. You seem to have nine lives, just like a cat."

"I take that as a compliment."

"So when did you find me out? What made you suspicious?" He looked around him. "And why don't you pull up a chair? Get more comfortable?"

"I'll stand, because the answer is simple."

"Suit yourself."

"You have no heart, Quinn, and from what I've heard, Hayes had one. So when everyone who knew and loved him talked about how differently he was behaving, I decided to pay attention. I came up short with any other explanation."

Ah!" he thought about it for a moment. "We were always different, Hayes and I, even as children. And not to sound maudlin, he was always everyone's favorite. Even our parents favored him. It was annoying."

"When did you decide to kill your brother?"

"The day he called me at our parents' and said he was flying to see me. The bank wrote him about the foreclosure and how the folks were losing the farm due to my mortgaging the place to the hilt.

"When he got there, the conversation was all about sending me to jail for forging our parents' names on checks. And how he had made a success of his life and why couldn't I? Of course, he was completely right. But why reinvent the wheel? Why not commandeer his successful life and abort mine? I'd thought about it many times before, even had come up with a plan. Now I had a chance to put that plan in action."

"So once he arrived, you dyed your hair red to match his, called him into the barn, killed him, set the barn ablaze with an accelerant, burned your hands, and took over his life. Just like that."

"Just like that. Always do the unexpected and do it grandly. No one would ever think I'd kill my own brother. And I was getting away with it until Jacques showed up."

"You knew him from Las Vegas, didn't you?"

"He was my big mistake. Never play poker when you're in your cups. It makes you talkative. I outlined my plan to him. One could say I bragged to Jacques over the card table a short time before I left to be my parents' caregiver. When Jacques read about the fire and how I had been "killed" in the same way, he thought it was too much of a coincidence. Once he came and saw me in person, he knew right away it was me."

"One soulless bastard meeting another."

"Why, Lee, how judgmental. But I couldn't let him even hint at the possibility of the switch. It would ruin everything."

"So you hired him because of the secret he had over you, not Connie."

"Correct. But given her history, it was the perfect answer now that my brother was dead. It also made me look like something of a gallant hero."

"You gave Jacques free run of the place. Why not? Posing as Hayes, you were going to close down the Institute, anyway. You didn't care if he destroyed its reputation in the interim by indulging in his sicknesses. In fact, I suspect you enjoyed it."

"I did. I truly did."

"What you were really after was Connie's money. Have her committed and it would all be yours."

"That dishrag was worth millions. Millions! Just there for the taking."

"But Jacques was spoiling your plans."

"He got greedy, no longer satisfied with his cushy job. He wanted half. Half of everything or he'd spill the beans. And he was becoming impatient."

"So you invited Patsy to be the guest chef this summer when the one scheduled became ill. You knew she would come to Hayes' aid. Then you'd kill Jacques, and put the blame on her."

"Two for one. I never liked that woman."

"You set everything up beforehand. Hid Connie's meds, gave her drugs, and messed with her head for weeks."

"Now that I look back, I realize I'd have broken Connie sooner if it wasn't for that miserable son of hers. I didn't count on him. If I'd paid more attention to her, I'd have noticed him hanging around. But there are only so many hours in a day. The Institute was very draining and I had to give Nancy some attention. After all, she was my very personal assistant."

"I'm sure she was taken in because for the first time, Hayes came on to her."

"It was so unlike my uptight brother. And she's surprisingly gullible. I even got her to copy Hayes' signature on checks and deposit them in the bank."

"In case you needed to shift the blame to her."

"Another woman ripe for the taking." He looked at me. "Present company excluded."

"After the scene Chef Jacques and Patsy had on Saturday, it was time to do away with him."

"Timing is everything." Quinn grinned.

"Sunday evening you forced sleeping pills down Connie's throat and called Patsy, who came running."

"And as usual, she took over, freeing me to take care of...other matters."

"Like going downstairs for a prearranged meeting with Jacques. You stabbed him with his own knife covered with Patsy's fingerprints, left the body where it was, took a quick shower, and changed into a pair of whites stored in the bathroom, just like I did the first day on the job. It only took ten or fifteen minutes, all in all."

"Well, aren't you a miss know-it-all."

"Not really. When both the pharmacist and the witness remarked you were dressed like an ice cream vendor, that started me thinking. It was Sunday. Your day off. You should have been in normal street clothes."

"An oversight on my part. But frankly, I didn't think anyone would catch that."

"To continue, you threw the bloody clothes into a black plastic bag probably to be disposed of off-site, drove to the pharmacy, and waited for the prescriptions to be readied. If someone questioned you about the missing few minutes, you could always say you were stuck in traffic. You created an alibi for yourself, but left Patsy without one."

"Ingenious, don't you think?"

"I could think of a few other words. I'm curious. Manuel Sanchez. What did he know that forced you to kill him?"

He shrugged. "Let's just say he saw something still useful and in play today. But not to worry, he was expendable. I had hoped you wouldn't find his body at all or, at least, not find it so quickly." He smiled at me. "Still, no hard feelings."

"Now that we've had our little chat, what's the real reason I'm here? Let's get to that."

Quinn pulled himself into a seated position. The ankle chain strained, going taut. Reaching behind him, he fluffed the pillow with care and leaned back on it before answering.

"Very well. In truth, I find myself short of cash. Hiring a good defense attorney is an expensive proposition."

"Excuse me?"

"And I thought the family, the boys, might be willing to help. I invited them to come, as well, to hear me out. But so far you're the only one with any manners."

"Are you friggin' kidding me?"

"You see, I have in my possession the very last journal their father wrote, the one he kept before he died. Ending, of course, last November when he passed."

"Where are you going with this?"

"So in a hurry! Very well. The last journal written by the dearly departed is most revealing. I never would have thought my brother capable of such thoughts and feelings."

He leaned forward conspiratorially.

"I think it was impending old age; his reflections on the past. The highlights are his innermost fears about Connie, a weak woman with little or no backbone, his all-consuming and continuing desire for Patsy, a world-renowned chef, and the sad disappointment in his sons' choices in life. There are a few other things I'd rather not mention, but might prove hurtful and embarrassing should they come out."

Here Quinn paused dramatically before going on. He tapped his head with a finger, as if he was thinking.

"I remember most of it by heart. But most importantly, it's all written down in nice, neat penmanship. The media loves things like that."

I finally saw where he was going with this and felt my blood pressure rise.

"You can't sell the journal, no matter what's in it. There's the Son of Sam Law, designed to keep lowlifes like you from profiting from their crimes."

"Why, you do me wrong, Lee. I wouldn't dream of selling it. But I might give it away or…" And here he paused. "Maybe I could be persuaded to return it to my nephews. For the right price."

"The fact that Wally and Pete haven't come to see you says they're not interested."

"They're not interested because they don't know what's in it. You know the saying, ignorance is bliss? Well, not in this case. I think the boys would be mighty upset if they saw what was in the journal, Lee, I truly do. This whole incident is very hot. Land sakes alive, I can see the headlines now; newspapers, the six o'clock news. Maybe even picked up by entertainment tell-all shows. Wherever scandal and dirt are truly appreciated."

"How do I know you're not bluffing?" I'd tried to keep the panic out of my voice, but missed by a mile.

"Do I sound like I'm bluffing? But rest assured, the journal is in a very safe place. For now. And I can get my hands on it at any time. Talk to the boys. See what it's worth to them."

"What number were you thinking of?"

"Two hundred and fifty thousand dollars. I hope that doesn't sound too greedy, but I need enough to hire a good attorney. And don't they want the complete collection? What good are any of the journals to Hayes' sons without the very last, most intimate, and possibly prophetic year? I ask you?"

Quinn didn't have to ask me. I had been bothered by the journal's absence ever since I'd discovered it missing from the cabinet in Hayes' office. It was one of my nagging niggles. A few days earlier, I'd even reinstituted another search for it. With Connie's permission, I'd spent a lot of time going through the Durand apartment while she packed to leave. *Nada*.

Of course, it wasn't there. The devil incarnate had it. And now he wanted to blackmail everyone with it.

I hate that.

"This interview is over." I spun around and left.

Chapter Forty-five

The Name Of The Roast

"Richard, did you put one of your gizmos on Nancy's car?"

It was a few minutes later and I was pulling out of the correctional facilities parking lot. This time no one tried to run me down. The day was looking up.

"If you mean a tracker, yes, your majesty," my brother replied. "Just as you requested, because this department has nothing better to do than bow to your every whim, even though the job is finished and –"

"Never mind all that," I interrupted. "Where is Nancy now?"

"Let's see."

There was a deep sigh then silence. Driving as fast as I dared on Highway 237 back to Palo Alto, I drummed my nails on the steering wheel in impatience. Finally, he came back to me.

"The car just turned onto the Oregon Expressway heading west."

"She left here about twenty, twenty-five minutes ago. I'll bet she's driving to the Institute. And on Quinn's orders. Thanks, Richard."

I disconnected before he could reply then hit one of my frequently called buttons. Gurn's place of business was about a half a mile from the Institute. He answered on the second ring.

"Hi, sweetheart. What's up?"

"Darling, I know it's still tax season, but can you drop everything and get to the Institute ASAP?"

"I suppose I can. Why?"

"I want you to stop Nancy Littlejohn from leaving the premises with anything larger than a toothpick. There shouldn't be anyone else there. Connie said she was moving out yesterday."

"I can do that. But what if she threatens to call the police?"

"Help her dial. I don't think she wants anyone to know what she's there for, Hayes' journal."

"On my way."

"I'll be there as soon as I can. Thanks, darling."

* * * *

Pulling into the Institute's parking lot, I saw three cars. I recognized Nancy's Saab, Gurn's Jeep Cherokee and the third looked like it could be Ms. Packersmythe's car, a steel-grey Honda Accord. Honda Accords, especially steel-grey in color, are prolific in the Bay Area.

If it was Ms. Packersmythe's car, what was she doing here? Everyone was supposed to be gone. This made me nervous. I didn't want any civilians involved, especially a pregnant woman.

I unlocked my glove compartment and pulled out my Beretta Tomcat. Sad to say, Lady Blue, my Detective Special, dropped into the briny depths of the Gulf of Mexico a while back. But that's another story.

When last at the Institute I had been outgunned; saved by Tío's frying pan. It wasn't going to happen again. Beretta in hand, I pushed the front door of the Institute open slowly and called out.

"Gurn?"

"In here, Lee." His reply, though echo-y and sounding far away, was quick and unguarded.

I lowered my weapon half way. "Everything all right?"

"Aces." That one word was our signal that everything was, indeed, all right.

I put the safety back on the Tomcat, returned it to its small holster in my pocket, and entered the foyer, talking all the time. "Who's the third car in the parking lot? Do you know?"

"Ms. Packersmythe's," Gurn said. "She arrived with Connie and her son right after I did; something about a missing teapot. They're upstairs and waiting for me to tell them when to come down. Being very cooperative. Unlike this one."

I crossed into the kitchens and eating area. Gurn was staring down at a seated but furious Nancy. She leapt up from the chair at seeing me. She commenced her snarling routine.

"You bitch! You'd better call off your goon and let me go. You have no right to hold me here against my will. I've a good mind to call the police."

"Goon?" Gurn looked at me with amusement. "I've never been called a goon before."

"You're free to call the police or leave whenever you like," I said, moving beside Gurn. "Although, when you go, you take absolutely nothing with you. You got that? You were terminated two days ago, with a very nice severance package. You cleaned out your desk at the time. There is nothing here for you. So I'll take the keys you used to get into the Institute and return them to their rightful owners."

I put out my hand. She was quiet, but her face showed she was doing some furious thinking. I looked at both her hands, drawn tensely to her side. One held a screwdriver.

"What's this?" I reached out and snatched it from her.

"Give that back to me," she said, making a grab for it, but I turned one way, as she went the other. Life is often about going in the right direction.

Gurn took a step between the two of us, facing the woman. "Play nice, Ms. Littlejohn. You didn't come in with that screwdriver. I know because I watched you enter the place. Ergo, it belongs to the Institute. You are not allowed to leave with anything that belongs to the Institute."

"I...I... Oh for heaven's sake. I don't have time for this." She looked at both of us. "Are you going to let me go or what?"

"Keys." I outstretched an empty hand. My other held on fast to the screwdriver.

With a sigh of exasperation, she removed a short lanyard wrapped around her wrist holding several dangling keys. Instead of handing them over, however, she threw them to the floor with a contemptuous snort.

"Ever the lady," I muttered.

Gurn looked at me. I nodded. He stepped aside and made a gentlemanly gesture to Nancy. I, too, made a gesture, but not so gentlemanly. We both watched her practically run to the front door, open it, and slam it behind her.

Gurn picked up the keys and looked at me. "Now what?"

"How long was she in the Institute before you came in?"

"Twenty seconds maybe. No more. I saw her going inside the building when I pulled the car in the lot. I parked and ran in."

"So she had just enough time to go to a drawer or the supply cabinet and grab the screwdriver."

"Right."

"Where was she when you came in and found her with the screwdriver?"

"Heading in the direction of the walk-in freezer." He crossed the room and stood in front of the massive appliance.

"Hmmm," I said. "Now what would you use a screwdriver for in a walk-in freezer?"

"Let's find out, shall we?" Gurn gave me a smile. He opened the freezer door and gestured for me to precede him. Southern manners at their finest.

Chapter Forty-six

Anatomy Of A Muffin

I stepped inside the ice cold freezer, square in shape and about the size of our master bedroom. All the frozen food Quinn had thrown away had been replaced. Icy mists wafted into the chilled air. I shivered.

Gurn bent down for a wooden doorstop on the floor. He reached up to the top hinge and jammed the triangular piece of wood between the hinge and the door itself.

"This should keep the door open a little more securely than using it on the floor. Hand over the screwdriver."

I did. Gurn looked around him while talking.

"So why did Quinn take all the frozen food out of here just to toss it away? You seem to know the man's mind."

"I probably should be insulted by that statement, but I suspect it was a diversionary tactic. Throw people off by making them look in any direction but the right one. Plus it was a great way to lower morale among the students and staff."

"It certainly did that," Gurn muttered. "Now where to start? Man, it's cold in here, even with the door open. What's here to unscrew?"

"Let's start with the walls."

Gurn nodded. He went to one side, I went to the other. Scanning the walls, we wound up at the rear of the freezer. I reached out to touch the icy metal.

"Look at these panels. Valves and dials. And the panels are screwed on."

Gurn came to my side and studied six rectangular panels, about two feet high and three feet wide each. "Those are control panels. In the event something breaks you have to be able to get behind them."

"I wonder if you could hide something in there?"

"I don't see why not," Gurn said, leaning in for a better look. "But let's find a panel with screws that look like they've been used recently." He dropped down on his knees and touched the lowest panel. "Like this one."

I squatted down beside Gurn, sorry I didn't have a sweater or jacket. Shaking from the cold, I watched his fingers twirl the screwdriver. Then my gaze traveled up his arm and to a face, intent and concentrating on the task. Maturity took hold of me.

His was a handsome face, with a square jawline, green-grey eyes, and chiseled nose. But it was also a face that showed the character of the man inside. A faint scar here and there revealed a touch of the pain he'd endured serving a country to which he'd more than once offered his life.

Gurn wasn't much like my father in small ways. But in larger ways he was. Both were men of honor. Both always strove to do the right thing, even if the right thing wasn't the easier choice. I took a shallow breath. Gurn would make a wonderful father. Words tumbled out of me.

"Darling, do you want to have children?"

He stopped what he was doing and stared at me.

"Now? Besides being a little busy, I'm freezing. Here, hold these screws I've pulled out."

I took them from his open palm but went on. "I'm serious. We've never talked about it. I just...I want to know where you stand on it."

He turned his focus back to the panel, and moved on to the next screw. "What brought this up?"

"Oh, I guess I've got babies on the brain. Everybody seems to be having one lately."

"Where do you stand on it, sweetheart?"

"I'm not sure. We just got married. I still feel like a bride. But we're both in our mid-thirties. Time may be running out. And if it's something you want, we should discuss it. I see how you act around little Steffi and –"

"Well, she's adorable and I've never been an uncle before. Besides, I see how you act around her. She's already got you wrapped around her little pinky. Who doesn't love a sweet, innocent baby? It would be inhuman."

He continued manipulating the screwdriver, absorbed in his job. Suddenly he turned and looked at me. "You want the truth?"

"Of course."

"I kind of thought we'd adopt someday, maybe take in one or two kids who need a chance at life. There are so many needy children out there, just begging to be loved. Of course, we might have our own, too. I'm open to all of it. Or none of it. But whatever we decide to do, I don't think the timing is here yet. If you disagree or think there's more to say on the subject, let's talk after dinner."

"No, I think we've said it. Let's table the discussion for some time in the future. We'll know when that is."

"You're sure?"

"I'm sure."

"Because we're in this together, Lee. You and me."

"For now and for always." I let out a frosty breath. "It's like I said, darling. I don't know what I want to do. And when you don't know what to do, do nothing. But I thought I'd get some feedback from you."

"Well, I'm good."

"That makes two of us. Meanwhile, I'll continue being a Big Sister. Those underprivileged girls are worth my time and effort."

"That's why I work with the Naval Reservists. It gives me a chance to help young men and women get a leg up on life, find themselves, begin to live up to their potential. So for right now, unless you're driven…"

"I'm only driven in my love for you."

I winked at him. He laughed.

"I love you, too. More than you can even imagine."

He kissed me lightly. His lips were cold.

"And now we've gotten this out of the way, can we get back to the job? I'm turning into a snowman. Here, take these last screws."

He dropped the last two screws in my cold, quivering hand and set the screwdriver on the floor.

He gripped both sides of the panel and gave it a tug. The panel lifted off to reveal pipes enclosed in insulation. An insulated wall sat further back at about a six- inches.

"Well, lookee here," Gurn said, reaching inside. He picked up a black nine by twelve book wrapped in clear plastic propped up against a pipe. He handed it to me.

I unwrapped it and looked at the spine. "The missing journal! This is probably what got Manuel killed. He must have seen Quinn hiding it. Is there anything else in there?" I glanced inside the wall. "What's that bag?"

Gurn reached in and pulled out a small, crumpled brown paper bag. He opened it. "It's jewelry. Not a lot of it, but what's there is choice."

He pulled out three gold rings set with precious stones and one diamond tennis bracelet.

"Is that it?"

Gurn ran a quick hand inside the wall. "That's it."

"Then let's get out of here. I have to meet Mom and Patsy for dinner, which is actually lunch, but that's what southerners call it. And, I'm freezing." I stood.

"I need to reattach this panel, sweetheart."

"Maybe we should open the rest of the panels just to make sure there's nothing else."

"Good idea. For all we know, this might be Quinn's private vault."

"Why don't you leave it for now until you get a sweater?"

"You don't need to ask me twice," he said standing.

Shivering, we moved to the exit.

"It's colder than a witch's nose in here," Gurn said, "as my mother would say."

"I've heard that expression, only using another part of the anatomy, darling."

We both laughed, while Gurn used the screwdriver to pry loose the wedge of wood from the freezer door. The door closed on silent hinges behind us. We both rubbed our arms and stamped our feet to warm up a little. Gurn turned to me.

"What are you going to do with the journal?"

"Same thing as with the jewelry, give it to Hayes' wife. According to his will, the Institute and business goes to the children, but everything else goes to her. That would include his journals."

"Do you think you should hand it over to Frank first?"

"Quinn confessed to everything. Frank calls it an open and shut case. I don't think this book will help anything. All it can possibly do is further hurt the Durand family."

Gurn deliberated for a moment. "I agree."

"Now that that's settled, why don't you call Evangeline Packersmythe and get those people down here? I've only got about twenty minutes before Mom will be burning the wires to find out why I'm not sideling up to the slop pen with her and Patsy."

"Sweetheart, you might want to rethink your creative interpretations of southern expressions. They're sending your mother's blood pressure through the stratosphere."

"They are? Hmmm." I mused. "That's too bad, because I just love them."

"Fight the urge," Gurn said, reaching for his phone. He glanced at the journal in my hand.

"What do you think is in there that's worth a quarter of a million dollars?"

"I have no idea. And I never thought I'd say this, but maybe some secrets are best left hidden."

Chapter Forty-seven

The Watercress File

Connie Durand held the three rings we'd found in the paper bag in the palm of her hand. Her face was unreadable.

"These were my mother's."

She turned to Henry standing beside her. She gave him a smile.

"Your grandmother. Here," she said, pushing them on him. "I want you to have them."

"Mother, those look very valuable. I can't. I –" Henry's protestation was strong, but Connie's will was stronger.

"Of course, you can. If the baby's a girl, pass them on to her. Or if you have a son..." Connie paused and gave Ms. Packersmythe a loving look. "Give them to him for his future wife. But whatever you decide to do, they belong to you now."

Without waiting for a reply Connie turned away and pulled the diamond tennis bracelet from the bag.

"This was a very extravagant gift from Hayes when we were first married." She looked up at me then turned to Ms. Packersmythe. "I never thought it was quite me." Connie thrust it into the other woman's hand. "Please take this, Evangeline, with my blessing. And don't say no. I will be offended."

"Why, thank you, Connie. It's lovely." Ms. Packersmythe's face showed surprise and pleasure.

The change in Connie was astounding. She no longer looked like a lost, frightened bird, too frail to stand on her own two feet. Her face was filled with color. A sense of vibrancy exuded from her. Just then her smile disappeared and she seemed to vanish into the recent past.

"Everyday something precious like this would go missing. And Hayes – Quinn – always pointed an accusing finger at me; I'd mislaid it, or thrown it away, or given it away and couldn't remember."

She touched the gold locket around her neck with her son's baby hair inside. "It was when this disappeared I knew it wasn't me. This was the one thing I knew for certain I hadn't misplaced or lost. I went looking for it. I found it in one of his bureau drawers, hidden in the back. When I confronted him, he said I'd put it there myself. I knew I hadn't. I knew. But in the past I was often so confused."

"He took away your meds, Mother," said Henry. "And your doctor found large traces of Rohybinal in your bloodstream." He looked at Gurn and me. "It's a drug, inducing paranoia and confusion."

"It had to be in the hot tea he gave me," Connie said. "Just like you said, Henry. I started throwing it away when he wasn't looking and my mind began to clear."

"That horrible man made you doubt your sanity, Connie," said Ms. Packersmythe.

"I know, Evangeline," said Connie, "but I should have fought back. I have to learn to be more independent, stronger. And I need to get back to work, back to my research. I'm going to fight for my job and tenure."

"We never thought he wasn't Hayes, not once," Henry said, taking over the conversation. "Mother kept telling me how different he was, but I blew it off." He shook his head, almost with shame. "All I could think about was how to stop him intimidating and scaring her half to death." He turned and looked at Connie. "I should have listened to you."

"It's not your fault, any more than mine. You and I finding each other is the only good thing to come out of this horrible nightmare."

"Now that we know Connie's a widow," Ms. Packersmythe said, stepping into the scene and throwing a massive arm around the smaller woman's shoulders, "Henry and I are going to insist she come live with us."

"But I'm not going to do that, Evangeline," Connie said, breaking free, with equal determination. "You two are going to get married, and raise a family, with as little interference from your husband's mother as possible."

Ms. Packersmythe and Henry started to protest, but Connie went on.

"I've thought about this a great deal for the past few days. I need to find my own life, be my own person. It's been so long. And with the help of proper medication and therapy, I should be able to do it."

"And help from those who love you, Mother," said Henry. "Please, don't shut me out. Especially now I've found you."

"Never again," she said and smiled at her son. They hugged briefly.

"I hate to interrupt," I said. "but I need to leave. What are you going to do about the journal? Are you going to keep it, read it, give it to Hayes' sons?"

Connie picked up the black book from the nearby table.

"After what little you've told me, Lee, I'm not sure I want to read it. I knew I wasn't Hayes' first love, but he did love me. I want to remember that."

She hesitated, seeming to reach another decision.

"But his boys might want to know what's in it. Maybe you should give this to Patsy and let her decide about whether or not her sons should see it." The last sentence was said more like a question, so I answered in kind.

"Are you sure?"

She considered. "Yes." Her answer, finally given, was firm. She handed me the journal. "You're certain Quinn can't tell the press what's in it?"

Gurn spoke up. "He can, but it's one thing to say somebody wrote something. It's hearsay and not very exciting. It's quite another to have the person's own written words. That's what the public wants to see and that's why he sent Nancy here to retrieve the journal."

"Right," I said. "Without this, he's got nothing, if he had anything to begin with. It could all be one big bluff. I wouldn't put it past him."

"What happens to Nancy?" Henry's features took a hard edge. "Will she be prosecuted for coming here and trying to steal the journal?"

"Not unless the Durands want to press charges," said Gurn. "Which I doubt."

"Besides, Nancy is going to marry Quinn," I said. "That should be punishment enough."

I looked at my watch. "I really have to go. I'm meeting Lila and Patsy. I'll give Patsy the journal, Connie. I promise." I turned to Gurn. "Are you coming?"

"You go ahead," said Gurn. "Now that I've warmed up a little, I want to check there's nothing else behind the rest of the panels." He gave me a light peck on the cheek. "It shouldn't take long."

"Thank you, darling," I said. "See you at home."

"If there's another screwdriver around, I'll help you," said Henry. "We can get the job done twice as fast."

The two men strode off, with Gurn mentioning something about a tool drawer. I turned to the two women.

"Sorry to rush off, but goodbye for now." I turned for the door, journal in hand.

"A moment of your time, Ms. Alvarez," said Ms. Packersmythe, coming up from behind.

"Oh, ah."

She came to my side and latched onto my arm. Propelling us both forward and out the building, she stopped only on the other side of the door. She looked back to make sure we couldn't be overheard before she spoke.

"We must have a word."

"I'm running late," I said, but my heart wasn't in it. I knew she wasn't listening.

"You have done me a great service. I will be forever indebted. Because of you, I know Henry to be a caring and principled man."

"It's quite all ri --"

"And now, as you know, I am getting married. I don't see us having a big wedding, just a hundred people or so. Henry wants to invite the orchestra."

"The entire San Mateo Orchestra?"

"I was hoping you'd help me plan the wedding."

"Plan the wedding?"

"You are good at that type of thing."

"I am?"

"And it's only right that you be my matron of honor."

"It is?"

"I knew you'd be pleased." She smothered me in a hug. "Not another word. It's done. I must get back to Connie now. Imagine, my friend being Henry's long, lost mother. It's a small world. But you and I shall meet later in the day. There is much to do for the wedding."

"Oh, ah."

And she was gone.

Chapter Forty-eight

From Russian Dressing With Love

"Lee, sugar," Patsy shouted to me from across the room. "I thought you'd never get here. Come on over."

Both women sat at a small table for four in the corner. Mom, dressed in a tan linen slack suit and hair pulled back neatly in a twist, sat opposite Patsy. The lady chef wore bright green jeans and matching long-sleeved blouse. A yellow bandana tied around her neck completed her vibrant look. Both women could have graced the cover of a magazine. Mom: *Vogue*, Patsy: *Hoedown*.

Patsy was, once again, ten times larger than life. Her words still reverberating in the air, I made my way through tables of diners toward the two. The entire restaurant was staring at us instead of eating. My mother just loves that.

Palo Alto's Il Fornaio is a frequent lunch spot for Mom, Richard and me, as it's only a block or two from D. I. I love the place and never tire of their chunky tomato soup. Or happy hour.

"Come here, girl." Patsy grabbed one of my hands as I neared. She pulled me down into a vacant chair. "Sit down. Talk to me."

"Sorry I'm late. First of all, congratulations, Patsy," I said. "I haven't seen you since that fateful day, but I hear you've finally been cleared of all charges. Hi Mom."

I turned to my mother and gave her a grin. She was downing the last of her martini. Given the situation, it might have even been her second; I was thirty-five minutes late.

"But they sure took their sweet time letting me go," Patsy said.

"It was a *complicated* case," Mom said. "Francis told me *much* had to be unraveled." Mom opened her mouth to say more but Patsy's voice rang out again.

"What's that you got there, Lee? It looks like one of Hayes' journals."

"Yes, the missing one."

I told the two women about my meeting with Quinn, what he'd tried to do, and how I recovered the journal. Both sat in stunned silence for a moment.

Then Patsy slapped her hand down on the table with gusto. The salt and pepper shakers jumped. So did Mom and I.

"Those damned *farkakteh* journals," Patsy spat out.

I tried to lighten things up. "I thought *farkakteh* was a Yiddish word, Patsy. How come you know it?"

"Oh, I get around. In case you don't know, it means crap. And that's what these journals are. I wish they'd all stay missing. Me and the boys talked about it and they feel the same way. They should all be thrown away. It's ghoulish reading somebody else's thoughts like that, especially when they're gone." She paused, reflecting. "I never did hold with Hayes writing them in the first place. You got something to say, say it out loud."

"And you are *quite* good at doing that," Mom said in an agreeable tone, extracting one of the olives from her empty martini glass and sucking on it daintily.

"Damn straight," Patsy said. Changing moods, she reached over and squeezed my hand with hers. "But don't think I don't appreciate your charging in there and saving my boys from any more hurt. They've had enough, losing their father like that. You're a good soul, Lee Alvarez. I don't want to hear nobody say you're not."

"Thank you, Patsy." I flushed at hearing her words, even though they were more along the lines of faint praise.

"Here you go," I said, setting the journal on the table. "Whatever you do with it, it's yours now."

Patsy picked up the book and dropped it on the floor. It landed with a thud.

"You know what? I want to see the Santa Cruz boardwalk before I leave, so I'm taking a boat ride down the coastline later today. I'll just toss that thing overboard when nobody's looking. Let the fishes read it."

"Wait a minute. You're leaving? California?" I looked at Patsy then Mom.

"Yes, Patsy's taking the first flight out tomorrow."

Yowzer, I thought. Is Tío going with her? I hadn't had the opportunity to talk to him or anybody else for several days.

Patsy was saying something and I tried to pay attention. She'd become serious, the volume of her voice lowering.

"When something like this happens, it makes you examine your life. Time to make some changes. I'm going back to Little Rock to restructure the business. Jolene and Wally already flew there yesterday. She was anxious to be with Rhonda. Jolene's a good girl. As long as she keeps her drinking under control. Wally, too," she added. "But I think they're going to make it."

Mom jumped in, turning to me. "We didn't want to talk about too much without you here, dear, but Patsy's been telling me that Peter's never been happy in the restaurant business. He wants to teach."

"I always knew that," said Patsy, "but I thought Petey'd learn to like the food game. But, no. He's been offered a job teaching at a charter school in Portland and he took it. That's the real reason he's been there so long, working out his contract. He and his wife are going to adopt Rhonda's baby and live in Portland. I see a lot of cross-country flying in my future."

She laughed. I didn't. If Tío was going to Little Rock with her, there'd be a lot of cross-country flying in my future, too. I tried not to freak out at the thought.

"What about the Institute?"

"It's the boys inheritance, but I'm putting my reputation and money behind it. We're leaving Dexter in charge. He's primed to run the place. And as soon as Brit graduates, she'll join him. I think Hayes would have been pleased."

Patsy took my hand again.

"I want to apologize for keeping so much from you, sugar, especially about my suspicions. I know I made your job harder."

"While we're making apologies, Patsy, I'm sorry I had to do things the way I did. I wasn't sure why the three of you kept lying to me. For all I knew, you could have been in on the murders."

"I can see why you'd think that." A huge sigh escaped Patsy. "When I worked side by side with the man, he just wasn't the same Hayes. I thought he was having a nervous breakdown. So did the boys. So we set up a secret meeting to decide what to do. I never knew Quinn all that well, but I never imagined…"

Her voice drifted off. She looked at me again. "It's just settling in now what Quinn did. I never dreamed anyone could be capable of doing all of this…for…" Patsy stopped speaking, as if she couldn't bring herself to go on.

"For the money," I said. "Connie's money, mostly. The Institute was secondary."

"But the building, itself, is worth quite a bit," said Mom. "Quinn had already put it on the market. Of course, the listing has been removed now."

Patsy shook her head. "How could I have not known from the git-go it wasn't Hayes? What kind of a wife was I?"

"I wouldn't feel too badly if I were you," Mom said. "Quinn was a *consummate* actor, as well as a sociopath. Playing the part of the loving husband, father, and distraught owner of the Institute seemed to come easily to him. Up to a *point*," she added.

"I agree with Mom, Patsy. I've read reviews from his acting days," I said. "They all mention how Quinn could bring tears to his eyes at will. And he had Hayes' very detailed letters and journals to guide him," I said.

"If any good came from this at all, maybe it's that Connie found her son," said Patsy. "I know what my boys mean to me."

Mom gave me an I-told-you-so look. I cleared my throat.

"There's been some coincidences in this case, which threw me," I said. "For instance, Ms. Packersmythe has known Connie for *years*, having struck up a friendship with each other at the public library."

"Although," added Mom, "Evangeline says mother and son kept their *relationship* a secret from her."

"Speaking of Ms. Packersmythe," I said. "You'll never guess what –"

Patsy's voice overrode mine. "So he hooked up with this Evangeline Packersmythe around the same time he found his mother?" She let out a soft chuckle.

"Seemingly so," said Mom, giving Patsy her full attention.

"She's about the same age as his mother, too," Patsy said. "Well, love comes in many ways. And men marry younger gals all the time. Turnabout's fair play."

"A valid point of view," said Mom.

Patsy stood. "Ladies, I hope you don't mind me cutting this short, but if'n I don't leave now, I'll never catch that boat for Santa Cruz. Now don't you worry about dinner. I already told them to put it on my credit card. The least I could do. You sure you aren't going to take any money for saving my lily white?"

"No, Patsy," I said, ignoring her politically incorrect remark. "We did it for Tío."

She shrugged, bent down, and retrieved the journal. She also picked up a pie box from the floor.

"Here, sugar," she said, handing the box to me. "This is for you. One of my possum pies. I baked it myself. Now you be sure to keep it refrigerated when you get home." She leaned over and kissed my cheek. "You come visit me anytime, sugar. You always got a free meal at *Sooie Cochon*." She looked at Mom. "You take care of yourself, Lila. You're a rare one, a bonified lady."

"Why, *thank you*, Patsy. It's been a pleasure meeting you," said Mom. She actually sounded sincere.

"Likewise, Lila honey, likewise."

Patsy also sounded sincere. Well, well, well.

Patsy hesitated then turned back to us. Her voice became soft.

"Hayes was a good man. The boys and I will miss him." She looked at the journal in her hand. "But I'm still throwing this overboard."

With no further words, Patsy Durand exited the restaurant more like the prow of a ship than a human being, the fellow patrons focused on her every move. A true star.

Mom turned to me. "Tell me there's not a *real* possum in that pie. And if so, *please* take it off the table."

"It's mainly pecans, chocolate, and whipped cream. But never mind that. Mom, is Tío moving to Little Rock?"

Mom laughed a little louder than usual, but she'd had a significant amount of alcohol. And in the middle of the day.

"Certainly *not*. He's home making dog biscuits for the animal shelter."

"But what's going on? Did something happen between them?"

"Liana, I *suggest* you go home and speak with your uncle. *He* will tell you in his own words."

"Does that mean you're okay if I leave now?"

"Yes. After forty-five minutes in Patsy's company, I could use, as *you* would say, some down time. I have my Kindle and I'll order a quiet lunch." She raised a royal hand for attention before going on. "The break will be *lovely*. And don't forget we're celebrating Richard and Victoria's two-year anniversary tomorrow. Francis and Abby will be joining us."

"You asked Frank?"

"And his wife."

"Well, well, well. Will wonders never cease? Have you two gone to a new level of friendship?"

My mother let out an exasperated sigh. "That is exactly the *type* of conversation you are to *avoid*. I expect you to be on your *best* behavior. Dinner at seven."

"On my calendar. Before I go, Mom, would you be willing to help me with Ms. Packersmythe's wedding? I got roped into being her wedding planner. And her matron of honor."

"Don't you think at this stage you can call her *Evangeline* instead of Ms. Packersmythe?"

"Not really. How about it, Mom?"

"I think *not*, dear," she said without missing a beat. "I did your wedding four months ago. *One* a year is my limit."

"Oh, lawdy."

A waiter appeared by Mom's side. "Are you ready to order, Mrs. Alvarez?"

"I *am*, Federico. I'll have the chicken marsala. My daughter will *not* be joining me. And bring me your *wine* list."

He toddled off. Mom turned her attention on me.

"Now hurry *along* to your uncle, Liana."

I spun around to leave, but Her Regalness spoke.

"And Liana."

I spun around again.

"Yes, ma'am?"

"I'm *very* proud of the way you handled yourself in clearing Mateo of any wrong doing. And Patsy, as well. It was a job well done. *Ordinarily*, I would have spoken to the board about giving you a bonus, but --"

"But as we're footing the bill ourselves --"

"It wouldn't be in keeping with the situation." Mom smiled at me; very warm, very loving, very unusual. "But it doesn't, in any way, *lessen* my pride in you."

"Why, thank you, Mom." I tried to take advantage of her mood. "And in light of that proudness, you're sure you don't want to help me out with Ms. Packersmythe's wedding plans?"

Her smile vanished. "No, dear, but I volunteer my notes. And that's *all* I shall volunteer."

"Double lawdy."

Chapter Forty-nine

A Farewell To Almonds

I entered the kitchen on silent feet. Tío's back was to me, busy at the stove. I stood for a moment, breathing it all in. The white café curtains in the three side-by-side windows over the sink had recently been replaced, as had the chairs' seat cushions. Their crisp whiteness against the crocus yellow walls gave a sense of peace I rarely experienced anywhere else.

It wasn't just the comforting familiarity, the room that with the exception of new appliances and freshening up hadn't changed in my lifetime. What I felt was a sense of continuity. Even the doggie biscuits baking in the oven smelled wonderful.

"Hola, Tío. *¿Cómo te va?*

My uncle turned, a broad smile lighting up his face. "How goes it? It goes well. I am almost done with the dog treats. Many happy wags of the tails tomorrow. But I bake for you, *mi Sobrina*, earlier."

He crossed the room, opened the refrigerator door, and pulled out a pie looking suspiciously like the one I was carrying in the box by my side.

Tío went on. "It is possum pie, but my way. It does not have the animal inside," he added hurriedly. "It is the name because it plays the possum."

I extended the box by the string that bound it. "Patsy gave me one a short time ago. Now I have two."

Tío looked at me in surprise then burst out laughing. "The minds that are great think the same."

"That's what they say, Tío." My voice was soft and filled with emotion. "Great minds think alike."

"*Dámelo,*" he said, commanding I give him the box. I handed it over and watched him return his pie to the fridge, as well as put in Patsy's.

"You will have for later."

He closed the refrigerator door and turned to me, with outstretched arms. I walked into his bear hug of an embrace. When we broke free, Tío looked at me.

"You and I, we have not had the alone time to talk, *Sobrina.*"

"I know, Tío, There has been so much paperwork to fill out and authorities to talk to. I've just been on the run."

"But no more."

"No more. I'm done."

"Then sit, *por favor.*"

I sat at the table, Tío taking a chair across from me. I jumped right in. "I understand Patsy's leaving tomorrow."

"*Si, si.* But we speak of that later. First, for all that has happened, *Sobrina,*" said Tío, "*lo siento.*"

"Sorry? What are you sorry for?"

"I nearly cost you your life. A life most *preciosa.*"

"You saved my life, Tío," I said. "Actually, you saved Gurn's. He pushed me out of the way and put himself in the line of fire. My men protect me."

I realized what I'd said. I drew myself up and sputtered.

"Not that I need protecting. I'm a pretty independent gal."

Tío fought back a smile. "It is good to be independent. But as the poem says, no man has the island."

"No man is an island, Tío." I stressed the correct saying.

"*Gracias.* No man is an island," he repeated. Tío waggled a finger in my face. "No woman, either."

"Point taken. And you're precious to me, too, Tío. So are you joining Patsy in Little Rock?"

His mouth dropped open at my question. "Why do you think I would do such a thing?"

My sputtering recommenced. "I thought you two were an item. In love. Sharing a life together."

Tío shook his head. "Always the romantic, *Sobrina*."

"But the cookbook you two are writing. The chefdom."

"What is this word, chefdom?"

"Just made it up. But you are both well-respected chefs --
"

"And this means what?"

"You have so much in common."

"Not so much. I enjoy the background. Patsy, she is at the center. She has the sparkle."

"You sparkle. I've seen you sparkle plenty. You can hold your own with her in the sparkle department."

He said nothing but stared at me. I rethought my position.

"What am I doing? I can't believe I'm trying to talk you into running away with her. But I love you, Tío. I want you to be happy."

"And I am, Liana. My happiness is here. With *la familia*. You and Gurn, your mama, Ricardo, Victoria, and now we have Stephanie Roberta." He leaned in with a smile. "You know, I hear your father in the little one's laugh. I remember from when he was as small. And then sometimes I see him when *la niña* turns her head just so."

"The same way? I had no idea."

Tío demonstrated and we both laughed. I felt my eyes brim over. Tío reached out and took my hand.

"My brother – your father – he lives on in her. That is the blessing of life."

"But don't you get lonely, Tío?"

"Not so much. I have the good life. And I have your *tía*, here." He tapped his chest over his heart. "She will always be *en mi corazón*. As will Roberto."

"They're in my heart, too, Tío. Always."

He pushed back from the table and stood, looking down. "We will talk no more of this. Patsy, she is a friend. A good friend. And whether I write the book with her or no, I go nowhere."

I let out a sigh of relief. "That's great, Tío. I don't know what I'd do if you weren't in my life."

"*Basta*. We say enough." Tío patted my hand before going on. "What I want now is to see the dogs eating the treats I bake and wagging their tails. And Tugger. I am teaching him a new trick. Baba, too, she learns it."

"You see, Tío? No matter how many feet your charges have, we all need you."

"And it is a blessing, *Sobrina*."

Chapter Fifty

Much Ado About Nutmeg

Gurn let out a moan. "I ate too much."

I stopped reading, rolled over, and looked at him across the king-sized bed.

"No? Really? How can four pieces of pie at one sitting be too much?"

Mock surprise was not lost on my husband. He put his hand on his stomach and looked at me.

"It was only three and a half. I couldn't decide which one I liked better, Tío's or Patsy's."

"So your goal was to keep on eating until you could make a decision?"

"Certainly. The pies were so different, but they both have the same name."

"It's a tradition with possum pie. Everybody adds something of their own to the recipe. Tío mentioned his cocoa beans were from Mexico. He said he added cinnamon, allspice, and chilies. Patsy's secret ingredient was honeysuckle, although I'm not supposed to tell."

"Well, if they ever do another bakeoff, save me from myself, will you?"

"I will." I tried not to laugh.

"How many pieces did you have?"

"Two. One of each. But unlike you, I didn't eat anything else for dinner. No fried chicken, mashed potatoes or coleslaw. In short, no KFC. You didn't notice?"

"I was too busy gorging myself."

He groaned again. I tried to return to my book. I was stopped by Gurn's voice, once more.

"Hey! I've got an idea."

He jumped out of bed and turned on the radio, lighting on a station that played forties and fifties standards. "Moonlight Serenade" by the Glenn Miller Band was playing. Humming, he came to my side of the bed and extended his hand.

"Let's dance some of the pie off."

"What? Here? Now?"

"Here and now." He bowed from the waist as if we were at a cotillion. "Is this dance taken, miss?"

Getting into the spirit of the thing, I tossed my book away, and swung my legs to the side of the bed. "No, kind sir. I'm all yours."

I glided into his arms, a familiar but thrilling fit. For a short time we twirled to the music, narrowly missing stepping on two curious cats that had leapt off the bed to join us.

"Tell me, miss," Gurn said, still in character. "Do you come here often?"

"Only when the fleet's in."

"Ah! You like us sailors." We spun several times, drifting to the center of the bedroom.

"So you're a navy man?"

"Yes, miss, a tin can sailor."

"Ah! That means you're on a submarine."

"Yes, miss." He dipped me.

"That must be exciting," I said when I came up.

"No, miss."

"Why's that?"

"I joined the navy to see the world." He half spoke, half sang the lyrics from one of a Fred Astaire wartime songs. I played along and fed him the second line.

"And what did you see?"

"I saw the sea."

We giggled then went silent. Our dancing became less comic, the romantic music lulling us into a rhythmic, soft sway.

I took in the scent of him and closed my eyes. For a moment it was just him, me, and eternity.

The song ended. Glenn Miller's band tooted the lively sounds of "In the Mood."

Gurn's face became animated. "What is that? The Charleston?"

"No, silly," I laughed. "Wrong decade. It's swing. You do the jitterbug. I'll teach it to you sometime."

He dropped his arm from my waist. Leaving me, he gyrated to the beat. I sat on the edge of the bed, waiting for what came next. Baba watched intently from the armrest of one of the two high back chairs in front of the bedroom's fireplace. Gurn crossed the room, swooped in, and picked her up.

"Come on, little girl. Let's swing." He spun around once, clutching the cat to him. I swear she looked more amused than surprised. Gurn held her up to his face, kissed the top of her head, and returned the feline to where she'd been. She resumed her meatloaf position.

"I think I prefer you," he said, coming back to me. He looked down at Tugger, who had jumped back on the bed, and came to my side. Tugs sat serene and regal amidst all this silliness.

"Sir," Gurn said to Tugger. "May I borrow your charming lady friend for this dance?"

Tugger meowed, which Gurn took to mean yes. I rose with laugher.

"Next time, I'm telling Tío to leave out the Kahlua in his possum pie."

"Did he put Kahlua in it?"

"Just a touch."

"Well, never mind. We're celebrating. All the clients' taxes have been filed, you found your killer, and all's right with the world."

He drew me into an embrace and then a kiss. A long kiss. When we broke free, he nuzzled my neck.

"So, miss, what are you doing for the rest of your life?"

"Spending it with you, sailor."

~~

Read on for the first chapter of
Book Seven of the
Alvarez Family Murder
Mysteries

Casting Call for a Corpse!

Chapter One

What a Housewarming

"Lee, there's a dead man in my bathtub."

The voice of my friend and world-famous actress, Gabrielle Darlé, made me turn in her direction. But I was oblivious to what she'd said.

Yes, I may have been physically standing in the doorway of my friend's living room, but my mind was at the San Francisco Zoo where earlier in the day I'd seen the debut of a baby Panda named Alice. Alice was so cute, she didn't even look real. Seeing her that morning made me smile the rest of the day no matter what.

And here was a big no matter what: having to listen to another world-famous person, author Desmond Slattery, drone on to an enraptured group of socialites and celebs about the true meaning of his book, *Unseen Passage*. Yawn, yawn.

Written twenty-five years ago and probably in its millionth printing, it was considered by those in the know as a literary masterpiece, sort of *Grapes of Wrath* meets *Planet of the Apes*. Since publication it has been required reading in every high school eleventh-grade English class. Thus, I plodded through it along with the rest of my stunned classmates. I still have no idea what it was about.

Sufficeth it to say, I had no idea what Gaby was droning on about, either, too full of meaningless metaphors, canapes, and champagne. Bit I smiled and pushed the flute of bubbly I'd been holding for her while she'd made a quick trip to the john back into her hand.

What I was paying attention to, however, was her elegant sheath and matching bolero jacket. Very haute couture and gorgeous, especially when worn by her. With Gaby's honey-blonde hair, green eyes, and the rubies glittering on her ears, the look was sensational.

Still ignoring her words, I continued to muse about the shade of red called Hibiscus Blush. Frankly, the outfit was a little too orangey to ever be seen on me, a tanned brunette with twilight colored eyes. Now if it came in a raspberry…

Wait a minute. Dead? Man? What?

I mentally slapped myself across the face, fighting back laughter. Silly me. "I'm, sorry, Gaby. You're never going to believe what I thought you just said, that there's a dead man in your bathtub."

"That's exactly what I did say." Gaby's words may have come out slightly strangled but were crystal clear. To make sure I got it, she added, "And he's wearing a tuxedo."

She grabbed my free arm and pulled me down the hallway. Champagne splashed on my hand, as well as the bodice of my new white lace, off-the-shoulder dress, not haute couture, but close enough. I was going to say something about being glad I wasn't carrying a glass of red wine when she opened the door to the bathroom and shoved me inside.

Shutting the door behind us, Gaby stared straight ahead, unblinking. Several hours before she had proudly given the Alvarez family a guided tour of her new home, which included this large guest bathroom. Modernized with all the latest conveniences it still harkening back to its early twentieth century beginnings. It was, in a word, gorgeous.

But I ignored the intricate designs of small black and white tiles executed by artisans of long gone. I disregarded emerald-green accent pieces scattered about by the let-no-cost-be-spared interior decorator. I gave no thought to the crystal chandelier shimmering overhead. What I concentrated on was the white, claw foot bathtub opposite the door and its formally attired but very dead occupant.

The man's head hung awkwardly over the rim of the tub, lolling to one side. His tongue protruded slightly through a slack, open jaw while dark, wide-opened eyes stared vacantly. In life he'd been somewhere in his mid-forties and tall, maybe six foot two. Long legs jutted up and over the back, revealing black socks worn above neatly laced patent leather dress shoes.

Sure enough, Gaby had called it. I could see the headlines now. *Dead man found in Broadway star's bathtub wearing tuxedo.* The man not the tub.

This can't be happening, I thought lamely. Weren't we in one of San Francisco's famed Painted Ladies, photographed so often the house and street it lived on were referred to as "Postcard Row?" Wasn't this a gala charity event given by one of Broadway's brightest stars, Gabrielle Darlé, with many of San Francisco's upper crust in attendance?

Didn't Lila Hamilton Alvarez, mother mine and She Who Must Be Obeyed, coerce anyone with a piggy bank to make the forty-five mile roundtrip drive from Palo Alto? Didn't that coercion include friend and Palo Alto Police Chief, Frank Thompson, who when last seen, looked as if he would rather stick a fork in his eye than be where he was?

The answers to the above were yup, yup, yup, and yup.

And here we all were, supporting a fundraiser for cleaner water in third world countries. It was no time for dead bodies in bathtubs, no matter how clean the h2o was.

Almost as one, Gaby and I leaned against the closed door, as if removing ourselves as far as possible from the sight without actually leaving the room. I took a slug of what champagne remained in my glass. Gaby did the same. Neither she nor I spoke.

Finally, I asked, "Who is it?"

"How should I know?" Her reply was decidedly snarky.

"This is your house, Gaby. It's a reasonable question."

I took another slug, draining my glass dry. Gaby did likewise.

"This is bad on so many levels," I said.

"Gee, you think?" Still snarky. But she shook her head and sucked in a ragged breath. "Oh my God, Lee. It *is* my house. But I didn't move in until a month ago." She revived for a moment. "It can't have anything to do with me. It has to be someone who knew the previous owner, Chip Gleeson. The corpse must be a friend of his." She pointed an accusatory finger at the occupant of the bathtub. "That man is an intruder!"

"Let me get this straight," I said, seeing a flaw in her reasoning. "You're saying a man dressed to the nines deliberately came in here to die because he mistakenly thought it was his friend's bathroom?"

"Exactly! It has nothing to do with me."

Denial is not just a river in the Amazon. But I completely understood. Two years before, Gaby had been swept up in the death of an international playboy with whom she'd been playing. She was a short-term suspect i.e., wrong place at the wrong time. I'm not the only one with a knack for that.

After a couple of days, his death was ruled as a self-administered drug overdose and Gaby was cleared. But the public had glommed onto her involvement. Yes, box-office sales of her then Broadway show went through the roof, but multi-media tattlers and paparazzi harassed her 24/7. Frenzied fans and non-fans sent thousands of letters, emails, and texts, some supportive, some not so nice.

Until the furor died down, she'd hibernated for nearly six months, coming out only to perform. I could understand her reluctance to become involved with yet another dead body.

I turned my attention back to the man. Even in death, you could tell he'd been good-looking and probably quite the ladies' man. Not my type, a little too flashy. But I try to be philosophical about these things. If everyone liked chocolate, what would happen to vanilla?

A clunky gold link bracelet on the wrist of the arm hanging over the side of the tub caught my eye. "That's odd," I said. "Very un-formal for somebody wearing a tux. The bracelet on his wrist. See?"

A flicker of something crossed Gaby's face. Recognition?

"You know who it is."

"No, no. Of course not," she protested. But the protest was weak.

"Gaby," I said, drawing out her name. "You know him. Who is it?"

She stood tall or as tall as her five-foot-two frame in five-inch spikes would allow. "I have no idea who the man is. I'm just rattled, that's all. I'm not involved."

"I think you are."

"No. I'm. Not."

Her lower lip may have quivered but she gave me a look of steel that would have won gold at the Olympics. I returned with my own look of steel. We stood there, steely gaze to steely gaze. A steel off. But mine was only worthy of silver.

"Alright," I relented. "We'll come back to it later. For now, you've got a dead man in your bathtub. At least we're in agreement on that. And we have to do something."

She turned to me, fear replacing steel. "You're right. But what? I've got a boatload of people out there thinking they're at a fundraiser not a funeral. What are we going to do?"

"First off, you didn't touch anything, did you, Gaby? In any way contaminate the crime scene?"

"No, no," she said. "I didn't go near him, I swear. I didn't even take a leak. I saw him there when I opened the door and just stared. He looked so....dead." All the time she was speaking she was, indeed, staring at the corpse in the bathtub.

I followed her gaze once more. She was right. I'd never seen a man look so dead. And I've seen one or two in my life.

As the in-house private investigator for Discretionary Inquiries, the family-owned business, my job description states I investigate Silicon Valley's white-collar cybercrimes. I usually accomplish this from the comfort of a desk while staring at a computer screen and compiling information.

Unfortunately, sometimes I stand up and leave my desk. When I do, I've been known to fall over a dead body or two. Case in point.

I handed off my empty glass to Gaby then reached inside my handbag for the phone. I snapped a quick succession of pictures with the camera, zooming in on the image of the corpse as close as possible from where I stood. Then I did a few panoramas to include the whole of the bathroom. It only took a few seconds to get fifteen shots. Gawd, I love these phones.

"What are you doing? Memories for your scrapbook?"

I was unperturbed by Gaby's return to snarkiness and took my glass back from her hand. "This is along the lines of you-never-know, pal." I took a deep breath to steady myself. "Well, we can't stand here all night. We've got to report this. Open the door."

She obeyed, opening it just enough for us to slip through. While exiting, I kept up my end of the conversation in whispered tones.

"Is there any way to lock this door? To prevent anyone else from coming in here?"

"Yes," she whispered back, reaching inside and pulling out an old-fashioned, large brass key from the keyhole. She held it up for me to see. "Now what?"

"Well, lock it, dufus."

"Oh, right."

"No one goes in or out until the police arrive," I said. "Is that clear?"

I blocked out the author's voice and sounds of laughter coming from an audience that had no idea what they were in for. I hit the number of the San Francisco Police Department on my phone. It is a number, unfortunately, I have on my speed dial. That's what happens when I get up and leave my desk.

Books by Heather Haven

The Alvarez Family Murder Mysteries
Murder is a Family Business, Book 1
A Wedding to Die For, Book 2
Death Runs in the Family, Book 3
DEAD...If Only, Book 4
The CEO Came DOA, Book 5
The Culinary Art of Murder, Book 6
Casting Call for a Corpse, Book 7

Love Can Be Murder Novelettes
Honeymoons Can Be Murder, Book 1
Marriage Can Be Murder, Book 2

The Persephone Cole Vintage Mysteries
The Dagger Before Me, Book 1
Iced Diamonds, Book 2
The Chocolate Kiss-Off, Book 3

The Snow Lake Romantic Suspense Novels
Christmas Trifle, Book 1

Docu-fiction/Noir Mystery Stand Alone
Murder under the Big Top

Collection of Short Stories
Corliss and Other Award-Winning Stories

Multi-Author Boxed Sets
Sleuthing Women: 10 First-in-Series Mysteries
Sleuthing Women II: 10 Mystery Novellas

About Heather Haven

After studying drama at the University of Miami in Miami, Florida, Heather went to Manhattan to pursue a career. There she wrote short stories, novels, comedy acts, television treatments, ad copy, commercials, and two one-act plays, produced at several places, such as Playwrights Horizon. Once she even ghostwrote a book on how to run an employment agency. She was unemployed at the time.

One of her first paying jobs was writing a love story for a book published by Bantam called *Moments of Love*. She had a deadline of one week but promptly came down with the flu. Heather wrote "The Sands of Time" with a raging temperature, and delivered some pretty hot stuff because of it. Her stint at New York City's No Soap Radio - where she wrote comedic ad copy – help develop her long-time love affair with comedy.

She has won many awards for the humorous Alvarez Family Murder Mysteries. The Persephone Cole Vintage Mysteries and *Corliss and Other Award Winning Stories* have garnered several, as well.

However, her proudest achievement is winning the Independent Publisher Book Awards (IPPY) 2014 Silver Medal for her stand-alone noir mystery, ***Murder under the Big Top***. As the real-life daughter of Ringling Brothers and Barnum and Bailey circus folk, she was inspired by stories told throughout her childhood by her mother, a trapeze artist and performer. The book cover even has a picture of her mother sitting atop an elephant from that time. Her father trained the elephants. Heather brings the daily existence of the Big Top to life during World War II, embellished by her own murderous imagination.

Connect with Heather at the following sites:

Website: www.heatherhavenstories.com
Heather's Blog:
 http://heatherhavenstories.com/blog/
https://www.facebook.com/HeatherHavenStories
https://www.twitter.com/Twitter@HeatherHaven

Sign up for Heather's newsletter at:
http://heatherhavenstories.com/subscribe-via-email/

Email: heather@heatherhavenstories.com.

She'd love to hear from you. Thanks so much!

The Wives of Bath Press

The Wife of Bath was a woman of a certain age, with opinions, who was on a journey. Publisher Heather Haven is a modern day Wife of Bath.

www.heatherhavenstories.com

Made in the USA
Monee, IL
16 November 2021

82275760R00193